The other boy handled the gun like a professional. He bent his knees slightly into a shooting position. Both hands were crimped tightly around the revolver, holding it at eye level. There was no wavering. No further bluster.

"Game over, you lose," he said. He was no longer screaming. His voice was calm. Cold.

Stephen started to move just as the shooter pulled the trigger; we heard the gunshot through the fuzzy audio. A single, crackling report. Stephen seemed to accordion into himself. He fell under the arcade machine and didn't move.

The other boy went into action, raced out of the room; his face came into view as he ran. A blurry view, because he was moving fast, but the image could be frozen. A picture could be created, good enough for identification.

One thing we could see clearly—the words across his T-shirt, in big crimson letters.

TOXIC AVENGER

But I didn't need that. I knew the face just as I'd known the voice. It was Jimmie. I'd just seen my brother kill another boy in cold blood.

If you enjoy this book…

The Journalist by G.L. Rockey

Techno-Noir edited By Jeff Marks and Eva Batonne

Amapola by Alan Heywood

Too Many Secrets by Linda Guyan

DEATH GAME

BY

CHERYL SWANSON

ZUMAYA PUBLICATIONS   GARIBALDI HIGHLANDS BC

2006

This book is a work of fiction. Names, characters, places and incidents are products of the author's imagination or are used fictitiously. Any resemblance to actual persons or events is purely coincidental.

DEATH GAME
© 2006 by Cheryl Swanson
ISBN 13: 978-1-55410-325-6
ISBN 10: 1-55410-325-8
Cover art and design by Martine Jardin

All rights reserved. Except for use in review, the reproduction or utilization of this work in whole or in part in any form by any electronic, mechanical or other means now known or hereafter invented, is forbidden without the written permission of the author or publisher.

Look for us online at http://www.zumayapublications.com

Library and Archives Canada Cataloguing in Publication

Swanson, Cheryl, 1952-
Death game / Cheryl Swanson.   — 1st Zumaya ed.

Also available in electronic format.
ISBN-13: 978-1-55410-326-3
ISBN-10: 1-55410-326-6

I. Title.

PS3612.A74D42   2006 813'.6   C2006-901315-2

DEDICATION

For Bob:
For then.
For now.
For always.

ACKNOWLEDGMENTS

A debut novel is a fragile creature that has to be coaxed into existence. Unless many people throw blessings (as well as time and attention) it will miscarry and never be born. My special thanks to my capable editor at Zumaya Publications, Elizabeth Burton, who was midwife at the birth of *Death Game*.

I would also like to thank the many individuals who assisted with research—far too many to enumerate. Finally, my gratitude to my *chiquita*, Carmen Alejandra, who watched endless reruns of *Sesame Street* while Mommie wrote.

Prologue

IT WAS AN EXPERIMENT," HE SAID. "AND I MUST SAY WE SUCCEEDED beyond our wildest expectations. We combined old-fashioned psychology with covert electronic warfare in a way the world has never seen before."

He poured a cup of tea.

"You killed a child," I said. "And the world never even noticed."

"The child's death was merely the beginning. It was regrettable, but necessary." He took a sip and paused to savor it.

A square of moonlight shone through the window. I could see his fingers gently holding the teacup. I tried to discern his features, but I couldn't.

"My sources tell me you're something of a technical wizard yourself," he said, "quite skilled at what you do." Then, as if he could not resist, "For a woman."

"Your sources are quite well informed," I said. "For fucked-up bastards."

His fingers tightened around the cup, but that was the only sign of anger he displayed. When he spoke again, his voice was as bland and pleasant as ever.

"Would you like some tea?"

I felt my mouth pucker, as if a nerve had been cut in my face.

They hadn't given me anything to eat or drink for two days; I wanted the tea so bad I could have killed for it.

"No, thanks," I said.

"No tea? You're sure?" He was faintly laughing this time.

I didn't answer. Don't give him the satisfaction, I was thinking. Don't give him the satisfaction of seeing you beg.

"You're not what I expected," he said, giving up on the tea and trying something else to make me beg. "I thought you'd be more like your little brother. So far, he's been very helpful to us."

It was not a surprise, but I pretended it was.

"Jimmie? What do you mean? Why would he help you?"

"I consider our use of your brother a masterstroke," he said. "It took a bit of planning, but we got him to deliver the first blow for us."

Jimmie's face came to me then. Intruding on me. Haunting me. My head felt light and hollow, and I was afraid I would be sick.

"Jimmie's just a boy," I said. "He has no reason to hate anyone."

"Hate has little to do with it. It begins by removing the subject's natural abhorrence to bloodshed. After that, the rest is comparatively easy."

I heaved a breath. Soon would come the blackness of my cell. Then the kicking and punching and the hands clutching and groping.

"Someone will stop you," I said.

There was a pause. When he spoke again, something new had emerged into his voice, the insatiable quality of someone moving deftly in for the kill.

"We won't be stopped because no one understands what we're doing. And when they finally understand, they won't believe it."

Chapter One

SOMEONE WAS SOBBING—NO, SHRIEKING. THE SOUND HIT ME LIKE A full-fisted punch in the stomach. I hurried down the stairs, banged on the door, shoved it open.

Jimmie stood inside his room, his red hair soaked—he'd just emerged from the shower. He held a wet T-shirt, his favorite; printed on it in dripping crimson letters were the words TOXIC AVENGER.

I hung there, just a few feet from the doorway, transfixed. The sound had come from Jimmie's computer. Something surged on the dark screen, something white and bloated that curled and writhed.

It was a naked human being. His skin had the pallid cast of someone who never ventured outdoors. Huge, baggy flanks, a grotesquely swollen belly—he was fat to the point of obscenity.

Porn?

But...

Gay porn?

A white silken cord dropped over the man's head. When it tightened around his neck, pulling him backwards, I could see his face. It was contorted. Ecstasy or pain? I couldn't tell. There was blood in his mouth; he seemed about to pass out.

3

Death Game

The cord slackened, he fell to his knees. Boots started kicking him. He rolled over, licked the boots.

Mother of God, I thought, and had to take a deep breath and look away.

Jimmie walked over, abruptly shut down his computer. He didn't meet my eyes, and when I asked him what he'd been watching he made a sort of choked sound.

"What *was* that?" I asked again. A vein pulsed in my forehead, but I kept hold of my temper, because I damn well had to. Any teenager on earth can beat you at whipping themselves up into a fury; but if you keep your ability to reason, the advantage is yours.

"Are you downloading porn off the internet?"

"It's not porn," my brother said. "You think I'm a total zip, don't you? A stupid, pathetic little loser. Someone no one would—"

He stopped. Crossed the room and leaned into his window, his hot breath fuzzing the windowpane.

His T-shirt was dripping. I took it away from him, draped it over the shower curtain rod. Up close, Jimmie reeked of some ammonia-laden soap, like he'd been scrubbing himself furiously and hadn't fully rinsed off. I stood a moment, reminding myself to stay calm.

I went back into the bedroom, stared morosely around me. Dirty clothing littered the floor—underwear, sleeveless T-shirts, jeans, all flung down in heaps or kicked around the room. The room was a running commentary on my brother's explosive moods.

Jimmie had moved in after Mom and Pa died, and ever since, his emotions had been pretty much confined to degrees and types of rage. Happiness rarely appeared on his face, and when it did looked like a guest who had shown up at the wrong party— out of place and uncomfortable. It would hang around for a few moments then flee.

4

A half-grown black-and-white cat padded into the room, tail in the air. Jimmie snagged her around her belly, tipped her over like a roller skate. She was his pet, but he'd been rough. She struck out, digging in her claws, plowing three bloody tracks down his arm.

He flung her on the floor. Stared at the blood. A moment later, he made a fist with his other hand, struck the wall. The cheap fiberboard barely withstood the blow. He struck it again; chips flew, a hairline crack appeared.

Blood dripped on the carpet; the cat was yowling; I had a hole in my house.

I took hold of Jimmie's arms, gave him a hard shake. "What's the matter?"

He just stood there, faintly trembling, like a wire strung too tight. His eyes looked exhausted—it was clear he hadn't slept. But then, Jimmie hardly ever slept. In happier days I'd joked with Mom that we should rig something up and feed him intravenously. Hooked up to a couple gallons of glucose, he'd never have to leave his beloved computer and videogames. He could just sit and toggle a joystick for the rest of his life.

"What's the matter with him?" my mother had asked me once. "He's such an odd kid. He never sleeps. How come he never sleeps?"

"Maybe he takes after Pa," I'd said.

Mom raised her head. "Cooper O'Brien, what are you talking about?"

Calling me by my full name meant nothing, but her eyes were blistering me.

I bit down on the words I wanted to say. Made a joke instead.

"Pa told me once he could never sleep through the night for fear the human species might not survive until morning without him."

Mom dropped her eyes.

Death Game

"Your pa's restless at night sometimes, worrying about the family," she'd muttered.

Worrying about the family, my ass.

I thought of all the nights in my childhood Pa had left the house in the wee hours. He'd slip out the side door, telling the dog to be quiet. I'd hear him, although he thought I was asleep. He'd slip back a few hours later. He thought he had us all fooled...

The accident happened ten months ago. My pa's Chrysler LeBaron was clipped from behind, went right off a cliff. I never saw Pa again. A coroner upstate told me he was thrown from the car, which then rolled on him. Pa was crushed; they could identify him from his dental records, no need to see his body. When I disagreed, he hung up.

Mom was still alive when the paramedics got there. They put her in a helicopter, and she made it to Stanford Hospital.

Beside her bed, on the sticky visitor's chair, I'd watched her die. Her face had been the gray of an old carp, her lips almost black. Her eyes, wide-open but unseeing, were the color of mud. Hitching, strangling noises came from her throat, but no words.

She died with me sitting there willing every struggling breath until, finally, she just didn't take the next one. We had never talked about what was wrong with our family. Why talk about it? There was no fixing it. With her death, there would never come a dawn when the damage could be undone.

The drunk had slithered away from the accident unharmed. He was a weepy bastard; he'd cried a lot at the trial. He hadn't meant to do it, of course. He hadn't meant to kill anyone. He just had this crippling gene that kept him sucking the bottle long past infancy.

Jimmie was looking out the window. A sea wind had peeled away the Golden Gate Bridge's usual shroud of mist. She was a-wing above the still dark city, towers seven hundred feet above the water, enough cable to circle the globe three times, eleven men dead raising her, and another lured every two weeks since into using her as a gangway to the void.

She was so beautiful that morning she was otherworldly, eerie—part elegy, part nightmare. A bridge in a dream.

Jimmie pointed at an alley opening into the street.

"That's where it happened. Remember?"

I didn't say anything. The night before the car accident, just after midnight, there'd been a commotion on the street. Two men had waylaid a woman, tried to rape her. My pa had been in the house. He'd heard screaming and raced out with a baseball bat.

"You can't beat two of us, old man," one of the woman's attackers said.

"Yes, I can," Pa replied.

He hit the first man a strong blow to the face with the bat. The man reeled backward, eyes full of disbelief. Took off, fingering his hemorrhaging mouth.

The one who had spoken hung behind, waving a blade. Too bad for him—Pa had pounded him to mincemeat with the bat, then slung him in the alley dumpster.

"When the cops showed up, they all wanted to shake Pa's hand," Jimmie said. His face turned reverential. "That was the last time I saw him. Pa was like...an awesome great person. A hero."

"He crushed a man's spine," I muttered. "Some hero."

The tip of Jimmie's nose flattened.

"Pa believed there were things you had to fight for, even things you had to be willing to die for, when the time came." He hesitated, said the rest of it in a rush. "He told me once that a true son of his would never let himself be called a coward."

There was something curious in his voice—urgent, perhaps frightened. I went to get antiseptic from the bathroom, spread it meticulously on his scratches. Wiped the metal threads clean and screwed the cap back on the tube.

"Look, Jimmie, Pa never would have wanted you to go around trying to choke people. If you did that because you were trying to qualify as brave in his book, you made a mistake."

"I didn't choke him," Jimmie said. "I hit him with a pizza tray. He called me a pitiful orphan. I did it to make him shut his ugly trap."

The incident had happened a month ago. The boy complained to the principal, and Jimmie had paid him back double with his fists after school. Drawing a week of suspension hadn't done anything to cool Jimmie's jets, either. He'd gone back touchy and moody, looking for the next skirmish.

He leaned forward on the windowsill, eyes traveling up and down the street. I considered the tight expression that had entered his face, the gathering current of intensity that filled his gaze.

He's a walking Hindenburg, I thought. Pure disaster in the making.

Out of the low-lying fog and gloom on the streets, two SFPD squad cars blasted, lightbars flashing. A pedestrian wrapped in a raincoat waited for them to pass then crossed the street. When the squad cars reached Park Presidio, they turned north, heading toward the bridge and the waterfront.

By the time the sirens faded, Jimmie had left the room, the cat at his heels. I kept watching the pedestrian until I was sure he was a cross-dresser from the whorehouse a block down the street. I knew the tilt of his head, caught sight of the frilly split-crotch fin du siècle unmentionables when a gust lifted his loosely wrapped raincoat.

The prostitutes never worked the streets on Monday mornings, but this one would be wanting a pint very badly, and heroin even worse. I'd talked to him—he chattered like a bird.

Had eyes like the clear blue sweets the Mexican children sucked.

I stayed in front of the window, thinking about my pa. Was he still out there? Hovering like a ghost in the darkness?

I was always looking...not for pa, but for his clothes. The disguise that concealed his identity. A dark suit and a crisp white shirt wrapped around a kind of inner madness. A silver-studded wristband fastened around a clenched fist. An appallingly fake blond wig sheltering eyes that had seen horrors. Two-tone leather shoes that had walked into thousands of strange hotel rooms.

Rambo-in-wingtips, I'd called him that time. To his face even. He'd smiled, which in itself had been a shock. He almost never smiled.

Just in case, I sent him a mental message. *Listen, old man. If you're still alive, it's time to come home. While you're mucking around, trying to save the world, your son is about to blow apart.*

A moment later, I shut my thoughts away. Went upstairs to dress.

*   *   *

The morning drive was maddening, as usual. I got stuck in a jam near the Wong Tai Sin Temple. Squeezed through an alley behind an earthquake shack, backtracked a few miles. Spun out in front of an electric bus on Geary and floored it.

When we got to George Washington High School, I expected Jimmie to jump out, but he sat without moving, his hands clenched. Someone in the line of cars at the drop-off curb tapped their horn. His head jerked.

He turned toward me, blinking rapidly, tearful, eyes not quite in focus.

"I'm scared, Sis," he said in a desperate way.

The horn went off again.

"Quit popping people in the jaw with pizza trays, and you won't have anything to be scared of," I said harshly. "Otherwise, the whole school is gonna be laying for you."

Giving me an angry look, he got out and slammed the door.

I watched him head through the swarming students. Those long, straight legs, that shock of red hair—he was a handsome boy, really. But he was walking with his usual self-protective hunch, and I knew he felt as ugly as a clod of dirt. His school counselor had recommended I take him to a psychologist. It hadn't seemed to help; the shame and self-loathing and enormous rage that had consumed him ever since the accident hadn't eased. Somewhere along the way, Jimmie had developed a desperate fixation on not being thought a coward. I couldn't fathom where that was coming from. Neither could the shrink.

"Jimmie!" I was out of the car, yelling. The stupid kid had left his knapsack behind.

He'd already disappeared, but a girl was passing by—Lauren, his biology lab partner. Her hair was fawn-colored, sleek. She wore it loose to the shoulders.

"Lauren, take Jimmie's backpack to him, would you?"

She tensed, her shoulders bunched. "No. I can't—"

"Really, it's okay." I glanced at my watch. Oh, shit. "Just take it."

I shoved it into her hands.

"It's dripping," she said.

I flipped open the buckles. Jimmie had stuffed his Toxic Avenger T-shirt inside. The front was stiff with soap scum. What a freaky-ass kid, I thought. Why'd he do that?

Lauren grabbed the T-shirt, stuffed it in the backpack. "I'm outta here...late!" she hollered as she ran off.

I made reasonably good time until I reached the Financial District. At the corner that held Shotwell's, where the city moguls congregate for after-hours brandy and cigars, the traffic congealed again. Complete gridlock—skyscrapers above, car bumpers below, as far as the eye could see.

I flipped open my laptop and started working. Soundtrack bombast filled the car—the roar of a truck engine, the squishing sound of tires on a wet street, a car door slamming, a woman screaming...

The traffic drifted a few yards forward; I moved with it. Refocused.

Up until a few months ago, I worked as a special effects artist at a large production studio north of the bay. It was a childhood fantasy of mine to work in films, and a child's dreams are not idle fancies; they are the means by which he creates the person he is going to become. At least, that's the line they fed us when we graduated from USC film school. In my case, I'd achieved my dreams, and all it meant was that my life had started to reek of desperation. Sometimes I thought if I had to work on one more bad movie I would tear my eyeballs out with my fingernails.

Two months before, personal injury attorney Rick Capra had talked me into getting out of the film business, going to work for him instead. Rick wanted me to create animated reenactments of accidents he could use in personal injury trials. According to him, these reenactments would help him overcome one of a personal injury attorney's biggest problems—how a jury can handle only so much yammering before they zone out, lose track of what's going on.

It wasn't just that. There's always at least one juror who has the intellectual capacity of a cauliflower. Wheeling a TV into the courtroom and showing a decapitated body, with the camera lovingly doting on bones poking through and arteries spurting, is sometimes the only way to get them to understand that this is *personal injury*, goddamnit. Someone really got injured.

I don't think I would have gone for it, but Rick hit me at a vulnerable time. My mother's dying, the drunk slithering off with a hand-slap—it had left me possessed by fury. And the studio had lent me out to Hideo Siri, a director who had the subtlety of a walrus with gas. In his last film he'd insisted that all the fast camerawork had to be done at an angle, an effect that made me want to get down on my knees and crash my skull against the floor. If I stayed any longer, I figured I'd have Hideo's brand on me, and that was closer to cinematic sodomy than I ever wanted to get.

Meanwhile, Rick kept pounding on me. My mother was past help, he'd point out, showing about as much subtlety as Hideo, but maybe I could help some other victim.

Sure, why not? What else was I going to do? Get a job at Sears shooting family portraits?

Only...Rick—Rick himself—was the stinger.

Seven years ago, Rick and I had agreed to keep our distance. It was an emergency measure, kind of like removing a blue flame from a test tube that is emitting clouds of yellow stuff, because otherwise it is going to blow up. We're both older, wiser—that's what you tell yourself when you go back to toxic relationships. We'll handle it better this time, isn't that what you say?

Yeah, right.

I snapped my car into a slot in the basement parking garage. Twisted the mass of red curls on my neck into a ponytail and fastened it up with a clip. There was a limo—regal-looking, white, with dark-blue leather—blocking my way to the elevator. The customized license plate said: LUDLOW.

I circled the limo, feeling my heart sink. When I got to the elevator, the owner was waiting for me. My gait faltered, but it was too late. Walter Ludlow took a step forward and pulled me inside.

He punched in the thirty-second floor. Then he added the privacy code that prevented the door from opening until it reached its destination. Then he made a single cry of distress and pain and wrapped his arms around me.

I didn't have the guts, or the presence of mind, to push him away. Once upon a time, Walter and I had a fling. A short fling, not very memorable, but still, I clearly remember seeing the

Grand Old Man naked in a post-coital moment, running his fingers through his thick silver hair.

The affair had affected me in strange ways. Something vital in me had died afterwards; something had been irrevocably finished. My destiny—that goddamn human destiny we all think we can elude—had been further and irretrievably complicated.

Right now, the Grand Old Man had a queer glassy look in his eyes. He smelled as if he'd neglected his morning shower, as well as his usual spritz of $400-an-ounce cologne, an almost unthinkable omission. His crown of silky smooth hair was awry and disheveled.

He was holding me tight, clinging to me, really, and I had no idea what to do. Why was it that Walter affected me so strangely? There seemed to be an inevitable doom in my relations with men; things always foundered. But Walter—there had been something in Walter that I'd never touched before in my life.

Let me tell you about the very rich. They are different than you and me—F. Scott Fitzgerald wasn't kidding. And even in the rarified financial air of San Francisco, Walter was something special. A powerful, supremely confident man, he owned a shipholding company that controlled half a dozen tankers as well as a hundred workboats that circled the globe. His home, five stories of glass perched on an ocean cliff, was as extraordinary a structure as I'd ever entered without paying admission.

"Something terrible happened, Cooper." Walter was breathing into my face. His breath smelled thick and fetid, as if he'd been vomiting. "Stephen is dead. The police found him just after six this morning. He had a bullet through his head."

He dropped his hands and stood there, not looking at me, not looking at anything. Everything stopped; even my heart seemed to stop beating. I put my hand out, braced myself against the elevator wall.

Stephen was Walter's son. A quiet kid. Shy, painfully

Death Game

underdeveloped for his age, never at ease, but a nice boy, really. Once you got him to open his mouth.

Walter's only child. Then came the thought; I couldn't stop it—the heir to everything. Dead.

I'd always liked Stephen. He hadn't been a particularly bright kid. Crashingly average, in fact. But he'd been the kind of kid who sometimes develops a backbone. Ends up surprising everyone, joining the Peace Corps or Greenpeace. Refuses to just sit around and live off his old man's money.

"He shot himself?" I asked gently.

It surprised me—and it didn't. For poor little rich kid Stephen, there must have been plenty of daily torment in not being able to live up to his father's expectations. In the presence of his awesomely impressive parent, Stephen had often seemed to me to be frozen with shame.

Walter flexed his hands and looked at them, as if their impotence shocked him.

"Not self-inflicted. At least I don't have that on my conscience."

There was a jerk as the elevator came to a stop. The doors slid open with a hydraulic whoosh. We had reached the thirty-second floor, but Walter didn't move.

"Walter?"

"I...need to tell you something, Cooper."

"Don't. Please—"

"The police aren't going to get to the bottom of this. The way Stephen was killed, it's the first time anyone has ever been killed that way."

I felt a twitch around my eyes. Tried to hide it, but he saw it.

"Damn you! What are you thinking? You don't think I had anything to do with Stephen's death?"

"No," I lied.

He followed me out of the elevator. "Why are you running

14

away?"

I stopped. "You said he was shot, Walter. You're not making sense."

He started crying now, the way men rarely cry—no sobs, but the tears falling fast. "The...the world has just found a new atrocity, a brand new way of killing."

"What are you talking about?" Outta his mind, I was thinking.

"What happened to Stephen, it's not going to be easy to figure out. And it's not over. No one is going to be safe."

I winced, shook my head. He'd lost his boy and he had a bad case of the crazies. Just like Bill Cosby. Just like John Walsh. Hell, just like a guy in a mobile home, hearing an unexpected knock at the door and answering it to find out his son was dead. Walter had turned into someone he probably didn't even know inhabited the same planet as he did.

An ordinary human being.

Walter's body tightened, his face flushed. He was trying to exert control over himself, doing his damnedest to bring the Grand Old Man back. It was his routine, his schtick, his mask— we all have one—and he did it like we all do, on autopilot.

But he also had his secret place. There was more to him, as there's more to any of us than we ever let on, and it was coming out now.

"You have to help me, Cooper," he said. "You've got to trust me; not—" He glanced at the door. "I need you. Before we go in, promise me you'll help."

I pushed open the door to Rick's suite and entered. Walter didn't follow. When I turned, he was still on the other side of the closed door, gesturing for me to come back. He wasn't asking, he was begging. Pleading. I stood, frozen into absolute stillness. Looking at upturned palms through whorls of smoky glass.

It was so strangely out of character for this regal man, and so human, it almost broke my heart.

Chapter Two

A HOT BREATH TOUCHED THE BACK OF MY NECK. I TURNED TO SEE TWO intense black eyes looking not at me but over my head.

"That's Walter, isn't it?" Rick asked. "Why isn't he coming in?"

He opened the door, tried to seize one of Walter's hands, shake it. Rick's gaze was naturally harsh—piercing—but he could soften it to great effect, and he did so now. He tried again to take Walter's hand, opened his mouth to offer condolence.

Walter dropped his hands. Clenched them at his side.

There was an awkward pause; then Rick turned on his heel and led us down the corridor to the conference room. He pointed at a high table, where a box of sleek, silver-encased surveillance tapes sat.

"Crissakes, I hope you weren't worried, Walter," Rick said, fidgeting. "I told you the *Sea Dream* surveillance tapes were safe."

Walter didn't respond. He made it clear through the slightest of winces, a raised hand, a turn of the shoulders, that he wasn't going to talk to Rick.

"One of the techs picked them up first thing this morning, that's the only reason they weren't on the yacht," Rick said.

Walter was busy looking through the box of tapes, but Rick

16

was unable to keep still.

"Don't worry. We'll get this...whoever he is, we'll get him."

"Tapes from the *Sea Dream*? What are they doing here?" I asked, confused.

"Stephen's body was found on the *Sea Dream*," Rick explained, dropping his voice. "The cops think he was killed there. Didn't he tell you?"

The *Sea Dream* was Walter's luxury yacht. It was both his personal toy and the party boat of the fleet he owned through his company, Sea Transport.

Walter lifted his head, looked straight at me. "I had no idea Stephen was on the yacht. He just ran out of the house last night. Jumped in a taxi."

His words were slow and deliberate, as though he were picking them one by one out of a cardboard box.

I waited.

He read my face, shook his head, clenched his hands slightly.

"We had...words, during dinner. The boy started bawling. Said he wanted to go to his mother's. I thought...let him go. I had his mother called so she'd know to expect him."

"He never got there?"

"He got there. But he did the same to her. Told her he was going back. Even when I figured it out, I thought he was holed up in a downtown hotel, sulking. He took off like that once. Went straight to the Stanford Hotel. Ordered room service and played his goddamned videogames all weekend."

A few moments later, Walter held up one of the tapes so I could see it. The label was handwritten, the letters awkwardly formed, but I could make out the words: STEPHEN LUDLOW'S STATEROOM.

He took a quick, gulping breath. "That's where the police found his body."

"I told you we had that tape," Rick said to him. "Whoever did this, they're bound to be on it."

Walter suddenly did something incredibly touching. Put his forehead down on the table, let it rest there while his shoulders heaved.

Rick took advantage of the moment to pull me out the door.

"God, I *hope* they're on it," he said.

A moment later, he ran his fingers through his black hair. He'd gelled it this morning—it was bulletproof, a helmet.

"You sleeping with that museum piece again?" he asked, giving an ugly laugh. "You spend last night making the Pacific Ocean roar with the Grand Old Fart? That the real reason he lost track of his kid?"

I felt like smacking him. "His son just died, Rick. Give it a rest."

He shrugged his bulky shoulders. Rick was good-looking but unrefined—rough-hewn features, a stocky build. A handsome peasant next to Walter's lean magnificence.

"He wouldn't shake my hand, wouldn't let me say a word, did you notice? He expects me to bob my head, be his little pissant, but I'm not good enough to offer him sympathy."

"So, bob your head. He pays you enough," I snapped.

Rick's company, Capra Security, had installed a covert surveillance system in the *Sea Dream* four months before. Tiny night-vision cameras were concealed in bulkheads, behind wall panels, in dropped ceilings in the staterooms. There were even trick ones that could see right through fabric, making it impossible for anyone to hide behind curtains.

Rick owned two businesses—a law practice and Capra Security, ran them both out of an echoey, marble-floored suite in an O'Farrell tower. The law practice employed one severely overworked paralegal and myself. The surveillance business kept six techs occupied. The techs were twenty-something immigrants with strong math and science backgrounds, the kind of young men who worked scooping up trash until they learned English. There was also a half-crazy computer genius with a doctorate from the University of Moscow.

Even though everyone worked for peanuts, there was the Class A skydeck office, as well as a lot of pricey computer software, film-editing and surveillance equipment. Somehow, Rick had not only made it pay; he'd turned it into a personal gold mine.

"You see the bloodhounds on your way up here?" he asked, changing the subject. "I thought they'd have shown up now. Well, speak of the—"

We could hear voices down the hall; the receptionist was greeting someone. A moment later, we met them. One pumped my hand while he told me his name—Detective Bernard Tuck. Pulling out the SFPD's blue badgeholder, he stuck it under my nose: Homicide, Marina Division

I didn't quite know how to take him. Something was off about the guy. His teeth were bonded, his hair thick with mousse, slicked back at the sides, a hint of a curl escaping on his forehead. Perfect hair. A Tinseltown grin. Maybe it was my film background, but Detective Bernard Tuck seemed less like a homicide cop to me than an actor pretending to be a homicide cop.

The other cop was older—late fifties—black. A neck like a tree stump; arms like fire hydrants. This one at least had the eyes: flat, giving nothing away. He told us his name—Detective Harry Harmon. Leaning his bulk against the conference table, which was approximately the size of an oil slick, he turned to Rick.

"What's the problem with these tapes?"

"What do you mean? There's no problem."

"Why weren't they on the *Sea Dream*?"

Rick shrugged. "One of my techs picked them up for debugging. It's regularly scheduled maintenance. Prevents system

Death Game

failure."

"We'll take them with us," Tuck said, scooping the box off the conference table.

"You can't. The playback system requires a fingerprint scan." Rick grinned. "You want to review these tapes anywhere but my office, you're going to have to cut off Cooper's finger and take it with you."

Harmon frowned. "Can't you register one of us?"

Rick shrugged again. "Not today. My computer expert isn't here. His wife is sick."

"Jala could go with them and play the tapes," I suggested. And so could you, I thought, didn't say.

Jala was the head of Rick's surveillance company. His real name was Jaluddin, but we all called him Jala. He was a twenty-something Yemeni who spread a prayer rug in the corridor and made us walk around him five times a day.

"Jala," repeated Harmon. "Is that who picked up the tapes from the *Sea Dream* this morning? I need to talk to him. We may have caught a break with these tapes; if so, I'll need a chain of custody on them. Besides, maybe he saw something."

"He's not here. All my techs took off about an hour ago, and they'll be gone for the rest of the day," Rick said breezily. He dropped his hands into his pockets, leaned against the wall.

Behind his head was a huge modernistic art piece—an isosceles triangle in fuschia and lime-green. It was ugly. And like the rest of the office, it radiated big money like heat from a stove.

"They're wiring a wine baron's cellars in Sonoma," he added.

"When are they coming back to Frisco?" Tuck asked.

Rick looked at him; so did I. Nobody from San Francisco called the city "Frisco." Hell, nobody who lived anywhere west of the Mississippi called the city "Frisco."

Rick caught my eye, grinned. I thought he was laughing at Tuck, figuring him for an idiot, but he had something else on his

20

mind.

"That means you're it, baby love," he half-whispered, grinning, his dark eyes snapping.

He'd spoken just loud enough for his words to carry. Everyone's head, including Walter's, came up. The knowing gaze of the men blistered me; I could feel my face go bright red.

Baby love, I thought furiously as I left. Rick, you are such an asshole.

When I came back, arms full of equipment, I expected the cops to be talking to Walter. But Walter wasn't in the room, and Tuck had insinuated himself next to Rick, close enough to nudge him.

"How'd you get into the surveillance biz, Mr. Capra?" he asked.

"Does it matter?"

"Most guys in surveillance get their start in the military..." Tuck hesitated, glanced at Harmon, who shifted his shoulders slightly. "Uh...you seem like a tough guy to me. You in the Marines when you were younger?"

Rick's face went still.

Tuck crinkled up his eyes, acted like he'd just had a thought.

"Some special group...Force Reconnaissance, maybe?"

There was a moment of dead silence.

"Jeez, were you one of those sharpshooting sons-of-bitches who like to eat babies?" Tuck laughed and stole another glance at Harmon.

"Never heard of it," Rick said, lying through his teeth.

"Never heard of what? The Marines?" Tuck grinned out of the side of his mouth with his teeth barely showing, like a possum.

Rick pushed Tuck in the breastbone with his fingers, forcing him to take a step backwards. Rick never talked about it, but he spent a couple of years in Force Reconnaissance after high school. He had killed a half-dozen men in close combat, and it had deposited plenty of snakes in his psyche.

He shook himself, like a dog shaking off an encounter with a skunk, turned his head my direction.

"Let's do this. Ready to roll, Cooper?"

The tone was light, his hands back in his pockets, but the skin around his mouth had gone taut and gray.

"Another minute," I mumbled.

There was a hidden video panel at the far end of the room. Rick flipped the switch; the modern art split down the middle and rolled away to reveal the screen.

"Cool," said Tuck appreciatively.

Harmon looked at him like he wanted to slap him on the head. From the beginning, I'd had the sense Harmon had told Tuck to play it a little Columbo-ish, a bit dimwitted. If so, Tuck was overplaying his role.

"What about Mr. Ludlow?" Tuck asked. "Should we wait for him?"

"Yes," I said.

Harmon turned my direction with a frown.

"Mr. Ludlow's grieving for his son." I said. "Starting without him would be callous. Uncaring."

I feigned a state of instinctive feminine politesse, and the three men—macho types—took it at face value. Turned their attention back on each other.

The shock of Stephen's death had sent me into limbo, made me wooly-headed, buzzy. But in the tech room, I'd woken up. Filled my arms with gear a sainted version of myself wouldn't have touched. The gear would allow me to surreptitiously feed a computerized copy of whatever we saw on screen to my laptop— there was a built-in patch panel under the lip of the conference table. By connecting the player and rigging a splitter, I could simultaneously send the signal output to the screen and my computer.

Walter, you said you wanted my help. So I'm helping.

The footage could be dissected for information later, right down to the individual frame.

My laptop was on a chair, and I'd tossed my jacket over it. Tuck was zeroed in on Rick. Harmon was watching Tuck. With any luck, I would get away with it.

When Walter sat down, holding a glass of water, I was almost done, wiggling a cable connect into an input port on the laptop with my left hand. Harmon glanced at me, eyes squinting. He couldn't see anything, but his cop instinct was bugging him. I flicked switches calmly, and his eyes shifted away. Video link in place? How about the audio laydown? Check...check...showtime.

But this wasn't some popcorn whodunit. I was about to run the first preview screening of my life where re-shooting wasn't possible. Where the film's hero—even if the pre-release polls said the audience overwhelmingly wanted him to live—wasn't going to be resurrected.

*   *   *

A small amber backlit box glowed in the center of the screen, counting: 01:00:00 SUNDAY 04/14/00. The numbers started running backward, racing through the fractions of seconds. Time code is always embedded in surveillance tape; by bringing it up, you can see exactly when something happened.

Harmon told me the coroner had put Stephen's time of death between eleven p.m. and three a.m. I slid a switch, and we were looking at a boy's stateroom, filmed the previous evening. From the perspective, the hidden camera was mounted above the only doorway.

The stateroom was stuffed with gaming and sports equipment, stacks of videocassettes, piles of CDs, an old-fashioned arcade-style videogaming device. In the corner was a twin bed, navy blue coverlet neatly tucked in. Next to the bed were a small desk, a laptop computer and a few books.

I edged up the sound, noticing that the audio laydown was lousy. There were continuous loud bursts of static.

As I worked on the audio, the screen abruptly faded into a sequence of flickers. A quick view of the room...a fade to gray...another quick view of the room.

"What's the matter with the picture?" Harmon asked.

"The camera has a motion sensor attachment. Every ten minutes or so, it shoots a couple of frames. A sample view of the room."

"Until something moves," Harmon said.

"Yes. Then it starts filming in real time."

Through the only window enough ambient light entered that the room stayed illuminated. Nothing interesting occurred until 24:56:04, when the time code stopped. The image of the room held steady. Something was happening.

We heard crackling sounds, hurried footsteps. A door opened. The audio hiss was still troublesome, but we could hear a voice over it. It was a sudden, furious voice, screaming out words that seemed driven from it by hatred.

"I have to do this. Fuck you. You knew that from the beginning. You knew it was gonna be me or you."

My fingers were on the audio controls, trying to fix the hiss. The voice...

My fingers froze.

The voice came again, still screaming.

"Fight, goddamn you. Put up some kind of a fight!"

Still that loud background hiss.

"Can you get rid of that?" Harmon asked.

"I'll try," I said. But I didn't try. Instead, I moved my shaking hands under the table. Clenched them into fists.

The tape kept rolling; someone walked into the stateroom

with the shuffling awkwardness of the very young. It was a boy, in a nice shirt and pressed pants. Another boy followed him. The second boy was holding an automatic pistol with his arms extended and stiff, at shoulder level.

From the camera above the doorway, all you could see was the backs of their heads, then an outstretched arm holding the gun. The weapon was pointed at the first boy, who now turned to face the camera. It was Stephen.

The boy with the gun kept his back to the camera.

Stephen wasn't wearing his big glasses, and without them, his face looked defenseless and extremely young. The skin beneath his left eye was twitching; a pulse beat hard in his neck.

He backed up a step. Then another. The waist-high arcade machine was directly behind him. He was crying—we could see his face contort—crying so hard he coughed up big, sticky globs of phlegm.

When he reached the arcade machine, he moved to the side of it. A few steps more, and he was against the wall. In a heartbreakingly futile gesture, he gathered up a big mouthful of phlegm and spat at the boy holding the gun. Then he put his hands in front of his face, stiffened and drew his shoulders up, as if to absorb the blow. Or maybe he intended, at that last moment, to try to feint, or run, or duck.

The other boy handled the gun like a professional. He bent his knees slightly into a shooting position. Both hands were crimped tightly around the revolver, holding it at eye level. There was no wavering. No further bluster.

"Game over, you lose," he said. He was no longer screaming. His voice was calm. Cold.

Stephen started to move just as the shooter pulled the trigger; we heard the gunshot through the fuzzy audio. A single, crackling report. Stephen seemed to accordion into himself. He fell under the arcade machine and didn't move.

Death Game

The other boy went into action, raced out of the room; his face came into view as he ran. A blurry view, because he was moving fast, but the image could be frozen. A picture could be created, good enough for identification.

One thing we could see clearly—the words across his T-shirt, in big crimson letters.

TOXIC AVENGER

But I didn't need that. I knew the face just as I'd known the voice. It was Jimmie. I'd just seen my brother kill another boy in cold blood.

Chapter Three

THE CAMERA STOPPED TRACKING AND RETURNED TO AN OVERVIEW SHOT of the room. The time code kept crawling, but there was no movement. Stephen didn't stir.

"It's over. Go back to the view of the shooter," Rick said.

I didn't move. Everything was fuzzy in my head. Rick got up, took a few steps, reached over my shoulder and stopped the tape. The screen went blank.

Jimmie. Oh, Jimmie. God...

Harmon was looking at Rick.

"It was over. You want to see the whole thing again? Or just the shooter?" Rick waved a hand at the screen.

A line of pain bored into my temple. Jimmie—

Harmon didn't reply.

Rick leaned over. "Cooper?" he whispered. "It was over, right? Tell him it was over."

But I didn't speak, couldn't.

Rick was looking at me, but not directly; he wouldn't meet my eyes. Instinctively, I reached for his arm. *Rick. Oh God, Rick. Did you see it was Jimmie?*

He moved away, and my hand dropped. I followed him with my eyes, trying to read his face. Had he recognized Jimmie? Was

27

he wondering why I hadn't admitted it? Mother of God, should I?

Ducking my head, I managed to get a slow reverse going. Harmon's attention had been claimed by Tuck, who was whispering something in his ear.

I stole a look at Walter. The moment the shooter appeared on the tape he had thrown his head up. There had been puzzlement—astonishment, really—on his face, but it had slowly faded. His eyes were red and murderous, glowing like coals. Thank God, Walter didn't know my brother. Otherwise, after what he'd just seen, he'd have had him sawed in half.

Jimmie. Oh, Jimmie...

I tried to think, but I wasn't tracking well. Agony kept stealing over me. Rick had turned the lights back down. I let the reverse continue, making certain it was out of focus. This time, Jimmie's face was an unrecognizable smear.

Rick leaned against the wall near the switch box, arms folded. His jacket lifted slightly with regular respirations. He was dead calm. Not shocked, not alarmed, not even surprised. How could he not have recognized Jimmie? He knew my brother, knew him well. So, why was he so calm? So...relieved. That was how I read him—relieved.

There was only one possible explanation. Rick had known Jimmie was the shooter before we saw the tape.

Realizing that brought me out of shock like a bucket of ice over the head. My fingers started moving rapidly over the equipment in front of me. I'd thoroughly indulged my suspicious streak, brought in a portable mixer box when I brought in the player and cables for the laptop download. A couple of extra video and audio links—it took only seconds to engage. Suddenly, there was a brilliant blaze of light from the screen.

"What the hell?" Harmon said.

Tuck glanced up. His eyes went blank.

On the screen, hundreds of freeform random lines jittered. A moment later, there was a fiery burst of red stage light, out of which drifted a stage. A guy with long hair hopped around the stage, hugging his guitar. Flames snapped upward in synchronized bursts. Amped-up music, as if we were in the middle of a wild rock concert at the Fillmore, flooded us from everywhere. Crazy sound—cranked-up bass, explosive percussion, bloodcurdling vocals.

"What is this?" Harmon yelled. "What's going on?"

"It's interference, a direct feed from a live broadcast," I yelled back. "I'll try to get rid of it."

Adrenaline surged through me. I killed the rock concert and switched to the image of a van cartwheeling and exploding. Pyrotechnic effects blazed. Tuck held his hands up over his eyes, stared between his fingers. His skin was lurid orange-red from the reflections off the screen.

I jumped up. "We're picking up broadcast signals—it happens sometimes in these skyscrapers." It was true enough, as far as it went, although I was the one doing the broadcasting. "We've got some equipment that can shield us. I'll go get it."

Harmon started to speak; he wasn't buying it. I shoved the audio to maximum. Then I was out the door, racing toward the reception area.

The girl at the desk was a temp; I didn't know her. She glanced up and widened her nostrils.

"Is something wrong?"

"Buzz the conference room after I leave," I said, pausing briefly. "Tell the cops they need to order a lockdown at George Washington High. If anyone asks where I am, tell them I had a personal emergency."

"Lockdown?" she repeated, as if she'd never heard the expression. "What's that?"

"They'll know what I mean," I said. "George Washington High School. Did you get that?"

Death Game

She stared at me, her eyes blank.

"This is important. Do you have a problem doing what I asked?"

"No problem," she said sullenly. Her bottom lip pushed out. Round vacuous eyes peered at me. Two empty blue balls—like marbles—were the last thing I saw before I was out the door and gone.

The streets were still clogged. Cussing and praying by turns, I snatched up the cell phone, thumbed the buttons.

"Razel here," he said.

"Something has gone terribly wrong," I said. "I need your help."

"You're making me all shivery, love. What's wrong?"

Razel was my tenant. More than a tenant, actually, after all the years we'd lived together. We're essential to each other, but not in a way that's easy to explain.

"You've got to get to Jimmie's school as fast as you can," I said.

"Whatever for?"

"You'll understand when you get there. There will be cops everywhere, classrooms locked up, a SWAT team, sharpshooters—" I was babbling, barely coherent. I stopped, took a breath. "Razel, please, I can't explain. Just go. The traffic is so bad I can't get there. Jimmie needs someone he knows. I don't know what he might—"

"You're fretting about nothing, darling," Razel said. "Jimmie's here."

"He ditched school? Blessed Jesus and Holy Mary, thank you," I said fervently.

"I don't see any reason to invoke blessings from deities," Razel responded darkly. "Ditching school is not going to get him into college and out of our hair."

"Is he still there? He hasn't taken off?"

30

"Jimmie!" Razel hollered.

Silence.

"He's not answering, but he's here. I just heard the refrigerator door thump."

I nosed my Fiat into a tiny gap between two cars. Slithered across the intersection in a turnaround.

"Make him stay put. How'd he get home, anyhow?"

"I have no idea. I just got home myself."

"Is he acting strange?"

Razel laughed. "My dear girl, he always acts strange. He's the psycho in your family, like I've always told you."

I felt a chill. Was he? Was Jimmie actually nuts? Did he have murder in him?

The phone clicked. Someone else was calling.

"Make sure he doesn't leave, Razel. Knock him down and sit on him if you have to."

"Oh, puh-leeze."

The phone clicked again.

"I mean it. Tie him up. Whatever it takes. Don't let him get away."

As I rang off he was muttering crossly, "Right. Right. I'm hardly a butch Marine in dirty overalls, love, in case you never noticed."

The incoming call was from Rick. I hesitated, wondering if I should pretend there was a bad connection and hang up.

"What's going on, Cooper?" he demanded.

"Stay out of it, Rick."

"Like hell I will. You owe me an explanation."

When I didn't respond, he softened slightly.

"That idiot temp came in mumbling you had an emergency. I told Harmon I'd find out what was going on. Where are you, anyway?"

"Uh, Rick, I can't hear—"

31

Death Game

"She said someone was locked up at George Washington High. Isn't that Jimmie's school? Is this one of Jimmie's pranks again? What'd the stupid kid do this time?"

He sounded genuinely aggrieved, not fishing for information, but I didn't trust him. I was certain he had recognized Jimmie on the tape. And I was equally certain he'd already known Jimmie was the shooter. In front of the cops, maybe he hadn't wanted to say anything, but why wasn't he admitting it to me now? Why the act?

"I don't appreciate you running out on me like this, Cooper—Yes, what? Okay, whatever,'" Rick said distractedly to someone else. He came back on the phone. "Harmon said he's taking the tapes and the player, they'll figure out how to make it work, so you're off the hook. That was weird what happened at the end of that tape, wasn't it? That interference? I thought for a minute you were doing that yourself."

He hung up abruptly. I had the sense that, whatever his initial purpose had been, he had regretted calling me almost immediately.

I was out of the Fiat before it stopped rumbling. In the darkness at the top of the garage staircase I heard something strange—a series of cracked high notes bleeding on the air. I stopped, tried to identify it. It wasn't like the sound I'd heard that morning. This sounded like an animal, bleating in pain.

My heart was pounding. I walked as quietly as I could through the cracked cement archway into the house. The stench of burnt pepperoni, onions and peppers met me just outside the kitchen; still-warm pizza dripped grease onto a paper plate. Water bubbled in a stainless steel pan.

I headed up the staircase, careful not to make noise. Near the top, I could see down the short hallway directly into the upstairs bathroom.

Blood was smeared on the ceiling and walls. Blood and water

swelled out over the lip of the toilet, dripped onto the linoleum floor. The plastic lid was closed, and something had been written on it.

Hearing movement from Jimmie's bedroom, I started that direction, looking for anything I could use as a weapon. A hammer lay next to the hallway telephone. I slipped it into my hand, let it hang loosely at my side.

An atavistic crawl had started in my intestines—someone was creeping my house, and I was about to catch them in the act.

I stopped a moment, but I couldn't hear anything. The door to Jimmie's room was slightly open; I pushed it a couple more inches with my toe. As I did, someone grasped the windowsill, sprang over it. Leapt agilely into the backyard below. Someone dressed in black slacks and a black jacket with a loose hood over his head.

He landed on the grass—the yard banked up behind the house, so the drop was less than six feet. Glancing both directions, he crossed the backyard garden in a few long strides. The clothes concealed the weight, but it was someone tall. It might have been a good-sized man or a very tall woman.

Or a tall teenage boy.

There was a gate to the alley, and he stopped. Paused a moment, looked back at the house. The hood cast a shadow over his face; I couldn't make out any features.

I whirled, thinking someone was behind me, but I was alone. The room looked untouched, as if whoever it was had just used it as an exit.

When I looked back into the yard, the person had gone. The gate was still swinging.

I put the hammer down and went back to the bathroom. It was worse than I had expected. Blood was everywhere, slung as if from a paintbrush. It dotted the porcelain sink, ran in zigzagging strings down the walls, oozed in thick clots out of the toilet.

On the toilet lid four words were written in blood: GAME OVER YOU LOSE.

I started to raise the lid, withdrew my hand. Went to the toilet paper roll and tore off a long section. Wadded it into a big square and went back to the lid and raised it.

I sucked the air into my lungs and looked aside for a moment. When I looked back it was still there—it had survived my refusal to believe in it.

I dropped the toilet paper into the wastebasket and turned to see Razel frozen in the doorway, his hand pinched around his mouth, his cheeks discolored.

"What…?"

"Don't look. Let's wait for the cops," I said.

Chapter Four

I TOLD HARMON FOR THE FOURTH TIME THAT I WAS CERTAIN IT WASN'T Jimmie who had killed and dismembered the cat. A uniformed cop was fishing the remains out of the toilet bowl with a net while Harmon and I talked in the hallway.

It was Jimmie's pet I'd seen in the purplish-red water, one dead eye of its severed head staring up at me. Entrails had bulged out of a slit running from its testicles to the side of its neck.

"None of this makes any sense," I said to Harmon. "Killing another boy. Killing his own pet." I pounded my fist on the wall. "Jimmie loved that damned cat!"

Harmon was looking at me. I was spooked. Thoroughly spooked, remembering how Jimmie had flung his precious kitten on the floor that morning.

"What's written on the toilet lid is the same thing your brother said on the surveillance tape," he said.

I staggered away, my heart beating so hard the pulse was visibly jumping in my throat. I'd held together until the cops arrived. The first group had glided in, sirens off so as not to spook the suspect, four cruisers homing in from different directions at once. The cops didn't need my permission to enter the house, since they were hoping to arrest Jimmie.

But Jimmie wasn't in the house, so technically, they weren't allowed to do an evidence search incident to a lawful arrest.

They wanted to search anyway, of course, and I thought about allowing it—for a microsecond. Then I demanded they leave. They backpedaled to the front stoop, except for one who evaded me and slipped upstairs. I found him crawling under Jimmie's bed like a snake creeping through the undergrowth.

It gave me the heebie-jeebies, seeing legs sticking out from under my brother's bed. When I yanked him out, he didn't apologize, just tried to convince me it was in my best interest to cooperate. But I was over the edge by then, and I made good use of the energy of my hysteria.

The second pack of cops came with sirens screaming, blue lights throbbing. No reason for quiet, since they'd been radioed the suspect had flown the coop. The commotion got my across-the-street neighbor, Crazy Sally, stirred up. She started throwing things out of her third-floor bedroom window.

"Piiigss!" she screamed. Her glittery eyes flashed, her tangled hair danced. "Fuck you! Get out of my neighborhood, piiigss!"

The street was soon overflowing with people and cars. A network news van raced up, tried to park under Crazy Sally's house. One of her large crop of teenagers—they had names like Dark Star, Shama Lana, Shortkut—started kicking it. The girl had spiky purple hair and the kind of boots that were capable of making a dent. A couple of siblings came down to help her, and the uproar slowed the cops' efforts to block the street.

Razel had told me that Jimmie had run out the front door carrying his backpack. Razel had gone hollering after him, but Jimmie easily lapped him the few blocks to Geary. Once there, he had cut across four lanes of midday traffic, raced another block and hopped onto an electric bus.

"I had to sit down for ten minutes to catch my breath," Razel said. "I was dying, my dear. I don't think I've run that far since I was in knickers. There were actual sweat stains around my socks."

I squeezed his shoulder and gave him a vague peck on the cheek, an attempt to console him. Razel was a short man with slightly bandy legs, hair dyed auburn to blot the gray. Past sixty and constantly bemoaning the fact. Sometimes you can just look at a person and know he or she is utterly decent. Razel was like that—ridiculous, outrageous, even occasionally a complete lunatic, but always decent.

When the homicide detail got their warrant, three evidence techs headed straight for Jimmie's room. The one who had been under the bed started taking lifts off every surface. Another grunt took photos, strobe popping. A third pulled the bookshelves apart. I had expected them to be cops, but they were FBI and not trying to hide it, wearing white coats with the letters stenciled on the backs.

One of them, obviously a specialist, was checking Jimmie's computer. I stood in the doorway, watching the computer screen as he ran through the various files. He was young, dressed in a rugby shirt and jeans under the jacket. He scrolled through a series of screens rapidly. Checking internet sites Jimmie had logged—*Doom, Mortal Kombat, Alien Shooter, Quake,* the usual list. Nothing seemed to catch his attention.

"Pretty nifty computer setup for a teenager," he said. "Broadband link, lots of horsepower. Your brother use it much?"

"For games," I said. "Uh, you find any porn on it?"

"Not yet," he said, turning back to the screen.

Harmon stuck his head in the doorway. Told me he had questions. We went to the front room, and he looked around for someplace to sit. There wasn't anything suitable. My grandmother came from a miserable, manic-depressive farm town in Ireland, and my front room was stuffed with her pass-down furniture—an armchair with floral upholstery that stank like it housed dead things, a fussy little loveseat with a spavined back, a Lady of Mercy corner table missing two of its corners.

Harmon fished a small pad and a pencil out of his pocket, planted his posterior on the floral armchair. I waited for it to collapse; he was approximately twice the size of anyone who had ever sat in it. When it didn't, I found a perch and stared at the floor.

He didn't bother with any warm-up questions.

"Your brother own a T-shirt like the one on the tape? The one that said *toxic avenger?*"

There was a longish pause.

"Ms. O'Brien?"

I raised my eyes. He had clamped his teeth together. There were mean lines on his face.

I tried to smile. "Call me Cooper, please. No need to be so formal."

He chugged a little more wattage into the scowl. "I'd prefer we keep our titles, Ms. O'Brien."

Fine. "Look, under ordinary circumstances, I'd tell you everything I know. But you're asking a lot—Jimmie's my brother, after all. And besides, this whole thing is weird. That guy who's with you, Tuck…"

"What about him?"

"He's a piss-poor imitation of a homicide cop."

"He showed you his credentials."

"Which I never asked to see. I think he did it to forestall suspicion."

Harmon hesitated a beat. "You insinuating something? Why don't you just say it outright?"

"He's not regular homicide. He's not even a cop. And he isn't from this city."

He didn't respond. I went on, hoping he'd get pissed, let something slip.

"And he's sure as hell not your usual partner—the two of you are as awkward together as a couple of junior-highers at a sock hop."

Still nothing.

"Tuck's a chickenshit undercover agent, isn't he? Hearts are fluttering in Foggy Bottom about Stephen Ludlow's murder, and Tuck got detailed to liaise with the locals."

I would have laid odds on it. Tuck's awkwardness, his calling the city *Frisco*—he was no San Francisco homicide cop. It was trying to replace Lassie with an animal cracker. Other branches of the Feds weren't even trying to conceal their involvement.

I didn't expect Harmon to admit it, but I did expect him to ask me what in hell I was talking about. He merely stared at me, like he'd kissed an ugly woman who drooled on him.

I tried again.

"Someone was tipped off—and long before Stephen Ludlow got shot. The FBI couldn't have been here so quick otherwise. And the State Department would never have gotten one of their spooks on the case so soon. So, why don't you level with me? Maybe I can help."

Harmon's stare had become so intense the bottom rim of his right eye twitched.

"Tell me what's going on. One kid gets shot, and presto—we've got SFPD, we've got FBI and we've even got a DSS agent, all in his house a few hours later." I held up four fingers and the opposable thumb, a movie gesture, something you do all the time on a set. "Even a knucklehead could read this scene. This goes way beyond one dead boy. No matter how important his father is."

I was trying to decide whether to tell him about Walter's strange words. Wondering if he'd heard them already, maybe long before I did. Those words, and my own background, were the reasons I'd had the sense Tuck was actually DSS—run out of the

State Department in Foggy Bottom. Most people, even law enforcement people—hell, even State Department people—didn't know about the Office of Security's existence. But I knew. Oh, yes, I knew.

"Do they think Jimmie could be some kind of a stalking horse?" I asked. "There's motive, opportunity and means—isn't that the investigator's mantra? What's the angle on a motive?"

"The T-shirt?"

I'm not on your leash, you prick. You want answers, you tell me something first. I froze up my forehead. Chomped my teeth down into what Pa used to call my mulish-Mick-Irish grimace.

"I'm struggling with temptation, Ms. O'Brien," Harmon said, shifting his weight in the chair. A lot of red was coming out under the brown. He was angry, but he was trying to control it.

"So, call a priest," I said rudely.

His cheeks stayed brown, but his eyes went crimson.

"I don't have a flying foreign fuck of an idea what you're talking about," he said. "And I don't care enough to try to figure it out. What I do care about is a fifteen-year-old boy who got popped last night. A perfect shot by someone who knew exactly what he was doing."

I didn't speak.

Harmon hesitated a moment. "Don't think I didn't realize you monkeyed with that surveillance tape. I've already got grounds to have you charged with obstruction. You start cooperating or you're going to spend the next two years scrubbing floors with female street dealers and women who pour hot water on their kids."

"I'm not going to help you railroad Jimmie," I said. Just try to lock me up, I was thinking. Rick will have me kicked loose in an hour.

In the folds beneath my breasts I could feel telltale dampness starting to gather, but I was pleased I had inspired genuine anger in Harmon. Now, maybe, we would get somewhere.

"Nobody's being railroaded. The camera doesn't lie."

"Bunk," I said.

I waited for that little lightbulb look that would tell me Harmon got what I was saying, but it didn't appear. A filmed image or reality—did he really think they were the same thing?

Our attention was diverted by a thump from outside; Crazy Sally had started throwing garbage. A black bag sailed through the air, landed on top of a cruiser, broke apart, showering the windshield with coffee grounds, orange peels and wadded-up toilet paper.

"Piiiigsss! Piiiigsss! Take that, you piiiigsss!" she hissed in triumph.

Harmon pinched his eyes with his fingers, as if he was getting a headache.

"This neighborhood is a real cuckoo's nest, isn't it? Who is that woman? She have any working brain cells?"

"That's Sally Starhawk," I said. "She doesn't need brain cells."

Harmon was surprised.

"Sally Starhawk? The famous rock-and-roll drummer?"

I nodded. "Fifteen years ago, she was headlining at the Fillmore. Now she does guerrilla gigs at BART stations. The rest of the time she does riffs in front of her upstairs window. You should question her—maybe she saw the guy who was creeping my house."

"You ever do investigation work, Ms. O'Brien?" Harmon asked.

"No. For the last seven years I've been too busy creating truck-sized dinosaurs that walk through jungles, pick up people in six-foot teeth and crunch them down like Mars Bars. And making it believable enough that sometimes even cops scream."

In other words, filmed forgeries of reality are pretty damn good these days, and that's probably what we've got here, you big prick.

The mean lines were back.

"Then what the fuck gives you the idea I want your advice about this case?"

I jerked my chin. "It's not just the questionable evidence. There's no motive. My brother had no reason to kill Stephen Ludlow. There's no connection between the two boys. I'll bet they never even met."

"They met on the *Sea Dream,* that's for sure."

"They met on a videotape that was *filmed* on the *Sea Dream,*" I said. "That's not the same thing."

Harmon looked bored. "My meter's running overtime. The T-shirt, Ms. O'Brien."

Silence.

"The T-shirt!"

I swallowed. There was no way to fudge this, not really.

"My brother had a T-shirt with those words on it," I said carefully. "But so do a hundred other boys. It's the name of a popular videogame."

Harmon seemed relieved I had finally answered a question. He drummed his fingers on his massive thighs for a moment.

"You told me you knew the Ludlow boy."

"Slightly. Very slightly."

"And Mr. Ludlow? Much more than slightly, I take it?" He was watching me alertly.

"Nobody has offered me a hundred thousand to be on *Sex Lives of Rich and Famous San Francisco Men,* if that's what you're insinuating," I said coolly.

"But maybe they should have."

I bit my lip. Felt the blood come surging up my neck.

"You said there was no connection," Harmon pointed out. "But there's you. You're a connection."

"Fuck you! Piiiigsss! Piiiigsss!" Another thump.

42

"Not guilty," I said. "This has nothing to do with me."

Harmon pointed at a glass-framed photo sitting on the Lady of Mercy table.

"I thought I saw that photo in Mr. Capra's office."

It was Heather's latest school photo—black hair as glossy as a sealskin, eleven-year-old eyes so bright and full of joy they almost glowed in the dark.

I cleared my throat. Attempted a casual tone. "You did. She's his daughter."

Harmon seemed amazed. "His daughter? Mr. Capra's daughter?"

I cleared my throat again. "And mine. Our daughter."

"Fuck you, piiiigsss!"

Harmon got up, walked to the window and shoved it open.

"Do you have an eggbeater for a brain?" he roared at the cop on the street. "Put that woman out of business!"

"We're trying to arrest her, Detective Harmon," the cop hollered back. "She's got her door barricaded."

Harmon stood at the window a moment. Came back abruptly and sat down.

"Ancient history," I said, before he could speak.

"What?"

"Rick and I. Ancient history. It ended almost eight years ago. We work together these days, that's it." I cleared my throat for the third time.

Harmon gave me his cold stare. "Where is your daughter? At school? Or does she live with her father?"

"She lives with me. She's at an art camp down in Monterey right now."

He was still eyeing me.

I jumped up. "Heather is an art freak, she insisted on going. She loves painting, making things out of clay, anything visual. She's…she's possessed when she's drawing. She's tone-deaf,

Death Game

barely passing in school, but she glows with a white flame when she paints—"

"You know where your brother was last night?"

I was nearly knocked flat by an unexpected surge of misery. This would destroy Heather. In spite of his sullenness, Jimmie was a prince to her, a prince who could do no wrong. I had picked up her photo while I was talking; my hands were so sweaty it almost slipped out of my grasp.

I could feel Harmon's eyes on my back. I swallowed.

"Jimmie was home last night. With me."

"All night?"

I swallowed again. My tongue felt thick and bristly.

"I don't know. I went to bed around eleven."

"He could have gone out after that?"

"It's possible," I admitted.

Harmon shut his notebook. He was done.

"Wait," I said, turning.

"What?" he snapped.

Two things happened at that moment. An older cop lumbered into the room, touched Harmon on the shoulder, said something into his ear. Hearing the distinctive *whump-whump-whump-whump* of rotors, I went to the window—a helicopter was landing in an empty construction lot up the street. As I watched, a man exited, shielding his face with his hat against the dust being kicked up. When he stepped out of the turbulence, he put the hat back on his head.

I was dumbfounded. He was a ghost, a dead man come back to life.

44

Chapter Five

YOU CUT YOUR HAND," THE OLDER COP SAID, COMING TOWARD ME, concerned. While I had been looking at the helicopter, Harmon had left the room.

"No, I..."

"You broke the picture frame," he insisted. "Your fingers are bleeding."

I'd gripped the frame so tightly the glass had snapped. I saw the blood, but I didn't feel any pain. I put the broken frame down, looked back out the window.

The man was coming south, toward the house. Drab suit under a beige topcoat. Tan felt hat with a black band. Two-tone wingtips. Wingtips? It wasn't possible. It couldn't be...

"Who is that?" I whispered to the cop.

He didn't look out the window. "You should go wash your hands. There might be glass in the cuts."

My fingers were dripping blood on the carpet. I wiped them awkwardly on a newspaper. The man was still walking toward the house.

"What's the matter?" the cop asked.

I tried to laugh, but the sound came out cracked.

"You ever thought you saw a ghost? And then wished it *was* a

45

Death Game

ghost? Because it would be so hard, so painful, to see the living person that even their ghost would be preferable?"

The man had stopped. Several others met him. Rambo, I thought. You heard me. You came home.

But I couldn't tell, not for sure; they were too far away. There were handshakes all around, a quick conversation. Slight nods and respectful demeanors—they were deferring to him.

"Who is he?" I asked the cop.

He glanced out the window. Shrugged. "Never saw him before. Why?"

"He reminds me of someone."

The man had turned around and was retreating back to the helicopter. Two of those he'd conferred with accompanied him, one on either side. He glanced over his shoulder, back towards the house.

The older cop was trying to be kind.

"You know, I wouldn't drive yourself nuts over this. Lots of kids from good families turn into bad-asses. It ain't that easy to figure out why."

The helicopter lifted off. It hovered a moment, then veered north. I watched it head over the bay until it became a toy helicopter, not quite real.

Harmon re-entered the room. He waited until the other cop left to drop a bomb.

"You know anything about handguns?" he asked, snapping off a pair of gloves.

I shook my head.

"We just found a loaded handgun in your tenant's workroom. It was stuffed in a trash receptacle next to a sewing machine, under some scraps of fabric."

Tuck stood behind him; dangling from his hand was a paper bag. Harmon pointed to the bag, and Tuck opened it so I could see inside.

46

"This belong to your brother?" he asked.

I felt like someone had socked me in the stomach. This was bad, real bad.

"Jimmie never owned a handgun," I whispered.

A flame had started to lick up in Harmon's eyes. "But it's not yours, is it?"

"It's the same type of semiautomatic pistol that was on the tape," Tuck interjected. "Unofficially, of course, until I get another chance to review the film. But I'd say that firearm was a Glock 17, or maybe a 19."

"Glock 19 pistol," Harmon said. "That's what we've got here. A very expensive gun, don't see them very often." He tried to be fair. "Your tenant? Could it be his?"

"My tenant would be as likely to keep a loaded gun in his room as a live cobra."

"How well do you know him?" Tuck asked.

"Very well. He's a close friend, not just a tenant."

"You trust him with a teenage boy in the house?" Tuck asked.

I could feel my neck blotching with anger.

"*Sieg heil,*" I said rudely to Tuck. "You are a bastard, aren't you? Whatever he is, at least he's not a slimy spook like you."

"You've really got a mouth," Harmon said to me. "You're not doing yourself any favors."

"X out the spies," I said to Tuck, ignoring Harmon.

Tuck made a strangled sound. Immediately turned it into a coughing attack, trying to cover his reaction.

"Hah!" I snapped my fingers. "I knew it. You *are* a DSS agent. What's your usual gig? Counterespionage?"

"X out the spies" was the underground slogan of agents who worked for the Diplomatic Security Service. The headquarters of the Office of Security and its DSS department were deep inside the endless underground corridors of the old State Department building in Foggy Bottom.

DSS is responsible for protecting foreign dignitaries in the United States from assassination attempts. They also help bring to justice terrorists, drug czars, organized crime kingpins and serial murderers, although the local police or the FBI always takes the credit. They are the best-kept secret in American law enforcement—and I wouldn't have known of their existence myself, except...

Well, except for Rambo.

My pa worked for the DSS—finally confessed to it while we were sitting in a seedy San Francisco bar, knocking back whiskeys.

"I've shook hands with presidents, prime ministers, a shah—once I even guarded Princess Di," the old man had said. "I've been to a three-sheet mezza, a hundred high teas and every McDonald's in the world." He looked at his Scotch. "I've drunk a thousand kinds of liquor—stuff from bottles with no labels, stuff from bottles with the wrong labels—and only got sick once. I've pulled bodies out of embassy bombings, chased a spymaster called Zia al-Haq through four kill zones and been to some very wild embassy and State parties. Uh, you're not going to tell your mother any of this, are you?"

I'd looked at him then, feeling surrealistic. He hadn't been wearing wingtips that night; he'd been wearing high heels. As well as a blond wig and a rabbit fur coat dyed powder-puff blue.

For years I thought my father was insane. I thought he had delusions of heroism. Rambo-in-wingtips—always sneaking out at night, trying to save the world. Most times, he'd come back in the early morning hours, but sometimes he'd be gone for months.

When I was twenty-eight, I'd been driving through Japantown late one night, near the Russian embassy. We were getting a film ready for release, and I had been working the night shift at the Optical Zone, my employer. I was about cross-eyed from the effort of getting a protoplasmic alien to emerge realistically from a checkerboard floor.

My trusty Fiat was giving me trouble, and I pulled over. Got out to check the engine. There was a cross-dresser on the sidewalk. He did a double take, almost fell into the street. It made me look closely at him, and that's when I realized who he was.

My pa.

He was doing undercover work in front of the embassy, concealing a bulky listening device in an iron maiden bra under the rabbit fur. But I didn't know that at first. At the time, I was just horrified. What do you say to your father when you think he's a cross-dresser? What do you say to your mother?

I got back in my car, but by then, Pa's cover was blown. We went to a bar, found a corner booth and talked it through. I don't know which of us was more embarrassed.

"Don't tell your mother," he repeated.

I took another big swallow of my Scotch. It was hard to look at him.

"You really think Mom doesn't know, Pa?"

"Of course not." He picked up his Scotch with a hand ending in half-inch red fingernails. Downed it in two gulps, then pointed at my empty glass. "Who taught you to drink like that?"

You did, old man. And you're wrong about Mom—of course, she knows.

The whisky had helped. And Pa seemed relieved he could talk about it. Occasionally, after that, when we were alone, he'd discuss what someone like him did in a general way. He'd always looked down on my job in film. Now that he was free to talk about his profession, he started to hint that maybe I should think about following in his footsteps.

Then came the car accident. After that, Pa started rearing up in my dreams and thoughts. Sometimes I'd even think I saw him. At night, I'd wake up, go to the window and look for him. Sometimes I'd sit for hours, staring out into the darkened street.

Death Game

There was always this lingering hope he didn't really die—the drunk had disappeared after the trial, and he'd had a very pricey lawyer for a lay-around in a bar. And that coroner who hung up on me—I'd never been able to track him down.

It occurred to me that maybe the DSS had suspicions the car accident was an assassination attempt. They might have thought that faking Pa's death was the only way to take the heat off him and keep the rest of the family from being progressively murdered.

*　　　*　　　*

The room had been silent too long.

"I don't know what you're talking about," Tuck said to me, having to say something. "But about this tenant…"

I was done. I walked around him and stuck my head in the hallway.

"Razel," I yelled. "Get out here and defend yourself. You're about to be slandered."

The bathroom door rattled, and he came out—he'd run down the hall to the downstairs bathroom earlier. I figured he'd had an urgent call of nature after seeing the dismembered cat. Probably a whole series of them, since he hadn't emerged since.

He looked a little green around the gills when he entered the room. He straightened himself up, wiped his top lip with the back of one finger.

"Just a little untoward indigestion," he said airily.

"Is this your handgun?" Harmon asked, showing it to him.

Razel stared at the semiautomatic pistol, his mouth an O.

"Well?" Harmon asked irritably.

"What would it mean if it was?" He gave Harmon a crafty look.

"It's a simple question. Just answer it."

"No questions are simple," Razel said primly. "E. M. Forster."

"Who?" Harmon asked.

50

"I may be just a worn-out fag to you, sweetheart, but I'll have you know I was reading the classics before my mum got me out of nappies."

Harmon gave his head a tiny shake, as if a gnat were buzzing in his ear.

But Razel wouldn't be bullied. He sat down. Gave his pants a discrete tug to straighten the seam.

"Razel, tell him it's not your gun," I said resignedly.

"I don't think it's my gun," he agreed. "Although it's possible it could be and I forgot about it." He yawned slightly. Covered his teeth with three fingers.

"Is that a yes or a no?" Harmon asked. "Stop wasting my time."

"I couldn't be sure either way, sweetheart," Razel said, straightening the other seam. "I'll have to think about it."

"You handle this," Harmon growled at Tuck. He yanked the bag holding the weapon out of Tuck's fingers and left the room. A moment later, I heard him roaring at someone.

Tuck nodded a few times and smiled his possum smile. Moved in close and put a light hand on Razel's shoulder.

"There's no reason for this to be unpleasant. Maybe it would help if I explained a couple things. We'll get a lab report on this firearm. We'll check fingerprints, registration. We'll know, eventually, so it's not like you're causing any problems for your, uh, landlady here."

"I said I had to think about it—don't rush me." Razel said, but his voice had weakened.

I went into the kitchen to wash the cuts on my fingers; it took a couple of minutes to pick the glass out and find a bandage. When I came back, Razel was admitting he'd never seen the gun before.

"Your landlady's brother?" Tuck asked, twisting his head to look at me. "He could have put it there, couldn't he? Maybe because he was trying to hide it? You don't keep your doors

Death Game

locked all the time, do you?"

Razel fidgeted a little. Tuck leaned close to him, narrow eyes glinting. There was a little buzz in the room.

"He never locks his doors," I said. "Why would he?"

"Well, I have four locks on my windows, and I do grease the windowsills with butter," Razel said, trying to hold up. He smiled at Tuck. "I'm a nervous wreck sometimes, thinking of all the murderers on the street."

"But your landlady's brother? He could have gotten into your rooms, right?"

Razel hesitated one more beat, and then nodded.

Before the cops left they took pictures of everything in Jimmie's room. Carried all of Jimmie's clothes and shoes out. By then, Razel had packed a suitcase.

"You're going to have to make a run for it," I said, peering out the window. The cops had left, but press dogs were all over the street.

"You don't think it's beastly of me? Leaving you at a time like this?"

"Hans is waiting," I said.

Hans, a Danish flight attendant with KLM, had just pulled his tiny rental car up at the corner. His chubby, worried face was framed by the window.

Razel fidgeted a bit.

"Sparks were flying in here. You were flirting with that slimy agent," I said, trying to lighten the mood with joking. "And all the time, Hans was waiting. You must be desperately horny these days."

"It's the consequence of old age," Razel said sadly. "You're always making an ass of yourself. Fidelity goes out the window." A moment later, he brightened. "Can you blame me for hoping? Those slim hips. That air of danger."

"That sneering grin. Those fuck-me-please eyes. That god-

52

awful aftershave."

"Yes," Razel sighed happily. "He was wearing Lagerfeld, did you notice? I was pretending I was in a smoky bar in Amsterdam, trying to withstand a slow seduction."

Hans honked the horn, and Razel startled a bit. He checked out the window.

"Enough news vans to cover an earthquake," he muttered. "You sure you'll be okay?" There was concern on his face.

I gave him a fierce hug. My chest was tight; my throat constricted. He leaned over to pat my cheek then darted out, reporters and cameramen in hot pursuit.

I immediately felt bereft. Razel had shown up at my front door seven years before, needing new digs because the last of his money had gone trying to keep his partner comfortable and pay for his medication. Heather, a sturdy-legged toddler, had followed him around while, bleary-eyed, feverish, he'd kept talking about the man he'd loved and lost. Catching the sadness in his tones, she had shoved her bedraggled, tattered Big Bird into his knees—her most treasured possession.

Razel finally took it. Started turning the bright-yellow toy over and over, like a dog worrying a stick, or a raccoon handling a corncob. As I watched him, he reminded me of a poor sick animal with its foot stuck in a trap, so wild with pain it couldn't figure out which limb hurt. I had the sense he'd been telling the same sad story to everyone he met—the kid server at the diner, the fat woman in the grocery store line.

I didn't expect to hear from him again, but he ended up signing a sublease, ignoring my warnings about flimsy walls and tubercular plumbing. He used half of my rented house as a place to both live and work. A window dresser by trade, he spent countless hours at his Singer, laboring over huge swathes of velvet to create swags and draping. Fussed interminably, pincushion dangling from his wrist, with his mannequins.

Considering his age and childless status, I thought Heather would make Razel nervous. She did, dreadfully, until one evening I walked in to find him reading his beloved Shakespeare to her, a funny section from *A Midsummer's Night Dream*. I watched, puzzled, while she settled against his bony shoulder and listened intently to every word.

Razel told me later that Heather had replenished his faith in humankind, worn perilously thin. An unusual child, mute and almost flash-frozen around ordinary people, she chattered endlessly with Razel, regarded him as her best friend. Knowing Heather, she'd stand by him through thick and thin for as long as he lived.

I was standing at the window in the front room, stupidly letting myself be seen from the street, when a flash exploded in my face. There were bangs on the back door—the press had the house surrounded.

Ignoring the racket, I drew a bucket of hot water and scrubbed the upstairs bathroom. My eyes burned from the ammonia; the water kept turning purple with blood as I washed the words off.

Game over. You lose.

What game? I wondered. And who had lost? Jimmie? But it was Stephen who was dead.

When I was done, I threw the gloves in the kitchen sink. Got a bottle of Scotch, sat at the kitchen table and knocked one back, neat. Threw another one back. My esophagus contracted, tears came to my eyes.

I couldn't figure it out. Who had been in the house? What had been their purpose? And where could Jimmie have gone? Dunno. Dunno. Dunno...

I felt like an idiot. How many times had I been blindsided in the past twelve hours?

I called Heather then, told her the exact truth but kept it

short. She took it calmly—so calmly I knew her father had already called her.

"Jimmie will come back, Mom," she said. "He couldn't have hurt anyone." She sounded untroubled, as if she was certain of it.

Then came the worst—nothing left to do. There was a picture of Jimmie on the fridge, holding his kitten—a mere fur ball then—grinning into the camera. Mom and Pa were next to him. Mom looked so real I could almost smell the lavender shampoo in her hair. Pa was holding his shades. His green eyes were intense, the skin under them slightly pale.

Staring at the picture, I felt as if someone had pulled the pin on a fragmentation grenade and thrown it right into the middle of my life. The explosion had blown everything apart. Sent pieces toppling over and over again into the far distance. Mom. Pa. And now Jimmie.

When night came, I took four pills and fell asleep with my head on the kitchen table. A long while after that—it was dark, I didn't know what time it was—I found myself in Jimmie's bedroom. I felt woozy, uncertain of how I'd even gotten there.

Jimmie's bed was unmade. I thought I would climb in, sleep there, but I ended up on the floor, huddled next to a portable electric heater. I didn't know what I was doing on the floor. I reached to turn heater on. I was confused; the air around me was misty and dim.

I got up to leave the room, or thought I did. I couldn't move. I had a sense that someone was standing or moving about nearby. I felt the way you feel when you sense, but don't see, someone near you on a darkened street.

Soon after that I smelt something like wet sulfur. There was a kind of dull haze in the room. The smell seemed to permeate everything.

The bad smell didn't alarm me because Jimmie's room often smelled of something horrible. Cold, congealed pizza scraps

Death Game

rotting in a corner. Rolled up underwear festering under the bed. Acne medicine, hair goop, jock itch cream, sweat-soaked tennis shoes...

I tried again to get up, but mists oozed around me. The air was so thick it blotted everything out. I felt wooly, semiconscious, surrounded by haze and murkiness—and the bad smell was stronger.

There was a silhouette in the room. A human silhouette. It was black with sparkling shadows behind it. I tried again to get up, but my feet felt wired together. Heat struck me, and I wilted back, tried to roll away, couldn't move.

Little tongues of red licked at me, grew swiftly, became ravenous and demonic. My spine was frozen. Whatever it was, it was bearing down on me and I...couldn't...move...

Fingers clutched my shoulder. The grip was strong but gentle, reassuring.

"What's the matter? Can't you get up?"

The hand stayed on me, but the grip turned fierce and shook me.

"Get up. You need to get out of here."

The hand pulled at me again. The next thing I knew I was outside the house on the street, looking at a black sky with a few stars sprinkled over it, wrapped to the chin in a scratchy blanket. I rolled over, started coughing and tried to get up.

"Just lay still, Cooper," he said, with exasperation. "The paramedics are coming. I want them to check you out."

"I'm all right, Rick," I whispered, my throat raw from the smoke. "What happened?"

I knew before he answered me, knew what had been teasing my nostrils the whole time. Not the smell of sweat-soaked socks or two-month-old pepperoni or anything else I had ever smelled in Jimmie's room before. This time it had been the smell of smoke.

Chapter Six

IT WAS RAINING HARD WHEN I WENT BACK TO WORK, A COLD, WET, horrible Friday afternoon; and the first person I saw was the last person I wanted to see—Walter Ludlow.

He was in Rick's private office, and he caught sight of me in the doorway, motioned me to come in. I entered, tried not to shiver. Rick's vast private office was blow-your-brains-out cold. A corner office, naturally. Mitered walls of floor-to-ceiling windows gave way to a spectacular 180-view of the city skyline, and the bay and ocean beyond.

I had assumed Walter was alone, but Rick sat across the room, looking out the windows. Looking through the walls of neighboring skyscrapers at the famous orange bridge, one of the few truly beautiful creations of an aberrant, apocalyptic century.

"Rick?" I was in a shitty mood. I badly needed to talk to Walter, but I just didn't feel like it.

Walter pointed at a leather sofa across from him, and I sat down. So many bad feelings were surging there was a kind of dizziness. All in all, I was almost throttled with misery—dizzy, nervous, confused, angry, cold. Especially cold.

"I'm sorry about what happened, Walter," I said. "I know it looks bad for Jimmie, but I don't think it's that simple. The two of us, maybe we can figure it out."

"I heard about the fire," he said, as if I hadn't spoken. "Was it an accident?"

I hugged my chest to warm myself. Didn't answer.

"Cooper?"

I glanced at Rick and lowered my voice. "Those things you said last time I saw you, Walter. What did you mean?"

"You think someone started the fire?" Walter's face had assumed a tiny frown, as if I were persisting in telling him a dirty joke.

"You called it a new...atrocity, a new way to kill. But Stephen was shot, and you already knew that. I don't—"

"The fire," he said sharply. "We were talking about the fire."

No, we were not.

Walter's paranoid behavior when I met him in the elevator had stayed with me. I'd wondered, at the time, if he had something to do with his son's death. All that nonsense he'd spouted, the way he'd said, "At least, I don't have that on my conscience." In Rick's office, he'd even admitted that he and Stephen had words. More than words—an argument that had sent Stephen running out of the house.

But after we saw the tape, Walter's face had been shocked, then murderously angry. I would have sworn, seeing his face, he had nothing to do with his son's death.

If so, he wasn't the type to sit back, rely on the cops to bring his son's killer to justice. He would be about the serious business of vengeance, and he'd have everything planned, down to the last detail. Nor would he waste time.

But then he said something that blew everything I was thinking to smithereens.

"Stephen's memorial service is next week, Cooper. I want you to come."

My blood instantly turned to ice. I bit my lips. "Walter, I...uh, don't think…"

"I'd appreciate it."

Words completely failed me. I flashed him a look.

"I would appreciate it," he repeated. He was looking softly at me. It was utterly insidious, Walter's look. He was saying: *I still care about you. I still want you. In spite of everything, I still want you, Cooper.*

Oh, God.

"If it's important to you, you know I'll be there," I said. I dropped my gaze to my hands; my head was reeling with this sudden change. Were we friends? Or enemies? He'd asked for my trust, but I'd never trusted him. Had that been a mistake?

I tried again.

"Walter, I can't stop thinking about the things you said the morning Stephen died."

There was dead silence in the room.

"I don't remember saying anything. I must have been in shock."

I took a deep breath.

"You asked for my help. You asked me to trust you, not…" I glanced at Rick. We'd been standing outside his door; I'd thought that was whom Walter meant.

"That's ridiculous, Cooper. You must be mistaken."

All of his tenderness—real or assumed—had dematerialized blindingly fast. Almost as fast as it had emerged. The coldness in the room had increased a hundredfold.

I repressed another shiver, admitted to myself the chill I felt was as much internal as external. Ever since the fire, I'd been frozen up inside. It was as if my mind had fled into a bunker deep inside my skull and was peering out at the wreckage through a narrow, armored slit. Seeing pictures of my family, I'd do a body count. One, two, three—Mom, Pa, Jimmie—dead or missing, all within a year.

Death Game

Luck of the Irish, I'd think, trying to make myself laugh. Only it wasn't funny.

When Walter prompted me again about the fire, I spoke bluntly, almost hostilely.

"The cops don't think it was an accident. They think someone started it."

Walter raised an eyebrow. "Who?"

"Me."

"They accused you of arson?"

I exhaled and stared into space.

"Of trying to destroy evidence they might have overlooked."

What were you trying to destroy, Ms. O'Brien? Something that might further implicate your brother? Do you realize destruction of evidence is a felony? That had been Harmon's opening salvo.

"How did it start?'

"A heater tipped over on a rug. It caught fire."

"It was accidental?"

"Of course."

"You're certain? But—"

"Absolutely fucking certain. It was an accident." I rarely interrupted the Grand Old Man, certainly not this coarsely, but he'd been jerking me around too much in the past few minutes. The fire had been purposeful—of course, it had been purposeful. In addition to the presence I'd sensed, the timing was too coincidental.

Maybe it had been Walter. He certainly seemed interested— very interested—in whether it had been considered an accident.

Walter had dimensions I'd never probed. The few nights I'd spent with him hadn't given me any window to his soul. Hell, all it had given me were hallucinations and enough Catholic guilt to sink a battleship.

Walter was a vast blank space to me, even more so since Stephen's murder. I couldn't figure it out—why did he care about the fire? What about his son's murder? He'd asked for my help, wanted an ally last time I'd seen him. Maybe he still did, but I didn't think so. He had something else up his sleeve.

I couldn't figure out what.

I wanted to run out of the office, but I tightened my mouth, licked my lips. I didn't really want Walter as an ally; I was too afraid of him. Between the two of them, Rick and Walter would tear me limb from limb. But I couldn't go it alone.

The insanity of this, the debased, frantic nature of everything, swam over me. I felt weak, inconsequential, brittle as glass, caught in the no-man's land between the two men. Rick, with the ghosts of the men he had killed standing around his bedside, was like a loaded gun with a hair trigger. Walter, for all his imperiousness and will to dominate, was subtle, essentially cunning, a planner.

Walter would never act purely out of passion, the way Rick did instinctively every day of his life. No, Walter would sing you a song of love while he licked honey off the knife he was planning to stick in your back.

"You said there was no connection. But there's you. You're a connection."

So Harmon had pointed out.

Maybe you're right, you big prick.

I looked at Walter, wondering if he had sent out his minions. Maybe they'd already tracked Jimmie down and were pouring acid down his throat. Afterwards, they'd cut off Jimmie's ears and send them back to Walter for his trophy case.

Men who own international tanker businesses don't bother with niceties.

I glanced at Rick. Overall, I preferred him as an ally over Walter. But Walter had asked me for help. Had almost begged for it. And if he still needed my help, then I had something to trade. If nothing else, it might persuade him to call his dogs off Jimmie.

A sick breach opened in me as I repeated, once again, the words he had said to me.

"Walter, you asked for my help. You said there was something—"

"I asked for your help? You're not making sense, Cooper."

Was he mocking me? I couldn't tell. Walter's voice was so cold it put a boundless chasm between us.

I licked my lips, looked back at Rick. But Rick was in a funk, face averted. He seemed to be watching raindrops roll slowly down the sheets of tinted glass.

There was a horrible feeling in the room.

Why was Walter denying his earlier words? Well, Walter being Walter, maybe I should have expected it. But what in hell was the matter with Rick? What could be so fascinating out those windows?

I wanted to get up, look out them myself. See if there were any clues out there.

When I glanced back at Walter, he had put his hand on his chest, sat up straighter, as if he'd suddenly felt severe pain. His face had paled, and sweat gathered on his brow.

"Are you okay?" I asked.

"It's nothing," he said, with an effort. He pulled out a handkerchief and blotted his forehead.

"Are you sure you're okay?"

Walter's lips had started to turn blue, and his skin was ashen. Sweat ran out of his hairline. He began swallowing deep in his throat, as if his lungs were laboring for air. I hurried out the door to get a glass of water. Brought it back, along with a few ice cubes in a cup.

When I returned, Rick was alone in his office. He was on his feet, standing in front of his wall of windows.

"Where's Walter?" I asked, going over to him.

"Went on to Sea Transport offices. He'd just stopped by for a moment." He sounded as if he was surprised I'd even asked.

"There was something wrong with him," I said. "He had some kind of a spell. Was he ill?"

"Ill?" Rick scoffed. "Walter's never ill." He shot me a sideways look. "You'll go to Stephen's memorial service, won't you? I'll pick you up. We might as well go together."

I stood for a moment, looking at him out of the corner of my eye. We hadn't spoken since the night of the fire. While waiting for the paramedics, he'd told me he'd driven over late, wanting to talk, and seen smoke coming out of the house. Pounded on the door and, when there was no answer, picked the lock. He'd put out the fire using the little red extinguisher I kept under the kitchen sink.

It had taken me almost a week to finally make it back to the office—I'd left Rick a message saying I needed a couple of days off to look for Jimmie. I'd kept running into cops when I'd cruise the places where the runaway kids hung out—The Haight, Polk Street, the Civic Center, the loading docks, the Park. The cops were doing citywide sweeps while I was hoofing it, passing around Jimmie's picture and an occasional tenner, asking for information.

I didn't know if the cops had any leads, but for me it had been a complete waste of time.

Rick was waiting for an answer.

"I think it's best I go alone. Thanks, anyway."

His lips twitched a fraction. His voice turned stubborn.

"You should go with me. Walter will expect it."

"Fine. Whatever you and Walter decide you want from me."

Rick ignored the sarcasm. He relaxed, stretched and un-hunched his shoulders.

"Don't run out of here," he said as I headed for the door. "We need to talk. You hear from that fucking flatfoot recently?"

"Oh, yeah. We hate each other so much, we're bound to end

up buds. That's how it goes in the movies, doesn't it?"

Detective Harmon had had me down to the Metro station house to ask more questions. I'd repeated everything I'd told him before. He'd called me again in the evening hours. More questions. Same answers.

"He have any idea where Jimmie could be?"

As if he would tell me, I thought sourly. The murder had made the front page of the *San Francisco Chronicle*, upper right corner, three-column head jumping to Section A, page 2: SHIPOWNER'S HEIR SHOT ON YACHT: ANOTHER TEENAGER SUSPECTED. The fire had even rated a front page story the next day, jumping to page 4: FIRE AT MURDER SUSPECT'S HOUSE.

The press hounds at the *Chronicle* had run several more stories about the murder, competing with the tabloids, who were making it all as lurid as possible. With the third story, the *Chronicle* had printed a photo of Stephen, his eyes obscured by big glasses and his skinny shoulders tensed.

There had been some debate about whether the local papers and the TV news were going to run Jimmie's photo. They had finally settled for a composite sketch a police artist made from the surveillance tape—there was Jimmie's status as a minor to take into consideration, as well as the fact he had no criminal record.

Rick was still asking questions, doing his lawyer bit, giving me the third degree. He seemed to think Harmon and I could have declared a truce.

I cut him off. "Harmon's only biding his time until he has my puny ass pitched into a holding cell. According to him, the DA is dithering about which felony to arraign me for first—obstruction of justice or destruction of evidence."

"Harmon's just playing you," Rick said airily, his mood lightening as mine darkened. "There's no case for obstruction. And if the DA goes after you for destroying evidence I can swear I found you in the victim's, not the perpetrator's, position, about to be turned into a crispy critter."

"Well, legal eagle, pass that along to Harmon next time you talk to him. Maybe he'll stop threatening me."

"Don't go," Rick said again as I was once more stalking towards the door.

But I kept going.

Chapter Seven

RICK WASN'T ABOUT TO LET ME LEAVE.

"Jala disappeared," he said just as I reached the doorway. "Damn fool," he added idly.

I whirled around. "What do you mean, Jala disappeared?"

He twitched a shoulder.

"He vamoosed somewhere. Probably took off for Vegas to gamble or ogle naked women."

"Well, that sucks," I said. "That was his terrible handwriting on the surveillance tape, wasn't it?"

Jala was only semi-literate in English, and his penmanship was atrocious.

"Big deal. He picked up the surveillance tapes. Then he went to Sonoma with the rest of the guys. The cops know all that. So what?"

"So, he was on the *Sea Dream* that morning. Harmon wanted to question him. Did he?"

Rick knocked the heavy Mexican silver ring he always wore on his left ring finger against the table. One of his classic stalling gestures—he called it his "oh-fuck, five-seconds-while-I-try-to-remember pause."

"He never got the chance," I concluded flatly.

Another light tap. *Ping.*

I regarded him with hostility.

"Jala didn't vamoose on his own. You told him to find a crack and slip into it for a while so he couldn't be questioned. Didn't you?"

He gave me a look. "Why in hell are you so hostile, Cooper? I saved your neck in that fire. You forgotten that already?"

Yeah, yeah, yeah. But you're not telling me everything you know about Stephen's murder. And you've got plenty to tell.

Rick, being Rick, was far too clever to implicate himself in any kind of a cover-up. The most I could hope for was to trick him into revealing something, in a roundabout way.

"Jala wouldn't go to Las Vegas," I said, keeping my tone even. "He's a devout Muslim."

He shrugged again. "All the more reason. Those fundamentalists can only stand it so long before they slip the leash and start fornicating and drinking."

"Jala is a genuine zealot, Rick. His father's a religious teacher in Yemen. He's hardly the evening-lap-dance-after-prayers type."

He yawned. "So, maybe that's the answer. Maybe his father told him to come home and mind the donkeys."

"Did he even have a green card? Or was he one of your cash-and-carry employees?"

He didn't answer, which was answer enough.

"If Jala left the country he'll never get back in."

He made a face. "Every fucking flea that ever wanted to nip the ass or suck the juice of America can get into this country. All they have to do is be patient. Hell, I spit out that window right now..." He pointed. "...a thousand illegals will get wet."

I couldn't disagree. The Chinese, the Saudis, the Filipinos, the Iranians, even the Iraqis and Sudanese, were using the Mexican connection to get into California. They massed in the border towns; coyotes ferried them north. Dumped them in the big coastal cities, where they had no trouble disappearing into the local scene.

Rick's phone buzzed and he picked it up, listened for three seconds.

"I know, I know, I know! I told ya, you'll get it soon." He listened for another three seconds. "I told you, *You'll...get...it...soon.*" He slammed down the phone, shook himself like a wet dog, as if to throw off the phone call. "Assholes," he muttered.

"Are you having money problems, Rick?"

"What?" He shook his head. "No way."

But he didn't explain who the assholes were or what they wanted.

When I'd first met him, Rick had been fresh out of the military, and his office had been the back of a rent-a-wreck Jeep. A lot of lean years had gone by. Then, suddenly, golly-gee, money had fallen out of the sky. It wasn't a matter of a business picking up. It was yesterday I'm a peon, today I'm a master of the universe. I just rented the fanciest goddamn office in the city.

I was pretty sure I knew how it had happened, but I'd never asked. I'd never wanted to know, actually. I still didn't want to know but felt I had to.

I put out a feeler.

"What's your monthly nut on this place? And all the equipment you lease," I said, thinking of the AVID machine I used to edit reenactments. "That must cost you a fortune."

He was silent.

"I never could figure out how you got so far so fast," I said. "No bank would finance you. A law degree barely means anything anymore. Remember all those...tough years?"

"You remember them? I thought you'd wiped your memory clean of the days when I was a fucked-up wreck. Forgotten we ever even lived together."

He wasn't going to get me off track that easily.

"What's the secret to your sudden success, Rick? You never told me how you finally broke out of the pack."

He didn't respond.

I glanced around the office.

"Walter set you up?" I guessed. "He's been fronting you. What is he? Some kind of a silent partner?"

Rick didn't answer.

"Is that why he comes over here? To keep an eye on his money?"

My voice and body language were mild, conversational, but I was breathing quickly.

Rick did not allow an eyelash to flutter.

"Walter's no friend of yours, not really. So he must be getting something back in exchange for risking his money. And it'd have to be something big, because Walter doesn't do anything unless it's big," I stood up, stretched. "Uh...what could you and Walter be doing, Rick? Nothing illegal, I hope?"

"You're way off the mark," he said. "Walter has never loaned me a dime." He frowned. "Besides, Walter would never get involved in anything illegal."

"Walter is the Prince of Darkness," I said, mostly to myself. "He lives in an international shadow world, like all self-made billionaires. The motives in that world are so above us you and I could never hope to comprehend them."

"Don't pretend you hate Walter," Rick said, flashing me an angry look. "I know better."

I opened my mouth, but he suddenly slammed his fist against the window.

"Fuck all—fuck all the Ludlow family! I'm sick of them!" He turned to pound his fist on his desk. "Fuck all of them!" He swept his arm over the top, knocking his lamp onto the floor, smashing the bulb.

Death Game

I stared at him and couldn't help but laugh.

"Well, glad you got that off your chest."

He picked up the lamp, looked at it, then smashed it down, cracking the base.

"Shit, how in hell do I get myself so fucked..." He stopped, took a breath and got himself under control. Sitting down, he stared morosely at the lamp he'd just broken. A desolate smile crossed his lips. "Okay, I'm broke, I admit it. That reenactment you've been working on? I can't bankroll the case any longer. I'm going to have to tell Bill he'll never get his day in court. We'll have to cut a deal with the fucking insurance boys."

I didn't know what to say; this was terrible news. The reenactment was of a woman who had been killed in a pedestrian accident. She was the mother of four, husband a fireman. She'd been in a coma for months, and Bill hadn't been able to take it—he was drinking and the kids were running wild.

A window installer's truck had run a stoplight, the installation company was part of a national franchise, the insurance company had deep pockets. Rick had been expecting a major win in a jury trial.

"Giving up on that case hurts," he said, and I actually saw water in his eyes. "Hurts in ways you can't imagine, babe."

It was an extraordinary moment, like the moment in a theater when an actor comes through the curtain to take a bow, having shed the character he or she has been playing like some second skin.

This was the real Rick coming out. Rick was driven, competitive as hell, even cutthroat sometimes, but also empathetic to a fault. Sure, he was an attorney, the scum of the earth. But he cared about his poor luckless clients—cared too much, actually. He attached his fate to theirs. Got hurt right along with them. It was the main reason he had never—so far as I knew—made much money as an attorney.

70

Successful personal injury attorneys are bloodless fucks. They have no problem cashing in on the misery of others.

I felt a brief, sweet moment of sympathy. I'd always accused Rick of having a Robin Hood complex, stealing from the rich to help the poor. But Robin Hood was a good guy, wasn't he? A hero?

Abruptly, I decided to level with him. I'd always known I would—eventually. Rick could be a real shit, but that was irrelevant. Historical beefs didn't count, not when it came to my brother's life. At least, that's what I told myself.

"I don't think Walter believes Jimmie killed Stephen," I said.

Rick's forehead puckered. "Of course, he does. It was on the surveillance tape."

"Which could have been doctored."

"You thought so? When you saw it?"

"No," I admitted. I could have missed the alterations, seeing it just once. But nights, whenever I wasn't looking for Jimmie, I'd been going through my copy of the tape, examining it frame by frame. It was possible the tape had been altered, through special effects, as a complicated photomontage done with image-processing software. The actual person who killed Stephen could have been digitally separated from the background and deleted—a painstaking job, since deleting a person includes deleting his shadows and reflection on objects in the room.

The problem was that Jimmie would have had to be filmed in front of a blue screen duplicating exactly the motions of the killer. Last step—and this was a big one—Jimmie's image would then have been detached from the blue screen background. Inserted in the place of the real killer.

But even if I could come up with some reason why Jimmie would agree to let himself be so filmed, effects this complicated always give themselves away. If the creator doesn't have enough skill or time or computer horsepower, even the casual moviegoer can detect them.

In this case, nothing had been immediately discernible, so I'd borrowed some equipment from an old work friend, a specialized oscilloscope called a waveform monitor that detected signal aberrations. Unfortunately, there had been no signal aberrations. It was pretty clear to me the surveillance tape was genuine. None of the images had been altered in the slightest. What was on the tape was what really had happened.

Rick was still frowning. "If Walter thought someone else killed his son, he'd have told the cops. Hell, he'd even have told me. Walter would never conceal anything like that. He thinks concealment is beneath him."

I started to argue, but Rick's face had gone black.

"You know Walter even told me when he screwed you?" he said. "Offhand-like, he tells me a year ago, 'Cooper and I, last night. Don't mind do you, Rick, ol' pal?' I can't even say he was bragging. It was as if it was a bit of business information he was sharing. As if I'd given him a legal tip, and he'd appreciated it, and did I have any other tips to share?"

There was an awful, dead silence. Then rage swept over me.

"At least I knew when Walter was fucking me," I screamed. "You're being fucked by him and you don't even know it."

A moment later, I realized I was out of control, had to pull back. If Rick thought he was getting to me, this would only be the beginning.

"I never acted jealous about you and Walter. That bothered you, didn't it?" he replied, unperturbed.

"You know, your ego would barely fit in the Basilica of St. Peter's in Rome," I said, still extremely agitated. "If you've been doing something underhanded for Walter Ludlow, it isn't just Jimmie who's going to be hurt. You're going to be crushed, Rick. You and I aren't in the same league as Walter. He could snap his fingers and have both of us destroyed."

"You're worried about me," he said, sounding surprised. "I'm touched."

"Damn right. You need someone to worry about you."

"Is that why you came to work for me? I admit I was surprised when you gave up your big fucking movie career. I never thought you would. Were you worried about me?"

"I quit because a medicated chimp could have done what I was doing," I said, but my tone was somewhat sheepish and he guessed the truth.

"You're a fool, Cooper," he said evenly. "You always were." And he gave me a look of reproof.

Yes, I am. About you. It's the deepest sadness of my life, but I can't conquer it.

I turned my head, looked west out the windows. The rain had petered out; a couple of oily clouds had gathered over the bridge. There was a tanker and a few commercial boats far out on the horizon, where it melted into grayness. For a moment, I feel a keen desire to be on one of those boats, bound for somewhere else. Headed for a different life entirely.

"I need to go to work," I said awkwardly, getting up to leave.

Rick had gone over to his desk, was fingering an electronic camera with fancy optics. He altered the settings slightly and motioned for me to come over.

"Don't touch anything," he said. "I just want you to see her."

She? Well, of course, "she" meant Walter's yacht, the *Sea Dream.*

The screen on the back of the camera showed a nice piece of eye-candy, nestled in a pricey slip at the St. Francis Yacht Club. But it was a sailboat; the *Sea Dream* wasn't in view.

"I must have bumped something," I said, flipping to the next picture. And the next. Close-up views of different sections of a boat's hull. Zooming out, I saw crime scene tape, realized I was looking at the hull of the *Sea Dream.*

Death Game

"What are you doing? I told you not to fuck with it!" Rick grabbed my hand. Readjusted the camera back to the first image.

"You took pictures of the *Sea Dream*'s hull? Were you looking for something?"

But Rick had got a board up his ass for some reason. He wouldn't answer me.

I looked again at the sailboat. The St. Francis was a billionaire's yacht club; no ordinary family cruisers allowed. Everyone's sense of self-worth was far too morbidly wrapped around their possessions for them to own a boat that didn't reflect the size of their bank account.

There was something familiar about the sailboat. Extremely familiar...

"Damn. Is that the *Mystic*?" I asked, astonished.

I kept looking. It *was* the *Mystic*. Or a sleek and gentrified copy of her. I was amazed. The last time I'd seen the *Mystic* she'd been a derelict, smelling like a pissoir and showing every day of her thirty-eight years.

"I had her rebuilt," Rick said proudly. "Just moved her to the St. Francis from San Pablo. She looks good, doesn't she?"

He had owned the sailboat for a dozen years. Shoddy maintenance had erased most of her value long before he got his hands on her, but he'd still enjoyed her.

"I barely recognized her," I said. "She reminds me of an old lady who just went to Beverly Hills and spent a million bucks getting everything lifted."

I meant it as flattery, but Rick was irritated.

"Okay, so the rebuild is mostly cosmetic. I've run out of bucks; I couldn't even afford to have her hull reinforced. She slams against something, she'll crack like an eggshell."

I kept looking at the sailboat. Rick had inherited the *Mystic* from his uncle, who owned a seedy boat dock business that was always in trouble with the taxman and the port authorities in

Long Beach. When the old man died, the *Mystic* was tied up to a rotting pier. There was nothing else left in the estate, and the *Mystic* would have been gone as well if the old man could have found a buyer.

I tried again to admire her, knowing how much it meant to Rick.

"Imagine what your uncle would think if he could see her."

"Yeah, he'd bust a gut, he'd be so proud," he sneered. "That sorry bastard spent most of his time making me regret I was ever born. Always trying to get me under his boots so he could kick me. Saying he wanted to make a man out of me."

"He taught you about the abuse of power and he tried his damnedest to make you exactly like him," I said uneasily, putting the camera down. "It's a poisonous gift fathers give their sons."

"He wasn't my father. My father doesn't even know I was born." His face twisted.

Rick's childhood had been hideous. He had a couple of sisters, maybe even a brother, but he never mentioned them. What he did mention was never getting enough to eat—he'd gone hungry for most of his childhood and he'd never gotten over it. I often suspected that one simple fact was the key to his entire personality.

He moved away from me. I started to say something else, but he waved his hand, making it clear that subject was over. He stared out the window towards the bridge and the mouth of the bay.

I picked up the camera, scanned the pictures again until I found a long shot of the *Sea Dream.* Yellow plastic crime scene tape was strung completely around her, a couple of uniformed cops were standing on her top deck. Zooming the image, I noticed a workman on a sling beneath the cops, working on the boat's hull a few inches above the waterline. The extreme close-up was so fuzzy I couldn't figure out what he was doing.

Death Game

When I looked up, Rick had gone completely still. He was staring northwest, at the mouth of the bay. There was a difference in him, as if something vital had left him.

I didn't bother to try to rouse him. He hadn't noticed me playing with the camera again because he was in his personal dreamland, no longer in the room with me. He was out there— on the water. Balanced on a whipsawing deck, a saw-toothed reef sliding by the port side. Measuring the wind, the currents, the tides with his eyes, his skin, his feet. Icy spray whistling past his ears.

I'd seen him pull this trick before. He'd stop talking, stop listening, drop completely out of the conversation. You'd look up, realize you were talking to dead air; Rick had unaccountably disappeared. His body was in the room, but his soul was out on the ocean. Headed for the sunset.

He spoke without looking at me.

"You want to crash at my place for a couple of days, Cooper? Your house must smell like the bottom of an ashtray."

I started to say something, but the words didn't quite clear my throat.

He moved closer. I felt something touch my arm, then my shoulder. I was briefly aware of some river of sensation running from my chest. There was a touch. A hint. A grazing. I could feel something—his lips, then his tongue...on my neck. My skin had turned excruciatingly sensitive. He turned and pulled me into him. His belly compact. His hips and thighs strong. His legs firm, taut. His lips parted, moist...

We kissed, tasted—I yanked my head away. Memories assailed me. Memories that were worms eating the heart.

"Tell me to stop," he whispered, kissing me again. "Just tell me." His face floated above me. "Anytime you want me to stop...all you have to do is tell me."

I was going to tell him to stop. For good. But I was starting to lose my balance, feeling his hands on my back, moving slightly, stroking. I felt giddy. Rocked to the core. I hadn't expected this, wasn't prepared. My body was vibrating, feeling thick and heavy and yet filled with light, trembling with its own current.

I wanted a moral victory, wanted to play the outraged female and fling myself away, but there was no embarrassment here, no awkwardness. We knew this part of each other too well. The door was shut and locked, the clothes moved out of the way effortlessly—no tugging, no rushing. He put his lips on mine again, opened them, and I had a decision to make.

He knew the battle I was having with myself, and he pulled away for a second. Measured me out one ironical wiggle of his eyebrows, one insulting half-smile.

"So, what about it, tiger? You want me to stop? Just say the word. Just tell me to stop."

I opened my mouth to tell him. This was Looney Tunes. This made no kind of sense at all.

"Well?" he asked, still holding himself back. Still smiling.

"Oh, hell," I said. "For once in your life, just shut up."

Chapter Eight

DETECTIVE HARMON'S OFFICE WAS SMALL AND SQUALID, DONE IN GRAY paint. It was on the second floor of the Marina Station House, a building that had a brave front but was not so charming inside.

Harmon was catching up on his paperwork when I pulled a metal chair in front of his desk and sat down. He wore a soft blue shirt with a buttoned-down collar, a knit tie and a tweed jacket. If he thought the nice threads would make him blend in with a crowd, he was wrong.

"What do you want?" he said. "I didn't call you."

I felt the skin on my face tighten. "I want to call a truce. There are things you don't understand about the Ludlow boy's murder."

"And you're going to explain them to me? I'm so thrilled I don't know whether to laugh or commit suicide." He opened his desk drawer, took out a box of paper clips, slammed it shut. "Hurry up. I'm busy."

I'd changed my tack, decided to behave like Little Ms. Integrity. Much good it was doing me.

I told him what Walter had said to me.

He made a face. "Pure bull-rinky. Some new way of killing?

78

The Ludlow boy was shot through the head, nothing new about that."

"That's what I thought. Except Mr. Ludlow is now denying that he ever said such a thing. So, I'm not so sure."

He turned his back on me, started rummaging through a metal file cabinet in the back of the office. There was a window. It gave a view of a warehouse with bricked-in windows.

"What if Mr. Ludlow caused that fire in my house?"

Harmon turned around, as if this question was simply too idiotic to be ignored.

"Mr. Ludlow is the person you thought you saw that night? Before the fire started?"

"That's not his style. But there are wheels within wheels—"

"I don't believe it. Why in hell would Mr. Ludlow want evidence destroyed regarding his own son's murder?"

"I think I was the target of that fire. Someone was trying to get rid of me."

"You're wasting my time, Ms. O'Brien. Say something worth listening to, or..." He made a scooting gesture with his hand.

"I've been looking for Jimmie and someone is tailing me. Mr. Ludlow could be behind that as well."

I wasn't sure, though. At first I'd thought it was Tuck, doing a little covert surveillance for his handlers. Then I'd wondered if it was merely a press puppy from the tabloids, a guy who'd hounded and pounded me incessantly ever since Stephen's murder.

Whoever it was, he wasn't heavy-handed. It wasn't a tight tail, nothing obvious. It was just that my instincts would tell me to stop and turn, and there would be some slug, jumping back out of my eyesight.

Harmon sighed. "I'm going to do something outrageous here. I'm going to give you a piece of advice, Ms. O'Brien. You need to get the hell out of this investigation or someone is gonna decorate their fireplace with your brains. You're dealing with people you don't understand."

"What do you suggest? I sit around shuffling papers and doing procedural dogshit?" I snapped. "While I'm kicking garbage cans over looking for my brother, your damn office is putting out press releases covering your collective asses. When are you going to actually solve Stephen's murder?"

I'd gone after Harmon in probably the only sensitive place he had, his professional pride. It was a dangerous thing to do—the man could crush me with his fingertips. But when you ain't got nothin', you got nothin' to lose.

He leaned forward. Fixed me with his cold eyes.

"We got this one solved. The physical evidence—"

"I don't care if the path report, the hair samples and even the digestive tract enzymes spell 'Jimmie O'Brien is guilty as hell,'" I said insolently. "You don't know why, you don't know where Jimmie is, you don't know how the boys even met—in fact, you don't know spit."

I was hoping he would feel compelled to defend himself. I'd sensed an enormous ego behind that huge forehead.

Harmon got up. For a moment, I thought he was going to try to throw me out the window, or shove his fist down my throat. The man despised me. You could see it in his body language. You could hear it in his voice. But I was right there, in his face. And I'd hurt his pride.

"It's time you faced facts," he said, trying for patience, probably figuring that was the fastest way to get rid of me. "Ballistics confirmed the Glock 19 we found in your house was the murder weapon. The slug that killed Stephen Ludlow came out of that gun."

This was bad, really bad. I hunched over in my seat, feeling slightly sick.

"Jimmie's fingerprints were on the gun?"

"No fingerprints. Handgrip was wiped clean."

I sat up straight. "Then you have no proof that Jimmie actually used that gun. Whoever creeped my house could have planted it."

"We lifted the shit out of your house. No fingerprints we couldn't identify. You made him up."

"I didn't..." Hopeless. "What about the surveillance tape? Did you have it checked?"

"Of course. Our forensic media lab authenticated it. That's routine in any felony investigation involving media evidence." He hesitated a beat. "We also sent the tape to a private facility for further checking. The imaging lab at Berkeley."

"They're good," I said. "What'd they say?"

"What we saw on the tape was exactly what happened. Your brother shot Stephen Ludlow."

My own evaluation of the tape hadn't revealed any alterations, so I hadn't been very hopeful. But something else...

"Is that routine? Having an outside lab double-check?"

He shrugged. "We did it because someone else raised a question that first day about the surveillance tape being altered to set your brother up."

Surprised, I scanned his face. "Who was that?"

There was a silence. I could almost feel the deliberations tick over in his brain.

"C'mon, Detective Harmon." I stood up. "Tell me and I'm out of your day."

He put his hands behind his head. "I see no reason not to tell you. It was Walter Ludlow."

For an instant, I had a lightheaded feeling of shock. It deepened, rippled through me. I muttered something, got out of Harmon's office. All the way home, I kept seeing Walter's pale, grieving face, hearing his words.

The way Stephen was killed, it's the first time anyone was ever killed that way. It's a new atrocity, a brand new way of killing.

*   *   *

I should have gone home to lick my wounds. Nothing altered on the surveillance tape, the Glock being the murder weapon—the physical evidence pointed straight at Jimmie.

There were a few niggling details, though. Thinking about one of them, I turned south on 32nd and drove to George Washington High School. The bell signaling the end of classes had just rung, and teenagers were rushing away from the school like there had been a bomb warning.

I was afraid I'd missed her, but she was in the parking lot, putting a key into the door of a brand-new metallic-yellow Corvette.

"Nice car," I said, getting out of my Fiat.

"It's my mother's," Lauren said. "She let me take it today." She squeezed her lips together then released them, as if she were making a decision. "I heard about Jimmie. This fat black guy, he, like, asked me a bunch of questions. Said he was, like, a detective or something," She said it like it amazed her that any black person would have the right to question her. "The school psychologist went to all Jimmie's classes, ya know? We even had, like, an assembly." She gave a sour smile. "Nobody, like, cared two cents about Jimmie, but now, like, the whole school's upset about it, ya know?."

"Could we go somewhere and talk? Get a Coke, or a cup of tea?"

She shook her head. "My mom would, like, kill me if she knew I was even talking to you, ya know? She said Jimmie could have, like, hurt me, those times we did homework at your house."

"Nothing's been proven against Jimmie, Lauren."

She smoothed an imaginary wrinkle in her sweater. She was

wearing a pink jewel-neck sweater and jeans with glued-on rhinestones. On her ears were two dangling stars suspended on pink leather chains.

"Well, my mother doesn't give a damn about that, ya know?. She's, like, the ultimate female supervisory unit. Ya know?"

"Lauren, we need to talk. You liked Jimmie, didn't you?"

She twisted a lock of her fawn-colored hair.

"I always thought he was kind of, like, sweet. Underneath it all, ya know?"

"Let's go get a Coke," I said. "There's a McDonald's up the street. How about we meet there in a few minutes?"

She nodded, reluctantly.

"I guess it would be okay."

I drove to the McDonald's, got a couple of Cokes with no ice. Sat at a booth in the corner where I'd have an unobstructed view of the door, something my pa had taught me without ever saying a word. A musky odor hung in the air—hot grease, sweat, spilled food. I was hungry, but McDonald's food...if I indulged, I'd better plan on picking up a bucket of Rolaids on the way home.

Lauren showed up just before I decided she'd ducked. Put a light-pink string purse on the sticky table and slid in. I pushed the Coke across to her.

"Thanks," she said and started sucking on the straw.

"What did Detective Harmon ask you?"

Her sweater was in place, but she tugged at it, smoothing it over her breasts.

"You mean that fat black guy?"

She'd done it again. Her tone was clearly contemptuous.

She made a face. "He asked me, like, where Jimmie was. I told him I didn't know, ya know? He asked me if Jimmie knew the kid who was killed. I told him I didn't know that, either."

"He annoyed you."

She smoothed the pink sweater again. Her expression had

turned flat. Ugly.

"That boy who was killed was, like, a billionaire Jew-boy, wasn't he? The Jews think they run this city, ya know? Maybe he, like, got what he deserved."

I'd read Lauren as a soft touch, but I'd read her wrong. In spite of the annoying Valley Girl act, she was hard as nails. And a bigot to boot.

"You did give Jimmie his knapsack, didn't you? That morning?"

The Toxic Avenger T-shirt had never been found. Jimmie had taken the knapsack with him, so it was likely he still had the shirt. More likely, he'd gotten rid of it.

Lauren shrugged. "I gave it to him, but, like, I only saw him for a sec, ya know?"

There was a long moment of silence while she sucked on her Coke.

"Well," I said conversationally, "I don't blame you for not telling Detective Harmon everything you know about Jimmie."

She looked me straight in the eye.

"I *don't* know anything about Jimmie." She finished her Coke, pushed the cup calmly aside. If I'd been a male cop, I think I would have bought it.

But I'd been a teenage girl myself. There is nothing more dangerous than a teenage boy, and there is nothing more devious than a teenage girl.

"You didn't want to take the knapsack—I almost had to force you to take it. That was because you were afraid of what was in it. You thought it contained evidence of a murder."

It was one of the niggling details—Lauren's reaction that morning. Her guard had been up for some reason. Until she'd seen the T-shirt. Then, she'd grabbed it out of my hands and run off. Maybe she'd decided—in spite of everything—she wanted to protect Jimmie.

Her face paled. She looked studiously at the booth diagonal to us, which was empty. Clasped and unclasped her hands.

"I'm not trying to get you in trouble, Lauren. But I need to know."

I was expecting...

I didn't know what I was expecting. But what she told me surprised me.

"It wasn't anything like that, " she said. "I mean, like, it's just that I, like, didn't, ya know, want to get in trouble. Jimmie...we're not lab partners anymore, ya know?."

"Why not?"

She raised a shoulder. Let it drop. "We, like, ditched lab a couple times a while back. Our biology teacher is, like, a bitch and a half. She split us up after that, ya know? Told us not to even, like, talk to each other."

"Where'd you go when you ditched?"

She pretended not to hear me. I repeated the question.

"Nowhere."

"You didn't leave campus?"

The fawn-colored hair swung lightly, and the feathered bangs lifted.

"But you must have gone somewhere."

There was a long silence. Her hands were busy, fingers rubbing against each other. I took them in my own. Squeezed them briefly.

"Lauren, Jimmie needs help. Whatever you know, you need to tell someone."

"You won't tell?" There was alarm in her eyes.

I shook my head.

"We, like, broke into the computer lab. There's no class in there, first period, ya know? This other guy, he, like, knew how to slip a credit card in, open the lock, ya know? The three of us used the computers to, like, play games." She pulled her hands out of mine. Her face hardened. "There's no decent PC bang near this stupid school. They're, like, all ghetto. Full of, like, Korean and Japanese gooks."

A PC bang was an internet gaming parlor. When he'd first moved in, Jimmie had had me drop him off at one occasionally. Hours later, I'd peel him out of a crowd of kids with their faces glued to screens. Eyes unblinking, bodies stiff except for the twitching finger, the hardcore gamers made me think of spectators at their own dismemberment.

Their T-shirts displayed names of popular videogames, or said things like: SAVE THE PLANET KILL YOURSELF.

"What kind of game did you play? Not, uh, *Video Basketball*, I take it."

She didn't answer.

"You watched porn?"

"Porn?" She seemed offended. "I wouldn't be caught dead watching porn."

"What kind of game?"

She told me it was a first-person shooter game, one of those where you're running around in a darkened room, shooting at someone. At the bottom of the screen there's a pair of hands holding whatever weapon you choose—a .38 revolver, a double-barreled twelve-gauge, a flamethrower, a rocket launcher, whatever. Shooter games could be played solo or against the computer or against other players online. Sometimes, you don't see yourself—you only see what you're trying to kill. Other times, other players are shooting back at you, and your view of the room keeps changing as you dodge.

"Jimmie always thought deathmatch games were cool," I muttered. A deathmatch was a multiplayer shooter game, played over the internet.

"They are," Lauren said. "They're awesome."

"Who bought the game in the first place?"

"Nobody. I mean, like, this was the kind you can, like, only access on the net, ya know? If the game's Deity gives you the password, though. Otherwise, you, like, hack into it."

"A bootleg game," I said thoughtfully. "But what do you mean by the Deity."

"The Deity is, like, somebody who develops deathmatch games. The programmer, ya know?" She sounded contemptuous.

I did—sort of.

"Jimmie was, like, playing *Doom* and this Deity cuts in. I guess he was, like, tripping on how good a deathmatcher Jimmie was, ya know? He emails Jimmie that he's, like, got this new kick-ass game, and he wants Jimmie to, like, be the first one to try it. A personal invite, ya know? That's really an awesome honor."

"Who was this other boy you mentioned?"

"Just a guy. I mean, I don't, like, want to tell you that." Her fingers moved nervously. "He'd be really mad at me."

"Who did you play against?"

She shrugged. "How would I know? I mean, it's not like you ever use your real name. You give yourself, like, a user name, like Trigger Happy Joe or Nazi Dave or…like, I called myself Jacqueline D. Ripper."

She grinned.

"There's nothing wrong with it," she said a moment later. "A lot of these games are used, like, by the Department of Defense, ya know? My brother was in the Persian Gulf and, like, he told me CENTCOM had, like, a whole combat game department on his base, ya know? Tons of programmer geeks. He said war and combat games were, like, General Schwarzkopf's religion."

"But you don't really know who this Deity is, do you? He could be anyone."

She shrugged.

"Who'd you kill, in this game? Demons? Aliens? People with little green heads?"

Death Game

"Kind of." A vein had appeared in Lauren's pale forehead, under the bangs.

"Who did you kill?"

She was tougher than I thought. Her eyes didn't change. She met my gaze without flinching.

I looked her over carefully. I knew something about games—the movie industry and gaming intersected at many points. Graphic technology invented for games had been adapted for the movies since the 1990's—and vice versa. The slashers, the sickest crazies to come out of Hollywood, got reborn in game format. And the games usually made a lot more money.

"There was something particularly warped about this game, wasn't there, Lauren?"

She didn't answer. But the fingers were moving again, giving her away.

"Tell me who the target was. Who were you trying to kill?"

She was gazing at two boys who had just walked into the side door of the McDonald's. One had eyes that were pig-like and the color of a tobacco leaf. The other boy was younger and smaller, wore glasses.

Lauren's head sank back on her shoulders, like that of a turtle retreating under its shell. When the boys got in line at the counter, I recognized the big one. Travis McLeod. He was a rangy redneck kid. The kind of boy you could write a fairly accurate biography of just by watching him swagger across a McDonald's.

"I need to, like, go home." Lauren's voice was whining and rasping. There was sweat on her brow, over the pulsing vein.

"That's the boy Jimmie clipped with a pizza tray. Do you know him?"

Silence.

I stood up. "Let's go talk to him."

"No!" Lauren hissed. She ducked her head lower, squirmed on the yellow vinyl seat.

88

"He's the one who broke into the computer lab for you, isn't he? That's probably why Jimmie and he got into a fight."

Silence again.

Travis had left the other boy at the counter. Gone to get a booth. There was a carton of milk on the floor—he kicked it as he passed, sending milk squirting onto the shoes of a short, frail-looking Hispanic man who was mopping the floor.

The man made an annoyed noise. He was probably in his fifties, and Travis was fifteen, but Travis towered a foot above him and outweighed him by sixty pounds.

Travis grinned and made an obscene gesture. The man was breathing hard, trembling at the insult. Travis laughed and threw himself into the booth sideways. Flipped off his baseball cap.

I took a fiver out of my purse, palmed it. Took Lauren by the arm and walked her to Travis's booth.

He looked up, eyes bored and suspicious.

"Hey, remember me?" I said warmly, with a fake smile. "I'm Cooper O'Brien, Jimmie's sister. We met in the principal's office. Uh…here, I'll take that," I said to the younger boy, grabbing a burger off the tray. I tossed the five-dollar bill in its place.

"What's that for?" he asked, looking at the money.

"It's for your seat. Go get yourself another greasy Big Mac and eat it somewhere else."

He looked sideways at Travis, grinned and walked off. I pushed Lauren down, shoved my hips against hers, forcing her to scoot in.

"Lauren was telling me this interesting story about a game she and Jimmie used to play," I said, still smiling.

Travis turned a furious eye on her.

"I'm betting you're the boy whose name she wouldn't tell me. The boy who used a credit card to break into the computer lab so the three of you could play."

"Stool pigeon," Travis hissed. "I'll pay you back."

89

Death Game

"Jimmie's in trouble, Travis," Lauren said, trying to meet his gaze. "Maybe we should help her."

"Jimmie's a prick," he said. "He deserves to have a flamethrower shoved up his ass. So do you. That's what happens to stool pigeons."

I reached across the table, grabbed his shoulder with my hand, squeezed. Leaned forward and stared malignantly into the pig eyes.

"You do anything to this girl and being thrown off the top of a four-story building is the least of what is going to happen to you."

"Riiiggghhhtt," he sneered. But he was a two-bit bully, all huff and puff. Jerking free of my grasp, he picked up the burger and started eating it, staring sullenly out the window.

"Your principal would be interested in hearing about your breaking into a classroom," I said. "Lauren here could probably charm her way out of suspension. But, Travis, you've got a history as a troublemaker. You'd be expelled."

He kept chewing and staring out the window.

"This deathmatch game...who were you killing?"

I didn't expect him to answer me, but he didn't hesitate.

"Subhuman pieces of shit," he said, sniggering, pieces of sandwich spilling out of his mouth. "And you don't call it killing, you call it fragging. *Eat lead, suckah!*"

"Subhuman...what?"

He sniggered again. "You blast beaners swimming across the Rio Grande. You frag them with a machine gun. *Eat lead, suckah!*" He yelled it again. No one in the restaurant even turned a head. His mouth split open in a big grin. I could see a piece of lettuce caught between his second and third molars.

"You pick up a big-ass, nasty gun and blast them to smithereens. Before they croak, they make a sound like a donkey braying." He took another bite. "And then the *ghet*-to apes. You frag their nappy heads. Those faggots die wetting their pants and screeching." He started laughing again. "The Jew-boys were the funniest. When you shoot them, they scream, 'Oy, vey! Oy, vey!'"

"It was supposed to be funny," Lauren interjected, wincing slightly. "We didn't take it seriously."

"Who's your school guidance counselor?" I asked, looking at her. "Heinrich Himmler?"

She shifted in her chair and had the grace to look ashamed of herself, but Travis only sniggered again.

I asked a few more questions but didn't learn anything. White racist teens of the world, unite, I thought, walking to my car, feeling like I'd been splattered with filth.

It was clear enough why Travis liked the game—it played right into his fantasies. And Lauren certainly wasn't the prissy little miss she pretended to be. The only point in her favor was that by the time I'd left she'd been sobbing, tears streaming out between her fingers, falling on the sticky table, mingling with the spots of grease.

I was glad she was crying, glad to see there was something human in her.

But Jimmie? Had Jimmie been a closet racist? Maybe, but...Jimmie had been pissed with the entire world. He wouldn't care who the targets were, so long as he could blow someone away.

My stomach had started growling—I hadn't eaten for eight hours—but there was never any restaurant parking in my neighborhood. Hell, there was never any parking, period. I drove home and walked to Clement Street. Wing Hing Seafood was my favorite market; everything on earth that swam, squirted or snapped could be found in their fish tanks.

I didn't feel like cooking, so I bought some carryout dim sum from a tiny, ancient Chinese woman whose eyes crinkled shut at the corners when she smiled. Sat on an iron bench and watched the moon rise.

Crowds of locals passed me. A group was partying across the street, creating a racket. I took a bite of Chinese dumpling, chewed it thoughtfully.

Maybe Lauren and Travis had told me the truth, maybe not. Lauren had convinced me—on the whole. But I'd already known about Jimmie's obsession with gaming. And I already knew how sick the games were. The basic plot of the deathmatches was the same as most action movies—buy a gun, kill a lot of people, screw a princess and repeat it over and over until your eyes drop out.

The party group was loud, and I got up and walked farther down the street, found another bench. The evening was unseasonably warm, and the Richmond District had burst into life. All around me, colorful markets tumbled out onto the sidewalks. Various famous city chefs would come by in the evening hours, squeeze the huge Mexican papayas, pinch the plump Thai eggplants, let their imaginations run wild over tangled bird's nests, salted duck eggs, black eel—a thousand other foodstuffs I'd never been able to bring myself to eat. After almost eight years in the district, I was still struggling to distinguish bitter melon from fuzzy melon.

The smell in the Richmond shopping area is offensive to some visitors, but I liked it. It's a musty, vegetable smell from the shops, coupled with salt and rotting seaweed, the bad breath of the nearby ocean. Underneath were smoky hints of burning incense—jasmine, honeysuckle and moonsage. The smell of old lust and renewal.

Jimmie had complained about the stink, but then Jimmie was a burb boy at heart—he'd never been comfortable in the city. Cities like Manhattan and San Francisco choose you; you don't choose them. If they choose you, you find them relentlessly interesting. If not, you'll never get anywhere near their soul.

In the burbs, everyone is expected to be a certain way, and

there's a lot of energy expended in making sure no one is any different. But in a city, you can go completely crazy, and it will pass unnoticed.

I'd always thought San Francisco was a breeding ground for madness. Especially in children, who, mostly, aren't prepared for extraordinary cities that roar down on them "You ain't shit, kiddo" when they're just walking home.

Children can adapt themselves to almost anything, but not to the white baffled noise of being supremely unimportant. Not to having to listen to constant revelers on the street, glass breaking, beer cans rolling on the sidewalk. And particularly not to seeing other kids their own age with their teeth rotting in their skull, their arm tied off with a belt, a syringe mounted in a purple vein.

I thought about Heather for a moment. She actually liked living in San Francisco—at least, she said she did. But Heather was, in her way, as extraordinary as the city itself. Most kids I knew living in crowded cities, if given wings, would take to the fucking sky.

I got up to go home, past the sound of the fiddle jig and cheers ringing out from the Irish pubs. The moon shone through the onion domes of St. Ignatius' Russian Orthodox Cathedral. My pa had said once that the upturned arms on the Russian church's crosses represented anchors in a sea of evil.

My neighborhood was occasionally dangerous—a few bloated sexual degenerates, an assault once a week or so, three or four murders a year. The Black House was only three blocks from my home, a decrepit purple-and-black Victorian where Anton LeVey, the founder of the Church of Satan, had lived and held rituals; it was good for a half-dozen ugly incidents a year.

But Richmond was Disneyland compared to the city's combat zone, the Tenderloin, a few miles east. You walk through the Tenderloin and the toughs are gonna toss you around like a football.

A boy in a green uniform passed me on the sidewalk, making a pizza delivery. I glanced at him—he could almost have been Jimmie. Red hair shone under the streetlight.

On closer look, he was nothing like Jimmie. The uniform was too big for him, hung over his hands. Jimmie had grown so fast in the year he'd lived with me he'd not only shot his cuffs, his hands had almost hung to his knees.

It took almost nothing to remind me of my brother; the reservoir was always filling. But it was a little different this time. Memory came alive, flayed my skin inch-by-inch. I saw not my sentimental musing about Jimmie but the real boy. Saw that flare of adolescent underlip, that vulnerable sneer that boys in their powerlessness assume, hoping it will mask their fear. Saw his shame, his naked embarrassment for not being as tough as he pretended to be.

He'd always affected to be weathered in the war zones, a genuine street kid. It had frustrated me, but I'd never paid his act a lot of attention. I'd thought of Jimmie as unhappy. I'd thought of him as dislocated, losing his parents far too young and far too quickly. I hadn't liked his self-pitying attitude—sometimes he'd made me furious—but I'd never noticed the cold light I'd seen in his eyes on the surveillance tape. I'd never seen the secret words forming that he'd screamed out just before he pointed the gun and pulled the trigger. I'd never heard the distant thunder of Jimmie's small but consequential war with the world.

Even the T-shirt—I'd thought the slogan harmless. Now I wished I'd let him wear his other favorite: I Love My Wiener.

When I got home, I thumbed through the mail. Bills and junk. I tossed the junk in the trash, put the bills in a drawer.

Cooper, you are in way over your head, I admitted regretfully, sitting at the kitchen table and addressing the part of me that cared the most for my psychologically scarred, terribly wounded brother. It's pretty clear you never understood him. Why don't you do what the pros do? Get someone to give you some psy-cho-lo-gi-cal insight?

Thought to action; I looked up the number and dialed Jimmie's shrink. Too late for him to be at his office, but I left a message on his voice mail, asking for the earliest possible appointment. After that, I watched some mindless reality show and waited for Rick.

He'd been coming over nights. Too late to talk, but I'd been sleeping in his arms in a way I hadn't slept for years. Sleeping as if felled with an ax, his arms around me, his warm cheek against mine, him stroking my face with his knuckles, his lips, kissing my fingers one-by-one...

But Rick didn't show up that night. I didn't call him, although I wanted to badly. The relationship had stayed strained—physically close but not emotionally intimate. Whenever I'd bring up Jimmie, he would act tense, strung on tight wires. The words would die in my throat.

I fell asleep feeling like I was hurtling backward, overwhelmed and disoriented. Dreamt of Jimmie's face, shining darkly, sadly, in my mirror. Behind that face was my mother's. *Save us, Cooper,* they whispered in the tones of ghosts. *Save us.*

Chapter Nine

IT WAS FILTHY-WET ON THE DAY OF STEPHEN'S MEMORIAL SERVICE. I took a seat in the very back of the synagogue, watched the rows fill with people. The air was stale and damp. There were no flowers, and the ventilation was poor.

The talk was appropriately quiet, but there were constant nods, handshakes—a cozy group. As Walter's friends and business associates filed past me, I slunk farther down in my seat, hoping nobody would recognize me, hoping they wouldn't make the connection. There was a part of me that felt like the village leper, the burglar tiptoeing away with the VCR.

There was no music; I'd heard that both flowers and music were contrary to Jewish tradition. A rabbi with a somber voice and thinning grayish hair said respectable things. Said them repeatedly. Jewish tradition requires burying the body almost immediately, and autopsies are frowned upon. Both had been violated in Stephen's case, thanks to the murder investigation. I wondered how much that had bothered Walter.

I'd known Walter was Jewish, although he'd never mentioned it to me. Ludlow, I thought, having to think about something. It didn't sound Jewish. Had Walter changed it? Or was that the work of his father? Or even grandfather? Maybe it had happened at Ellis

Island, some immigration official scribbling down a wrong spelling.

My mind wandered.

The rain clicked against the roof, and there were no windows. The damp, cave-like feeling of the synagogue made me feel insubstantial, cut off from everything. The dreams I'd had the night before—they wouldn't stay out of my head.

All of a sudden, I had a vision, palpable and immediate, of Jimmie. I saw him as he'd been on the surveillance tape, a gun in his hand. He carried himself as if his whole body ached, ached with a fixed determination that dared not flag. On this day I become a man, he was thinking.

Jimmie! I wanted to scream. Stop! For God's sake, stop!

But he kept going. There was another boy with him. He was thin, sparrow-like—Stephen. The two boys were looking at each other, as if this insane situation was perfectly logical and reasonable and inescapable...

The rabbi was chanting, and many joined him, chanting in an ancient tongue, a language that to me had always sounded like the voice of mystery itself. I tried to get some sense of the majesty the ritual was meant to inspire, but all I could think was *Why? Why? Why?*

That vision of Jimmie and Stephen stayed with me the entire drive to Walter's house, hovering in the air above me like a ghostly vision. Both boys moved so unerringly toward the murder—Jimmie so murderously cold, Stephen making no effort to defend himself.

Walter's street was lined with cars with thrashing wipers, a long file of chrome and lacquer; tag-end—my tiny, plebian Fiat. Across the street, a black gardener wearing a discolored jacket and tattered tennis shoes toiled in what had become a downpour.

A valet took my keys. I caught my lip between my teeth, yanked my raincoat around me and trotted through the privacy gates and down the steps to the front door. I had a bad case of the jitters. It was the occasion, naturally. It was also my inferiority complex. I was the duck among swans, never a comfortable place to be.

And...it was the house. Walter's house. That was the crux of it.

I took a few hesitant steps forward, feeling as I always did when I entered that house—like I'd landed on another planet. Someplace where the gravity might be different, or what looked solid might suddenly start sinking. As always, I had a hard time believing what I was seeing. I kept turning my head, looking right, left, up and down. Vertigo assailed me; my head spun.

The best way I can describe the place: a citadel of glass. A hundred feet long across the front, five stories tall—three stories up, two down. The top three floors, the public areas, were wrapped in sheets of glass. Highly reflective black marble covered the floors, stainless steel staircases led to suspended lofts. The house was perched on a cliff overlooking the bay and the ocean beyond. On a bright day, shafts of light would flash off the waves, reflect through the interior and bounce off the staircases and mirrors like tracer bullets.

Visions and images pressed on me as I stood there, memories of the first time I'd been in the house. Walter hadn't turned on the lights. His thick crown of white hair had glinted, serving as a signal beacon, as I followed him. His voice had kept fading as his long strides outpaced me.

He'd come back, taken my hand, laughed.

"You're not going to chicken out on me?" he'd asked, as if we were two guilty teenagers.

"No," I'd said, hopelessly ill-at-ease. "Why don't you turn on some lights?"

He'd laughed again, pulled me close. So close I could see him looking intently into my eyes. I blushed, felt faint. The sea was pounding that night, pounding and pressing as if waves were going to crash through the window into his bedroom, pull us both back out into the blackness. It had been part of the strangeness of that night and was now irretrievably mixed up in my feelings about the house—that unbounded feeling of the ocean below, the stars hanging above.

There'd been that night, a few others—not enough to merit a formal goodbye. Walter had ended it, not me. Not that he'd said anything. He'd simply...never made another attempt. It hadn't broken my heart, but it had been...there'd been a few sleepless nights.

I climbed the main staircase slowly, resisting the impulse to clutch the railing for support. The sky was overcast, sealed off, and I felt suspended in grayness.

Walter stood at the head of the stairs, surrounded by a small group. He shook my hand, said a few distant, polite words then headed downstairs. I followed, caught his arm.

"Walter, I wondered if we could talk a moment? Privately"

He kept going, talking through clenched teeth, switching off his public voice and letting anger show.

"It's been horrible, Cooper. Horrible. Stephen's body...the police still haven't released it. Nothing in the casket, nothing to bury, what's the point? But I went ahead anyway. I thought any kind of a service, at least that'd bring some closure."

He'd reached the bottom of the staircase. He put his hand briefly on his chest.

"I've been thinking about Stephen all the time. Thinking and thinking. That's all I do anymore. Could I have done something—"

He broke off; a fashionably dressed middle-aged couple were shaking his hand.

"Yes, thank you for coming. Food's downstairs, be sure to stay for that." Another couple. "Oh, yes, thank you for coming. Thank you."

"Walter, why have you been avoiding me?" I'd left a half-dozen messages on his private number since I'd talked to Harmon. He'd never returned them.

"I'm not. I'm just…" Another couple was approaching. "Not now. I'll get back to you."

When? After Jimmie's found with Drano poured down his throat? Have you found Jimmie, Walter? Is that why you've been avoiding me?

I didn't believe it. Not anymore. It wasn't that I would put it past him. It was that Harmon had said Walter asked him if the surveillance tape was altered.

The day after I'd gone to Jimmie's school, I'd driven to the Sea Transport offices in Oakland harbor. Snuck past the security guards at the entrance desk and prowled the corridors. I'd never been inside the building, and the size and grandeur of the place awed me.

The offices were full of windows, like Rick's, but Sea Transport Limited was tenanted in four floors of a high-rise building not just a tiny corner. From the windows, you could see the city of San Francisco, laid out across the bay like a gorgeous table setting of crystal and sterling silver. San Francisco was never the same, no matter how many times you saw her, or from what angle. Clouds had been massed along the horizon. The sun filtered through them, touching here and there with a flash of light.

One of the security guards, a guy with a pencil mustache, eventually nailed me while I was standing in front of one of the windows, thinking hard. I'd already made it up to Walter's private office, only to be told he wasn't there. I hadn't bought it, but his secretary called security and I'd raced away. A moment later, I'd changed my mind, dawdled in front of a window. Let the security guard catch me—maybe Walter would come down to prevent a scene, keep me from being arrested.

100

But the guard had merely herded me to the elevator and downstairs. I'd gotten nowhere, and I wasn't able to think of any other reasonable plan to get near Walter.

I'd pinned my hopes on the service; but the house was full of people, and Walter wasn't making it easy. He kept moving, looking harried, making the rounds, tending the various conversational groupings, giving orders to the help. Drifting behind him, unnoticed, I started to feel sinister. A small, sinister shadow, trailing behind a man with whom I had once performed the act of love. And now there was death between us as well. What else could happen? What was left?

Eventually, he disappeared into the private part of the house, locking the door behind him. I gave up waiting. Climbed to the top loft.

I didn't see Rick, but I felt his vibrations. He was there. Somewhere.

It was bad news. I didn't want to see him.

The rain had stopped. Gray tunnels of spun glass and smoke were rising from the ocean. One of them spun slowly over the north tower of the Golden Gate Bridge. I swallowed—the bridge was so beautiful that afternoon she was like the edge of a very sharp knife.

Something drew my attention, made me look. Rick stared at me from across the room. He wore a dark suit, white shirt with French cuffs, pale blue tie. As usual, his dark, almost black, eyes had that uncommon raw glitter of life and passion. Those eyes had always held enormous power over me.

Seeing him, I was nearly knocked flat with longing. The feeling was overwhelming. To my horror, my nipples sprung erect and hard under my dress. My skin turned hot—so hot I was almost afraid I would cry out. For a moment, I could almost feel his touch, see his face coming close to mine, his mouth parting, his fingers making a slow circle on the back of my neck, his head

Death Game

moving downward, his tongue sliding across my skin…

He shifted his eyes away. Driven by simple animal magnetism, without thinking, I'd started across the room toward him. By the time I was halfway across the room, he'd put his back to me.

I stopped. Blessedly, the sexual arousal was passing, but the aftermath left me throbbing like a bell after an alarm.

Rick was talking energetically to a man standing near him, a man he had ignored before. I moved away with faltering steps. I could hardly breath.

Jazzed, smarting—reeling, actually—I staggered to a large glass trophy case. Inside the case were toy-sized replicas of the Sea Transport fleet. The company's insignia flag stretched along the back of the case. A pretty flag: green background, a large ST in white on a diamond-shaped field, a gold bird flying above it. The ST was obvious: Sea Transport. Why the gold bird? I tried to feel interested.

Rick's reflection appeared in the glass, as if I was looking into a foggy mirror. His gold cufflinks sparkled as he waved his arms around, telling a joke. I caught the dull flash of his Mexican silver ring. A few people gathered around, attracted by his sudden energy; they were laughing appreciatively.

The crowd had gotten bigger as well as noisier and more convivial. Rick looked less out of place than I would have expected in this rich crowd.

A server walked by, glasses of double malt whisky on his silver tray. Another server, who looked like he'd been starched in arrogance, carried shrimp, crab, smoked salmon, tender slices of raw beef.

I took a whisky. As I was debating between the beef and shrimp, a girl snagged my elbow. She was gorgeous, one of those sleek blondes, with quick greenish carnal eyes, full lips; hair swinging down her back, legs as long as those on a newborn colt.

"I know you," she said, smiling. "What are you doing here?"

"You have any catsup? Could you go steal a bottle for me from the kitchen?" I asked the server, ignoring the girl. My mood was heavier than titanium. I was trying to lighten it by poking fun at myself.

The girl laughed, and I turned to look at her. I didn't know her. I didn't know anyone in this rich crowd—she must have mistaken me for someone.

Her grasp on my elbow got tighter.

"Come with me," she hissed.

She made an imperious gesture to the server, and he nodded submissively, took the plate I had just loaded with beef and shrimp and carried it away.

"Wait a minute. I'm hungry," I called after him.

"And I'm Kim," the girl interrupted, still laughing. "Walter's bastard daughter. Let's go have a cozy chat."

Well, hell, I didn't even know Walter had a daughter. I shut up and followed her.

She led me to the elevator at the back of the loft, and we descended to the very bottom of the house. Double doors stood open, and she closed them behind us. It was a guest suite, apparently hers, at least for the moment. Women's clothes were thrown all on the sofa. A tiger-print thong hung out of a bureau drawer. No windows, but there was a fireplace, a long arc of granite with gas logs under it, lit and crackling.

"Walter's very ill, did you know that?" she said, dropping into the sofa and kicking off her shoes. "Some kind of heart problem. The doctors say it has started progressing very rapidly recently. He may have no more than another month or two."

"I'm sorry to hear that," I said. I was feeling—I didn't know what I was feeling. A lump the size of a dragon's egg had gathered in my throat.

Kim's eyes brightened mischievously. "Didn't he tell you? Isn't he worried, when the two of you..." She grinned.

103

My shoulders tightened. It wasn't the insinuation...okay, it *was* the insinuation. But it wasn't *just* the insinuation. It was the woman herself.

Her eyes were very bright, as if she was hoping for a reaction. When I didn't say anything, she shook a cigarette out of a gold case, snapped a tiny lighter.

"Do you smoke?" she asked, holding the pack out to me.

"I quit," I said.

She grinned again and carelessly blew smoke at me. "Do drugs?"

"I quit that, too."

Another beat passed while she gazed at me.

"Is Walter any good in bed?"

"Can we stop playing games?" I was finding it hard to talk. My chest was tight, my throat constricted. *Walter? You're dying? Why didn't you tell me?*

"I like playing games," she said, smiling.

"I don't." I got up.

She stubbed out the cigarette. Sat up and looked contrite.

"Don't leave. I tend to joke when I shouldn't—it's one of my problems. Stephen was a nice kid. I don't mean him any disrespect, but I barely knew him."

I didn't say anything.

She took a breath. "And my father, I'm really sad about that. I mean, I adore Walter, he's a marvelous person." Her face was sad; her eyes sparkled with tears. "Unfortunately, I haven't lived with him since I was eleven. My mother was a hysterical bitch. She queered me with my father."

She'd done it perfectly; she should have sold me completely. But after a moment, as if she couldn't resist, she spoiled the illusion.

"How'd it feel when I told you Walter was dying? Did it hurt?"

I didn't answer. What in hell was wrong with this woman? Was she bipolar? Schizophrenic? What?

She twitched the still-glowing cigarette in a black marble ashtray. There was a ring of red lipstick around it.

"You don't love Walter, though, do you?"

"What business is that of yours?"

She shrugged and smiled. "So, I'm impudent. So are you. The cops think your brother was the one who killed Stephen, isn't that right? So what are you doing here? Snooping?" She wagged her finger at me as if I was an errant child. Laughed.

"It's not out of disrespect," I said. "Walter requested it."

Kim wrinkled her nose. "Oh, well, that explains it."

It explained nothing, of course, but it's one of the things people say when they want to talk about something else. Barely taking breath, she launched into a rapid-fire rundown of her life. How she'd tramped all over the world. The stage work she'd done in London, in a play I'd never heard of. How she was at loose ends at the moment, looking for something to do.

While she was talking, she snuggled deeper into the sofa cushions. Put her arms behind her head. She wasn't big-star material—too bulldoggy around the jowls—but she'd pass, in most of the movies I'd worked on. She wasn't the spitting image of Walter, but she looked enough like him I had no trouble believing she was his daughter.

"I'm going back upstairs to mingle," I said, standing up abruptly in the middle of one of her stories.

I thought she'd be offended, but she smiled and asked for my phone number.

"Your home, too," she said. "I'll call you some evening. I'm kind of lonely in this city. We can go get a drink together."

She was disarmingly charming and sweet at the moment.

"I mostly work evenings," I said, thinking I would puke if I actually had to have a drink with this woman.

She lifted an eyebrow.

Death Game

"You needn't be afraid of me; I'm not coming on to you." Her eyes flicked over my cheap college-leftover dress, and her lips puckered.

"I never thought that," I said, meeting her gaze and trying to conceal how much I disliked her.

"You did." She jeered at me, grinning and wagging her finger. "I don't blame you, though. San Francisco is, like, the gayest city on the planet—everyone's always coming on to somebody."

I didn't speak; there was nothing to say.

She pushed her hair back. "Was your kid brother gay, by the way?"

I was near the door, but I stopped dead. Turned to stare at her.

"I don't think so. Why?"

"Well…Stephen was. And Walter…" She shook her head. "That was the worst thing possible to him. When I heard about the shooting, I thought that might have been the reason. I thought maybe Stephen and your brother were gone on each other and had a lover's quarrel."

My jaw dropped. "Is that what your father thinks?"

"Walter would never tell me that." She smiled charmingly again. "I tend to be pretty mouthy, did you notice? Christ, do you think I should see an analyst or something?" She laughed.

I almost bit, but I clamped my lips together.

"I like to get things off my, uh, chest," she said, pointing at her ample endowment and laughing. "Uh…how'd little brother and Jimmie meet, anyway?"

"That's a good question," I said. "Nobody seems to know."

She suddenly turned coy. I waited for her opinion, but she didn't give one.

Kim had gone back to smoking when I left the room. I climbed up to the top loft, leaned over a railing, feeling sick. The tide was coming in, cold, slow and ruthless. Looking down on the roiling black water, it got me in the gut. How had an awkward, withdrawn boy like Stephen felt, having such a poisonous sister?

And his father, the Grand Old Man. So fucking noble of Walter to be dying without letting anyone know. No doubt he'd even told Stephen to keep it a secret. Could he have been that inhumane? To his own son? Or maybe he hadn't told him at all. Kept Stephen guessing...

Stephen had always seemed so lost—droopy, listless, half-strangled with timidity. Like a pet bird left to languish in a gilded cage. I'd always thought it was just his natural personality, coupled with the massive sense of inferiority Walter brought out in anyone who spent thirty seconds with him.

But maybe there was more to it. How long had Stephen known his father was dying? Under the pressure of knowing and yet having to keep it a secret, had he wanted to die himself?

A voice caught my attention. Rick was in the loft below me. A woman came up to him, whispered in his ear—Kim. He turned, put his hands on her shoulders. She glanced up; I would have sworn she knew I was watching.

I dodged back, hoping Rick hadn't seen me. Took a staircase down to the main floor.

Walter, looking paler than ever, was near the front door, mobbed by people making their adieus. *I don't know you, Walter, I thought. I don't know what sort of man you are. How could you not tell me you were dying?*

He took my hand, shook it, never once looked at me. That was the final straw.

I shoved past him, splashed back to my car through the rain. The damn valet had parked my Fiat four blocks away.

Chapter Ten

RAZEL WAS SITTING IN BED, RELAXING. I GOT IN BED NEXT TO HIM, pulled a fuzzy blanket up to my chin. He was wearing briefs and dark elastic socks attached to calf garters, an improbable outfit, and he had made it worse by wrapping himself in a faded Oriental blue silk smoking jacket that had slipped away to reveal the few hairs that grew on his sternum.

He had opened a bottle of wine, and he poured me a few inches in a plastic glass.

"Poverty chic," he said, indicating the wine label. "Two-ninety-nine a bottle. Got ten of them at Trader Joe's. Help me celebrate."

"Bloomies' windows next. After that, the world," I said as we clicked plastic.

Razel had been commissioned to do the windows at Gumps. He'd lacked any kind of window-design work lately, and Gumps was the real deal. I was happy for him.

"I just met Stephen Ludlow's half-sister, and she told me Stephen was gay." I reflected a moment. "I suspect she's a bit bicoastal herself, so she should have gotten that right. But I'm not sure I trust her. She also thought Jimmie was gay."

"Heavens," Razel said.

Cheryl Swanson

He took a sip of wine, slid down and closed his eyes. He was half-gassed. In a moment, he'd be asleep.

I punched him lightly on the arm. "So, what do you think? Is Jimmie gay?"

"How would I know? Do you realize…" He flicked open his eyes, gazed at me with comic plaintiveness. "I don't think Jimmie even knew *I* was gay." He tittered. "Imagine that."

"Oh, hell, Razel." The wine tasted like kerosene. I put my glass down. "What about Jimmie?"

"Tell me first what you think of the wine."

"An aftertaste like a field of flowers," I said. "Now, what about Jimmie?"

"You mean it tastes like kerosene. You always were a dreadful liar."

"Stay awake, and I'll stop lying, I promise. What about Jimmie?"

"What difference does it make? Unless you believe gays are more likely to kill then straight people, which belief is so naive it makes me extremely tired." He yawned the third time.

I twitched a shoulder. "It's not that. You didn't know my pa. Thinking about Pa finding something like that out would have been terrible for Jimmie. That alone could have sent him around the bend."

"Ah. The horror of horrors. The fate worse than death," Razel said. "Having a son who is one of *them*." He made a face at his plastic cup.

"Exactly."

Razel had closed his eyes again. His face was remarkably unlined for a man in his mid-sixties.

"Your pa passed from this mortal coil a year ago, love. Surely, that ended his influence over the poor boy."

"Pa isn't dead," I said without thinking. I was feeling jittery and downcast after my meeting with the lovely Kim. It

109

Death Game

just...slipped out.

When I dared to glance at him, Razel had pulled himself back up. He was looking at me, an eyebrow raised.

"I mean he's not dead in Jimmie's mind," I amended. "The memory of Pa is still manipulating Jimmie somehow. That's all I meant."

"I don't get it, darling." He studied my face, and he no longer looked as tired.

"Jimmie...hero-worshipped Pa. He thought Pa was Superman."

"Superman," Razel repeated doubtfully. "I'm afraid I never got to Nietzche."

"I don't mean Nietzche's superman, I mean *Superman*." I spread my arms like I was flying.

"Superman?" Razel shook his head slightly. "You know, I have absolutely no grasp of American pop culture. Who is Superman?"

"It doesn't matter. And Pa was more like Lex Luthor, anyway," I mumbled.

"Lex...?"

"I was the girl, so thankfully he never tried to make a man out of me. But with Jimmie he was a real ass-racker. 'Go to your room, dumbhead!' If I heard him holler that once at Jimmie, I heard it a thousand times."

I yelled the words for added effect, but Razel ignored my yelling. He was giving me a blue-eyed look that was as pure and uncomplicated as sea air.

I kept going, talking fast and loud.

"If Jimmie ever stepped out of line, Pa would make him do pushups till he dropped. Make him run until he couldn't feel his legs. Pa wanted Jimmie to fear him. Worse, he wanted Jimmie to like him *because* he feared him. Pa was the kind of fucked-up hero America needs during wartime, but that we don't know

110

where to put when the battles are over."

"Well, darling, no one has to understand Nietzche to know how much you hated your pa," Razel said dryly.

"I loved him," I said, tearful suddenly. "I still do. Terribly. But I loathed the way he treated my brother."

I wiped away a tear with the edge of the sheet.

"Have you ever realized how indescribably god-awful it is to have a hero for a father—especially for a teenage boy? There was no way for Jimmie to ever measure up, but the poor kid never, ever stopped trying. I remember once Pa was trying to teach him jujitsu. He spins him twenty feet in the air then picks him up and jeers, 'You really are a mama's boy, aren't you, dumbhead? Why don't you just start wearing panties like the girls? You'll never get the hang of it.'"

"And of course, Jimmie never got the hang of it. No matter what he tried, Pa could always do it, and a hundred times better. It made Jimmie feel like the dumbest, weakest boy on the planet."

"That was boring, boring, boring," Razel said, when I finally ended my turgid diatribe. "And you didn't fool me a bit." He turned his head, cocked an eye at me. "Who did you bury in Pa's place in the family crypt? Someone who deserved it, I hope."

I ignored him. "Do you realize that the very night before the murder, Jimmie and I had an argument about Pa's idiotic concepts of bravery?" I thought a moment. "Y'know, when I look back on the year Jimmie lived here, I no longer see him at all. All I see this pale, pathetic shadow of Pa, a shadow that was programmed not to think for itself, just to try to follow some asinine code of bravery...and..."

"Well, then, I don't know what you're worried about," Razel said calmly. "If that's true, then the poor boy couldn't possibly have killed anyone."

"What do you mean?"

Death Game

"Think of it this way. Weren't you just saying your pa programmed your brother not to think for himself?"

I nodded.

"Then he couldn't have killed someone. Not unless he was programmed for it first." He smiled devilishly.

"Programmed to kill," I repeated.

"Exactly."

"Do you actually have something specific in mind?" I asked irritably. "How could that be?"

He shifted a silk-encased shoulder. "I don't know, that's for you to figure out, Sherlock."

For a moment, the room was silent.

"I know you and Jimmie talked once in a while. What did you talk about?"

"I never listened, love."

"But you talked, I know—"

Razel made a face.

"Well, I hated the way the poor boy dressed, so I tried to help him with his wardrobe. He was nice-looking, you know, quite a nice figure."

"Chester the molester," I moaned. "That's all I need."

Razel waved off the insult. "I had a discard, an Armani jacket that would have fit him beautifully. It had just the tiniest hole in it, nobody would have noticed. I went in his room to see if he wanted me to tailor it for him. He was staring at his computer screen, and..." He shuddered slightly at the memory. "This fat, naked man was rolling on the floor and screeching while he was being whipped, or kicked, or something. And there were actually points being totaled—it was some kind of game." He shuddered again. "So uncivilized. I just couldn't see the poor boy in Armani after that."

"I saw something like that. But I didn't see any points."

"Well, it was just a game, my dear," Razel said, sensing my

112

alarm. "He was always playing those games. Blowing things up. Shooting and clubbing and axing and, uh, castrating. I never understood the appeal." He sounded both slightly pained and flummoxed.

"No one understands teenage boys. Not even teenage boys."

"But these computer games are so...coarse."

I sighed. "Adolescence isn't a stage boys go through; it's a catastrophe. The day they turn thirteen they wake up and have four pounds of testosterone where they should have a brain. They become like poisoned rats, and they're at these stupid shoot-'em-up games day and night, killing each other over and over, like crazed animals."

And not just the boys, I thought, thinking of Lauren.

Razel wrinkled his brow, as if his sensibilities had been offended.

"I know it's breaking your heart and all that, but I haven't missed your brother. If I could prove him innocent I would do it in an instant, but I don't think I could bear another year with him in the same house."

"I don't think you'll have to worry about that. The cops have all but got him nailed," I said gloomily. I told him about the gun. "And I can't figure that out, either, Razel. Jimmie couldn't have bought a gun legally, he was too young. So, where'd he get it?"

Razel was falling asleep again.

"Darling, how deliciously naïve you are," he mumbled. "Half the people in this neighborhood would sell you their soul for a nickel."

"Their soul, maybe. I'm talking about a gun."

"A gun would cost more, that's the only difference."

He slid down in the bed, waved for me to leave.

"But...okay, say Jimmie did shoot Stephen. Wouldn't he have ditched the gun? Could he really have been stupid enough to bring a gun he killed someone with back to his house and try to hide it?"

Razel didn't answer. Maybe he was already asleep. Yes, Jimmie could have been that stupid. It was utterly pathetic, but Jimmie as an adolescent had exhibited no capacity to think for himself.

I went downstairs and pulled the curtains aside. Crazy Sally was at her upstairs window, playing her drums. She caught sight of me, pointed both sticks at me—a signal she wanted me to come over. I shook my head—the very last thing I wanted at the end of this horrible day was a visit with Crazy Sally.

She slammed the drumsticks against the window, hard enough to make to make the glass reverberate. Okay. Time to get over there. Pronto.

I grabbed an old jacket from the hook by the front door and trotted across the street, grumbling that I was tired of being the neighborhood caretaker. Cold wet air blew down my neck, and water ran under my collar. The cheap wine wasn't settling well on an empty stomach.

And I was having one of those uncomfortable self-critical moments.

The truth is, you could recite the phone book through most of the films I'd made, and it would hardly detract from them. The plot was just there to get you quickly to the next person to get jumped, mutilated, raped or blown up. Hell, in half the movies these days, the entire script could be shrunk to a one-page memo outlining pyrotechnics and facial tics. So, how was I any better than Jimmie?

Crazy Sally met me at the front door.

"You stupid bitch!" she screamed. *"You almost burned the block down! I should throttle you!"*

She stood there, glaring. I'd taken a half-step backwards, wondering if she was going to try to punch me. She got violent sometimes.

But this time she couldn't have if she wanted to. She looked shaky and weak, white as paste.

"Sally, did you take your meds?"

Her shoulders slumped. "I can't find 'em," she mumbled. "Fuckin' kids probably took 'em and sold 'em."

"Okay, okay," I said soothingly. "I'll help you look."

I went inside; her place looked like a twister had hit it. The floor was strewn with cigarette butts, empty Dr. Pepper cans, a bottle of Wild Turkey, a quarter-key of pot in a plastic baggie in the corner. Everything but her pills.

Crazy Sally trailed after me, hindering more than helping. Her wild hair hung over her shoulders; she wore a yellow-and-pink tie-dyed muumuu. Her feet were clad in gray sweat socks, one rolled up, the other half-off.

"Where's your purse?" I asked. "Maybe they're in your purse."

I unearthed a vinyl zip-up purse from behind the radiator; there were enough bottles of pills in it to inventory a small hospital. I fished through them—uppers, downers, who-gives-a-crap-arounders—gave up and handed her the purse. She peered at the bottles foggily, unscrewed one, threw a fistful of pills down her throat.

"You want some water?"

She shook her head.

"You want some coffee?"

She nodded. I went into her kitchen and found a jar of instant in her cupboard.

"Harold walked out on me last night," she announced. "He said he hated my drums. Asshole. He thinks music is synths and drum machines."

Her face tightened, she was going to cry. She ran a trembling hand through her hair.

I told her to sit down. The name Harold didn't ring a bell—

the last man I'd seen her with had been Latino, copper-skinned, name of either Jorge or Roberto. He'd worn bowling shirts, worked in a music video store called Dr. Boomboom. He'd left after kicking the hell out of her.

"What would you have done?" Crazy Sally asked me.

"About what?" I scrubbed out a saucepan with a ring of dried food on it. Filled it with fresh water from the sink.

"About Harold. He said it's either him or the drums. I said I ain't taking no orders from no fucking man. Since they shut the Downtown Rehearsal Building, I got no other place to practice. Five hundred bands out on the street, you believe that? This city is going to the dogs. So he splits. What would you have done?"

"I guess I would have thought about whether I wanted to be alone again. And whether maybe I could understand that not everybody digs rock-and-roll."

"At least my man didn't try to burn my house down," she spat, her hostility reviving.

I handed her a mug of coffee. *At least my man didn't try to burn my house down? What the hell did that mean?*

"What are you saying, Sally? You think Harold started the fire?"

She shook her head.

"Not *my* man," she said, "*your* man. Whasisname. I saw him."

"You mean Rick?" I asked, even more puzzled.

She nodded.

"Saw that fuckin' gas-guzzling car of his, saw him get out of it in his skanky clothes, saw him jimmy the lock and walk right in your house. Happened the night after those pigs showed up at your place." She took a sip of coffee. "I thought they were going to bust me. Ended up, though, the pigs just told me to be cool, they just had a few questions to ask. They walked right by that quarter-key, didn't even see it." She grinned and pointed. "Or maybe they did, and just pretended they didn't," she added reflectively. "Some pigs is almost human."

"Rick came that night to talk," I said. "He smelled smoke, that's why he went in."

Crazy Sally shook her head emphatically.

"I was sitting at the window that night. That bastard was there long before the fire. The sirens didn't start wailing until after. "

I felt woozy. "You sure? Don't bullshit me, Sally, you could have been drunk or dreaming that night."

"I was mostly sober and I'm positive," she said. "One hundred percent."

She must have read it in my eyes. She patted my shoulder.

"Better face it, honey," she said. "He's tryin' to get rid of you."

Chapter Eleven

JIMMIE'S SHRINK LEFT A MESSAGE WHILE I WAS AT STEPHEN'S SHIVA saying he was free Sunday afternoon. It was an odd time for an appointment, but he'd been renting office space from another psychiatrist and had decided to give up the space, semi-retire. To see him, I'd have to make an expedition north.

I took me two hours and ten minutes to get to his front door. I would have gotten there sooner except the town signage was missing—northern California is filled with inhabitants who sneak out and remove road signs. On a busy weekend, in the tule fog, there will a seven-car pile-up on the 101, everyone looking for an exit sign that doesn't exist.

The radio was on KPZP, a country music station. Merle Haggard crooned on about his dog, his ex or his days in the pen. I winced, shut my ears.

The shrink let me in the house through his kitchen, which smelled of freshly baked chocolate chip cookies. He was retired military and a very cool customer. He'd only seen Jimmie a few times, but I'd kept hoping chemistry might develop. My other two choices had been a slim, well-dressed, thirtyish Indian who'd stared at Jimmie with humid eyes and a seventyish woman with large wattles erupting beneath her chin. No chance of chemistry there.

"Sorry to hear about Jimmie," he said.

Nate Jordan didn't look the part of a retired army colonel—more chin fuzz than a grizzly, a ponytail longer than my own. He had on a green Hawaiian shirt with pink flamingos printed on it, baggy shorts and Timberland boots.

He was a clinical psychologist, and went by doctor "only to my patients below the age of ten." So he'd said, telling me—since I wasn't a patient—to call him by his first name. But I'd always addressed him as Colonel.

He'd told me to cut it out—he only used the title when he needed something from the commissary down in the city—but I kept using it. In spite of his renegade looks, he was pure colonel.

He led me into the family room. The windows were open, and a family of California quail ran through his backyard. The feral cats had killed all the quail in the city—as well as the wood ducks and any other bird that nested on the ground and wasn't big enough to peck the damn cats' eyes out.

The colonel settled into a chair, pointed to one for me.

"Tell me what's up, Cooper. Yack away. I'll interrupt when you start repeating yourself."

An undersized Jack Russell came in, snarled at me, teeth slavering. The colonel dragged the dog, which was the size of a well-fed rat, up on his lap.

"Has delusions he's a Rottweiler," he explained. "The only human being he likes is my wife. Go on. Go on." He waved a hand at me.

I started talking. Kept talking. I'd meant to just hit the highlights, but before I was done I had told him everything.

There was silence afterwards. The terrier had laid his head in the colonel's lap. Tiny, evil brown eyes watched my every move.

"Jimmie was absorbed in violence, Colonel," I said. "But I don't think...I can't believe he was a killer."

Death Game

Lines creased the colonel's forehead.

"I only had a few sessions with him, and not a lot came out, to tell you the truth. One thing I never got to the bottom of was what happened at the trial that followed your parents' accident. Didn't Jimmie speak at the sentencing hearing?"

I shrugged. When the day came for the victims to speak, Jimmie had gone the limit. He'd even gotten his hair cut before he spoke. Worn the suit he'd worn to the funeral, and carefully pressed his only white shirt himself.

I'd spoken first, asking for the maximum sentence. Memories of watching my mother die had made my voice harsh, my words short. I no longer believed in the system. The trial was a shuck; I expected the guy to get what he got—a handslap.

But Jimmie had that simple, eloquent, unshakable belief in justice that only the young possess. Armed with passion, he carefully detailed how much the drunk had taken from him. From me. From Heather. I'd been proud of him. Very proud. For a moment or two, I'd even thought the judge would listen.

"We go home afterwards, and Jimmie goes berserk," I said, winding up the story. "You know how teenagers are, how they have all these assumptions about the world being a meaningful place, about fairness?"

The colonel glanced into my eyes, and I was surprised to find that I was angry.

"That judge might as well have butt-raped Jimmie. This poor kid spills his guts out, and he makes some patronizing comment. He'd already made his mind up to give the guy a pass." I lifted my chin. "Jimmie couldn't handle it. He lost his innocence in one fell swoop, that day in the courtroom. He was withdrawn before the trial, but never vengeful. Never the slightest bit mean. Afterwards, he wanted to sever every artery and blood vessel in the drunk's body. Stuff the judge's head in a dumpster.

"But he couldn't do anything, just file tamely out of the

120

courtroom. I think he felt so completely fucking helpless he couldn't stand it anymore. He wanted to take vengeance on everyone—kids at school, me, any authority figure, whoever the hell he thought he was killing in his games. Mostly, I think he hated himself."

"I know he was absorbed in first-person shooter games. How bad was that? He barely mentioned them to me."

"After that shuck of a trial? Total immersion. Like he'd jumped off a bridge and never came up." I told him about the deathmatch that Lauren, Travis and Jimmie had played. "That's what he was doing in the weeks before Stephen Ludlow was shot. You think there could be a connection?"

The colonel looked out the window briefly then looked back. The quail had disappeared, but a wind was blowing in the trees, making shifting patterns of shadow and light.

"I don't see how there could be."

"But Stephen was Jewish. And they were killing Jews. And the judge, in the trial, he was a Jew." I'd told Jimmie that myself, angry, said you could always trust the Jews to rise to the top. Why had I said that? Because there was a part of me—a part of all of us—that opens to darkness.

The Colonel gave me a keen, long look. "Jimmie wear Nazi regalia? Put swastika insignias on his wall? Hang out with skinheads?"

"Not that I ever saw."

"They were killing blacks, as well. And Hispanics."

I nodded.

The colonel's mind had turned to something else.

"Your brother and I got into another area that seemed to upset him. He hero-worshipped his father. Whenever he thought I doubted his pater's courage, he'd come unglued. I had to tread very lightly."

I laughed uneasily. "Unfortunately, he was telling the truth. Pa was the bravest man I ever met. An old-fashioned gung-ho hero, a fuck-the-motherfuckers person."

"Which means exactly what?"

"Do you fear death?"

"Of course."

"Everyone I know fears death more than anything else, but Pa actually looked forward to it. He saw it as a long paid vacation where he'd never have to think about what a fucked-up mess the world had become."

"What was his profession?"

I only hesitated a moment. "Counter-espionage."

The colonel raised an eyebrow. "Heady stuff, if you can stand the loneliness."

"Pa found it intoxicating. To him, it was like carrying on an anonymous affair with a stranger. He held all the power. He could walk out on his family any time he wanted. He didn't have to be reasonable, compromise, see anyone else's side, share, cope. He missed birthdays, holidays, anniversaries. Hell, sometimes he'd disappear for months at a time. Mom had to do all the banal family stuff—wipe our noses and clean up our puke—while he was off walking on the dark side of the moon."

"You told me before that he never physically abused Jimmie. Are you sure about that?"

A sense of loss and bemusement was flooding out of me.

"Pa wasn't like that. I mean, hell, it would have been better if he *had* hit us—it would have clarified things. But his own father had beat the crap out of him, and he said he'd cut his hand off before he put us through that, no matter how much we aggravated him.

"Jimmie was timid as a little kid, easily frightened. When he started puberty, Pa decided he was a mommy's boy, and it was up to him to toughen him up. He never let up on him after that. Made him feel like a little shit. All in the name of making a man out of him, of course."

"Sometimes God doesn't deliver kids to the right parents."

I didn't respond. It was too true. Fuck you, Pa, I thought. Would it have killed you to give Jimmie an occasional kind word?

"Killing someone isn't the real appeal of first-person shooter games," the colonel said, changing the subject. "That's a popular misconception. The real appeal, especially to teenage boys, is titillation. Sexual arousal."

I was taken aback. "You've got to be kidding."

"Mind you, since you're not one of my underage patients, I'll admit that I've got nothing against sexual arousal." He grinned. "But I got problems with a society that teaches teenagers to get their sexual arousal by immersing themselves knee-deep in dead bodies. You want a beer?" He had gone to kneel in front of a small fridge. He pulled out two cans of Budweiser.

I nodded. "I don't get it. Are you saying that killing someone produces…"

"Sexual arousal? Damn straight. Especially if it's explicit, obsessional, frenzied killing, like you see in these games. And like you see in modern action films, for that matter. *I'm* not saying it, though—the research says it."

He tossed me a beer.

"I'm not buying this," I said. "Violence on a screen gets tiresome. Even kids mostly get tired of it, go on to something else. They don't go out and start imitating what they see."

"You're right. The vast majority of children, even if they were somehow forced to watch twenty-four hours a day of screen violence, would never kill anyone. But they'd sure as hell be desensitized. Grow up lacking empathy, and indifferent to pain and suffering. And there's always the worst, worst cases. Kids who get exposed to violence and find it enjoyable. They not only learn how to kill, they learn to like it."

I stared down at my hands. Columbine, I thought. Two

Death Game

seemingly normal boys from nice homes, on a rampage that most experts had linked to their incessant violent-game playing.

I hadn't heard the sexual connection, but it was hard to discount. To a teenage boy, flooded with raging hormones, what could be more sexually exciting then killing endlessly, with no consequences? For the first time I thought I understood why Jimmie had sat endlessly in front of his computer, pulling on a phallic-looking joystick with the empty-eyed look of someone whose spirit had been extracted out of his flesh.

"This isn't just speculation," the colonel said.

I glanced up, realized he was holding a chrome-plated automatic pistol. Pointing it at me. At my head.

"Don't worry," he said. "It's not loaded. I'm just using it to make a point."

I twitched uncomfortably in my chair. Nutty old coot.

"You heard of that fourteen-year-old boy, Michael Carneal, who fired into a prayer circle?"

I nodded.

"He approaches this circle of children. Fires eight rounds. He targeted a different child with each round, and he never missed. And most of them were head shots, the hardest shot to make." He spun in a circle, clicked the trigger eight times. The eighth shot would have gone right through my skull.

He tossed the pistol to me. "You think you could shoot as accurately as Michael Carneal, Cooper?"

I caught the gun awkwardly. It was heavier than I expected. My pa had had a couple of sidearms, but he'd kept them in a locked cabinet.

"You've never held a gun before, have you?" He went to the window, flexed the stiffness out of his back. When he turned around to look at me, his eyes were full of humor.

"Nope."

The humor died.

124

Cheryl Swanson

"Neither had Michael Carneal. Until the day of his rampage." He went back to the refrigerator, pulled out another beer. "Here's something remarkable, Cooper. In the recorded history of conflicts involving firearms, there has never been a feat of high-speed precision marksmanship against human targets to match Carneal's shooting of those children in Paducah. Not by a criminal, a cop, a citizen or a soldier. Ever."

I licked my lips. Stared at the weapon in my hands.

"Stephen Ludlow was shot through the forehead. A perfect shot, the cops said. I always thought that shot would be too hard for my brother to make."

"Michael Carneal learned to be a near-perfect marksman through simulations. He knew nothing about real guns, but he was a master at shooting games. Just like your brother."

"Oh, fuck," I muttered sadly. Jimmie had looked extremely professional in the surveillance tape. It had been one of those niggling details that had made me think he couldn't be guilty. Something that had made me doubt what I was seeing, because how could he have learned to shoot like that?

Well, he'd learned the same way Carneal had.

The colonel threw me a curve.

"Don't mistake what I'm saying here. It's not easy to kill, not for most people. The human body reacts to the stress of killing another human being with all kinds of psychosomatic reactions." He shrugged. "I'll drop the shrink-speak. Basically, they puke their guts out afterwards. It's hard to get even trained soldiers to accurately aim a gun at another human being."

There was a silence. His jaw hooked forward in a peculiar way.

"I was a soldier for years. One night, I almost killed someone. We were cornered in a marsh in Nam. The VC were trying to flush us out. Just after first light—" He stopped. Laughed and pointed at his rear. "Still scares me so much you couldn't drill a flaxseed up my ass with a sledgehammer right now. Just from thinking about it."

He folded his arms and put them behind his head. Laughed again. "Anyway, we see this squad of VC pointing their rifles at us. We jump up, point our guns back. Nobody moves. Eyes burning, lips quivering, we all stand there, waiting to die. What should have happened is that every blessed mother's son of us should have died with a hundred bullet wounds in us. Instead, both sides start to slowly back off. No one fired a shot."

I whistled. "Weird."

"Not a bit weird. I heard the same story a dozen times when I was over there. After the war was over, it was one of the things that spurred me into becoming a shrink. I wanted to learn why killing someone face-to-face was so difficult."

I was perplexed. Killing is difficult? Even for soldiers? "I thought the whole point of being a soldier was to kill."

He shook his head. "When you look at the historical evidence, when you're considering face-to-face, short-range battles, what you find out is that most soldiers are trying *not* to kill the enemy."

I made a skeptical sound.

"Let me give you the statistics. In Nam, it took an average of fifty thousand rounds of ammunition to kill one enemy solider. And that's nothing. Go back to another conflict. In World War II, less then one percent of the fighter pilots accounted for virtually all the enemy aircraft destroyed in the air. In spite of all the fables, it turns out that most fighter pilots never shot down anyone or even tried to do so. Just like my men and those VC, once we all looked in each other's eyeballs, we found that we simply could not kill."

This was fascinating stuff. "So how do soldiers bring themselves to kill?" I asked.

"Most soldiers kill only under compulsion. They'll shoot once they're fired upon, or when directly ordered to do so. And even then, plenty of them make sure not to aim their guns. If it ever comes to killing face-to-face, a lot of soldiers, in spite of themselves, become conscientious objectors."

I was still fascinated, but I'd lost the connection to Jimmie.

"One of Jimmie's high school friends told me that the military was deeply involved in computer games. Was she right?"

"She talking about operant conditioning? Used to train a military assassin?"

"I don't know. What's operant conditioning? I've never heard of it."

He waved his hand. "The modern military mostly uses computer and video games to plan tactics and execute war strategies. They call them war games. That's common, it's gone on for decades, and it's harmless. But some branches of the military also use games to condition responses in deadly force situations. It's called operant conditioning, which is a fancy term for a game that is used to successfully indoctrinate soldiers into the business of killing.

"What they do is immerse a soldier repeatedly in simulated high-stress training exercises. By doing so, you can create strong memories of the correct responses that can be recalled by the subconscious under extreme conditions."

"Okay, give it to me again. In English."

He laughed. "I'll do better than that. I'll give you an example. You create a game where your soldier is in a foxhole. Targets pop up on the computer screen, pointing guns at him. If he shoots, the target drops. Otherwise, he's the one who drops. Pretty soon, he's shooting reflexively, precisely mimicking the act of killing, and he's doing it without thinking."

"You said you could train assassins," I said, groping. Something was starting to add up—but what? "Some soldier pretending he's in a foxhole isn't an assassin."

The colonel didn't respond. He seemed reluctant to go on

with it. He sighed, ran a hand over his brow.

"Our military doesn't admit to it, but particularly gruesome interactive simulations have been developed and used in certain military sub-groups to turn an ordinary person into a trained assassin."

I was taken aback. "How do they accomplish that?"

"They start by making the targets more realistic. As close to a real kill as possible. The Israelis, for instance, they frankly admit they use targets in their combat games that look as much as possible like real human beings. Other groups, they saturate their trainees in gruesome simulations of people being killed or injured in violent ways. Some even put their conscript's head in a vice. Make them look at simulations of killing repeatedly.

"The goal is to force the trainee to disassociate their emotions from such a situation. It's a form of classic Pavlovian conditioning. A kind of systematic desensitization."

I took a breath. "What about using real killings instead of simulations?"

"What do you mean?"

I was excited. "Having the trainee watch real people being killed. Repeatedly. Wouldn't that be the ultimate desensitization?"

He shrugged. "Sounds gruesome, but you're right, that would be the ultimate desensitization."

"Has it been done?"

"Sure, it's been done. During World War II, the Japanese military would take a prisoner and gather their young unblooded privates around him. One private would bayonet the prisoner to death while the others watched. Then, they'd bring in the whores for a reward. Pretty good training, actually."

And pretty fucking sick.

He was done, and we stood up. I reached to pet the dog, which condescended to wave the extreme tip of his tail.

"You're not very good at hiding your feelings," the colonel

said. His face softened slightly. "You're dying inside because you believe your brother's a killer, don't you?"

"Yes," I said sadly. Tears threatened, and I ducked my head slightly to cover it.

The colonel was quiet for a moment. He gazed thoughtfully over my head, as if he were accessing some private store of knowledge.

"You could be wrong about your brother," he said clearly, calmly.

"What?" I jerked my head up.

"So what if he pointed the gun and pulled the trigger? That's not the same as killing, is it?"

"What?"

He tucked the terrier farther under his arm, took my right hand, placed the pistol between my fingers. Turned it so the barrel was pointing at his chest.

"Now tell yourself it's loaded and pull the trigger."

"Be serious."

"Do it!"

I did it.

"Am I dead? Am I even wounded?"

The terrier's guardianship instinct was so offended he had leapt directly at my face. If the colonel hadn't been holding him, I would have lost a hunk of my nose.

But I wasn't thinking about the dog. Instinctively, I had turned the gun slightly aside. Aimed away from the colonel a split-second before I pulled the trigger.

I looked at the dog, looked at the colonel. The dog was going crazy, yelping and clawing and snapping.

"If he was my dog, I'd think about putting some Thorazine in his food," I said.

"Yeah? Not a half-bad idea."

He was laughing as he closed the door quietly in my face.

Chapter Twelve

I WAS SURPRISED TO SEE KIM THE NEXT DAY AT WORK, BUT NOT THAT surprised. I was in the employee lounge at noon, eating a soggy tuna on rye, when she stuck her head in.

I eyed her over the limp edge of my sandwich. Felt my jaw tighten.

"You're here to see Rick?"

She fiddled with a gold earring. It was in the shape of a heart with an arrow through it.

"I met, uh, Mr. Capra, at Stephen's funeral. He told me he was looking for a receptionist, and I told him I wasn't working right now." She grinned complacently. "He hired me on the spot. He's such a nice man."

"He's a shark," I said, extinguishing the sandwich in another bite. "He eats pretty little girls like you for breakfast."

She sucked her teeth a moment.

"Could you introduce me around?" she asked. Her tone was exactly the same. Either she hadn't heard or was determined to misunderstand me.

I couldn't think of an excuse. I grunted and balled up the paper the sandwich had been wrapped in, threw it in the trash.

"You're itching to meet the other animals in this zoo? Okay,

130

but you may regret it."

Her grin stayed locked in place, even though, unfortunately, it turned out my words were prophetic.

When we reached the corridor leading to the tech room, we heard a commotion. Two of the techs were in the midst of a violent argument. One of them was Jala's replacement, Waleed Alomari.

Jala had always been well-groomed, very cognizant of dress, even slightly urbane—a young yuppie for Allah. Waleed was another sort entirely.

He dressed worse than a city cabbie; his black turbans smelled like he dipped them in an open sewer. He was mid-sized, with long arms, a weak chin, a big beak nose and bulging brown eyes. The first time I'd met him, I'd reached out to shake his hand. He'd looked me over, frowned and spat on the ground.

It wasn't that Waleed didn't like women. His face gave him away—it was full of secret places, roadmarked with lust. He'd passed me too close in the hallway once, touched my breast. I'd stiffened immediately, took his hand and flung it away. His stare had hardened; he'd spat on the floor again.

He was the kind of man who I figured knew the address of every whorehouse in the city and its rates. It wasn't too hard to imagine this gorilla out on a regular nightly jaunt, looking for the youngest, most childlike American whore to violate. It wasn't hard to imagine him settling for a sheep, a dog of uncertain pedigree or a black Nubian goat back at home when nothing else offered.

Waleed was shoving a thin gold disc against the office code wizard's chest.

"It isn't finished! Take it! You must take it and finish it!"

Viktor Kirnov kept his arms folded. He made no effort to take the DVD.

"Hurry," Waleed said excitedly. "You must hurry! We have

Death Game

little time."

Viktor was also a big man. Tall. Powerful. Square face. Closely cropped light hair. He unclasped his arms, knocked Waleed's elbow aside with a flip of his hand. The DVD slipped away, hit the floor on its edge, spun through a pile of gear. The room was full of equipment that should have been put away: electronic cables, video cameras, keyboards, computer monitors, computer mice, recorders and players.

Tsk-tsk, I thought, looking around the room. Waleed was not proving to be a very good replacement for Jala.

"You son-a-bitch. I know what is wrong with you! You want more money. You think I am Mister Pay! Mister Pay!" Waleed's voice was shrill. He danced around, flogging himself into a ludicrous rage.

Viktor growled something I didn't catch.

"You do what we say. Or you will be killed a thousand times!" Waleed shouted. He danced around some more. "I kill you ten thousand times if you don't!"

Viktor reached out a powerful hand and grabbed Waleed, who was a good four inches shorter, around the neck.

"I will tear your fucking face off your fucking skull if you don't shut up," he said. He put his hand to his face, and his finger traced a long, ugly centipede-shaped scar that ran horizontally across his forehead, below his almost-white hair. It was a weird movement, suggestive of the threat he had uttered, but it could have been coincidental. Viktor often traced that scar—apparently unconsciously—with his fingertips.

I had stayed quiet, not frightened but curious. My hand was on Kim's arm.

"Steady as she goes," I whispered in her ear.

She shook me off, shuffled her feet. Both men swiveled their heads at the noise, belatedly realized they were being observed. Waleed's eyes were startled, aghast. Even Viktor seemed a little discomfited.

I went to retrieve the DVD. It had rolled under a lab bench, and I had to get on my knees to reach it. Backing out from under the bench, I bumped into Waleed. He was standing over me, his feet widely planted.

"Give it to me," he ordered.

I couldn't get off my knees, not with him standing there.

"Move back," I said. "Let me get up."

"Give it to me!" he yelled, bending his face down to within an inch of mine. The man's eyeballs were popped, traced with red veins, the whites the color of mayonnaise left out in the sun. It was the closest I'd ever been to him. A stench lifted off his flesh, sharper than a whiff of arsenic. If he'd ever taken a bath, it was because it had rained on him.

Viktor was leaving the room. He whacked Kim with his shoulder, where she stood in the doorway. I couldn't tell if it was purposeful or accidental, but she didn't protest. She just stood there, rubbing her shoulder, her weight on one foot, looking serenely unconcerned.

Waleed had snatched the DVD back by then. He swiveled his head to look at Kim, and their eyes met and held. She stopped rubbing her shoulder and curled her lips into a flirtatious smile.

To my amazement, Waleed blushed violently. A moment later, he made a gesture toward her that was subject to a couple of interpretations, the most charitable one that he was imagining himself yanking the zipper of his pants open and urinating on her.

Kim's grin widened, as if she found this amusing.

I'd reached her by then. "Let's get out of here before we both have to get rabies shots," I said, not bothering to lower my voice. Spinning her around, I marched her out of the room.

She was laughing. "I thought you were joking about introducing me to the zoo animals."

Death Game

"Yeah. Couple of circus acts, aren't they?" I kept my hands on her shoulders, hustling her away, thinking hard.

Kim narrowed her eyes. "What was that about?"

"Some argument. Who cares?"

"That big white-haired creep? The one who could win an ugly contest? He reminds me of a guy I once knew in the Ukrainian mafiya."

"How would you know someone in the Russian mafiya?" I asked, nonplussed. She'd even said it correctly—mafiya, not mafia. She hadn't got that from watching CNN; the talking heads never got it right.

"Ukrainian," she corrected. She raised her green eyes and gave me a limpid and transparent look. "My mother had a boyfriend, this Ukrainian bloke? He was in the mafiya."

I didn't say anything. I was thinking of the obscene gesture Waleed had made. Much as I hated ratting out an employee, the man had pushed it too far. Waleed needed a ticket out the door.

I asked Kim for her take was on Waleed, whether he was mostly all bluff. She blew out a breath. Lifted her eyes to mine.

"What do you expect of a towel-head? I mean, I wouldn't wipe my ass with the whole race. So far as I'm concerned, Arabs are proof that Abraham fucked goats."

I scowled. "That's a friggin' stupid thing to say. Waleed's his own category. He's not part of any race. I'm not even sure he's human."

She frowned slightly. "I wouldn't worry about him. I want to know about the big guy. What does that Viktor fellow do here?"

"Some kind of programming that involves visual editing," I said vaguely.

Viktor could crank out code and editing work at a prodigious rate, and what I'd seen of his work was jaw-droppingly good. But I hadn't seen much of it.

We did a quick lap around the office. Stopped in the tiny law

134

library, where Rick's newest paralegal was working among the ghosts of trees. Kim smiled briefly at the woman, didn't extend her hand.

"Uh, Cooper?" she said. "I'm dying for a smoke."

The paralegal was the timid type, in her mid-forties with hair gone completely gray. She froze motionless at Kim's rudeness, red streaks running up into her cheeks. I lingered for a moment, to cover the awkwardness, and also to ask her if she'd had any problems with Waleed. When I caught up with Kim, she was standing in front of the editing room, asking what was inside.

The editing room had a security panel. Punching in the code, I flipped open the door, meaning to shut it again immediately. End of tour. Get lost.

"It's padded, like a cell," Kim said, shoving past me. She tested the rubberized floor with a high heel. "Who works here?"

"Me," I said. "It's *my* padded cell. Let's go."

She lit a cigarette.

"You can't smoke in here."

"Rick told me you used to work on films. You think I would have a shot at a good role? If I went to Hollywood?"

I snatched the cigarette.

"You smoke in here, and Rick would be within his rights to throw you out a window," I said heatedly. "Smoke particles get into the computer drives, they're ruined."

She was unperturbed. "You surely are protective of Rick," she said, grinning.

Well, at least she'd dropped the *Mr. Capra.* I gave her a point for honesty.

I passed her, caressed the computer console with my fingertips. The wall in front of us was crammed waist-level to rafters with recessed video screens. Under my fingers were dozens of rows of jog-shuttle-slide switches that controlled the monitors, the visual effects palette and the audio layback.

Death Game

Beneath that was the workstation, the brains of the great beast.

It was not nearly as sophisticated a set-up as the equipment at the production studio, but pretty damn cool nevertheless.

Tour over, we headed down the corridor to the reception area. I expected Kim to make a beeline for the elevators and a chance to smoke. Instead, when she arrived, she stopped dead, unbuttoned the front of her skirt, reached down and adjusted her underwear while I stood there.

I was determined to be fair, to be impartial, to be just, but I found her disgusting. She glanced at me, a teasing smile on her face.

"What?"

"Very fetching," I said.

Her face twisted into ugliness, and she rebuttoned her skirt. A moment later, she struck back, started to do a slice-and-dice on me.

"Rick's not bad looking, don't you think?"

"Uglier than a monkey's ass," I said, turning away.

I felt like running a wind sprint back to the editing room and bricking myself in for a week. She stood in front of me, blocking the way. I grabbed her by the belt and yanked her sideways. When I got to the editing room, I punched the code, entered and closed the door.

I had a lot of work to do. By making a supreme effort, I got lost in it. When I looked up again, it was past six o'clock. On my desk in the tiny cubicle I used as an office was a stack of paperwork—four days' worth. I'd taken a lot of time off looking for Jimmie.

By the time I collected my things to go home, the emergency nightlights were on; the corridor was bathed in a weird bluish glow. When I passed the editing room, I heard Viktor caterwauling at the top of his lungs. He stopped, started again, stopped again.

Well, hell.

I stood outside the doorway, feeling one of those impulses you learn, as you get older, to ignore. The shenanigans I'd witnessed in the tech room had triggered my curiosity. My nose grew an inch while I stood there.

Viktor was at it again, sounding like he was just getting revved up. He was in love with opera—Russian opera, naturally. He'd sing along at the top of his lungs. Once, I'd even come upon him in a savage bout of weeping. I hadn't paid any attention—code wizards are invariably strange animals. It goes with the territory, at least in America, where programmers are solitude-seeking geeks. And when you're talking an explosively talented programmer, someone like Viktor, you expect them to be half-mad.

I had about as much natural stealth ability as a pregnant elephant, but I thought I could get away with it. The racket would cover my entrance. The hallway was dim, so Viktor wouldn't notice a change in light level when the door opened.

My heart started to beat faster. Ooze in, ooze out—what could be easier? Viktor would have his back to me; he was singing his head off, besides being busy working.

But still, I hesitated. I'd seen an ugly side of Viktor in his little contretemps with Waleed. I'd always thought of him as a peaceful crazy person, but peaceful crazies do not threaten to tear someone's face off.

Telling myself my curiosity would be the death of me, I slipped inside.

The back of Viktor's cropped head was right in front of me. I looked over it at the screens, to see what he was doing.

He wasn't working; he was watching porn.

Jimmie's porn. Only worse.

Reflected in multiple screens was the same obscenely fat naked man I'd seen on Jimmie's screen the morning after Stephen's murder, only this time he was standing and pissing.

Death Game

Pissing for all he was worth. He wasn't relieving himself—his stance was oddly rigid, and his lips were drawn back in a rictus of terror, as if he were staring at something so terrifying it had caused him to lose control.

He kept pissing. A big, steaming pool formed under his feet. His mouth had fallen open, saliva hung from his lips in thick, obscene strings. Other people—not their faces, just their hands—came into the camera's field of view. Sets of hands forced the naked, drooling man to lie facedown in his urine. Rubbed his face, his nose in it, as if he were an animal.

The camera zoomed in, the hands disappeared. The man was alone again, left there lying facedown in his own piss. After a few moments, he dragged himself up on his knees. It had to be the same man. He was round-shouldered, with a sagging belly, the deathly pale skin of someone who never ventured outdoors.

He wasn't left alone long. The sound of doors opening made him turn, but not fast enough. His left leg went from under him; a stick the size of a baseball bat had struck it. Another bat hit him squarely in the spine.

A knife flashed, cut the fat man's throat. There was no telling who did this—whoever held the knife wore a silky white hood. An orange band around the forehead held the hood in place. There were eyeholes, and the eyes looked strange—hot, glowing, immense. His hand nestled around the dead man's throat. His fingers rubbed gleefully in the bloody flesh. He leaned over him, laughing...

I slipped open the door. *Got to get out of here, got to get out of—*

I felt a hand on my shoulder and gasped. Turned to see scowling eyes appraising me.

"What's going on, Cooper? Why are you still here?"

I couldn't breathe. I wanted to speak, but couldn't form a single word. I put my arms around his neck and hid my eyes against his chest.

Rick picked me up and carried me back to his office. Dropped me on the sofa and opened a cabinet, took out a bottle of Scotch and poured us both a drink.

"Easy, tiger," he said, sitting next to me, watching me gulp the whiskey. "You have to drive home tonight."

I put the glass down and told him what I'd seen.

Rick knocked his ring against his leg.

"Damn fool," he muttered.

I sat, looking at my palms. The alcohol wasn't helping. I could still see the crazed eyes of the man in the hood. See his unblinking, insane stare as he caressed the slit throat, rubbed his fingers excitedly in the blood.

"You have any idea what it was?"

"I don't know. But whoever the poor man was, he was tortured and killed."

"Hardcore porn," Rick said irritably. "The jerk's getting his jollies here so his wife won't catch him with it at home."

"A man was killed, Rick. His throat was slit and he bled to death."

"A snuff film? And that pompous Russian twit is watching it on my nickel?" His dark eyes were unblinking, as if he was thinking hard. "Snuff films are illegal. Viktor downloading it and watching it in my office—that could get me in trouble."

He wasn't the only one thinking hard.

"What kind of project is Viktor actually working on?" I asked. "Isn't he supposed to be creating training videos on test equipment for oil rigs?"

Rick stood up. "Yes. And he's right on schedule. He's a goddamned genius, you know. He'd have no problem watching ten channels of smut while simultaneously deactivating a bomb."

While I'd been working at OZ, I'd seen a fair amount of porn—special f/x people have some of the most cheerfully dirty

Death Game

minds you'll ever encounter. It was par for the course to watch porn while you were working. Being that I was usually the lone female, and a Catholic schoolgirl to boot, the guys would dump hardcore porn on my computer as a practical joke.

But there had been a half-dozen screens lit up in the editing room. Now that I was thinking more clearly, I wondered if the fat man being killed—scenes of *that*—was what Viktor was working on.

Rick was in front of the windows.

"Actually, I'd appreciate it if you don't mention any of this to Viktor."

He arched his back slightly, hunched his shoulders. He'd taken his drink with him, and he took a big swallow.

"I have to. I need to tell him that snuff films are illegal."

There was silence.

"Cooper?" He looked over his shoulder.

When I'd leaned back, the fingers of my left hand had awkwardly slipped behind one of the cushions. There was something down there, something hard and regularly shaped. I probed more deeply, turning the object around in my fingers, feeling the edges. I was pretty sure I knew what it was.

"Uh…is Kim still in the office?" I asked.

"This late? Course not." Rick had turned around to face me. He grinned. "Hell, it's so late I don't even know why I'm here."

"When'd she leave?"

"She barely worked at all. She took two hours for lunch," he complained. "Walter wanted me to give her the job—he thought it might steady her, if she had something to do. You know she's his daughter, don't you?"

"She told me."

"She can't type, can't spell, already screwed up the filing." He poured another, waved the bottle my direction, but I shook my head. "She's a sweet kid, but rather basic."

140

I didn't respond.

"What's the matter?" He had picked up something—some slight vibration from me.

"Nothing." I smiled slightly, a forced smile. "Well...uh, past time for me to go as well."

He stared at me. "You were going to say something a minute ago. Why don't you want me to talk to Viktor?"

The object was an earring; I was sure of that now. I let my chin drift over my shoulder, shot a look at what my fingers were cradling. An earring in the shape of a heart with an arrow through it.

I dropped it as if it burned my fingers. It slipped behind the cushion, disappeared. It doesn't mean anything, I told myself. Kim was in Rick's office, sitting on the sofa. The earring fell off, and she didn't notice.

But I could smell her expensive scent all over the leather cushions. And I knew Rick. Oh, yes, that was the trouble—I knew Rick.

I'd gotten up to hide the tears stinging my eyelids. I stood in front of the window, trying to distract myself.

"You're so goddamned beautiful," I muttered to the dark, velvety city.

When I'd first moved to San Francisco, there'd been times when I felt the city was almost sentient. She reminded me of a beautiful woman, quivering with life, intelligent without purpose, excitable and sexual, with a heart that actually beat.

I kept looking out the window, snuffing my tears, refusing to let them fall.

"Can I ask you a personal question, Rick?"

"Depends on how personal," he replied, nervous.

"Why did you want me to work for you again? Was it that you felt you needed one more time to prove to me what an absolutely shameless bastard you are?"

Death Game

He laughed awkwardly, kept laughing. He was making certain I knew he was going to take this as a joke.

Chapter Thirteen

SLEEP, THAT MOST NATURAL AND INEVITABLE CONDITION OF THE HUMAN metabolism, had stopped coming to me on any terms. I spent the nights lying alone in a square of moonlight, my palms damp against the sheets, my breath loud in my chest, my mind filled with monstrous shapes and ideas.

Well, hell, as usual, I'm not going gently into this good night—

I went downstairs and revved up my old graphics workstation. It had been loaned to me so I could do visual editing at home, and OZ had neglected—thus far—to reclaim it. I'd had to return the specialized oscilloscope, but the same friend had given me a copy of some video authentication software.

I loaded the program then downloaded the file containing the feed from the surveillance tape into it. Watched lines jitter up and down the screen. A light-green line, the original signal, rose and fell like a heartbeat. Just above it was an acid-green line.

I watched them, expecting nothing. Expecting a big fat zero—what all my other examinations of the tape had revealed.

But this time, there was…something. The lines didn't—exactly—match up.

I blocked out all the other visuals, zoomed in tight. The same

143

discrepancy occurred. I stared at the screen. *Tell me I'm wrong, that I'm not seeing what I think I'm seeing.*

But I was.

I got dressed as quickly as I could. Tossed down a cup of coffee and a piece of toast for breakfast and drove straight to work. At seven-thirty Rick came in to find me searching his office, looking through his law books. Methodically, I pushed each one aside to look behind it, then flipped it open to see if a hole could have been cut in the pages and something inserted. Put it back on the shelf. Went to the next.

He put his briefcase on his desk, watched me a moment.

"What in hell are you doing, Cooper? Tell me what you're looking for, I'll tell you where it is."

He was preoccupied. War-weary, as if he were suffering from battle fatigue. We'd left late the night before, but this was more than just ordinary tiredness. There were lines in his face I hadn't seen before.

I dropped a book, and it banged on the floor. He winced. I expected him to object again, but he didn't.

I finished the last of the books, looked around for something else to examine. I'd already done a pretty thorough sweep of his office. Theoretically, I could have missed something—I hadn't looked in the ventilation ducts, for example. There was a locked cabinet behind his desk with a television in it—I hadn't opened that. Maybe that would have netted something, but probably not. If he had anything concealed in his office, he would have protested my search more strongly.

I leaned against the bookcase and waited until he looked up.

"I'm looking for the surveillance tape," I said. "The one that shows what really happened to Stephen Ludlow."

Rick shook his head, as if he had been thinking about something else. Thinking so hard that he had struggled to regain his focus.

"The cops have that."

"They have a videotape. It's not the original. It's a copy. I want the original."

"What are you talking about?"

"The tape you had me show Harmon the morning after Stephen was killed was a copy. It wasn't the original tape."

He made some kind of noncommittal grunt. Started fiddling with the brass latches on his leather briefcase, snapping them up and down. Snap. Snap. Snap. He glanced sideways at me, but I stayed put, my arms crossed over my chest.

He pressed a hand against his stomach as if his ulcer was acting up. Exhaled heavily and pressed again. Got up and went to the credenza behind him, opened a drawer and fumbled out some pills.

While his back was turned, I opened his briefcase and thumbed through the contents. He didn't turn to look and see what I was doing, although he must have heard me moving the papers inside. He gave me plenty of time to shut the briefcase before he turned, but I didn't bother.

He sat down again. Frowned at the open briefcase but didn't ask about it.

"Where'd you get this crazy idea about the tape?"

"I'll give it to you in a nutshell," I said. "That morning you had me show it? I rigged a splitter to send the signal output from the tape to my laptop."

"What?"

"I made a copy. I checked it carefully for image alterations, but I never found any. Then, last night, I looked at that downloaded file with some software that analyzes the origin of signals. I found small irregularities in the cross pulse signal. What's called a windup signature."

"Windup," he repeated, as if he didn't know what that was.

"It's a change in the signal," I said. "It only happens when

Death Game

something is being wound up, getting up to speed. Finding it on that file meant that the images didn't come directly from a camera. Instead, some other playback system had to get up to speed to make a copy from the original."

I spread my hands. "I don't care if you understand it or not, Rick. I don't make mistakes about stuff like this. What you had me show the cops wasn't the original tape. It was a copy. I want to know why it was copied. And I want to see the original."

He flipped two tablets in his mouth. Got up again and poured a glass of water.

"Your fingerprint signature was on file, so you could have viewed the tape before any of us got there." I said. "But you insisted I show the tape. You never let on to Harmon you could have shown it."

He didn't respond.

"And you were also goddamned insistent that I stop immediately after the shooting. As if you were afraid of anyone seeing what happened next." I'd been in shock, so that had passed me by at the time. But I'd thought about it since.

There was a long pause. When Rick finally spoke, his voice sounded as if he was doing his best to be patient.

"I'm not going to argue technical stuff with you, Cooper. Let's agree, just hypothetically, that the surveillance tape you showed the cops was a copy, not the original. Let's also agree that I might have been the one who made that copy. Do you understand why it might make good sense for me to do that?"

"I can think of a couple of reasons."

"Stay with the obvious one."

"You did it for the same reason you'd automatically copy an important document or record of any kind," I said reluctantly. "To make sure you had a backup in case the original got lost or damaged. A way to protect yourself from someone else's incompetence. Or some unforeseen accident."

146

"I looked at the tape before you and Walter got there, I admit that. When I saw…Jimmie, I made a copy. I was going to tell you that Jimmie was the shooter, but I didn't have a chance. When you ran out, I realized giving Harmon a copied tape could cause problems."

"So, you switched the tapes back."

He nodded. "I gave Harmon the original. I didn't want it to come back on me. Or, uh, you."

I sat quietly for a moment, wondering if he was lying.

He'd gone back to snapping his briefcase latches. Snap. Snap. Snap. He looked as bad as I did. In fact, he looked worse, like he'd run a marathon the previous day.

"If you don't believe me, call Harmon yourself. If you spotted this, his forensic lab would have, too. Or you can tell him what to look for. I've got nothing to hide," Rick said.

I remained quiet. Gazed at him.

He punched the pager for the wireless intercom.

"Kim, get the SFPD's Marina office on the phone."

"I believe you." And I wasn't lying. It explained why I was the only one who spotted the wind-up signature. Harmon had had the tape thoroughly authenticated—he'd even sent it off to Berkeley's imaging lab. But they'd had the original, so there was nothing for them to find. In fact, all along Harmon had had a different tape than I had. The only question was—why?

"Never mind," Rick said to Kim. He shut down the link. "It wasn't illegal, immoral or even unethical, Cooper. I was just being cautious. You should understand that." He sounded aggrieved. "You admitted a moment ago you basically did the same thing yourself. You also made a copy of that tape."

"I do understand it."

He relaxed slightly.

"I understand a lot of things… now."

It was pretty clear this was a leading comment, but he didn't

Death Game

follow up on it.

"If you gave Harmon the original surveillance tape, what did you do with the copy I showed?"

"I destroyed it. There was no reason to keep it."

I went to the door. When I got there, I paused.

"You told me Jala picked up the tapes on the *Sea Dream*. Then, poof, he disappears."

"And I told you I had nothing to do with that."

"Hate to be brutally frank, Rick, but about that, at least, you're lying through your teeth."

A thick, bifurcated vein stood out in his forehead. I heard him inhale.

"I'm not going to let you involve me further in this, Cooper. You need to start thinking with your head, not your feelings. Once Jimmie's arrested, I'll be glad to help him any way I can. Maybe we can get him off with an insanity defense."

"I don't want Jimmie to get off," I said bitterly. "And you've got it wrong, Rick. All wrong. I'm being objective—totally objective. The evidence against Jimmie seems airtight, until you look closely. Then you realize that everything surrounding that evidence is suspicious. The man who retrieved the surveillance tape is missing, the tape itself was copied before it was viewed, and the cops have a different tape than the one they saw in the beginning."

"The city DA is a smart cookie. He doesn't even need the surveillance tape. He'll make the case on other evidence. There's the gun that was found in your house."

"And maybe that other evidence will prove equally tainted."

"Look, I don't blame you for caring about your brother. But, babe, when it comes to you and me—" Abruptly, he got up, reached out and pulled me to him. Kissed me hard on the lips. "There," he said, shoving me away when he was done. "What does that tell you?"

148

"You've never kissed me like that." My lips were bruised, hurting. My upper lip was bleeding where he had bit me.

"Yes, I have." He reached for me again. He had me by the back of the neck, kissing me, pushing his body into me, his hands hard on my back, under my skirt, in my underwear....

I yanked away.

"You aren't kissing *me*," I said bitterly. "Who are you kissing, Rick?"

He didn't answer.

I made an abrupt movement. *You lying, cheating sonofabitch. You don't have to say a word. I know. I can tell from this new style—rough and ugly. What does she do while you jam it in her? Whip your sorry butt?*

Rick tapped his Mexican silver ring against the desk, tried to smile.

"What's wrong? Me and you, no matter what, we've always—"

"Here's the matter what, Rick. There's a kid in a crypt in a Jewish cemetery I keep thinking about. A kid who had his body carved up before it was laid to rest, in violation of his religion. And another kid, who's got my stubborn streak and his mother's eyes. I'm hoping that kid is at least still alive. You're not going to distract me from trying to finding out what happened between those two lost souls."

Not this time.

The smile faded. He glared at me, and I returned the look.

"You know, being with you has been like being buried under ice. But what did I expect from a Catholic girl. But then the Grand Old Man comes along and you hand it away on a platter."

"I did to you what you did to me," I said. "You showed me the path through the ocean."

"What do you mean?"

"I mean I go to bed nights, dream I've fallen into the ocean. I open my eyes underwater, and see a thousand women floating by me, all dead. And you're fucking every one of them."

"Always loved this about you, Cooper," Rick said, staring at me. "You take it to the hoop. No room for compromise, for moral shadings, for elbowroom. It's always all or nothing, either-or, black or white. It's a world of extremes played outside all known margins. It sounds sincere, but it has no relation to life on earth."

"I'm my father's daughter," I said. "He was a moral man, but he wasn't flexible."

* * *

After my ugly conversation with Rick, I went to my cubicle in a blind rage. My hands shook, and I felt cold all over.

In a film, I thought, this would be the time for the hero to come running after me. Utter a meaningful, life-affirming line, like, "I know we had a fight, darling, but the day is young and life is long. I desire you passionately, and I'm giving the blond chick the shove. Should we find an empty hotel room and have a nooner?"

Being that it wasn't a film, Rick never came near my cubicle. Not the rest of that day or the next. In fact, he stopped talking to me entirely. He'd see me in the corridor, pass by with his eyes averted, pretending I wasn't there.

Rage is a good antidote to depression, and my rage energized me to keep looking for the missing surveillance tape. For almost a week, I poked around the various cabinets and closets diligently, but I didn't find it, and I became convinced I wouldn't find it—not without someone telling me where it was.

Tricking Rick into letting that information slip wasn't possible, but there was another option—Viktor. If anyone knew the tape's whereabouts, or why Rick had copied it, that person would be Viktor. The techs in the office knew enough to do installations, but Viktor was a code genius, could program in multiple languages as well as handle sophisticated visual editing tools. He had a PhD from the University of Moscow, a school that is no slouch when it comes to creating advanced graphic environments.

Fear all over me, a brick on my heart, I tapped on Viktor's private office door a week after my conversation with Rick. My mouth felt grimy, and I kept swallowing. It was the equinox, and in another hour, spring would give way to summer. In San Francisco, that meant we'd have another month of raindrops, a few sunny days, and then the really miserable weather would set in—summer.

Viktor didn't respond, and I tapped again. Somewhere in the distance was the sound of a floor buffer—the night cleaning crew was hard at work.

At my third knock, Viktor flung the door open. Planted his huge bulk in front of me, wearing a don't-bother-me glare. His face warmed up slightly when he saw the bottles I was holding.

"Krista," he said, taking the bottles of Kristall Vodka. "Krista," he repeated, caressing the labels. "*Ya tebyla lyublyu*, Krista."

I didn't need to know what he was saying to know he was pleased.

I trotted out a prepared story, said it was an Irish custom that friends share a drink to celebrate the coming of summer. Everyone's gone, we're working late hours…how about I come inside and we take a couple of nips?

I was pretty sure he would go for it. When I'd first started working for Rick, Viktor and I had had a couple of afterwork sessions in a scruffy bar. Swilled cheap, watered-down booze, traded insults and told plenty of lies about our talents, which is the equivalent of a great evening between technical types.

But Viktor wasn't in a sociable mood.

"Irish custom?" he snorted. "Krista is Russian custom—Irish drink rotgut whisky." He slammed the door in my face.

Death Game

I should have left. The only excuse I can think of is that there is a persistent myth that a mysterious alchemy happens to Slavs when they over-indulge in vodka. Too many snorts and they compulsively whisper all their secrets. Tell you everything that comes to their mind, in a drunken haze of bonhommie.

At least, that's how the myth goes...

Some part of me was screaming to give up what I was planning. I'd seen how Viktor had handled Waleed, and the memory of watching the fat man so brutally killed hadn't left me. Whenever my mind was still, it would come to me, and drops of pure animal sweat would ooze onto my brow.

But the beating and killing of that moronic-looking fat man had something to do with Stephen's death. At least, I was pretty sure it did. How else could I explain why it had also appeared on Jimmie's computer? And like Stephen's murder, the fat man's had been cold, calculated.

Insane.

It wasn't the fat man I remembered so much anymore. The eyes of his killer, the man who had slit his throat and rubbed his fingers in the blood—those eyes never wholly left my thoughts. They had even started to drip into my dreams.

I stood outside the closed door once again, feeling terrified—and also pissed. Viktor was in there, hugging two bottles of premium Russian vodka to his chest. Vodka that had cost me a solid hunk of what was left in my wretched bank account. I went to the employee lounge and retrieved two thick, short glasses. Tapped on the door again.

He opened it, but he was clearly not happy I'd returned. I pushed in anyway, noticing he had already opened a bottle.

"Let's have a toast," I said, picking up the bottle with sweaty fingers. I was hoping he didn't know me well enough to recognize the signals I gave off when I was frightened.

He flopped down in his big desk chair.

152

Cheryl Swanson

"*Za khokhlov!*" he shouted, after I poured us both a shot. He slammed the Krista down the hatch. Banged his glass down for me to refill.

"Long life to you, a wet mouth and death in Ireland!" I yelled, a toast Pa used when Mom wasn't around. We knocked glasses, and then I knocked my glass against my teeth.

"Ha!" Viktor roared. He slapped his big hand on the metal desk. Slammed the second Krista after the first.

He produced a packet of crackers out of the bottom drawer of his desk. Ripped the cellophane off with his teeth. Spread brown goo with his forefinger.

Scotch is my poison—if I have to drink vodka, I prefer about two drops of it per drink. With my having no head for it, the Krista wasn't resolving itself harmlessly. I was starting to feel like I'd been sniffing high-grade coke.

Viktor didn't seem affected, except that he was more garrulous than usual. He told stories incessantly, cracker crumbs and brown goo spilling out of his mouth. He was halfway through one about something called *banyas,* which he said were Russian bathhouses.

"You rub yourself with honey. Big banya woman whips crap out of you. You don't die of heart attack, you don't have to see doctor rest of life." He thumped his belly. "Cleans out liver. Excellent for digestion."

"You pay for this? To get whipped?" I was cheerfully horrified.

He waved his huge hands. "Two hundred rubles. Measly seventy-five cents."

"I wouldn't pay to be whipped," I said. "Why would anyone want to be whipped?"

He shrugged. "In America, everyone wants to be comfortable all the time. In Russia, is different. I live once in closed city, and it—"

"Closed city? What's that?" I asked idly.

153

Death Game

Viktor didn't answer, and I freshened his drink. My only hope of survival was stealth. Whenever he looked away, I poured the lethal stuff from my glass down the side of his desk into his dead potted plant.

Viktor took another huge mouthful. Started a weird story about a pile of army caskets that got mixed up with boxes of ammunition in some godforsaken country where the Commies got their living asses kicked.

"Where was this?" I asked, vaguely interested. "You never mentioned you were a soldier."

Viktor made a face. "The Desert of Death. Afghanistan."

My ears sharpened. "Is that why you and Waleed had that, uh, argument? Isn't he from Afghanistan?"

"Waleed is *khoklov!*" Viktor spat out.

"In English?

He grinned maliciously. "*Khoklov* means fat stupid yokel. Big idiot."

"You said *'Za Khoklov!'* in your toast. You were calling me a yokel. A big idiot." I tried, failed, to feel aggrieved. I was really getting drunk.

Viktor shrugged. "You wish me death in pigsty Ireland."

I pointed at the red tracks across his forehead, just below his hairline. Two parallel scars about two-and-a-half inches apart. "Those scars? Are they war wounds? You get those in the Red Army?"

Viktor appraised me coldly. Took a gulp of the Krista and fixed me a cracker, licking the brown goo off the edges. After I took a bite, he grinned. "Krista goes down good with leetle horse fat on crackers, yes?"

I didn't realize this was meant to be a joke, until Viktor shoved my shoulder with his hand, to get a reaction. He'd barely exerted himself, but I'd had to rachet my fingers around the bottom of my chair and grip it like a vise to retain my seat. A moment later, he ran his hand through the short, white-blond hair on his forehead, tugging at it, as if he wished he could pull it over the scars.

"So, uh, what is it between you and Waleed?" *And why do I care about your answer to this?* I took another swallow of the Krista. There was some reason, but at the moment I couldn't remember it.

"As a boy, I go to war. As a man, I go to Moscow University," he said loftily. "Meet my wife there. Have I shown you picture of my wife, Natalya?" He retrieved his wallet from his back pocket, extracted a much-thumbed snapshot. "She study music at Moscow University," he added proudly. "Very talented. Natalya was also greatly talented in…" He waggled his fingers, screwed up his face like he couldn't remember the English word.

"Piano? Was she a pianist?"

"No, no." He put his thumb and second finger together to make a round O, shot the second finger of his other hand through the O repeatedly.

"You don't mean she was…" I paused delicately, felt my face blush.

He beamed. "She and her sister visit dachas of Soviet leaders. Work at orgies. Big swimming pool with glass walls. Dolphins swim with naked girls. She tells me all about it. She has much influence in those days."

I took the photo from him. The woman in the photo had the perfect facial structure of a Greta Garbo—it wasn't hard to imagine her the cynosure of Communist party bigwigs a couple of decades ago.

"Natalya is…no longer happy," Viktor said sadly. He slipped the snapshot back in his wallet. "She used to go out all the time, but now she does nothing. Everything is left for me to do."

"Why? Is she ill?"

But talking about Natalya seemed to have darkened his mood.

155

He bumped his heels on the ground a few times. Sloshed the vodka around. When he started talking again, there was no longer any content to it. Or, if there was, I couldn't absorb it or remember it.

What I did remember, later, was is throwing both our glasses against the door. Viktor leapt up, grabbed me around the waist and raised me so my legs dangled.

"No one sees us," he said, laughing. "Maybe I squeeze you to death like stuck pig. You can die right here, not pig Ireland."

"Do it slowly, you big Cossack. I want to enjoy it!" I hollered gaily. When he dropped me, I thought my ribs were broken. He was even stronger then I expected—one swing and he could break my skull.

Viktor was still laughing. He kept laughing—and I laughed with him. He turned to look at me, straight in the eyes. For the first time ever, my eyes met his directly, with no shadow between them. I expected humor, or maybe ferocity, but that wasn't what I saw. His eyes were distressingly sad, full of tragedy.

A moment later, they took on that soft look eyes get when the brain behind them has just gone absent. Viktor slid to the floor, rolled languidly over and ended up lying on his back with his head to the side, his eyes shut. His face relaxed slowly.

I leaned over his wastebasket and stuck my fingers down my throat. When I'd emptied as much of the vodka out of my stomach as I could, I touched my head. It felt spongy, as if my fingers might go right through my skull.

Viktor's breathing was loud and regular. I pushed against the small of his back gently with my foot.

He didn't stir.

In the top drawer of his desk was the key to his file cabinet, and I started there. Dozens of manila folders, which I pawed through quickly. Boring diagrams and blueprints—to my blurry eyes, they looked like blueprints of a bridge. There was also a

156

schedule—columns with dates and names of various seaports. Even more boring.

I tossed everything back in the cabinet. I was after the duplicate surveillance tape—that was the point of this little escapade.

The desk contained boxes of crackers, potato chips, a red-and-gold tin of caviar, plus a few rolls of stamps. No videotapes. Two of the four drawers were completely empty. I slammed the bottom one shut with irritation. Felt the adrenaline race as the noise reverberated round the small room.

Viktor groaned and rolled over; his head landed in an awkward position. He was in a deep sleep. If I left him like that, he'd wake up with the worst neck-ache of his life. Stripping his jacket off a peg on the wall, I started to roll it up, planning to slip it under his head.

My fingers felt something in a pocket—a thin, round object. I smoothed out the jacket and pulled it out. A gold-fronted DVD— a high-capacity recordable optical disc. It was unlabeled, just like the one I'd retrieved from under the lab bench that Waleed had snatched away. Was it the same disc?

Impossible to tell, but the grooves were darkened, so it wasn't a blank. I slipped it inside the waistband of my pants, put the jacket under Viktor's head. Stood up.

I glanced around the office one last time, wanting to be certain I'd done a thorough search. That's when I saw it, poking out of the air conditioning register, up near the ceiling. I took two steps over to it, lifted my head...

It was a bad discovery, perhaps the worst I could make, but it was too late to do anything about it.

Chapter Fourteen

WHEN I PUSHED OPEN THE GLASS OFFICE DOOR THE NEXT MORNING, Kim sat at the reception desk looking at a box of long-stemmed red roses. Same flowers he always gave me, I thought, passing by without a word. Rick never had any imagination.

His office door was closed when I went by, but fifteen minutes later, she buzzed to say he wanted me. Weaving carefully back down the corridor, I went in and sat down. A dancing balloon of intense yellow light was flashing on and off behind my eyeballs.

"You tied on a real beaut, didn't you?" he asked, grimly focused on me.

I mumbled something, examined my palms to avoid his eyes.

"Little Miss Sobriety," he said. "And to think you used to lecture me about my drinking."

"I could curse myself right now, Rick, but I can't take moralizing from you." The yellow balloon was brighter. I pinched my eyeballs to make it go away.

He went to his office door and slammed it.

Irritation struggled to break through the inner lethargy. I felt dizzy, exhausted, like I was in a horrible dream. Rick opened a door of the cabinet behind his desk, revealing a large surveillance monitor. I knew what was about to happen, but I watched him

Cheryl Swanson

anyway, wondering if he felt any shame, any embarrassment about spying on us. It was illegal, wasn't it, to snoop on your employees? Maybe not, but it was repellent.

The screen sprang to life when he activated the remote. Not CNN, no has-been movie star peddling garish jewelry. It was strictly a receiver, used to display live or recorded feeds of digitized images from different sites.

He kept flicking until he reached the view of Viktor's tiny private office. Viktor's features appeared, then my own, as he squeezed buttons, forwarding the time clock rapidly.

The lighting was poor, and Viktor and I were significantly distorted in most of the views. Whenever we moved, little pieces of us slid off the screen—the concealed camera I'd discovered wasn't nearly as high quality as the cameras on the *Sea Dream.*

I stopped thinking like a critic as Rick skipped the tape forward. In no time at all, he had hit all the high points—me drinking with Viktor, talking with Viktor, laughing with Viktor, searching the office with Viktor passed out and lying on the floor. There was an audio feed, but he kept it off, as if he had already listened to our conversation and saw no reason to do so again.

When he was done, he tossed the remote on his desk. Turned and stared at me as if I were so dirty I need to be mucked out, ventilated and scrubbed. He was waiting for me to say something—defend myself, maybe—but I didn't speak. I couldn't think of anything to say.

There was a longish pause while nothing happened. The silence lengthened, to the point I was tempted to rest my head on my hands. I didn't. I decided, all in all, it was better to stay upright.

"I'm canning your ass," Rick said, direct as a bullet now he was finally speaking. "Clean out your desk. I want you out of here in thirty minutes."

That roused me a little.

159

Death Game

"You're firing me?" I didn't believe him.

"What'd you expect? You think you have a right to get one of my employees drunk and then search his office?"

"I wanted the copy you made of the surveillance tape," I said doggedly. "I thought Viktor might have it."

"And I told you a week ago, when you were snooping around in my office, I destroyed that tape."

"You didn't tell me the truth about that, did you?" I stretched my hands toward him. My voice had caught in my throat, turned hoarse.

He didn't respond.

"Rick, everything you've told me since Stephen's murder has been bullshit." Having nothing more to lose, I decided to take a flyer, hope against hope he might actually level with me. "What are you afraid of? What's really going on? What is Viktor really doing?"

He looked at me coldly. "Stay on the point, Cooper. This time you've gone over the line. You've violated every rule I can think of about how an employee should behave." A moment later, the fury came out. "You must be off your rocker to act like this. No, don't argue with me. I've got no option. Pack up your stuff and leave the premises. Right now."

"You're really giving me the boot? Seriously?" My tone was incredulous.

"Give me one goddamn reason I shouldn't." His voice was low, compelling. It sent unpleasant buzzes through me.

My lethargy was gone; I was shivering. Tingling almost to the point of nausea. Rick stared straight at me. His eyes seem to enter me—dark eyes, the kind that go back in time, channels of memory...

I took a deep breath. "Here's one goddamn reason," I said, speaking in a voice so strained I barely recognized it. "We can't get away from each other that easily, Rick. Remember? We're still

160

married. I'm your wife."

His face went rigid with fury. "And you never trusted me. Not from the very beginning."

"I did," I said, stricken. "When we were first married, I trusted you completely."

His eyes narrowed with an odd light. He came to his feet with his arm thrown forward, finger pointing at the door.

"Get out," he said hoarsely. "I can't stand the sight of you anymore! Get out of my office! Get out of my sight!"

*   *   *

Twenty minutes later I drove home, the meager contents of my desk boxed up and sitting in the passenger seat of the Fiat. Rick is right, I told myself abjectly. I never trusted him, right from the beginning.

Rick and I met during a coed tag football game on the grass behind the film school at USC. When I joined in, he knocked me down. I was immediately suspicious that the full-body tackle he landed on me was as accidental as a tidal wave.

He reached out a hand and pulled me back up. After the game, he insisted on buying me a beer so he could apologize.

He never did get around to that apology. Instead, over beer and pizza, which I paid for, he told me his life story. Explained how he didn't have the bucks to travel so he'd joined the Marines. Got selected to be in Force Reconnaissance and learned a few things about surveillance. Quit the Marines, stumbled through a couple of nothing jobs and eventually started his own security company. How he was doing really well, hiring himself out to private eyes, working nonstop, making a lot of dough.

I didn't believe much of his story. For one thing, everyone in the bar knew him, kept coming by to slap his hand. When was he working, if he was spending so much time in a bar? And he looked, frankly, even poorer than I did—jeans ripped by wear,

Death Game

not by style; a sweat-stained baseball hat; running shoes splattered with motor oil.

But I liked him anyway. Compared to the pasty-faced film school students I'd been dating—USC was very hip then, full of earnestly idiotic Spielberg wannabes—Rick was a jolt of electricity. It wasn't long before I wasn't listening so much as feeling.

I'd taken amphetamines plenty of times, but that was nothing compared to the bug-eyed, empty-bellied rush I felt being around Rick. Being near him created little stirrings all over my body. Made the blood start to move faster in my veins. He was one of those people who can gather up all the energy in a room and shine it on you. Make you feel the light blazing into every pore.

Later, I realized that he was, quite simply, the most potent man I'd ever met in my life. Maybe it was his god-awful background, maybe it was his lack of any decent parenting, maybe it was that only someone with magic inside could have survived. All I knew was that when I was around Rick, he brought me so alive I felt like I could count every cell in my body with my fingertips.

After he told me his story, he led me out to his scabrous Jeep Cherokee. Showed me his surveillance equipment—a couple of portable cameras, including a trick one with a night-vision scope. It was then I found out he had plans for me beyond a free meal and a flop in the hay. He saw me, a starving film student who knew her way around cameras, as super-cheap labor to exploit.

He kept talking as I played with the cameras, waving his hands in the air, flipping a bird at a car that whizzed by too close. His words had started to carry an assumptive tone, but I wasn't certain what he thought I had agreed to do.

He was certain, though—I was going to take over his snooping business for him, because he wanted to go to law school nights.

162

I said no way; I had film classes to attend. He said that was okay, we'd work around that. He'd work days, and I'd work nights. And maybe, in a few months, he'd make me a partner.

I quit after two weeks and every two weeks after that for a year. The physical danger of surveillance work was a big part of its appeal to Rick, but I wasn't keen on it. I had my shoulder separated, cracked three of my ribs, had a hole bit in my butt by a Doberman. And one night, a half-stoned guy, who had supposedly busted his back, caught me filming him dancing outside a Long Beach club. He threw the camera I was holding into the sewer. Tossed me in after it. I was five months pregnant.

I had a serious talk with Rick that night.

Neither of us was ready to give up on the business, but we stopped the onsite surveillance work, switched to installing surveillance equipment instead. That was much safer, but not any more successful. Rick kept his promise and made me a partner before we got married, but all that meant was that I was equally on the hook for the bills.

When Heather was almost three, a job offer with OZ came through, giving me a chance to finally start doing what I'd gone to film school for. By then, Rick had finished law school and was trying to set up a personal injury practice in Los Angeles. To bring in a few extra bucks, I took a reasonable job for a woman with a small child—teaching swimming at the YMCA. Heather toddled around after the older kids on my swim team. Afternoons and evenings, I worked the surveillance business.

While I was reasonably happy, Rick was disintegrating. Neither business—surveillance or law practice—went anywhere. I took charge of the phone, typed up what he needed for his meager law practice. He haunted the hospitals, hung out in the emergency rooms, passing out business cards I created on our ancient printer.

As the bills piled up, anxiety started to nibble at him like a famished rat. He would start the day off as if determined to get somewhere. Determined, by sheer force of will, to pull himself up by the bootstraps. He'd start early, his face set, fierce, and come home late, drunk. Not drunk and noisy. Drunk and quiet. I'd find him slumped over the kitchen table, his eyes open and staring, looking as if he would have traded his soul for some rest, for sleep. And it wasn't just his face that turned haunted. His voice was raspy, as if he were breaking up inside.

Then came a very ugly time, when Satan seemed to set up housekeeping in his soul. My happiness disappeared; I started to feel frightened and guilt-ridden. It seemed completely reasonable to me that I was to blame. I had slipped up, saddled him with a kid when my first job should have been to make sure his life went smoothly. Rick was failing—he thought he was a failure, at least, in those early years of trying to turn his practice into a paying concern—and it was all my fault.

There was plenty of precedent for these feelings. From infancy, I'd been nurtured on the belief that women, especially mothers, had to be perfect. A mother, a true mother, committed a crime against nature if she didn't drop to her knees to beg her husband's forgiveness after he tried to knock her head off. The Roman Catholic Church, my gene pool—shit, the entire country of Ireland—they all reinforced the message that a woman should adore her husband and try to make his life easy, no matter what. Rick had married me no doubt in part because he wanted that naive advocacy, that mindless hero-worship.

One day, I returned to our apartment early after taking Heather to visit my parents for the holidays. Rick had stayed home, telling me he had things to decide, that he was thinking of giving up his law practice. I remember it was a warm day for December, the sun glowing dirty pink on the horizon.

When I came into the apartment, a young woman I didn't recognize was stretched out on the tatty sofa. All she wore was one of Rick's T-shirts and a nervous look. Rick was in the kitchen, but he came out in a hurry when he heard me come in.

There was no scene; everyone behaved with painful naturalness. Heather displayed the Christmas toys her grandparents had given her. The woman went into the bedroom, retrieved her clothes and Rick drove her away.

After they left, I felt waves of intense emotion sweep through my body. Anger. Grief. Fear. Jealousy. Rage. I would pack my things and go—I must go…go immediately. Go before my courage failed me.

When he came back, he told me the woman was an old friend. Her flight had been cancelled, and she was using the apartment to clean up before going back to the airport. I listened and agreed it was a pity the airlines were so unreliable over the holidays. Two weeks later, the woman was in the apartment again.

This time they were in the bedroom, didn't notice that someone had come in. Heather was sound asleep in her room. I took her to the closest park, and she scampered through the trash-strewn grass, wandering back and forth, while I kept kneeling to retch in the urine-soaked bushes.

Rick broke up with the woman—or told me he did. Not that it mattered. Soon enough, he was covering her card with as many others as he could pull from the pack. Sometimes, I pretended I was unaware; other times, I tried to reason with him. When I got desperate, I threw a fit. Yelled and screamed.

Nothing worked.

When you're young, you think things can be patched together again. You think you can reshape and refigure the past, keep the good things, discard the rest. But the crack between Rick and I just kept spreading, widening beneath my feet. It didn't matter how hard I tried to resurrect the shattered dream. Everything was slipping through my fingers.

By the time Heather was three-and-a-half, reasons no longer mattered. I'd heard somewhere there was a force, a law of nature, that hurls things apart. Things diverge; things separate—you can't stop it. What created the final split was the job offer from OZ. I was excited when I told Rick about it.

"You're moving to San Francisco? Just like that?" he said.

He was angry, and his reaction had surprised me. He'd told me repeatedly he wanted to move to northern California. He thought there were more opportunities there, but we couldn't afford to move. I tried to present the job offer that way, but he blasted me.

"What are you proposing?" he asked icily. "That I live off my wife?"

I stood for a moment with my head sunk, eyes fixed on the ground.

"I want Heather to grow up seeing her father as much as possible," I mumbled.

"You're using this as an excuse to leave me." There was a panicked, haunted tone in his voice.

I lifted my head, steeled myself. "It's the logical conclusion, isn't it?"

I'd decided it was best to be casual. Pretend I didn't care. What's love, if not pretending? I thought bitterly.

"Don't you understand that a man can love one woman with all his soul and still crave something different once in—"

"It's my dream, Rick. I'll be doing what I've always wanted to do."

"We're staying in LA," he snapped.

I shook my head.

"Baby love, we can patch things up. We can—"

"No."

"I'm dying," he said, his voice going flat, his face turning ashen as he sensed my determination. "I'm dying here, Cooper.

166

Help me out."

Oh, the feeling, the feeling as I watched him. It felt like my soul was breaking apart. I reached out, but I pulled my hand back immediately, let it fall.

It was over. It had to be over.

But it wasn't.

We didn't divorce; we separated. Rick wrote up the legal agreement—a post-nup, he called it; and at first I thought he was joking. But he carefully detailed it all out, all our little financial arrangements. He got the TV, I got the kitchen table, he got the surveillance equipment—a pathetic totting up of the forks and spoons.

I told myself I hadn't been ready for marriage, and Rick hadn't been, either. But we'd done it, and there was Heather and…well, surely, she deserved that we give our marriage this final chance. And then, I was a Catholic, and well…

What it all really meant was that divorce was failure, and we couldn't, *wouldn't* admit defeat.

In San Francisco, loneliness was a constant problem, so I dated occasionally. Not often. I couldn't quite see the sense of never going out, but I'd never found anyone I liked. All my instincts were against hanging my heart out there for someone else to stomp on.

By the time Rick moved to San Francisco, I think we were both certain it was only a matter of time before we'd do the formal thing. Get divorced. But the years went by, and we seemed trapped in a kind of limbo. Neither of us had the intestinal fortitude to sever the marriage.

I kept telling myself I had extracted Rick out of my heart. Obliterated the infection. Cauterized the wound. All that was left was ancient keloid scar tissue, the remnants of barbed hooks removed from flesh. How little I knew in those days about love. How little I knew about the heart's infinite capacity for pain.

Chapter Fifteen

HEATHER WASN'T READY WHEN RICK CAME TO PICK HER UP. IT WAS Saturday afternoon, and he wore casual clothes, very of-the-moment in style—an unstructured dark linen jacket and a matching linen-blend sweater. He mumbled something, headed straight for the front room and looked out the bay window. His car—a lovely thing, all Brazilian walnut, German engineering and Italian leather—sat under a handwritten handbill. PARC YR GAS-HOG HERE YUPIE SCUM AND WE'LL BUS OUT YOUR % ^ &*$ WINDOS! WE'RE REKLAMING THE NEIGBORHUD!!!!

Crazy Sally made up a new sign every weekend.

"You don't need to worry," I said, watching him. "Not unless you see a woman in a tie-dyed muumuu out there with a sledgehammer."

He didn't respond.

It was a windblown afternoon, leaves flying in the air; a condom stuck in the chain-link fence across the street flapped. Rick's eyes had gone to the condom, and his jaw clenched slightly.

"You want some coffee?"

"I don't have time."

"You have time. Heather's not going to be ready for twenty

168

minutes yet. I'll go start a new pot."

When I came back, he was making an effort. He'd sat down, picked up a magazine and was thumbing through it.

"Did Heather enjoy art camp?" he asked without looking at me.

"She loved it, but I cried myself to sleep every night."

"Horseshit. You never cry," he said bitterly. "I thought we agreed *I'd* bring her back to the city."

"I have plenty of time now that I'm unemployed. I didn't think you'd mind."

He tossed the magazine down, went back to look out the window. No sign of Sally, but two of her freaky kids, morose-faced, dressed goth, leaned against the chain-link fence.

"This is the kind of trashy street my mother made her living off of," he griped. "I never liked Heather living here. It's too dangerous."

"Actually, it's one of the safest streets in the city ever since Pa broke a man's back a year ago. The word got around."

He didn't say anything.

"And the cops cruise by all the time now. We're getting so much cop traffic even the honest people are feeling nervous."

That got his attention.

"The cops are looking for Jimmie? They think he might come back here?"

I shrugged. "There's also a sneaky-looking operative cruising the block. He drives a government-issue Chevy, parks a different place every day."

I'd knock on the guy's window with my knuckles when I sighted him. Maybe he was just an ordinary undercover cop, but my instincts told me he was DSS. He'd look up from his newspaper, and I'd smile, wave, pretend to talk into my wristwatch. The first time, he'd folded his newspaper and driven away. The last time he'd just made an obscene gesture and gone back to reading.

Rick got out a pipe. Lit it and started smoking.

"Mock me all you want, Cooper," he said. "But I don't like having my daughter live in this neighborhood. I don't like her growing up having to cope with punk kids and cross-dressing whores and rapists and mounds of trash."

"Then you better move her out of America entirely," I said. "How about...I know—Antarctica."

After that, I let him puff in silence. I hadn't seen him smoke in years, not since he got his ulcer and the doctor told him to stop. The doctor had also told him to cut back on the drinking, and that had seemed effective as well.

He picked up the magazine, went back to flicking through it, but it was clear his mind was elsewhere. Since he wouldn't meet my eyes, I had a chance to study him.

He'd aged in the past few weeks; his features had been pared down, become crueler. The curve of his neck, his profile were flint-like, and there was a light in his eye I'd never seen before. A brutal greenish light.

"I hope you've thought about it. I made the right decision. It's best we don't work together," he said, squirming a little under my gaze.

I mumbled something meaningless.

"Have you filed for unemployment? That'll tide you over, and if you need a few extra bucks, maybe I can loan you something."

"I know I'm a low-rent person to you, Rick, but I'm not a bum. Don't offer me charity."

"If we got divorced, you'd have child support, at least."

I sat down next to the Lady of Mercy corner table. Didn't say anything.

"If you had a steady monthly income, maybe you could move."

I sat with my head cocked like a priest's who is feigning

attention to the ramblings of a penitent. Time to get real, I thought.

"I want you to tell me something, Rick. Just this one thing...that's all I want to know. How did Stephen and Jimmie meet each other?"

"Beats me."

"They didn't go to the same school; they didn't run in the same groups. So, how'd they meet?"

He shrugged his bulky shoulders. "You're talking teenage boys. There are a dozen ways they could have met and nobody known about it."

"Name one."

"What difference does it make?" He took another puff on his pipe. "That kid brother of yours is a natural-born killer. The way he murdered, so coldly. He barely acted like a human being."

"Jimmie hasn't been arrested yet, much less tried and convicted. Maybe you should withhold judgment."

"You saw the tape. I don't know what else it's gonna take to convince you." He sounded reasonable, but a moment later he was on the offensive. "You should have kicked him out of your house. At least, made him get a job and take responsibility for himself. You're damn lucky he didn't get himself a bazooka and a case of antitank grenades and blow his high school sky-high. That's what you were afraid of, wasn't it? Why you blasted out of my office that day? Left me to deal with Harmon."

"Jimmie's fair game now, is that it? You can finally tell me what you really thought of him?"

"He was a mixed-up kid since he was born. A loser," Rick said coolly. "He had a good background, parents who looked after him, but he didn't appreciate it. Compare his mother to the bitch who brought me into this world."

"He's not a coward, and I think whoever killed Stephen was a coward," I said bitterly. "I've still got some hope it wasn't my little brother."

When Rick spoke next it was in an unguarded way, as if he was talking to himself.

"I hated having Jimmie living with Heather. Those two shouldn't even be on the same planet, much less walking around the same house." He fidgeted, seemed to make a decision. "All I've worked for, it's been to make sure my daughter never had to go through what I went through." He raised his voice, assumed a self-righteous tone. "And then you take in that punk brother of yours."

I gave him a flat, dark look. I was feeling…I don't know. Plenty. Plenty had been going around in my head about Rick recently, and most of it was rancid and rotten and suspicious.

I went to the coffee table, lifted five magazines off the stack. Unearthed a DVD, which I'd quickly concealed there when I saw Rick at the door.

"What's that?" He reached for the DVD, but I pulled away.

"You know what it is," I said. "It's a copy of Viktor's…snuff film. You lied about that from the beginning, didn't you, Rick? That's why you leased that goddamn expensive AVID in the first place. Not for me—I was cover, in case the DSS, the SV or the CIA or any other of the phone book full of secret agencies in this country ever got nosy. You wanted that equipment for Viktor."

So he could manufacture—what? What was Rick involved in? If I knew the answer to that, I would know the answer to everything.

He didn't say anything.

"Was Walter Ludlow in it with you? Using your dirty little business to add to his billions?"

Never underestimate the power of sheer fucking money, my pa had always said.

But I felt like I was in the dark about everything and badly needed some light. Walter would kiss the ass of every cross-

172

dresser in the city before he'd get involved in porn. I could see Rick peddling porn, even snuffies, but not Walter. It just wasn't his style.

But what else could it be?

While I was talking, Rick reached for the DVD again, but I backed away. He followed, had me almost up against the wall when the outside door banged open and there were footsteps in the entry.

Razel poked his head in the arched doorway.

"Where's our baby? Is she wearing the Big Girl blouse I gave her?" he asked eagerly. Adjusting from the glare on the street to the darkness of the room, he didn't see Rick. "It still smells like smoke in here," he complained. He swung the shopping bags he was holding. The head of a geisha poked out of one bag, the tail of a golden dragon out of the other. "Heather will want them in her room, next to the airplane fuselage." His round pale face gleamed like a cheerful puffball. "I'm teaching her to be ultra chic."

Rick came forward, gave Razel a press of the hand and a social smile. The smile only moved his lips; his eyes said, "Kindly disintegrate."

"What'd he mean, calling Heather 'our baby?'" he asked the moment Razel left. "You let that peacock's ass call my daughter 'our baby?'" He had thrown his pipe in the fireplace and was moving around the room in tight little circles.

"Keep your voice down." Razel was on the staircase, the bags bumping after him. "What if he hears you?"

"I hope he does hear me. I'm not letting some psychotic old fag buy clothes and collect trash for my daughter. You put a stop to that, or Heather's not going to be living here." His voice was loud, obnoxious. He sounded like he was about to blow his stack.

I was annoyed. "When did you join the homo patrol, Rick?" I didn't take this burst of self-righteousness seriously. Or his anger. Rick could turn his anger on like a tap when he had a use for it.

173

Death Game

"I mean it, Cooper. With what happened with your brother, a judge could easily be persuaded this isn't a fit home for a child anymore."

"You're threatening me," I said, amazed. "A moment ago you were trying to bribe me and now you're threatening me."

He stopped dead a few feet from me, breathing hard.

"Horseshit, I'm not threatening or bribing anyone. And I'm not sponsoring any kind of pornography. Not snuff films, not soft core, not even a Playboy Channel." He wasn't selling it; he could tell that from my face. He changed tactics. "For crissakes, Cooper, if you're right about Viktor I'll bust that big ugly mug right back to Siberia."

He was directly in front of me. I held the DVD tightly; he wasn't reaching for it, but he was fully focused. On the alert. He was angling in, ready to knock me down, acting elaborately casual to hide it, but he was balanced on his toes. And he was strung as tight as a piano wire. As I watched, a muscle jumped spasmodically under his left eye...

"Keep your distance," I said sharply.

In spite of my efforts to stay calm, I felt like busting his chops. My temper was starting to flare. *Just let him try to snatch the DVD from me—I'll bust* him *back to Siberia.*

Heather came in. Read this lousy movie scene right out of the set-up in front of her. Read my crummy feelings right off my face.

"Mom, what's the matter? What's going on?"

I was struggling to control my temper, and I didn't answer her. She turned to her father.

"Dad? What's wrong?"

She accepted our arguments without comment, usually, but this was more than an argument. Both of us were quivering with suppressed, murderous rage.

When her father didn't answer her either, tears started trembling in her eyes, ready to fall. I put my hand on her head.

Cheryl Swanson

My red hair is as naturally unruly and untidy as crabgrass on a city lawn, but Heather had her father's dark hair—thick, straight and beautiful. I felt guilty, guilty as hell. Why is it that when parents lose their way, children always take it on the nose?

I stroked her head, spoke gently. "We're just...trying to settle something. Nothing for you to worry about, Heather."

She yanked her head away. "You're just trying to protect me. I hate it when you do that."

I turned to face Rick. "I apologize."

My words were for Heather's sake, and so were his.

"Just a little tiff, honey," He forced a light tone. "Lovers' quarrel."

"No, really..." I was annoyed. This was one thing I never joked about. I never wanted to mislead Heather, get her hoping for reconciliation.

"Your mom and I always work things out," Rick said, raising her chin with his hand. "Don't cry, sweetheart. The three of us, we're a team. No matter what."

He gave me a false smile, and I returned it. Heather's face started to clear.

"Ready to go? You got every minute of the afternoon planned for me already? Gonna drag your old dad around until he's so tired and beat he's begging for mercy?"

She hugged him. "I'll go easy on you, Dad."

"Go out to the car, honey," he said. "I want to ask your mother something." He waited until she was out of earshot. "You want to give me that DVD now?"

"Was I right, Rick? You've reinvented yourself? Screw trying to be a good lawyer, you're gonna make it as a porn king?"

"Give me the disc, Cooper," he said. His mouth had formed a tight line, and his nostrils dilated slightly.

"How does it connect to Stephen's death?" I asked. "Tell me that, and I won't keep it." At least, I won't unless I need to for

175

Jimmie's sake.

I expected him to deny there was a connection, but he didn't. Instead, he tried something else. He put the fingers of his right hand around the Mexican silver ring, held it tightly.

"For once in your life, trust me," he said, sounding smothered. "Give me the damn DVD. Let me handle this."

"Sorry."

His eyes looked intently into mine. I had a sense that if Razel wasn't in the house he might try some strong-arm tactic, in spite of Heather waiting in his car across the street.

"You're fucking Kim Ludlow, aren't you?" I suddenly asked. About some things, Rick could fool me, but not about other women, not when I could see into his eyes.

"Crissakes, if I am, you've got nothing to talk about. You were fucking her father."

I felt a sudden burst of sadness. "You're a fool, Rick. Walter only wanted me because he was in some kind of idiotic competition with you. When I figured that out, it was over."

"I don't give a rat's ass why Walter wanted you. What I care about is why you wanted him instead of me. You wanted him because he was rich. Refined. Cultured." His voice was bitter. He'd stopped holding the ring and stood with his hands jammed in his pockets, like he was afraid if he took them out he might be tempted to do violence. "You married me as a social reclamation project. You always wanted a rich man, but when I got there it was too late for you. Too late and too little."

"You're out of your mind," I said. "I got involved with Walter because I've always been stupid when it comes to men. Just like my mother. I should have known better. My pa told me the straight-up truth about that. He said life was just to humiliate you and dash your dreams and the only way you could handle it was to never get your hopes up. But I didn't listen to him. I loved you, and when we broke up there were days when I couldn't think about it or I feared I would stop breathing. After being with you, spending time with someone like Walter was like being with a...dead man."

Rick's eyes flickered, but he didn't speak. He had grown very pale, as if I had touched a nerve.

"For your own sake, Rick, get away from Kim," I pleaded. "Stop being such a jerk."

"What if she's in love with me?"

"It's a measure of your own blindness you even think that. She's not capable of love. The most you can hope for is that she's just enjoying herself. Working off steam. If it's not that, she's got something planned so horrible you and I can't even imagine it. Some humiliation that is gonna make you wish you'd settled for a picture of her and masturbation."

His face turned fuchsia. He took a step back, as if I had slashed him with a knife.

"Sorry," I said, already deeply regretting my words. "I'm so sorry, Rick." I ran my tongue around my teeth. "I shouldn't have said that."

"Give me the DVD, Cooper," he said, sounding...humiliated. "Please trust me. Please. There's no other way."

"No."

As I said it, I felt resolution forming. Rick turned away, sensing that resolution. He was finished with the conversation, finished with me as well. A clock chimed softly near the fireplace. My mother's clock, a termite-eaten timepiece she'd inherited from her mother, of course. It was twenty minutes off; it had never kept decent time.

Rick had gone out the door. He crossed the street to where Heather was waiting while I stood rooted in front of the window, watching him. Heather looked over her shoulder at me, circled by his arm. I stepped back behind the shadow of the curtains so she couldn't see me. The staggering size of what had probably been

Death Game

destroyed, of what was being wrenched away from me, brought a whirling sense of desperation.

Rick, I thought. Oh, my God, Rick.

*   *   *

That evening, around six o'clock, Heather called.

"Mom? Dad took me to this private school that's in northern Sausalito. There's a big field around it. They've got cherry trees and a swimming pool and horses kids can ride."

"Sounds great, honey," I said, barely listening.

"Best of all, they've got this special art program going," she continued, her voice excited. "You can go on field trips or paint or do collages outdoors. Dad said if I stayed with him, I could go there."

My heart went to my feet with a thud. "Don't you want to just relax for a bit? School starts again in May, you know." Heather was on one of those twelve-month schedules, instituted to lessen the crowding problem in the city schools.

"It will just be for a month," she said quickly. "When school starts, I'll be back with you."

"You sure you want to do this?" I tried to keep my voice neutral, tried not to let her hear my disappointment.

"You don't mind, Mom? I mean, I'll see you on weekends."

"Let me talk to your father, honey."

There was a long pause before he came to the phone.

"She can't live with you. She's never lived with you," I said.

"Of course, she has. Don't be ridiculous." His voice was heavy and distant.

"An occasional weekend. An overnight. This is different. You don't know her habits, Rick, you don't know her needs." The words came pouring out. "She comes downstairs and eats her breakfast without ever uttering a word. You talk to her, and she won't eat. She's upset all day. And...she hates having her artwork praised," I added desperately. "She'd much prefer it be made fun of. She wants to be told she should give up art. That all her paintings suck. That she'd make more money as a female wrestler. It spurs her forward. Otherwise, she withers. You don't know even these basic things about her."

"She's an art prodigy," Rick said proudly. "She should be told how great she is by qualified teachers. It would encourage her."

"There's no such thing as an art prodigy." I wrapped the phone cord around my hand, tighter and tighter, until it was cutting off my circulation. "Child prodigies come in only two classifications—music and mathematics. And I do tell her how great she is. I praise her for cleaning up her room, having good manners and helping around the house. But I don't praise her for doing what she loves.

"There're far too many destroyed gifted kids in this city. Destroyed because their parents try to live through them. Mostly they get into hard drugs at puberty, end up living on the streets. Rick, you don't know anything about children. All you know about Heather is what you want her to be. You've never thought about her as an individual in your whole life."

Just like Pa with Jimmie, I thought. And look where that ended.

"I'm not getting into a battle with you over this, Cooper," Rick said, so dully I wondered if he had been drinking. "I'll send my housekeeper over to get her things. When she comes by, you can tell her anything she needs to know about Heather's...diet, or whatever."

"Rick, tell me I'm wrong. Tell me you really want Heather with you. Tell me you're not doing this just to pressure me."

"I'm not even going to dignify that with a response." A moment later he couldn't resist. "That disc is stolen property. If I have to use legal channels to retrieve it I will."

"Fat chance," I said, giving a bitter laugh. "If I let Harmon get

Death Game

a whiff of what's on that disc you'll have to pull every string you have to stay out of jail yourself."

There was a longish pause. "What do you want from me, Cooper?"

"I want to know what in hell has happened to you. When did you decide to stop even trying to be a fucking decent person?"

He got off instead of answering, and Heather came back on the phone.

"You don't mind do you, Mom?"

"No, honey. I'll miss you and all that, but it'll be okay."

"I'll miss you, too," she said.

"I did a great job raising you, you know that?" I tried to sound happy. "You're a toughie, not a wuss like me."

She sounded happy in turn. "Yeah, you are a wuss. But Dad always looks out for you, so you'll be okay."

I felt a hand squeeze my heart. "Goodnight, honey."

"You want me to say goodnight to Dad for you?"

"Uh, ask him to get back on the phone, would you, honey? I'll tell him myself."

And Heather went to do my bidding—she was the kind of child who would not have neglected such a commission—but Rick didn't come back on the phone.

Chapter Sixteen

THE NEXT DAY WAS THE ANNIVERSARY OF MY MOM'S DEATH. I WENT TO church, said every Catholic prayer I remembered and prayed for Jimmie, except for lapses when my mind wandered. Before I left, I even prayed for Stephen, a half-crazy, retroactive prayer asking God to relieve the suffering he experienced before his death. Maybe God is bounded by time or space as we are, but it doesn't seem likely, so I asked Him to anesthetize Stephen's senses, to numb the terror he felt in his final moments.

I walked out of the church feeling worse, not better. For weeks I'd been imploring God to help, and the more I begged, the more I felt like a child who constantly whined and needed to stop asking.

When I got home, a bright yellow Corvette was in my driveway, its tail blocking the sidewalk. Lauren wasn't inside. She was huddled on my front stoop, looking miserable.

I opened the garage, but the Corvette was too long to fit inside. I left it half in, half out, found a place for the Fiat three blocks away and jogged back to the house.

"I wondered when you were going to show up," I said, huffing a little.

"I can only stay a minute," she said. "My mom thinks I'm,

181

like, at the library."

"No boo-hooing this time, okay?" I said cruelly, letting her in and tossing the keys on the Our Lady of Mercy table. Maybe I shouldn't have been so heartless, but I didn't think it would inflict any permanent damage. I also thought that Lauren needed to learn that tears weren't the best way to get what she wanted.

"I hate Travis," she said.

"I do, too," I said cheerfully. "But you don't need to worry about Travis. He'll get what's coming to him. Some woman will marry him and blow his TV up, tell him he's got to spend one hour a day doing something useful. Or he'll have a live-in girlfriend who pops out triplets and skewers him for child support. Someday, someone is gonna teach him how stupid it is not to respect women."

She almost grinned.

"He's such a dillweed, ya know? He keeps threatening me, but I don't, like, care anymore. I got something I, like, need to tell you about Jimmie."

"And Travis doesn't want you to tell me?"

"Oh, it's not that. He just likes to..."

"Scare you."

"Yeah. Only it's, like, not working, ya know? Instead, I'm getting pissed with him." This time she did grin. "What makes a guy act like that? What makes him so mean?"

"A sense of inferiority," I said. "Males know we're better than them. The good ones don't care, in fact, they enjoy it. The rest try to even the score with physical power and brutality."

"Jimmie wasn't like that," she said.

"I don't know what Jimmie was like," I said, sitting down. "Why don't you tell me?"

She settled into my grandmother's ancient chair. Wrinkled her nose a little as the cushions puffed out dust and insect carcasses.

"You knew Jimmie and I, like, made love, right?" she asked.

"No," I said. "And please don't tell me you're pregnant."

"Gawd no," she said, sounding prudish. "I'm on the pill."

"Good."

"And I don't think…I mean, it was only once. Well, twice."

She twisted her fingers together. She was trying to act cool about it, but she was upset.

"It's nothing to hate yourself for," I said. "It happens. But you shouldn't be in such a hurry to do it again. Give yourself some time to grow up. Besides, boys are mostly rope-a-dopes, aren't they?"

She fidgeted a little. Picked a scab on her arm. "Jimmie wasn't."

I stayed silent.

"Jimmie…" She gave up on the scab, started twisting her fingers again. "I said things about Jimmie that, like, weren't true. That game we were playing? He stopped playing it."

"Because he thought it was racist?"

She seemed shocked. "No. It was, like, just for fun—I told you that. But there was another game he got into, ya know? He was, like, such a freak about it he couldn't be, like, bothered with the game Travis and I were playing anymore, ya know?"

I was perplexed. "Another game? What was it like?"

The fingers were still twisting. "I don't know. Jimmie, like, tried to play it at the computer lab a couple times, but he, like, couldn't make it work. He said he didn't need to, that he could, like, play it right in his bedroom." She frowned. "He started talking like he might, like, actually kill someone, ya know? Only then he said he never would, that it would, like, just make everyone hate him even more, ya know?"

"Why did you want to tell me this, Lauren?"

But, of course, it wasn't this she'd wanted to tell me. It was just her excuse for coming over. What she'd really wanted to tell

Death Game

me about was having sex with Jimmie.

I talked to her a little more, trying to help her. I'd lost my virginity when I was about her age—a highly unpleasant encounter on the back of an Appaloosa pony. It had taken me almost two decades to see the humor in it.

The truth was that it had shattered something inside. I'd lost my sense of girlishness way too young, that powerful connection to my childhood. But I'd been afraid I'd be singled out as the only girl in my peer group who didn't know what having sex was like.

Lauren had been seeking sympathetic ears, but I got the sense she was doing fine. She seemed to genuinely care about Jimmie, which meant he'd probably cared about her.

"When you said Jimmie started talking like he could kill someone, what did you mean?" I asked her just before she left.

"I gotta go," she said. "My mom will be, like, majorly pissed if I don't get home right away."

"Stop it," I said irritably. "You tell me something, and then you start this deaf-and-dumb routine. Trust me. Or don't trust me. But cut out the act."

There was silence. I had backed her mom's car out of the garage, and I was holding the keys. When she reached for them, I dropped them into my other palm and closed my fingers around them.

The skin of her face tightened. "Jimmie said you were a bitch. He said you, like, started every day with a nervous breakdown." She was breathing hard through her nose.

"I am like that. Sometimes." But it hurt, hearing her repeat the words.

She hesitated. "He also said you had, like, a soft heart. And that if anyone ever tried to hurt you, he'd, like, dump a ton of garbage in their life."

I sighed. "I think Jimmie was way more frightened than he ever let on."

184

"Well, duh. Do you think the cops will kill him? If they find him?" She was looking up at me, her face filled with a pinched light.

"No," I said, "that's not likely to happen, Lauren."

"I'd, like, do anything to help you find Jimmie, ya know?" She was blinking rapidly, and her cheeks were full of red discolorations, but she didn't cry.

"What I said about crying, you didn't need to take that seriously. That's just my hang-up."

She thought about that. "No, you were right. It doesn't help," she said, as if she had just reached a profound metaphysical conclusion.

*   *   *

I had a late dinner engagement, but I left early, just after eight o'clock. Made a few loops through back roads in the Presidio then popped out on Park Presidio. Headed south, straight for Golden Gate Park.

I took that route because the Presidio is a great place to spot a tail. The two-lane roads are usually empty, and they double back so you can see a long distance behind you.

When I got to the eastern part of the park, I pulled the Fiat off the road behind some scrub. Walked to a circle of bluegums that seemed to be emitting smoke. The sun had just set, and a group of homeless teenagers had built a fire and were roasting some meat. I strolled around until I found one I recognized, a boy named Doug.

"Have you seen my kid brother Jimmie?" I asked him. "I have another picture, if you lost the last one." I reached in my pocket.

"We're having a barbecue," Doug said. "Someone got a hunk of beef, and it's like the Bible says about sharing and shit. We're all family."

"Don't you remember me?" The park was the place I visited

most often, looking for Jimmie. It was only a couple miles from home, and he knew it like the back of his hand. It wasn't as if I thought he was still in the park, or even in the city, but I kept thinking he might have passed through—and maybe one of the teenage drifters had seen him.

Doug was buzzed—naturally. Still mainlining, although he'd run the alphabet soup with hepatitis and didn't have enough of a liver left to keep a cat alive. I snagged a few other throwaway kids, steeling myself to resist their stories of deteriorating health and cravings for drugs.

It was a dud, as usual. I was leaving when a girl came running up.

"That suburban reject runaway whose picture you gave to Dougie?" she said. "I saw him." She grinned at me. Her eyes were blue, the whites tinged red from reefer hits. "It was a couple weeks ago. On Jackson. He was dumpster diving. But...uh, he wasn't taking stuff out. He was putting something in."

She opened her leather jacket, and I saw she had on an over-sized T-shirt. Crumpled between her small breasts were two words printed in dripping scarlet: TOXIC AVENGER.

My heart lurched. I reached out to touch the shirt but quickly withdrew my hand.

She was staring at me.

"You want it? I'll sell it to you. Maybe you'd like a memento of your pain-in-the-ass brother?"

"Those look like bloodstains," I said, almost whispering. There were tiny brown spots sprinkled on the front, beneath the red lettering. The last time I'd seen the shirt it had been wet, and badly wrinkled. Could I have missed the tiny spots?

"Just spaghetti sauce," the girl said. She was yanking the shirt over her head. "Someone stole my Enema Of The State shirt, so I need to buy something else."

I fumbled out a couple ten-dollar bills. She took them, ran

186

off. I heard her hollering to someone, "Let's hitch a ride to Happy Donuts. They've got the best turkey on rye in the city."

As I was leaving the grove, I stumbled over another girl, lying under a wet blanket. A boy with his head shaved was trying to have sex with her, and she seemed unconscious. I told him to leave her alone, and he told me to shut the fuck up.

When I didn't move, he jumped up, licked my cheek. Then he snapped his fingers, close to my eyes. He was just a kid, about Jimmie's age, probably no more than fourteen or fifteen. There were safety pins stuck through his skin—in his nostrils and all along the side of his cheek.

I walked a dozen yards away, pulled my cell phone out of my pocket. Called a number Harmon had given me to make a return call, late. While I waited for him to pick up, the girl woke up. Started to slam a crushed pill into her arm with a blunted knife. Her teeth were completely rotten, nothing but stubs. The boy saw me watching and snapped his fingers at me again.

Harmon answered, realized it was me, said a few choice words. I told him what I was watching, and he growled at me to call 911.

"And I think I found my brother's T-shirt. The one he was wearing when Stephen Ludlow was murdered."

Silence.

The boy had lost interest in the girl. He'd got up, wandered away. I started toward my car.

"Did you hear me? I'm sorry to bother you at home, but this could be important. I found the T-shirt."

Harmon didn't respond. He'd be interested in the T-shirt, so he must not have heard me. Maybe he'd tossed his phone aside, gone back to whatever he'd been doing. You sonofabitch, I thought angrily. How many times have you called me at home, trying to get information or just generally bullying me? I'm not fond of you either, you know.

Death Game

"The T-shirt!" I hollered. *"Jimmie's T-shirt!"*

Over my hollering, I didn't see or hear the blow coming, which was a pity.

Chapter Seventeen

WHEN I GOT TO THE RESTAURANT, YOSHI STOPPED MID-SENTENCE, yanked his square-rimmed glasses down on his nose, and stared at me.

"You look like a pilot in the Imperial Japanese Air Force," he said. "Somebody try to break an oyster open on your skull?"

"Very funny," I said, sitting down across from him. "And possibly even accurate on both counts. But you mixed the metaphors." I lifted a hand to touch the aching bump behind my ear, decided to leave it alone.

"Bad scene, mon," Yoshi said, shaking his head.

He'd been talking to a kid waiter who was about four feet tall and wore black, flapping slippers. He finished the order in Japanese, and the kid flapped away.

"So, spill it. Who whacked you on the bazoo?"

"I don't know," I said.

As muggings go, mine had been minor. When I'd woken up, facedown in the dirt, there'd been a long bout of nausea and puking, more the result of fear than injury. My purse was in the car, so I hadn't lost any credit cards or money. In fact, the only real damage was that Jimmie's T-shirt had been taken.

Yoshi scratched his moustache. "You didn't see who hit you?"

Death Game

"No. But I'd had a little dispute with a wannabe rapist. Maybe it was him," I said without interest. I was trying to decide if I could actually eat anything.

I'd almost blown off the dinner, wanting to go home and put some ice on the injury. Would have, if I hadn't needed to talk to Yoshi so desperately.

I'd called him the day before, asked if he could spare a couple hours. He'd said to meet him for a late dinner and he'd picked the place, one of those supremely dumpy ethnic restaurants that seventy years of urban redevelopment have passed over without touching. This one oozed authenticity, all the way to the polyethylene booths, the stench of deep-fryer oil and a giant video screen playing Japanese anime.

I'd first been introduced to Yoshi at Optical Zone, where he had a well-deserved rep for being a big eater. Taking Yoshi out for dinner, even in a cheap place like this, meant I'd be living on breadcrumbs for weeks.

Dull brown eyes with uptilted edges lit up after I told him about the T-shirt being taken. Yoshi had shoulder-length hair and would be a dead ringer for Mike in *Doonesbury* if he weren't Japanese.

"Hey, maybe it was the snake. Maybe he bopped you."

"If you mean Rick, it wasn't him."

"You get whacked from behind and you don't know who it is, but you know who it's not." He sounded disgusted.

"If it was Rick, he would have taken this." I slipped Viktor's DVD out of my purse. Held it up by the edges. I'd left my purse in my car, but I'd had the DVD on me, in my jacket pocket, thinking that was the safest place. When I woke up, it was still there.

Yoshi turned to look at the anime while I fed the DVD into the laptop. I'd watched the fat man be tortured and murdered until it had all become about as gripping as watching melba toast go stale. I needed a new set of eyes, and a trained brain.

190

Cheryl Swanson

Yoshi wasn't just a wizard in the special f/x business. Even half-comatose, he was smarter than anyone I'd ever met.

I put my laptop on the sticky table. Flipped the machine around. Yoshi took a cell phone call, kept watching the anime. He'd yet to glance at the laptop screen.

Anime is about as interesting to me as the Home Shopping Network. Maybe I'm not smart enough for it, I don't know. A few minutes went by, Yoshi argued with someone about deadlines, the deal memo and reshooting, and I thought I'd lost him entirely.

Déjà vu set in. It could have been me doing the arguing—we were always a couple hundred thousand over the top sheet and three months behind at OZ. Sometimes it got to the point where we would work nonstop, sleep in shifts.

Yoshi clicked off. Told me he was working on a sci-fi.

"The primary effect is taking buckets of dirt and throwing them across the screen. The director has a real hard-on for dirt. And the cinematographer—if he can even get a job afterwards I'll eat my own dick."

"You miss me," I said.

"You deserved to have your skull cracked, Cooper," he said. "Why don't you just hang a sign around your neck—Kick me around, I'm too stupid to get a divorce. Why'd you go back to that jerk?"

"I didn't go back to him," I said. I pointed at the laptop, where the fat man was about to get garroted. I didn't want to talk about Rick with Yoshi. Or the mugging, for that matter. Maybe it had been Rick—he could have missed the DVD. Or one of Walter's minions. Or one of Tuck's compadres. The guy in the government issue Chevy, for instance. All of them wanted to get their hands on the T-shirt, and none of them would have been particularly fussy about how they went about it.

I hadn't seen the tail for a few days, but someone could have planted a homing device in my car. Or creeped my house and planted one in my clothes, for that matter.

The truth was, I didn't have a fucking clue who it was. Like almost everything that had happened since Stephen's murder, the finger of suspicion seemed to point simultaneously at everyone and no one.

Yoshi flipped his mop of hair out of his eyes, resettled his glasses and obligingly looked at the laptop screen.

"Shit, I don't want to see some fat slob get popped. Not just before I eat."

He shoved the machine away in disgust. The kid waiter came back, bringing endless platters of food, all of it smelling like nothing I'd ever put in my mouth before. Yoshi snapped a set of disposable chopsticks apart. Dug in.

"I didn't know you went in for snuff films, little girl," he said, after a couple of minutes. "That was the real deal. I thought you were still in the nursery in your entertainment taste. Watching Disney with Heather."

"Heather wouldn't be caught dead watching Disney," I said. "And I don't think it's just a snuff film, Yoshi. I think it's something much weirder."

"What's weirder than a snuffie?"

I pulled the laptop back into view, punched a sequence of keys. The man with the garrot moved in response to my keystrokes. Pressing one sequence, I made him move backwards and away. Another sequence, he moved forward, dropped it over the fat man's head. Repeating that sequence, he tightened or released it over and over.

"Well, hell, I know what that is," Yoshi said conversationally, after we went back to eating.

"Some underwater crustacean?" I asked doubtfully, looking at what was between my chopsticks. "A deep-fried pencil eraser?" I put the rubbery morsel in my mouth. Vainly tried to swallow it.

Yoshi burped, patted his chest.

"Not the food, you nincompoop. The DVD. It's a bootleg game program." He hit his chest with his open palm. Burped again.

"A game made out of a snuff film? That's incredibly sick."

He shrugged. "Not the usual fare, I grant you. Not something you're gonna see written up in *Bitch X*. But there's a ton of weird bootlegs out there. Most are so raw you could fertilize the ground with them. This game I saw a few years ago? You play being General Custer, and you go through a storm of arrows to rape an Indian maiden. You rip her clothes off, tie her to a tree and jam your prick into her while she screams. The more virgins you capture and rape the more points you get."

"Lovely," I said.

"And a big moneymaker. I heard it outsold Nintendo when it first came out. And then there's this other one called *Beat 'em and Eat 'em*. You—"

"I know all this," I said. "And I'm the one with the sensitive stomach, remember?" Putting my napkin over my mouth, I spat the morsel into it. Whatever it was, my teeth hadn't made a dent.

I told Yoshi about the game Lauren, Jimmie and Travis had played.

"You have any idea who could have developed something like that? You think he lives in this area?"

He shrugged. "Some skinhead, out of some quasi-legit political group. Maybe he's in a high-rise in Berlin, or maybe he's living in some shack in Montana. Who knows? Making a game isn't like making a film." He grinned. "No site-specific infrastructure or schmoozing required."

"But this area is where all big video and computer game companies are."

"So what? Games aren't tied to the Bay area, like films are tied to LA." He pointed at my laptop. "Besides, the codeslinger who did that sack of trash had to have access to snuff footage.

Can't quite see those diddle-brains at Electronic Arts creating snuffies in a backroom in Redwood City."

He had started playing with the program. Almost immediately, he found things I hadn't discovered after dozens of hours of trying.

"You only got a little piece of this," he said cheerfully. "Someone wrote a huge program. Name of..." He kept working, straining my little laptop, making it whirr. "Named it Enigma, so your programmer's English-speaking. Or pretending to be English-speaking. And here's something really weird."

On the screen was something I hadn't seen before—a dark-walled room about thirty feet long. In it were a long series of radar screens, each with dials and mounted on separate podiums. We heard a buzzer sound, and the image disappeared. The screen turned fuzzy.

"Where'd that come from? That looks like some kind of control room. Bring it back."

He tried, but almost immediately the laptop crashed.

"Program's unstable as hell," Yoshi said, disgusted. "And like I told you, you only got a little piece of it."

"Try again," I urged. I was slurping up the last of a bowl of glistening noodles. I washed them down with tapioca pearl tea.

Yoshi got the room back on the screen again. This time I managed to count the radar systems—six—before the laptop crashed again.

"That's the best I can do," he said.

I thought about it a moment. Six radar systems? What kind of an operation would need six radar systems? A military bunker? A huge transport plane? An ocean-going military vessel? And what in hell did radar systems have to do with filming the murder of some poor dimwit?

None of it was adding up.

"You visited Russia a couple years ago," I said, veering from the subject, but not really. "Did you hear of places called closed cities?"

Yoshi shimmered his hands like a voodoo man. "Sure. Spooky places. Spooky as hell."

"Why spooky? And what does it mean—'closed?'"

"We're talking major weaponry, Cooper. End of the world stuff." His voice had changed. "You sure you want to know?"

I nodded.

He gazed absently at a far wall. "They were filled with genius-level scientists, all skilled at creating methods of terror and weapons of mass destruction."

"But they're not inhabited anymore?"

"Not since Mikhail Gorbachev's reform initiatives." Yoshi had turned serious, as serious as he ever got. "You know, Cooper, glasnost changed the map of the world, and it wasn't altogether a good change for the West. The USSR falling apart left a big empty place, big enough for a hell of a lot of blowback. I heard there were twenty-seven thousand nuclear warheads suddenly up for sale after perestroika. To the highest bidder."

"But these scientists?"

"Not quite twenty-seven thousand of them, but they all went up for sale as well. They needed jobs and they were all experts in the various methodologies of terror. Unfortunately, they weren't familiar with what the legitimate global scientific community was doing, or how they might fit in."

"But they'd still find employment," I said, feeling chilled. "As fucked up as this world is, they would find employment easily."

"Yeah. And you can imagine their new employers. Militant organizations. Extremist groups. Warlords. People who kill for God or for profit."

"Or, apparently, ordinary American businesses," I said, almost in a whisper.

"Hey, you look scared," Yoshi said suddenly. "Lighten up." He was looking at the anime again.

Death Game

"I am scared," I said, slipping the gold disc back into my purse. "I'm starting to hope that my brother really is a child-killer, not something worse."

Yoshi glanced back at me and frowned. "Like, that is a foul thing to say, girl. What are you talking about?"

I shrugged. "How'd you know about these closed cities?" I asked, changing subjects. "You visit one?"

"No way. KGB still blocks access."

"Then, how'd...?"

"Washington Post? CNN? Tass? The Drudge Report?" Yoshi raised an eyebrow. "Probably all four. A cloud of anthrax vapor was released from one of the biochemical factories in one of them. Killed sixty-four poor yucks who were walking by on the street. It made the news big-time a few years ago." He switched the topic then, started talking again about the film. "This one has me weeping for humanity, Cooper. The hero is such an idiot, you root for the aliens to finish him off. I'm telling you, making it is keeping me doubled over in pain.

"Take care of yourself," he said a moment later, getting up to leave. "They come after you again, they might slice you into sushi and finish the job."

His attention was distracted; he swiveled his head. A petite older Japanese woman came out of the kitchen and straight for us—fast. I did a double take when I saw she had a glistening meat cleaver in her hand.

When she reached us, Yoshi reached down, gave her a big hug, lifting her right off the floor.

"Your mom?" I asked needlessly, as he deposited her carefully back down on the sticky linoleum. She had Yoshi's sideways grin and dull, uptilted brown eyes.

"Yeah." He grinned at her. "She put me through Princeton. Wouldn't think a skinny-assed ape like me would have such a beautiful mother, would you?"

Chapter Eighteen

RAMBO-IN-WINGTIPS, WHERE ARE YOU? I THOUGHT LATE THAT NIGHT AS I stared at the ceiling. If you're ever going to make another appearance now is the time. At the very least, you son of a bitch, give me a ring.

I went downstairs and checked my machine, just for kicks. There were the usual messages from homeless kids, all of them claiming they had information about Jimmie, and all of them obviously lying. I sat down at the kitchen table, my head on the table, and had almost fallen asleep when a message informed me Walter Ludlow wanted to see me.

My head jerked up. I let out a perfectly controlled, high-pitched scream.

Well, gee. Not Rambo, but almost as good.

I spent the rest of the night wide-awake, listening to dry thunder—a storm was brewing somewhere out on the Pacific—the beads of my rosary twisted around my fist. Belatedly, it'd occurred to me I should pray. Might as well cover all the bases.

At first light, I pulled into Walter's driveway. A burly guard came out to the front gate carrying an umbrella. He opened the car door, but when I tried to get out, he said, "Don't be cute. Stay put." He flipped open his cell phone and called the house. When

197

Death Game

he was done, he said, "This way, please, Ms. O'Brien."

He left me in the hands of a brunette with a spray of daffodils in her hand. After looking me over as if she thought I might be there to steal the china or silver, she put the daffodils down, walked briskly through the house, her heels ringing on black marble tiles. Led me down a flight of stairs. Opened double doors to a large room.

It was Walter's study. There was a desk in the corner, some bookshelves, a wall of photographs. I'd been in the room before, and I glanced at the photos of the Sea Transport fleet. Through the windows I could see a narrow strip of deck. Beyond that was the ocean.

A nurse stood in front of a leather couch, pouring coffee out of a silver carafe into a china cup. An old man lay on the couch with a quilt over him.

"I was hoping to talk to Mr. Ludlow," I said to the maid.

She raised her head, gave me a deliberately blank look and shut the double doors behind her.

With a sinking feeling, I advanced to the couch; the man made no effort to rise as I approached. It was apparent that, this time, there would be no revival, no return of his energy. Silent and exhausted, his face sunken and appallingly aged, Walter looked at me from under the blanket.

The nurse hovered, and he waved her away. She made reference to required medication, and he told her to leave. In the silence that followed, I stood awkwardly, not wanting to look at him.

"Sit down, Cooper. I didn't want you to see me like this, but we need to talk." He made a gesture, indicating a chair opposite the couch.

I couldn't speak. Tears stung my eyes. If I hated someone my whole life I wouldn't want them to die looking like this.

"Doctors are here every day now. I may have no more than a

week or two left."

"Walter, I don't...know what to say."

"I don't dread death, Cooper. Not anymore. After Stephen was killed I kept fighting for a little while. I thought I owed it to him, to stay alive long enough to find out what happened." Walter's face contorted, a spasm of pain. He took a deep breath before he continued. "He was a good kid, wasn't he? A really nice boy. And he was my son. My son."

His voice had gone soft; you could feel a father's simple love and longing for his child in the words.

He hitched himself up a bit, hardened his voice. "He was also my heir, damn it. I was planning to leave him the whole shooting match. I knew he wasn't a genius, but he'd have done okay. Everything I worked for all these years, at least it wouldn't have been a complete waste."

I was looking at the table beside the sofa. On it rested dozens of prescription vials, a plastic-wrapped hypodermic. The room smelled of uncontrolled diarrhea and ammonia, a corrupt bouquet that reminded me of my mother's last hours.

Walter sensed my thoughts, and his face turned bitter.

"It's tough having anyone see me like this, Cooper, especially you. That's why I never returned your calls. Being in love with you, it made me feel young again. And now...I feel old. And sick."

"It was wrong, wasn't it?" I asked sadly. "What happened between us? Somehow, it set in motion things that shouldn't have been set in motion."

"You regret it? You never felt anything for me? That's why you broke it off?"

"I didn't—"

"Rick told me you didn't want to hurt me. I didn't blame you, but I thought—" He'd caught my wrist gently in his frail bluish-white fingers. There was a probing look in his eyes.

Death Game

I thought back to how we had wrapped ourselves into an inseparable knot that first night, collapsing inside each other.

"*Ananku*," he whispered to me at three o'clock in the morning, with the waves crashing beneath us, the stars shining through the window.

"Ananku?" I murmured, half-asleep, not understanding.

"I learned it years ago. It's a word the Tibetans use to mean love that is dangerous," he said. "Love that lures you over the edge into the realm of falling things. It's why I built my business. Why I traveled the world." He laughed. "Hell, it's why I was enough of a lunatic to try to climb Everest and learn the word in the first place." There was a pause. "It's why I wanted you," he whispered.

He ran two hands over me then, caressed my thighs as one would caress the flanks of a lioness.

*   *   *

Walter had dropped my wrist to reach for the coffee. His hand was so shaky I had to hold the cup for him.

"Thanks," he said briefly, taking a sip. "We have some things we must talk about, don't we, Cooper?"

But he didn't talk. His head dropped back. He wasn't looking at me any longer; he seemed utterly dispirited.

I waited for almost a minute and still he didn't speak.

"Detective Harmon told me you thought the videotape was altered," I said. "Why?"

This roused him a bit. "I had a good reason for it at the time. In the beginning, I didn't believe your brother killed Stephen."

"Why not?"

"Because I was told Stephen was going to be killed. By someone who had no connection with your brother. They told me my son would be killed in a way that no one on earth had ever been killed before. That it was a new atrocity, a brand new way of

200

Cheryl Swanson

killing. And that no one would be safe from it."

I looked at him, blinking, deeply astonished. The same words I'd heard him utter—what?—a scant six weeks before? *The way Stephen was killed—it's the first time anyone in the history of the world was ever killed that way. The world has just found a new atrocity, a brand new way of killing.*

The words he denied having said later, when we were in Rick's office. Now, maybe I would find out why he'd found it necessary to lie.

"At first, I didn't take the threat seriously," he said. "When you make the kind of money I've made, you learn how to evaluate these things. You learn to recognize if it's a credible threat. If it's possible for this person to do what they're threatening to do. The threats that were made against Stephen— they didn't seem credible to me. Not at first."

"But then he was killed."

"Yes. So I rethought everything. But it was too late." His forehead creased. "I blame myself that Stephen slipped away that night. If he hadn't left the house it might never have happened."

"You think he faked getting upset that night? Planned the whole thing? So he could get lost for a while?"

"I don't know."

"Did he run off a lot?"

"No. Just that once before. He was a good boy, Cooper. But he had no...friends. Didn't know how to relate to anyone. Wasn't comfortable, really, unless he was alone."

And maybe he didn't know how to relate to anyone because you were so cold with him, I thought.

But it was long past the time when saying anything would help. And who was I to talk, anyway? What about the way I'd treated Jimmie?

A single seagull drifted in from the sky. Landed on a spar that projected from the house and tucked in its wings. Walter looked

201

Death Game

at the gull through the dancing rain.

"Frankly, teenage boys are hard to figure out. Your brother, for instance—did you have any idea he was capable of murder?"

"If anyone had asked me, I would have said it was impossible."

"You thought he was a normal boy?"

Normal? You're talking teenage boys. You think any of them are normal? But I didn't say that to Walter.

"I don't make strong claims of mental health myself, Walter, so who am I to judge?"

He kept waiting. Wanting a real answer.

"It's not so much whether Jimmie was capable, Walter. It's how it happened. Two boys meet in the middle of a night, in a place where no one can interrupt them. One of them kills the other, apparently for no reason, but it's all captured on film..."

"That's it. That's what I thought," he said eagerly. "It looked planned. Like a set-up. Like someone compelled your brother to shoot Stephen."

I could feel my breathing quicken. "But how is that possible, Walter? You saw the surveillance tape. There was no one there but Stephen and Jimmie."

He didn't respond.

I leaned forward. "Walter, who wanted Stephen dead? If I knew that, maybe we'd be able to find out if the murder was planned."

He shook his head, didn't reply. Sick as he was, he wasn't going to allow me to cross-examine him. He wasn't going to tell me what I really wanted to know.

I tried again anyway, from a different angle.

"What about these threats, Walter? Did you ever find out who made them?"

"It doesn't matter. I know now they were empty threats. Just as I'd thought from the beginning."

Cheryl Swanson

"But who made them?"

He shook his head.

"Why won't you explain yourself fully, Walter? Who are you protecting?"

But he'd gone inward; I could see him imposing control on himself. Whatever this was about, it was private stuff. He was not going to tell me anything further.

As if on cue, the nurse came in.

"It's way past time for your pain medication, Mr. Ludlow," she said, filling a syringe with fluid. "Mr. Ludlow needs to rest now," she added to me, her meaning clear.

Moving his head forward, Walter gave me a ghost of a smile.

"Sorry, Cooper, I've been remiss. I didn't offer you any refreshment."

It seemed condescending, transparent, unworthy. After all we've been to each other it came down to this? Politeness? A meaningless social gesture?

"Walter..."

Our eyes met. I didn't know what to say. Neither did he, but I know we were both thinking the same thing—*This is it, the last meeting.*

"Walter..." I said again, almost strangling. I reached out to him, but he didn't respond; his eyes didn't even blink.

My brother's fate—I know it has the priority to you of a hangnail. But how can you let a boy, who could be completely innocent, spend his last moment of life convulsing in a box? You want to face your Maker with that on your conscience?

But I didn't say it, couldn't. Walter wasn't looking at me anymore, and the man with the umbrella had come in—Pete, a bodyguard. He herded me back to the front door. I made some protest, but it was useless. Pete knew his business, and it wasn't as if I was going to be able to choke the truth out of poor, dying Walter.

"Get off," I said, shoving Pete away when we got outside. He was overachieving at his job, hanging on to my arm.

I returned to my car. It was cold—not bitter-sharp cold like the Midwest or Northeast, but northern California cold, damp and vapor-locked. One of those days when the air was so thick going outside felt like drowning.

The roads were skiddy, fogbound and terrible, but I didn't hesitate when I got to the main street. I turned south. Pushed the Fiat to its limit. After the talk with Walter, I was in a new phase. Whoever he was protecting, they were still out there, which meant the game was still going on.

Game over, you lose. I saw Stephen crying, spitting, falling...and I saw something else. I saw Jimmie, the fragile bone structure of his face caving in, the front of his skull slowly erupting into a bloody mist.

Chapter Nineteen

THE HILL WAS STEEP, SO I CUT MY WHEELS IN AT THE CURB WHEN I parked. Natalya Kirnov lived in one of those areas of the city that look like newsreel footage of the Warsaw ghetto. There were no pedestrians, but in front of her apartment building was a man wearing blue Nikes with a silver slash. He had a cell phone glued to his head.

Viktor and Natalya's apartment was on the fourth floor. The elevator wasn't heated, and I got off of it shivering. I consulted the scrap of paper and knocked on the third door on the left.

A woman's voice answered.

"I work with your husband," I said. "May I come in?"

She opened the door but left the chain on. It was a gesture—the door looked flimsy enough to push off its hinges with one shoulder heave.

"Viktor is not here," she said. It was Natalya. Her English was thickly accented but understandable.

"I know he's not here," I said. "I want to talk to you."

Natalya unhooked the chain and let me in. I walked straight to the window and looked out; the dark blue carpet felt crunchy, like the padding was bubble wrap. I was looking to make sure the man with the Nike swoosh and cell phone had moved on. The

205

Death Game

only living thing I saw was a big feral cat, nosing at a dead rat.

"Viktor has a problem. At work?" Natalya sucked in her lip. She was still attractive, the shape and contours of her face finely drawn. But there was a white core of fear somewhere in her, and it showed in her expression and the self-protective hunching of her shoulders.

There was an old upright mahogany piano in the corner of the room. I went over and plunked a few keys.

"Do you play?" I asked her.

"I have...had...few students," she said, with a nervous cough. "They came here for lessons."

I noted her use of the past tense. Turning my head, I could see through an open door into the bedroom. There was a suitcase open on the bed, folded clothing piled neatly around it.

Her eyes followed my line of sight.

"I am packing to go back to Russia," she said.

I sat down, and she perched on a chair across from me. She hadn't invited me to sit, and her eyes were extremely wary.

"You're leaving immediately?"

"Tomorrow."

"You and Viktor are splitting up? Perhaps," I suggested, "because of his office romance?"

"Pfffftt," she said, suddenly erupting. "That is why you are here?" Two bright smudges of color appeared on her cheekbones. "So what if he occupies himself with another woman in the office? I am not jealous. Jealousy is petit-bourgeois thinking."

I was quiet a moment. 'I hate Russians,' my ass, I thought. I knew there was something...

"What's the woman's name?" I asked, to confirm it.

"Viktor does not tell me; I do not ask. Maybe it is you." She curled her lip.

"No," I said sadly, "it can't be me. I don't do sex anymore."

She stared at me a moment as if she had no idea what I was

talking about, then dropped her gaze.

"This woman, she is this to Viktor." She snapped her fingers. The color in her cheekbones had become ever more intense. I had the sense that Natalya, in spite of her protest, had picked up a few bourgeois attitudes about sex since she'd been living in America.

"I try to help by teaching piano, but..." She shook her head. "It does not so well pay. I am not technical, like Viktor, or I would be able to earn more."

"If you're happy together, why are you leaving?"

She shrugged. "Viktor tells me to leave. I ask him to reconsider, but he says no, I must go. He is going to be fired? That is why he tells me to leave, so I will not know this? Is that what you come to tell me?"

When I didn't answer she knelt next to me and took my hands in hers. Gently chafed them.

"You have nice hands," she said. "Hands like this usually do not belong to a person who is cruel. You have influence? Viktor must not lose his job. Viktor works...feverishly. All the time. In Russia. Here. He is a brilliant man."

I sat, helpless. She was begging, and I felt like a criminal. No, I felt worse then a criminal.

"He must not go back," she said, jumping up. There were tears in her eyes. "If he goes back to Russia, he will go back to prison. He will be a *zek* again."

Her emotion had given her another coughing spasm. She got a handkerchief and put it over her mouth while she coughed.

"I have a cold in my chest," she said apologetically. She coughed a few more times. "You know this word *zek*?"

"I know it. I've read Solzhenitsyn. You mean a political prisoner."

"Solzhenitsyn—that old fool," she spat with contempt. She coughed one more time. "I must trust you. I must tell you. After

Death Game

Viktor and I marry, years go by, and then Viktor is sent to the Kolyma Peninsula. Seven hundred miles from Moscow. A prison fortress. Viktor is tied to a rope and made to drag great logs up inclines. Tied into a leather harness, his body and his forehead made tight with leather straps—"

"A leather strap?" I asked, surprised. "That's what caused those scars?"

"Yes," she said. "They come from the years where he is tied into harness, his forehead crossed by the strap."

"Tell me the rest of it."

"He is made fast in this harness, his feet sliding and slipping on snow...like a beast. An animal. My husband, who has three degrees from Moscow University. Treated like an animal. Solzhenitsyn." She made a sound like she was spitting. "My husband is loyal, always loyal to Russia. To the Party, in the old days. Not a traitor like Solzhenitsyn."

"If he wasn't an enemy of the Party, then why was he in prison?"

"This was 1989," she said. "Viktor was loyal, but what they ask him to do after he comes out of university is ugly. Viktor did not want to do it." She shrugged hopelessly. "So they make him a prisoner for years, in harness. Finally, he says yes, he will do it. Then they send him to another terrible place."

"A closed city."

She only shuddered, but it was all I needed for an answer.

"Why send him to a closed city? What did they want him to do?"

Natalya started to shudder again; then, abruptly, her eyes widened with shock. I heard a snapping sound behind my head. Turned and saw a rush of color and felt a cord yank tight across my neck.

*   *   *

208

It would have been over immediately if not for Natalya. She threw herself on the man's back, bit deep into his left ear. He twisted desperately, trying to get it out from between her teeth while she clawed at the back of his head and neck. He didn't let go of me, but fighting the two of us put him off-balance, made him slacken his hold enough that I could drag all of us into the kitchen.

When I got to the sink, as though it had a life of its own, my hand grabbed a meat-cutting scissors out of a knife block. Stabbing over my right shoulder, I caught him squarely in the front of the neck with the razor-sharp point.

I put all my force behind it, pushing and twisting until his head snapped sideways. A jet of blood hit the sink, and I turned to see the watery electric shock in his eyes.

He was bearded, his eyes already going milky, but I recognized him.

It was Jala.

He slipped to the floor, the cord he'd wrapped around my neck still clutched in his hands. The scissors had opened his carotid artery—he was bleeding to death, his chest heaving as his dying heart pumped out a scarlet tide. His body convulsed with long, racking shudders.

Natalya lay across the room, her hands pressed hard on her stomach, panting, blood on her lips. Just before I'd stabbed him, Jala had backhanded her across the room; she'd slammed against the wall so hard I feared she was injured internally. I was reaching for the phone to call 911 when I heard footsteps.

Two more men materialized through the gaping door with the broken chain. The first was the one I'd seen outside with the cell phone glued to his ear. He halted just inside, startled to see Jala twitching on the kitchen floor, his neck a mass of gore.

The other rushed past him, straight at me. It was Waleed, and I saw rage in his simian eyes as he came after me with a blackjack. I threw my forearm in front to me, but it barely

Death Game

deflected the blow. The blackjack whopped across my shoulder, and the blow sank deep into bone. The muscles in my chest and side quivered and seemed to collapse.

I clawed at him weakly, overwhelmed by impotence, by terror, the strength in my arms temporarily gone. He hit me again on the shoulder. This time it was a rock-solid blow with his full weight behind it.

The next instant, he brought the club down on my head. It crashed off the back of my skull, setting off internal pyrotechnics, making vivid flares in front of my eyes. Colors started flashing in front of my eyes, swirling designs.

It must have ended with another thump on my head, or my head crashing back against something solid enough to knock me out. The colors swam in and out of the back of my head. Then they disappeared completely.

When I woke up, I lay facedown on the floor of a van, trussed up like a chicken. Rope was tied around me in an effective figure eight; it bit deep into the flesh of my arms and legs. Electrician's tape had been wound across my mouth so tight I was gagging on my tongue. For a good long time, I believed I was dreaming. Then my brain came further awake and made it clear that I was not.

I was revoltingly uncomfortable. There was a scruffy carpet scrap on the floor, and my face was mashed into it; the interior of the van smelled like decomposing rubber. I couldn't raise myself, not even an inch. My head ached with a massive dull throb.

Waleed was driving and talking steadily, a hard flow of some language I couldn't understand. I assumed it was Arabic, but it could have been Farsi, Pashto, Kurdish—one of a dozen dialects and languages. I heard Jalaluddin's name mentioned and something that sounded like *shalah*.

He braked often, going around curves, making me slide around. It was an old panel van, the interior stripped bare, the walls streaked with orange rust marks. There were four bubble-

210

type portholes in back for windows, but they were blacked out so no one could see in.

I tested the knots, but whoever had tied me up knew his way around a rope—pulling on them only made them tighter.

I kept slipping in and out of a semi-conscious state. Once I felt some fresh air. Realized a window had been rolled down. I got a glimpse out the driver's side, saw ocean and knew we were traveling north.

The road kept twisting and turning. I dozed and woke in pain and fear. My veins swelled from lack of circulation, and my muscles started cramping; but the worst part was the growing urge to retch. The tape had been wound so tight it was making me constantly drool. I kept swallowing the saliva, but it was sticky, tickled my throat. And Jala's blood was everywhere on me—my hands looked like sponges from an operating theatre.

The urge to vomit got stronger and stronger. I had to control the reflex. If I started retching, I could choke to death. In a cold, detached part of my brain, I considered whether that might the best solution. Strangling in my own vomit might be the only chance I had of a merciful death.

The trip lasted so long that by the end of it only primitive responses were getting through. Dumb, instinctive resistance to puking. A fog-like bewilderment. A flash of Jala's body, twitching on the kitchen floor, followed by horror. The memory made me want to vomit all the more. But I couldn't. I couldn't...

The rear doors finally opened, and someone climbed in next to me. It wasn't Waleed or the other man; it was a youngish man who had a paunch on him that would have made an incipient mother of twins proud. He cut the rope that bound me to the floor with a buck knife, dragged me out of the van, dropped me on the dirt. Took a couple of breaths then slung me over his shoulder.

He walked, my face bumping against the rolls of fat on his

back. Fat Boy, I thought. Stop wheezing like you're dying. I don't weigh that much.

I turned my face away from his body, wondering where we were. It was nearly noon, the sun almost directly overhead. My hair hung over my face, and I kept shaking my head to get it out of the way, hoping to recognize something in the terrain.

We were on a broad open sweep of empty land. It shelved down and was covered with scrub grass and a few stunted trees. There was a broken-down corral farther down the slope, rusted-out troughs for feeding livestock. Some kind of old ranch, perhaps a sheep ranch?

Wherever it was, it seemed to have been long since abandoned. I could see no sign of anything living. The place had a degenerated feeling. It was gritty, almost featureless.

Fat Boy kept wheezing and moaning as he carried me. He climbed onto the porch of a primitive building with a flat roof, his back popping audibly. Roughly cut plank floorboards squeaked underfoot as we entered a narrow hallway. I got glimpses of workrooms, a mechanic's bench with various tools. Farther along was a kitchen. Men were in some of the rooms; heads swiveled as we went by.

Waleed opened a locked door with a key, and Fat Boy dropped me to the floor, took his knife again and cut the rest of the ropes. He straightened, grunting a sigh of relief, and stretched briefly, hands on his hips. He gave me a brief curious look, with no particular malevolence to it, before he shambled out the door.

Waleed ripped the gag from my mouth. It tore a chunk of my lip, but I breathed hard and gratefully; my lungs were aching for air. My hands were purple, bloated with lack of circulation, the skin dead to the touch.

He gathered up the ropes, threw them out the door and then locked it. Hunkered down until his eyes were on a level with mine. There was spit on his lips and in the corner of his mouth, and he had a high, wet gleam in his eyes.

"Nice day for a drive, Waleed," I said matter-of-factly. "But you should have asked me first."

I saw his focus travel from my breasts to my thighs and back again. He licked at the saliva.

"Whore," he said softly. His voice was eager, and his lips drew back from his teeth. "I kill you soon, whore. I kill you now if you try to get away. Why don't you try? Why don't you fight me, whore?"

His hands clenched and unclenched and his nostrils flared with pulsating regularity. I had seen the change in his face when he knelt down next to me, saw the vast, twisted load of hatred he carried. It wasn't the face of a man; it was the face of an animal. Not even a furry mammalian animal—something reptilian.

"Well, I can't say you never took me anyplace interesting," I said, looking around the closet. I felt fear, plenty of it, but there was no percentage in letting it show. Not until I couldn't help it.

A gloating grin had settled on Waleed's face. He reached for my left breast and groped it. He moved closer; his breath smelled rank—acrid and metallic. He said something, described a depraved act he wanted me to perform on him.

"Another time," I said, pulling away and trying not to let the shattering horror I felt show on my face.

He fumbled with his zipper. He was panting. When it came out, it was varicosed with veins, protuberant, dark-colored, with an oily sheen. I had stopped trying to joke, looked at the wall in front of me steadily, trying not to think of what was going to follow, resolved not to cry, not to beg, no matter what. The man was evil. This wasn't sexual lust; it was darkness and vengeance and the need to humiliate a woman.

His mouth was askew with concentration, his hideous wheeze was in my face, his breath was rank and eager. He crawled on top of me, his left hand grabbed my larynx and squeezed. I clawed at

Death Game

him, dug in my heels, tried to roll away, to kick him. He braced his forearm under my chin, squeezed so hard I thought I would lose consciousness.

I wrenched myself sideways, started screaming and thrashing. My screams were despairing, and I was shocked when the door reopened and a shaft of bright light entered the room. Waleed, panting, said something over his shoulder, probably a request to whoever had opened the door to go away, mind his own business.

But Fat Boy—it was Fat Boy, I realized, as he stepped inside—grinned widely. Refused to leave. He didn't try to stop Waleed. Instead, he folded his arms across his chest. Stood there grinning, a voyeuristic glint in his eye.

His presence unnerved Waleed—apparently, he couldn't stand being watched. It had unstiffened his dick. He yanked up his zipper, stood reluctantly, looking baffled and angry.

At the doorway he turned.

"I'll be back, whore," he hissed. "Then I fuck you, when no one is watching. Afterwards, I kill you." He shut the door and locked it.

The room they'd left me in had a bucket in the corner for a toilet and a blanket for a bed. Nothing else. I scrambled over to the bucket. Retched. Retched endlessly, over and over again. When I had emptied my stomach, I collapsed onto the floor.

A few feeble rays of light, coming from a low-wattage light bulb overhead, kept the closet faintly illuminated for an hour. I heard doors bang in the distance. The sound of someone urinating loudly in a toilet. The clump of heavy footsteps.

The light went off, and soon after I heard the keening wail of prayers. They were uncannily clear—a high-pitched babbling followed by a chorus of voices chanting. They pounded out each syllable like a drum. It was beautiful. I wanted to despise it, but I couldn't. How could they have twisted something so beautiful into something so corrupt?

214

While they prayed, I tested my prison. Ignoring the ache in my cramped muscles, the numbness of my hands, I worked my fingers over every surface. There was no handle on the inside of the door, just the back of the lock. No nails driven into the walls that I could pry off and use as weapons. The plank floorboards were warped, and I found splintered places. Wedging my fingers into a tiny hole, I tested it to see if I might actually be able to lift one of the boards, tear it out.

While the vocal drumbeats continued, I started pulling. I disturbed a large, fat spider, and he crawled over my fingers. I pulled until my teeth gripped my lower lip and sweat stood on my forehead. I pulled until my hands ached and my fingers were bruised. I pulled as if I was in a crypt, in a coffin, and I had to get out or die of suffocation.

No good. There was no possibility of tearing anything free; the boards were strong as iron.

My chest went tight. I threw myself back down, rolled up in the blanket. I began searching for mental signposts, something to think about that would keep me calm. I couldn't find any, but fortunately, shock was setting in. A fatigue so overwhelming as to be sedative entered my body.

I didn't fight it; I reached for it.

Chapter Twenty

THE NEXT THING I HEARD—IT WAS PROBABLY SOMETIME AFTER midnight—was a soft scratching sound. Waleed, I thought, opening my eyes in the darkness, come back in stealth now that Fat Boy wasn't around to interfere.

Something hot and awful started to rise in my body. I stared at the door, thinking of Waleed's groping hands. I waited, listening, my mind whirling crazily. My breath clogged in my throat as the silence held, spun out…

The tiny scratching noise came again, right next to my cheek this time. A mouse was creeping by. I'd seen him earlier, crouched in a corner. He turned his head and stared; tiny, reddish eyes blinked in the gloom. I made a feeble movement, and he scampered away.

You're not handling this so well, Cooper, I thought. You should be steeling, bracing, hardening yourself for what's ahead. Instead, you're turned to a mass of quivering jelly…by a mouse. You're in the hands of drink-your-blood men who treat women like dogs. You're in hell, and you can't get out, so you better find some intestinal fortitude.

The rest of the night I didn't sleep. I thought about five little words: get me out of here, get me out of hell. Get me out of here, get me out of hell. I thought about all the innocent people who lived in countries filled with men like my captors. Who lived fearing their children's blood would be painted on the walls, their women raped and abused, the graves of their dead desecrated. Who didn't want to live there but couldn't get out.

We're in it together, I thought. All of us. Get me out of here. Get me out of hell!

It became my mantra, my prayer, my drumbeat in the darkness. It was the litany of millions of innocents on the other side of the earth, who lived in stony wastes and deserts and dung-colored villages. I learned later the words they used: *Tal'eeni m'n hal jaheem! Tal'eeni m'n hal jaheem!* Get me out of here. Get me out of hell! Different words, but the same meaning: *Tal'eeni m'n hal jaheem!* Get me out of here. Get me out of hell!

A slight increase of warmth in the closet told me night had finally passed. If it had seemed endless the day that followed was time without end. There was a sick ache in my head, and as the hours wore on, it got worse. The closet trapped heat; bluebottles emerged, started buzzing, buzzing. They beat against the walls, landed on my sticky face, crawled in my hair. I'd kill one by slapping it with my palm, and two more would appear.

Sweat ran under my clothes until I could smell myself. With nothing to eat or drink, my thirst kept growing. My mouth turned parched, and my throat tightened.

Occasionally, I heard conversations that started up then ended, like broken threads. They were in languages I didn't understand. There was nothing to do, so mostly I thought about the past. Not about the recent past—that was too painful to contemplate. The distant past. Pa loomed large in my thoughts.

Pa had never tried to teach me martial arts, like he had Jimmie, but he enrolled me in a basic self-defense course when I was fourteen. We'd go together every Wednesday night. I hadn't wanted to go, but he insisted.

Death Game

The session I remembered most was one in which a female instructor—a slip of a thing—had held off two men. She hadn't used fancy kicks or judo holds. She'd simply kept the men from getting her in an armlock or a chokehold by continually slithering away and resisting.

"You can't learn self-defense in twenty weeks," Pa said to me afterwards. "What I want you to learn, Cooper, is how hard it is to subdue someone who is resisting. Even a girl like you can wear out several men, just by resisting. You get in trouble, you use whatever you got at hand to attack your assailant. You pick up a baseball bat, a brick, a rock. There may come a time when you don't have anything to fight with, but you can still beat them if you can out-endure them."

As the day wore on, my thirst grew until it overwhelmed all competing stimuli. I couldn't feel the pain in my head anymore. I couldn't feel the ache in my muscles. I couldn't think. When I closed my eyes, gray worms squirmed against my eyelids.

The mouse kept moving closer, and I finally grabbed him. He squirmed hysterically in my hands, terrified, desperate. It would be easy to choke off his breath, but then what? Could I really eat him? Could I really drink his blood, hoping for moisture? I let him go, telling myself there weren't enough calories in his tiny body to keep me alive.

I groped inside for reality. Why had I grabbed the mouse only to let him go? Was it a sign I was starting to lose my grip? Was I slowly going insane?

A few hours after nightfall the second day, the door to the closet finally opened again. It was Waleed. His shirt was open at his throat, and he held a gun, an automatic with a blued finish on the grip. He gestured with it. Said something to me.

I sat without moving, my heels drawn against me. My bones felt hollowed out by dryness. My blood moved sluggishly, as if my veins were clogged with lead. Waleed spoke in English, but my

218

brain had to work over his words before I understood them.

"Get up," he ordered again. "We're going to meet him."

We went outside, where it was dark and the air was cold. I stumbled downhill along a dirt path; Waleed jabbed the gun in my back when I hesitated. We went past the empty corrals to the edge of a field. In front of us was a water tank on metal braces, next to it a small electric generator.

Stars glittered overhead. An almost-full moon. Far-distant lights, but they are scattered; we weren't near civilization—there was no pink glow in the darkness, signaling a city. Sniffing the air, desperate for freshness, my nose detected something—the smell of the salt. Somewhere out there, in the shrouded distance, was the ocean.

The old hulk of a building loomed in the darkness in front of me. Waleed prodded me with the gun to go through the doorway. The walls inside were unpainted drywall streaked with water stains, the floor plywood, the ceiling bare beams. A particleboard partition had been erected, and I saw several cast-iron beds behind it, all neatly made, army surplus blankets tucked tight. Against one wall was a long table with several computers.

Waleed took me into another room, a big one. There was no light, but moonlight streamed through a large window. We entered past a low couch. At the other end, a metal chair sat in front of the window with a pile of ropes behind it.

Waleed told me to sit in the chair. Put my hands behind me so he could tie them.

I sat, let my head hang. Slumped my shoulders. My breathing had quickened, but he didn't notice. He thought my energy was sapped. He thought I'd become spiritless, weak, the good little prisoner.

What he didn't know was that there was a cataclysm of desperation building in my chest. The large personages of my life—Jimmie, my mother, Heather, my pa, especially my pa—

circled around me like multiple moons, exerting deep tidal impulses. When I felt the gun flick away from my spine as he reached for the ropes, I spun sideways in one convulsive movement and kicked the back of his legs below the knees.

There was enough desperation behind the kick to make it a hard chop. Waleed stumbled and fell, screaming. It was a strange scream, a whistling, furious sound. It was not pain or fear. It was humiliation mixed with violent exasperation.

I was hoping to get the gun, but he rolled over, came to his feet clenching the weapon tight. His scream had turned into words.

"I kill you, whore! I kill you!" His eyes were wide, filled with murderous rage. "I kill you—"

"Ten thousand times," I said, licking my dry lips. His face was only a few inches from mine, and our eyes locked. I felt short of breath, giddy. I had a maniacal impulse to laugh, so I did. The laughter came through my parched throat—an arid chuckle as dry as the Sahara.

I was pressing my luck, but I hated the man so much I didn't care if he pulled the trigger. What did it matter? I was dead anyway.

Another man heard the commotion and ran into the room. He was a strong-bodied, dark-skinned young man, nice-looking except for a rabbit mouth he couldn't quite manage to close over protruding teeth.

"You kill without orders, and he will be angry," he said nervously.

Waleed shoved me down again. Quickly fashioned a slip loop that held my legs to the chair, yanked on the rope and tied the knots tighter than necessary.

He and Rabbit Mouth left, but I wasn't alone for long. Two other men entered, stood flanking the door as if they were waiting for someone. Someone important—they were braced, like soldiers at attention. It was too dark and they were too far away for me to see their expressions, but I could smell their fear. Feel the tension in the air as they waited.

My fit of bravado faded; my courage drained right out of my pores. The last two months had all been leading up to this. Ever since Stephen died, ever since Jimmie had flown the coop—this was the end that had been looming. As the minutes ticked by, I could feel the sweat running down my body; and a sound started in my head like the whirring of the ocean inside a seashell.

Chapter Twenty-One

H E WAS SMALLER THAN I EXPECTED. UNCONSCIOUSLY, I HAD BEEN expecting a robust man, someone imposing in girth and manner. This man was not only thin, but he walked so softly I couldn't hear his footfalls. The shadows in the room made his face indecipherable.

He settled on the sofa. Another man entered carrying a tray with a tea service. He put it down and backed out of the room, bowing, cringing, making obeisance. The man on the sofa sat calmly, without moving, without speaking. Eventually, he put his hand over the top of the teapot's spout, as if to check for steam.

The moonlight shone through the window, made shifting patterns of shadow on the walls. The man had a sense of theater, I gave him credit for that. All I could see of him in the dark cold room were the pits of his eyesockets.

Strangely, I wasn't all that frightened, perhaps because the lack of water had altered my blood chemistry. My body felt limp, drained; and my thoughts kept rambling. I just couldn't stay focused on fear, only how thirsty I was. I licked my lips, tried to work some saliva into my throat.

"I enjoyed the ride up here," I said. "But the movie stank."

To my amazement, he chuckled.

I counted to a hundred in my head. Then two hundred. I felt weird, like I was floating. Detached.

"It's your turn," I said, when the silence had stretched almost five minutes. "We've got at least one thing to talk about. You could explain why you had Stephen Ludlow killed."

"The murder of Stephen Ludlow was an experiment," he said. His voice sounded cultured. His English was perfect, although slightly flat-toned. "And we succeeded beyond our wildest expectations. We combined old-fashioned psychology with electronic and covert warfare in a way the world has never seen before."

"You killed a child," I said. "And the world never even noticed."

He took a sip of tea and paused to savor it. "The child's death was regrettable, but necessary."

He kept talking, and I felt my soul sink. Ever since I'd been kidnapped, it had been clear that some grand obsession was in operation, something for which Stephen's murder had been merely a prelude. Stories had glimmered in my brain. Atrocities I'd heard of, read about; others my pa had described. Babies thrown from bridges in sacks, used as targets as they fell. Talented, educated girls pouring petrol on themselves and lighting it out of despair. The death of hundreds, thousands— hallowed five times a day by renegade clerics and political fanatics in incomprehensible sentences.

He asked me several questions, but I refused to answer. Taunted me with the tea, which tempted me, even though I was certain it was a trick. There was no point to showing him any respect, so I didn't. My insults barely registered, and he revealed nothing.

His concentration on me was intense. While I floundered mentally, he was carefully evaluating. Evaluating…and calculating how he could use me.

Death Game

He was clever. So clever I thought he'd never tell me his name, but I was wrong.

"I knew your father," he said. "When he first met me, I had a Nicaraguan *cedula*, under the name of Zia al-Haq, given me by the Sandistan government." He chuckled. "I raised a holy ruckus, and the cedula was genuine, so the INS inspectors insisted I be let go. He tracked me for years, caught up with me again in Bloomington, Illinois, where I was picked up for false identity papers. But I was released before he got there."

"The Great Satan America," I said. "For demons and infidels, we're remarkably trusting."

I thought of what Pa had told me of Zia al-Haq. He was born into the Arab Diaspora community of Chicago. He and his family had felt disenfranchised in their new home and alienated in a strange culture. When he was eleven, his father was murdered coming out of a mosque. The family had moved to Kuwait, then to Germany, where Zia had been educated.

Zia had gotten a degree in electronic engineering in Hamburg. Then had come the shadow years, where there was no record of where he was or what he was doing. Nobody much cared, not until 1989, when he was implicated in laying the groundwork for a terrorist master strike.

A young strung-out teenage girl, in love with him, had secreted a barometric bomb in the cargo hold of a passenger aircraft. Miraculously, although the bomb punched a hole through the hold wall, the Austrian Airlines pilot was able to make an emergency landing in Vienna.

Zia al-Haq had next tried to bring down an El Al aircraft, but the El Al's armor-reinforced fuselage was able to absorb the explosion, and the aircraft had made it safely into Tel Aviv.

Zia al-Haq had struck a library attached to the embassy building next, killing a half-dozen people. Then had come a mujahedin-style commando assault on a prison in Pakistan to release his cousin.

The man was an artisan, constantly conjuring up recipes and plots to topple buildings and planes and governments. The man was also a butcher, his dreams littered with the dead, his thoughts soaked in blood. His potential for cruelty was far beyond any concept I had ever had about how people acted, his goal nothing less than turning off all the lights in the world, one by one.

When I was brought back to the closet, there was a brown grocery bag in the corner. The mouse was rooting furiously through it. I picked the mouse up by the tail, tossed it aside. There were two plastic bottles of water, a bag of potato chips, gooey chocolate cupcakes, an assortment of candy.

I unscrewed a bottle of water and started gulping; it ran uneasily down my esophagus, as if it did not know where to go. I huddled over the bucket, lost a brief struggle with my stomach.

I drank more cautiously after that. When I was sure my stomach had settled, I started in on the cupcakes.

The mouse quivered in the corner. Breaking off a few sticky crumbs, I tossed them to him—my hunger was abating, and there was no reason to be greedy.

My meeting with Zia al-Haq had made at least one thing clear—he had some use for me. Some plan. Just like he'd had a plan for Jimmie.

I knew your father.

Jimmie and I had been marked for attention, probably at least a year before, because of the family relationship.

Stretching out on the hard boards, I twisted the blanket around me, stared upward, contemplating the dimness of my prison. *Get me out of here! Get me out of hell! Get me out of—*

I couldn't finish it. All I could do anymore was wait. Wait for what came next. My courage, my defiance had departed. Vanished. I'm not going to out-endure them, Pa, I thought

Death Game

numbly. I know the limits of my strength, and I'm beyond them.

*   *   *

Another day went by. The men had relented completely on food and water. I had little appetite—everything tasted foul. I ate it anyway. The meals were a combination of the worst foods produced in America—Peanut M & M's, Reese's Cups, greasy potato chips, Twinkies and chocolate cookies.

Our junk food is going to kill them, if nothing else does, I thought. I was trying to make myself laugh, or at least smile at the idea, when Waleed came back. He was freshly shaved and smelled of lotion. He took me down the same trail as before, hustling me along, not allowing me to dawdle this time. He was extremely wary, and I knew he wasn't going to let me fool him again.

When we arrived at the big house, we went up a flight of stairs to a study. There was a man in the room, sitting behind a metal desk, closing a manila folder. He was dressed western, and he had a fine-boned face, skin olive in tone and black hair. There was nothing unusual about him except his eyes, which had a hollowed-out look. It was a look words cannot even describe, a look I have only seen in artists' renderings of people who have lost their souls.

"I hear you have eaten," he said in his soft, polite voice. "Do you feel better?"

Waleed prodded me to sit down in front of the desk then stood guard at the doorway. I folded my arms across my chest. Zia waited patiently, but I refrained from saying anything.

After about thirty seconds had elapsed, he spoke again. "We have received the order to begin."

There was anticipation under his flat tones, and his breathing was a little uneven; but it didn't alter the precision of his English.

He impressed me—I couldn't help it. His demeanor was

almost courtly. If you didn't look closely into his eyes, you would think he was moral and gentlemanly. And who would notice his eyes? I had seen executives with that same look. I'd seen surgeons with that look. I'd seen God-besotted preachers and Jesuit priests with that look. It is the look of intelligence and power carefully utilized to do its worst. The look of runaway megalomania, swallowed up in endless hatred and contempt, coupled with bottomless courage.

"From now on," he ordered, "you will do exactly what you are told. Otherwise, you will be killed instantly."

"You can go fuck yourself. My old man had you on the run once," I said. "You're going to make a hash of whatever you're planning this time as well."

My words were bombast; my heart beat with fear. I had a watery feeling in my gut.

Zia gestured to Waleed in a leisurely way. Waleed came forward, open-mouthed, his face jittering with excitement. I eyed him, brushed my hand under my arched throat, and simultaneously clicked my tongue against my teeth, the ultimate Arab gesture of disdain.

He raked the pistol across my mouth as though he was wielding a hammer. My bottom lip burst against my teeth. A socket of pain raced deep into my throat and up my nose. I bent forward slightly, with my mouth open, wondering if my lower jaw had been unhinged. A long string of saliva dripped out of my mouth. A gout of blood spattered.

"You see, we have many ways to break you, if we had time," Zia murmured. "I assumed you were intelligent enough that we would not have to use them."

The blood kept pooling in my mouth, my lower lip had almost been torn in half. I spoke the words carefully, "Do your worst. I've said my death prayers."

Waleed hefted the gun again, but I was ready for him this

Death Game

time. I sucked in a big mouthful of blood. Spat it directly in his face. Spittle and gore splattered forehead, dripped into his eyes.

There was a moment of stunned silence as he raised his left hand and wiped his face. I watched him closely, not expecting an opportunity to get away, simply having decided my death would be easier if I was killed resisting. Or maybe, in the midst of everything, I just needed one moment of pride and honor.

Zia said something to him. It was sharp—a command. Waleed cringed like a beaten dog. Grabbed the back of my shirt, lifted me off the chair and hauled me down a corridor. Zia followed. We passed a series of doors before going out the back of the building, heading towards a tumbledown shack. A sickish-sweet odor came from it; hundreds of flies buzzed in the open doorway. I tried to stop, but Waleed yanked my hands from the doorframe. Slung me inside onto the floor.

Viktor's body lay spread-eagled between four heavy steel pegs driven through the flooring; he had been held down with handcuffs and chains, which were still attached to him. He was naked, but his body wasn't white. It was red and bloody from exposed muscle tissue. He had been flayed alive.

His mouth hung open, and his face conveyed a sense of shock, as if, in the midst of the torture, he had been astonished at what was happening to him.

I knew it was useless, but I put my fingers on the outthrust wrist below the handcuffs. Then I held my hand in front of his mouth. Nothing moved against my palm, no faint breath of air; but the wrist was warm—warm enough to tell me he had not been dead very long. His fingernails were bloody; the plank floor showed marks of desperate clawing. Tiny wormlike rolls of skin hung from his arms, his legs and his naked chest; the skin had been carved from him with sharp knives, like peeling an apple.

I looked at his face again. His eyes were bursting out of their sockets, as if the terrible infliction of pain had sent them bulging from his head.

I stayed kneeling beside him for a moment; then I shut his eyes with my fingers.

"He was no longer useful," Zia said in his cool voice. "We needed his help for awhile, but in the end we had no use for him."

My eyes were watering, and I rubbed them quickly, pretending there was something in them. Waleed was grinning again, but Zia's face stayed detached. His terrible, calm eyes considered me thoughtfully for one final brief second.

"You have heard of what psychologists call psychological transference? Children who are treated badly, they grow up twisted. They love the father who tortured them. They would even die for him." He laughed. "You will do what we say now, because we have taught you to be afraid. But, were you worth it, I could do much more. Turn you so you would see me as a great hero. Love me like a father."

His voice was soft, his manner assured, but there was a hint of frustration in his tone.

"One problem," I said weakly. "My father already tried that game on me. It didn't work."

But he didn't heed me. He was already leaving the room, his steps slightly hurried. He knew he had one enough; there *was* no strength left in me. What comes next? I wondered. Oh, God, oh, God, this has gone beyond the rim of madness. What next?

Chapter Twenty-Two

THEY DIDN'T TAKE ME BACK TO THE CLOSET. INSTEAD, WE WENT AROUND the side of the building, and they put me in the van with the blacked-out windows. Waleed and Fat Boy got in front, Waleed on the driver's side. Four men climbed in the back with me. One of them was Rabbit Mouth, the others I hadn't seen before. I was bound and gagged, but they allowed me one privilege. Instead of lying prone like the last time, I was allowed to squat on the strip of mangy carpet.

Before we left, they loaded a strongbox into the back of the van. When they opened it to check the contents, I saw what it contained: holsters, ammunition, pistols, what looked like disassembled automatic rifles. There were also flares. An axe. Extra jackets.

None of the men showed any particular hostility towards me. Squatting there, virtually knee-to-knee, they barely looked at me; but it gave me a weird, primitive tingle being so close to them. Their faces were reservoirs of mindless purpose that made me shudder.

They were all clean-shaven, with Arabic features. Some had dark skin; others were almost fair. They were young, full of brio, had shoulders you could break a two-by-four across.

I imagined them as children, boys squatting with doubled-up legs, rocking back and forth on stone benches, endlessly reciting hate-filled slogans. Listening to some terrible, chanting voice proclaim death to their enemies, inferiority to their mothers and sisters, and feeling exalted by it. Full-grown now, they were puppets in human bodies. Any real semblance of having a distinct personality, of thinking for themselves, was beyond them.

They spoke only occasionally and rarely in English. Their eyes were bright, and they seemed excited; but I saw no nervous gestures. No playing with objects, turning them over and over. No gnawing on fingernails.

After we started moving, the man nearest me put his hand to his face, offended by my stench. He said something, and Fat Boy turned his head, eyed me, held his nose and guffawed loudly.

After a few hours of travel, the men slumped over and went to sleep, or at least into a heavy doze. Fat Boy threw his head back and snored open-mouthed. Once I got used to the swaying motion I dozed myself, dozed for a long time. Woke up with a nasty jolt when the van stopped.

We were in a poorly lit, mostly empty parking lot, strewn with trash. The finger of an eroding dock pointed out into water, hulks of old boats tied up to it. A BEER-BAIT-BOATS neon sign hung over a strip of murky buildings cast glittering shadows like reflective spangles on the black water.

That was all I saw before Fat Boy snapped open a tarp, pushed me flat and rolled me into it. He heaved me onto a handtruck, strapped me down and wheeled me away. The slap of water against wood told me I was being trundled along the dock like provisions. The tarpaulin I was wrapped in smelled like rotting mackerel.

When we stopped I was dropped into something that sank and dipped under me—a boat. The rocking got more violent as the men jumped in, bringing with them something heavy and rigid,

Death Game

which I assumed was the strongbox. There was a short conversation, a loud motor started up, and we powered through the water at a fast clip.

After about ten minutes, the motor was cut; the bow nudged gently against something, making a scraping sound. The men climbed out, making the boat rock, leaving me behind.

As soon as I was sure they were all gone, I twisted my head out of the tarp. We had tied up behind a large sailboat, anchored about a half-mile out.

Being left alone brought some of my cockiness back. I wiggled back to the stern of the launch, cautiously sat up, hoping I could use a sharp edge on the motor to cut the ropes…

"Aaaaaaaaaaah!"

A scream unwound like a curl of paper in a party blower. A man jumped down from the sailboat, kicked me in the side, grunting from effort. I collapsed back on the launch floor, but he wasn't satisfied. He leashed a rope around one of the cleats, fastened me so I couldn't move.

Time went by. Planes winked overhead. The sky turned a pure limpid blue. Clouds started swirling whitely as the sun lit a fire on the horizon. A flock of pelicans skimmed over the surface of the waves. Dawn, I was thinking when someone snapped the tarp, revolved me out of it. A knife flashed. He cut the ropes, hurried me into the sailboat's cockpit and down the stairs.

Waleed was waiting for us. After fastening my hands to the mast, he pushed me down, squatted next to me.

"When I kill you, I will put this inside here and fire it." He had a gun, and he rubbed the snout against my pelvis. "It is a good way to kill whores. They scream and die slowly."

He continued to amuse himself, telling me about other whores he'd killed. Rubbing the butt of his gun against my thighs and groin, pointing it at my breasts, putting it against my temple.

Ignoring him, I looked around the salon. There was a large

stern bunk, a table for eating, two side bunks you could sit on, a nicely fitted out galley. Near the staircase was the head, and a private cabin had been tucked beneath the gunwales. Everything was custom-built and almost brand-new. I'd never seen any of it before, but something about the boat was familiar.

Waleed was upset by my lack of attention, and he jabbed the gun harder. It hurt, and I made the mistake of turning and looking into his eyes directly. A pinprick of hatred as bright as a drop of blood was in the center of each eye.

I saw him killing me as a hog is butchered in a pen. As a viper is clubbed in a pit. It was clear that the restraint laid on him had been lifted. He described again how he was going to kill me, and there was a victorious sneer in his tone.

"What big heroes you all are," I said to him, unable to contain myself any longer. "You kill women and teenage boys. What's next? Terminal cancer victims and six-month-old babies?"

The growl of an approaching motor kept him from answering. He heaved regretfully to his feet and headed up the ladder. There was a slight commotion as the newcomers got aboard, the sound of clattering footsteps, muttered words of greeting.

When I heard a woman's voice speaking English, I looked up. Kim was descending into the cabin. She didn't seem surprised to see me. Instead, she looked pleased. Her face was alive, full of animation.

There was a man behind her, standing at the top of the stairs, waiting to come down. It was Rick, the bones of his skull sharp under the stretched skin

We looked at each other for a long, clockless moment. His eyes were large, empty, his expression stiff and unreadable. He stared at me as if he barely knew me.

I'd gone into shock. I was shivering, shuddering, feeling my body twitch and my teeth click. Rick spoke a few words softly into Kim's ear. She shook her head, pulled away, but he put his hand on her arm and pulled her back gently. He stroked, as if he were calming a restive animal. He spoke again, his lips touching her ear.

She gave a little rippling movement, and he turned to look at me again. We locked eyes with each other for another long moment.

"I remember you used to say you would kill me if I left the toothpaste cap off one more time," I said when I could bear the silence no longer. "But I never thought you meant it."

"Are you still telling jokes, Cooper? Do you have any idea what kind of trouble you're in?"

"Heather," I asked quickly. "Is she safe? They didn't..."

My voice failed; I was pierced by fear. Heather had been threatened, that had to be the explanation. That was the only thing that could have leagued Rick with these conspirators. He'd been blackmailed.

"Heather's fine. She's perfectly safe," he said, and from the way he said it, without flinching, I knew it was true.

I took a long breath.

"You'll be fine, too," he added. "Just don't cause any more problems."

He spoke in Kim's ear again. They continued their tête-à-tête until she shrugged acquiescence. Rick went back up into the cockpit, while Kim brushed past me, snapped open a cabinet and pulled out some clothes. She tossed them on a bunk and started to untie the knots.

"You look like you've been dragged behind a horse, Cooper," she observed cheerfully. "And you smell worse than an open sewer."

"Really? I'll write a letter of complaint to the beauty spa," I said. My hair, sweat-soaked, matted, clung to my face. I blew a breath into the strands; they had darkened with filth to a muddy brown.

She handed me clothes and a towel.

"Rick suggested that I let you take a shower, and considering how bad you smell, I guess he's right." She led me to the head, opened the door, checked the medicine chest and the service locker beneath the sink. "You've got three minutes," she said, grinning as she closed the door. "Then I'll send Waleed in there after you."

I stood naked under the shower. Let water boil over my scalp and sluice down my body. Turned off the water. Wiped my slick face with my palms and took a deep breath through my nose. There was a small porthole in the head; squinting through it I could see pygmy figures on the shoreline. Headlands above, reaching up in green tiers to...

Well, hell, it was Mount Tam. So that's where we were. Back in San Francisco. On a finger of the bay, just above Sausalito.

I yanked on a pair of khaki pants and one of Rick's old shirts, inspected my face in the mirror. It was scored with welts, but the only serious damage was my lower lip. I fingered the swollen hole with its gaping red edges—a doctor would have insisted on stitches.

My eyes were bloodshot as well as fixed and absorbed in a way I didn't recognize. I look like someone who could stab a scissors into a man's throat, I thought, feeling a chill. Worse, I looked like I might even feel a certain satisfaction in doing so.

While I was dressing, a click and a growl from overhead told me the *Mystic's* motor had been started. The electric winch began pulling up the anchors. By the time I was back in the cabin, we were already powering out of the anchorage.

All the men were up top, but Kim was still in the cabin. She'd set an orange juice drink with a couple of cubes of ice in it on the galley table for me. She hummed a tune to herself.

I took a sip—fire and fruit and it burned all the way down. I winced.

Death Game

Kim eyed me over her own glass.

"Used some of Rick's stock. Figured you needed something to buck you up." She took a short mouthful of her drink as she continued her assessing glance. "You don't seem surprised to see me."

"How could I be surprised? You gave me plenty of warning."

"I never lied to you," she said. Her nostrils had flared slightly. She looked extremely well. Full of vitamins. She was wearing her usual exotic perfume; my nose picked up the scent of orchids. She was so clean and shiny I could feel dirt reforming under my fingernails just looking at her.

She shrugged. Long blond hair swung freely over her shoulders.

"What happened is as much your doing as mine. In fact, you might even end up profiting from it."

This was intolerable; I cut her off with a two-handed gesture.

"Don't bother trying to enlist me. I saw what happened to your last confederate. Your friends skinned him alive."

She shifted her head slightly. Didn't reply.

There were the sounds of a torrent of line being pulled out. With a great flapping the sails were hoisted overhead. We had rounded the high ridge that blocked Sausalito from the ocean winds, and Rick was raising the mainsail and a working jib. I could hear him, issuing orders in increasingly exasperated tones. Shoes thudded overhead; shouts and curses sounded; things splashed as they fell overboard. Through the open hatchway I caught glimpses of the men scrambling around in the cockpit.

"Didn't you hear me?" I asked Kim. "They skinned Viktor Kirnov alive. Because they no longer had any use for him. What further use do they have for you?"

She took another sip of her drink, yawned slightly and stretched. There was a feral, self-satisfied look on her face. A westerly breeze caught us, and the boat started to lean. She

236

Cheryl Swanson

angled her legs out over the double-bunk in the forward berth, let her rump slide down and sprawled against the pillows.

"How'd you get mixed up in this?"

"It was the damnedest thing." Her face had turned meditative. Dreamy. "I met this guy in London in 1997. Almost a dead ringer for Keanu Reeves, y'know? God, he looked so good in a wet T-shirt." She shook her head. "He asked me to fly to Bagram. Pick up something for him and bring it back."

"Bagram?" I was confused. "Isn't that in Afghanistan?"

The drink sat in the crook of her elbow. She ran a polished red fingernail around the edge of her glass.

"It was a place where there were miles and miles of white poppies sparkling in the sun."

Poppies?

"You agreed to courier heroin? From Afghanistan? Don't you read the newspapers, Kim?" I couldn't believe she'd fallen for this.

She stuck a finger in the glass, lifted it to her lips and sucked.

"Kim?"

She rocked her hips, gave a tiny shrug. "I never read a newspaper in my life. He offered me a lot of money and all I had to do was take a weekend trip. When I got there, a guide met me and we took a narrow-gauge railroad to a town called Landi Kotal. They were selling smack for fifty dollars a kilo. Can you believe that?"

I'd heard of Landi Kotal. The drug manufacturing capital of the world.

Her face distorted suddenly, as if a bad thought had interrupted a pleasant memory.

"On the way back, my guide sold me out. I was arrested and thrown in prison. I found out that the punishment for drug smuggling was public execution. They threatened to behead me."

"Were you surprised?"

237

Death Game

She lifted a shoulder, let it drop. "I wasn't even frightened. I knew my father would get me out."

"Kim, don't you understand? It was a sting, and you were bait. They weren't after drugs, they were after leverage on your father."

She lifted her chin. Glowered at me. She was proud of her intrigue. Unwilling to face that she had been a stooge.

"You're twisting everything around," she hissed. "You're just like my father…making it all my fault. 'Kim, how could you have got involved in this? Kim, how could you have disappointed me so much? Kim, how could you have been so stupid?' Well, who's the stupid one now?"

Her voice was low and savage, and I realized I'd got it wrong. So had Walter. This wasn't a stupid woman; she'd guessed it was a sting. Gone along for her own reasons.

"What'd Walter have to do to spring you?"

She waved a finger at the open hatchway. Rabbit Mouth and Fat Boy had just scurried past, pursued by Rick's shouted orders.

"Those guys—he transported them. A few other towel-heads. Gave them secret passage on one of his boats. Walter made a big fuss, but, hell…" She lifted the hair off the back of her neck, looped it behind an ear. "…a thousand illegals come into this country every day. Who cares about a dozen more?"

"Kim, get the fuck off of it," I said, incensed. "You know better than that. These men aren't illegals. They're terrorists."

She sneered at me. "You think I'm simpleminded, don't you? Well, I heard how you cut a hole in poor Jala's windpipe, so how are you any better than a terrorist?"

My head throbbed, and something rose in my throat.

She twined her hands behind her head. "Most people would kill if they had enough guts. Some goody-goody old woman, she's so bitter when she finally kicks off that she'd really prefer the world blew up with her. Some working stiff, he's wetting his pants every night, dreaming about severing every blood vessel in his

238

bosses' bodies."

Her eyes glittered happily. "See, here's reality, Cooper. Everyone's a terrorist. In their heart."

"Thanks for sharing your unusual philosophy," I said.

She missed the sarcasm and actually smiled.

"Everything changed after Walter agreed to help." A sly look came over her face. "I was let out of prison. Taken around, introduced to all kinds of people."

"People like Viktor."

She seesawed her head. "I'd already met Viktor. I told my friend in London how my feebleminded kid brother was gonna inherit half the maritime world, while Daddy's little girl would be lucky to get a rusted-out pile of scrap metal. He said he knew this computer whiz in Russia who might be able to change that. That's when I met Viktor."

I was trying to rein in my temper, play it cool, but it was difficult. This grinning female—she was so titillated with all this. So stimulated and thrilled. As self-satisfied as if she'd run a race, been awarded a trophy and was standing on the finish line, reliving her triumph.

"He already knew all about your father," I said. "He'd been fed that information before he even met you. He was a dangle, someone who is used to catch another person up in something that can be used against them. It's a confidence trick as old as Methusaleh. And you guessed that from the beginning."

But she still wouldn't admit it.

"That's your opinion," she said, not at all offended. "It's true, it didn't turn out the way I thought it would, but Viktor had something to offer that was very clever. And I was smart enough to know how to use it."

"Clever?" I felt like shaking her. "Say ghoulish, Kim. Say horrible and fiendish and evil. Viktor had created a computer game that used real people as targets."

239

Death Game

She laughed, as if she thought I'd said something amusing.

"Children can usually fly under a government's radar screen, that's what Viktor told me. He and these other scientists were working on a program that would brainwash a teenage boy, turn him into an assassin. Program him to be sent after a pre-selected target. The Russians used simulated targets first; using real people came later." She gave a tiny shrug. "The people they used for targets were undesirables. Crazies. Cripples. Mentals. People no one would miss."

"Plenty of those around," I muttered.

She missed the irony; the sly smile was back on her face.

"It was tailor-made for Stephen. He was forever playing computer games. All I had to do was tell him I was playing this new deathmatch game, all hush-hush and, anyway, much too sophisticated for him. When we were ready, I gave him the access code. Viktor took it from there."

And Jimmie? Jimmie got an invitation off the internet from Viktor, and he swallowed it hook, line and sinker.

She sighed, stretched her legs. Wiggled her toes.

"You ever play shooters? Viktor's game wasn't much different, not in the beginning. You blow people away, you get points; when you get enough points, you move up a level." She grinned. "But with Viktor's game, the highest levels are real. You're strangling these ugly mentals. Or shooting crips. All of a sudden, they don't just look real, they are real."

"No consequences for murder. Become God in three easy lessons. No wonder it was irresistible." I was thinking about something else, however.

She shrugged again.

"Who cares about people like that? It wasn't any worse than gathering up a bunch of stray cats and burning them in an incinerator. My little brother had plenty of hatred and rage inside," she added, smiling. "My father made Stephen feel like he was nothing."

As did my pa with Jimmie.

She found a cigarette in her purse, lit it.

"Shooters are addictive. I used to play them all the time. And this one…it wasn't long before I couldn't stay away from it. You'd be amazed—it gives you a buzz to know you're really…sort of…participating in a murder. Your hands start sweating, your heart pumping. Seeing someone piss their pants they're so afraid of you, lick your shoes and beg for mercy—it's a real trip."

She drew in a deep breath of smoke, sent it up toward the ceiling. Sighed comfortably.

"Viktor kept teasing Jimmie and Stephen. He had them convinced it was a huge tournament, and they were ahead of everyone else. Eventually, it came down to the two of them, and then he told them they would meet face-to face. Have an incredible duel. Their own personal deathmatch." The tip of the cigarette smoldered between her fingernails. She flicked away some ash. "I was worried that Stephen wouldn't have the stomach for it, not face-to-face—and I was right.

"I drove him to the *Sea Dream* that night, but he lost his nerve long before we got there. He was blubbering, asking me if Walter was dying, saying that he wanted to die, too. I'd told Walter I'd caught Stephen in the sack with the bodyguard's boy." She laughed. "You should have seen Walter tighten his lips."

She mimicked the Grand Old Man, did it perfectly.

"Stephen couldn't deny it; he turned scarlet, said he wanted to go to his mom's." She laughed. "He took a taxi, but he called me later. I told him Walter wanted him to die. That he was ashamed of him. Didn't want to leave his precious company to a pussy faggot."

She flicked more ash. "There were two guns on the *Sea Dream*, but I'm sure Stephen never even picked one up. Maybe he was in God mode, thought nothing could harm him. Maybe he didn't care. Who knows? He was such a stupid kid."

I was furious with Jimmie suddenly, furious enough to think of my kid brother with an intensity and rage I could have done without. Stephen's instincts that night had been those of the lemming, to jump over the cliff needlessly, caught up in a family drama of death. But Jimmie's instincts had been those of the vicious predator, the one that bites simply because he is cruel.

And then I stopped—because instincts are predictable, and Jimmie's instincts had never been vicious. Lauren's words: *I always thought he was kind of sweet. Underneath it all.* Jimmie *was* sweet underneath it all. I'd spent hundreds of hours thinking about him since the shooting, and I would have staked my life on it.

I sucked in a breath. It was an extraordinary plot, grotesque and fetid and macabre—and also careful and elaborate and sophisticated. Jimmie had been caught up in a net, tricked and needled and enticed. He hadn't initiated anything; all his actions had been pre-staged for him.

But had he really gone through with it?

Kim was still talking. I listened more carefully, wondering how much of what she was telling me was actually true.

"We wanted the deathmatch to be on the *Sea Dream* so it would be filmed," she said. "Otherwise, Walter would have suspected me. We needed proof I had nothing to do with it."

"But the cops could have traced Jimmie's action back to Viktor. And on to you."

She shook her head vehemently.

"There was no link. None at all. I never met your brother. Never spoke to him. And Viktor? All Jimmie knew was that there was some shadowy guy named Deity, hanging out in cyberspace. He doesn't know his name, doesn't know where he lives, has no idea what he looks like. And besides, Viktor never told Jimmie to kill Stephen. He just led him up to it. It was like—what do they call it—the perfect murder?"

She was grinning again. She enjoyed this, telling me all the details. There had not been very many chances in her life for her to impress anyone with how smart she was.

"There was a link—Jimmie's computer. There would have been a record of internet sites he logged on to, including the one where he played Viktor's game."

She took another drag on the cigarette. Spoke through a mouthful of smoke.

"We took care of that. That was Viktor you saw in your house, just before the cops got there. Jimmie ditched the gun on the *Sea Dream*, so Viktor took it and planted it in your house. While he was there, he deleted the links between the game and your brother's computer." She grinned. "He was double-checking Jimmie's computer when you showed up. He wanted to go back that night, to make sure he'd deleted everything. I told him a fire would be a better idea. A fire would take care of everything."

"Including me," I said.

She met my eyes, didn't flinch.

"You said Walter would have suspected you. Why would he think you would kill your own brother?"

There was silence; smoke drifted upward.

"I loved my father and he...loved me, until my brother came along." A spasm of hatred passed over her face. Her mouth twisted. "After that, I was just crap. An abortion that should have happened but didn't." She shook her head. "I tried to win him back. When I was ten and Stephen was a baby, I filled a tub with water and dropped him in. I thought if Stephen was gone, my father would start loving me again."

Sweat had broken out on her forehead. The hatred grew, turned to fury.

"After that, he sent me away. Sent me to Europe to live with my mother. He was my father, he was rich; he could have made my life easy. Instead, I go to my mother. My mother, who was a slut, who everyone fucked, just like he had. It was a bad life, and he sent me to it and never cared what happened to me."

She sat up, threw her cigarette into the sink, where it made a quick sizzling noise.

"He never really loved me! How dare he! Fathers are supposed to love their little girls! But he didn't! He loved Stephen!"

Her voice had turned furious, raging. Spittle ran from the corner of her mouth. She wrapped her arms around her chest. Started rocking furiously. She reminded me of a small child having a tantrum. A murderously angry child.

She turned sideways, bumped her head against the sidewall. Tears spilled from her eyes. Her head hung down; bright hair cloaked her face. I thought of the shock she'd been subjected to—a shock equivalent to a moral volcano for a ten-year-old. Being removed suddenly from a sheltered, luxurious environment. Sent to live at the mercy of a woman who couldn't or wouldn't protect her.

With the force of insane logic, Kim had justified the murder of the brother who supplanted her with a motive as old as the Greek tragedies. It wasn't the money, it was something much more dangerous—vengeance. Vengeance against her father for rejecting her. Vengeance against the brother who supplanted her.

It was more than that, though. Kim had experienced her father's love as cruelty. Seeking more of his love, she had returned what she thought love was—cruelty. The sins of the fathers—was there ever a truer expression? Generation after generation, the children never stop paying dues.

But I didn't have sympathy for her. If Walter had been Judas Iscariot mated with Delilah he couldn't have produced a more traitorous child.

Kim's rocking ceased abruptly. The crying ended and was

replaced by her usual sly grin. The grin was amiable, her face soft—she reminded me of Jennifer Anniston. She was a true narcissist, and like all narcissists, the intensity of her suffering was only exceeded by how quickly she could recover from that suffering. To an outsider, looking on, it was almost comic.

A comic atrocity, that is. Kim, having no core of strength, could only prove she did by destroying others. You couldn't outflank a woman like this. Automatically, without the slightest need to understand why, she would clutch and rend and destroy anyone within her reach.

"I tried again, when I grew up," she said, the irrepressible smile suffusing her lips. "Hired someone to kill Stephen, but he bungled it. Walter thought I was behind it. He told me that if I ever injured a hair of precious little Stephen's head he'd write me out of his will. Cut me off without a penny."

She wet her lips with her tongue. She'd taken off her jacket, slid down on the bunk again; her breasts were stiff against her shirt, the nipples like pennies.

"Walter is gonna die any day now. And I'm going to get it all. His hundreds of millions. His precious company." She parted her bright-red-lipped mouth into a smile, looked directly at me. "The bastard daughter is gonna get it all. She's gonna inherit the earth."

The air in the cabin was starting to feel unbreathable. It was more than just the thick smoke; there was an emanation of evil coming from this woman. I felt like I was sharing space with a grinning succubus.

I affected a careless manner. "These men didn't get into this just to make you rich, Kim. They have another agenda."

She didn't respond, but I saw something in her eyes. She knew. She knew what it was all about, what was ahead. And what's more, she didn't care.

A cold shudder ran down my back. The concentrated essence

of all the madness in the world could have taken residence in her, and she wouldn't have flinched. She was living in a chiaroscuro world where no one really existed but herself. Where all the rest of humanity was obliterated, their voices drowned out by the constant howl of egotism in her head.

"Why did they want Viktor working in Rick's business?"

She didn't answer, so I asked the question another way.

"Why did Rick hire Viktor?"

"He didn't," she said softly. "I did."

My mind jerked. *What?*

"But Viktor worked for Rick."

Kim crossed her legs, sat up and gave me another of her little cat grins.

"And for me. For the past couple years, I've been a full partner in everything Rick owns."

I felt the jerk again. "What?"

"Walter gave me a lump sum of money when I turned twenty-one." She wrinkled her nose disdainfully. "He told me to put it in safe investments and live off the income. But I didn't see any reason to settle for a piddling seven thousand a month, not when Rick knew a way to turn it into real money."

"How'd you even know Rick?"

"Walter and I were having dinner at Absinthe. Rick saw us from across the room, came steaming over. Walter didn't introduce him, just kept talking, lecturing me about investing the money, saying it was all he was ever going to give me. Rick wouldn't go away." She laughed. "I could read him like a book. He wanted to fuck me right there, on top of the oysters and pea soup."

She flicked some ashes on the floor of the cabin. "I got sick of Walter's drivel, got the key and went into the ladies room. Rick followed, happened right there the first time."

And I know when Rick first brought up you lending him the

246

money—one minute after he zippered it up.

"Rut and run," I said. "That's Rick's usual style, you know."

"Not at all," she said, offended. "He was in love with me. He wanted to get married, make it legal, but he wanted Heather to get a little older before he divorced you."

I breathed air through my nose, gritted my teeth, felt the side of my face twitch. How was I any different than Kim? Rick had made fools of us both.

But I didn't have it exactly right.

"Walter was pissed as hell when he found out. That's what I liked best about screwing Rick, to tell you the truth, that it upset my father." Her eyes narrowed viciously. "Shit, I'd screw an orangutan if I thought that would cause Walter to suffer." A moment later, she tossed her head and smiled. "Truth is, Rick's just another fuck anymore. One day I thought I was in love with him, next day, I wasn't. That's the way it is with me. I get bored easy."

She got up and cupped her hand on my shoulder. Sat down and shifted so that our legs touched. Placed her hand on my thigh.

Her fingers were burning a hole in my leg. I had smothered my pride, knowing she held all the cards, but I felt nauseous. There was a kind of greasy, repulsive taste on my lips. For the first time in my life, I knew how hookers felt.

"Think about Rick," Kim whispered, moving closer, pressing her breasts against me. "Think about him watching us do it. It's the only way he'll ever look at you again. Or how about we let Walter watch? If he's not dead already."

Her mouth was red and cold. What was lurching up out of the pit of my abdomen must have shown on my face. She couldn't resist the impulse to humiliate me.

"Frankly, I'd cut myself open, tie my intestines to the back bumper of a bus and be dragged to death before I'd spend a moment in the sack with you," I said. "And I wouldn't care if Robert Redford himself promised to watch."

She shoved me away. Got up and tossed away her drink; rivulets of juice ran down the stainless steel side of the galley sink. The soaked cigarette lay on the bottom like a fat white worm.

"Shut the fuck up," she said. Then she grinned again. "I don't need you and I don't need Rick. I'm going to be so rich I won't need anyone." She was reveling in it, her face lit up with satisfaction.

The boat straightened suddenly, throwing us sideways. We were under the Golden Gate Bridge, which shielded us against the wind for a moment. When the boat went back to leaning deeply, I clambered over the forward bunk, looked out the porthole. The downtown towers of San Francisco lay behind us. Inbound boats were cutting fast wakes around us.

"Where are we headed?" I asked Kim.

No answer. When I turned my head, I was alone—Kim had gone up into the cockpit.

Rabbit Mouth came clattering down the steps a moment later. I was getting out of the bunk, but he screeched at me to stay put. Pointed at the ropes still lying in a pile near the mast. The message was clear—stay put or be tied up.

I moved back to look out the porthole again. We were angling out toward Point Bonita, a finger of blackish-brown rock that thrusts out a half-mile into the ocean. We were bearing south, down the coast. I got a final view of a jumble of rocky outcroppings—sharply pointed, rough boulders with frothy white waves slapping them. Behind it all, the San Francisco skyline glittered in the sun.

Where were we headed? To what end? For what reason?

My imagination went here and there with a bound. What was the point of all this? I could think of nothing...nothing.

I wanted to believe I could figure this out. That I could come up with some solution, some explanation. But I had no ideas at all.

Chapter Twenty-Three

As TIME PASSED THE PACIFIC OCEAN TOOK ON AN OILY LOOK. A FEW wisps of fog floated just above the water, like shapeless ghosts haunting the ocean expanse. The prevailing wind outside the Golden Gate wind funnel is a northwesterly. It blows steady, and it usually blows hard. It did this day as well, raising a short, dirty chop that beat us over to starboard.

The *Mystic* leaned over at a steep angle, and was moving in that painfully slow, corkscrewing motion peculiar to blue water that makes so many people go swimmy in the head on the open ocean. The men suffered—they would come below, find the motion was worse and go back up into the open air. Rabbit Mouth was the only consistent company I had, and he wasn't a talker. The only sound I heard from him was a snap when he checked the clip on his gun.

Rick eventually came below to check the navigation equipment. He was concentrated and silent, intently focused on what he was doing. His face was steady, his lips compressed; he didn't glance my direction.

"I always imagined you were Robin Hood," I said, "stealing from the rich to help the poor, and here you turn out to be Prince John, the bad guy. You certainly let your little brain think for your big one this time."

"And we're sure as hell not in Sherwood Forest at the moment," he growled without turning his head. "So shut up."

Kim came down occasionally to use the head or get something to eat. Once she took a short nap. I didn't speak to her, and I didn't try to speak to Rick again, either.

As the hours went by, I stopped feeling angry, stopped feeling frightened, stopped feeling much of anything. My emotions shut down, and so did my mind. I felt cut loose, disconnected. At noon someone handed me a plate of food. I ate it mechanically, didn't even notice what I was eating.

Just past four o'clock I heard a throaty sound—the distant growl of diesel engines. I glanced out the porthole; an oceangoing tanker was laboring up the coast. Nothing unusual—tankers often made the coastal run. There were depots dotted all along the Pacific coast.

The boat approached slowly. Tankers are slugs, even when they're empty. This one was so loaded she showed almost no freeboard, and she was going six knots at most. She wasn't a supertanker, not one of the giants of the sea, but big enough, nevertheless. The three-island kind—three raised sections on a long deck. When she got close enough, I could read her white-lettered name off her sleek black side: the *Luista.*

As we closed with her, I noticed she was bearing straight for us. That's what made me realize the *Mystic* was in the shipping channel.

I jumped up, amazed. You stay the hell out of the shipping channel when you're a small boat. You cross it quickly and stay clear afterwards. Boats like tankers have stop-for-nothing skippers. You get in their way you're asking to be mowed over.

I waited for Rick to veer off, but he maintained his course. As the gap between the tanker and the *Mystic* lessened, my amazement turned to fear. The tanker paid no attention to us.

According to maritime rules, we were expected to get out of *her* way—large commercial and military boats always have the right-of-way over small craft, on the premise that big boats aren't as maneuverable. They can't stop or change course quickly.

As the hoarse sound of the tanker's diesels increased, the men in the cabin opened the strongbox, collected what was left of the weapons and went into the cockpit. Wondering what was going on, I moved to the foot of the steps.

I heard a loud pop and a sizzling sound overhead—someone on the *Mystic* had fired a low-altitude flare. A moment later, I saw an orange, smoky trail across the sky. More orange flares followed. Then came a parachute flare, curving a tight arc of red light. It went the highest, fell slowly, held in the sky by its small parachute.

While the pyrotechnics burned, I heard Rick and Waleed, their voices raised.

"Hail the tanker! It is time to hail the tanker!" Waleed urged. He pointed at the VHF radio rig hanging on the boat's steering column.

"To hell with that. This scheme of yours won't work," Rick responded, waving a hand at him in disgust. "I'm not going along with it. Not anymore. Forget it. It won't work."

His frown against the ocean glare was creased with worry. The tanker was closing rapidly. In another minute, maybe less, we would be in serious trouble.

"Do what I tell you!" Waleed screamed. "Hail the tanker! Do it!"

Rick's hands tightened on the helm.

"It won't work," he repeated stubbornly.

Waleed shouted at Fat Boy and pointed at the VHF radio.

"Find Channel 16! We can't wait any longer!"

Fat Boy flipped the handheld microphone free and started fumbling with dials. I saw Rick's shoulders tense. Channel 16 is

Cheryl Swanson

the international distress frequency and has a range of fifteen to twenty-five miles. We would easily be heard by the tanker, which was now less than a quarter-mile away.

Waleed took the mike, started shouting into it.

"*Mayday. Mayday.* Tanker! Tanker *Luista*! We are in front of you! Come in! Come in!" He released the button and waited.

We heard the radio stutter, but the tanker didn't answer. Waleed yelled at Fat Boy to make sure the radio was on Channel 16. Then he tried again.

Still no answer.

"You might as well give up. They are not going to answer. Let me change course," Rick said.

"*Mayday. Mayday.* Come in, tanker. This is *Mysss-tic*," Waleed wailed into the microphone.

"They won't stop," Rick said, furious. "Even if you convince them we're in trouble, all they'll do is relay our position to the Coast Guard and continue their course. They'll expect the Coast Guard to send a chopper or a boat to pick us up. You can't stop a commercial tanker in the open ocean with a fool scheme like this. I told you that from the beginning."

"If there is someone over the side, they'll stop," Waleed hissed. "No time for Coast Guard chopper then. If someone dies if they don't stop, they have to stop. It is the law."

It wasn't exactly the law, but he was close. Nautical convention and international law require ships to do whatever they can to help vessels in distress. Only when a would-be rescuer would endanger his own crew is he excused from this responsibility.

Waleed handed Rick the radio.

"They are not listening to me. You tell them there is a man overboard. That will make them stop."

"They'll be able to see from their deck there's no one in the water," Rick pointed out, striving for a reasonable tone. "I'm veering off."

253

Death Game

He started to turn the helm, but Waleed yanked it away from him, barked something—an order, apparently—to a man who was built like a fireplug, with thick, muscular shoulders and forearms. He clattered down the staircase into the cabin, shoved me aside, tore the ladder from the hatchway. There was a door behind the ladder; it opened into a compartment that contained the motor.

Fat Boy handed him an axe. Yanking the door open, he started smashing the blade of the axe against a cable. There was a loud ping as the steel parted. He jumped back.

An instant later, the *Mystic* lurched and the steering wheel spun. Rick grabbed it, stopped the spinning, but the boat kept lurching, didn't respond.

"What'd you do?" he screamed. "Goddamn you! Did you cut the steering cable?"

The steering cable connects the wheel to the rudder. If it's broken, there is no longer any way to control the boat.

The *Mystic*, at the mercy of the waves now, wobbled dangerously. The sails fluttered, started flailing. Rick's sprinted to the bow; he had to get the sails down before they tore themselves to pieces. I stuck my head up; he scuttled around, unhooking and reattaching lines and tackle, the sails beating at him. The boom came free and swung straight for him. I saw him stumble, fall to his knees, get flipped backwards...

The heavy boom kept going, plunging across the deck, lines from the tackle under it snaking and zipping with enough force to tear out an eye. The moment it passed, I clambered completely up into the cockpit, trying to see if Rick had fallen overboard.

As I scrambled past Waleed, he grabbed my hair, jerking it the same way you'd snap a dog's leash. We were sideways to the ocean rollers, and the deck heaved and rocked. The boom swung back and forth, making everyone duck. One of the men crouched behind the helm, yelling into the microphone, demanding that

254

the *Luista* stop and help us. His accent was heavy, so heavy the words were barely intelligible.

Waleed pulled me down on my back, my head against the teak flooring.

"Are you a good swimmer, whore?" he asked, panting hard, his foul breath in my face.

"I used to teach swimming at the YMCA," I said defiantly, kicking and clawing at him, trying to break free.

It was the wrong answer. Waleed grunted something, and one of the other men grabbed a rope and looped it around my legs. Knotted it behind my knees.

Kim had moved into the extreme back corner of the cockpit, where she was safe from the swinging boom. She held to the steel railings as the boat went up and down. Watching me get tied up, she started laughing, highly amused.

"Now that whore," Waleed said, spinning around and pointing at her. "It will be more convincing if we have two victims."

Kim kept laughing, showing no concern. She was still smiling when Rabbit Mouth grabbed her arms. She leaned forward, breathed into his face, leered at him. It was as if she had no concept that a man's aggression towards her could be anything but the force of lust.

Fat Boy grabbed her legs, and they stretched her between them. When they started tying her, it must finally have penetrated. She screamed, something high and inarticulate; I saw Rick raise his head at the sound. Dozens of yards of white canvas flailed around him. The boat pitched sideways—she had caught a wave broadside.

The movement threw me against the railing, and Waleed took advantage of it to roll me over the side.

For a split second I didn't have any sense of motion at all; I felt suspended, adrift in a bubble. Then I felt the wrench of the cold black water. The shock of it knocked the air from my lungs.

With my legs tied, I couldn't swim in a normal way, but I could do a kind of humping thrash that propelled me through the water. I used that and my arms to swim frantically upwards, fighting the downward pull of my heavy, waterlogged clothes. When my head broke through the surface, I grabbed some air then curled back down into the water.

There, safe from the buffeting of the waves, I yanked off my shoes and socks. Then I peeled off the jacket and Rick's shirt, the slacks were caught under the rope.

With my next breath, I worked on releasing my legs; but the knot was complicated, and I couldn't see it. I fumbled with it, awkwardly reaching behind me, bobbing up to get air. I was still struggling when something solid landed on me.

Kim.

She grabbed at my shoulders and neck, grasping and clawing. A wave broke across us, burying us in water. When I came up, another wave broke across my face, and I gagged on a mouthful of seawater.

Kim clung to me, choking me, shoving me under, trying to get as far out of the water as possible. I spat water out, tried to make her listen.

"You can stay afloat with your arms!" I shouted. "Kick your shoes off, Kim! Use your arms!"

I thought she heard me, but I was wrong. Her terror had reached the point she was past listening. Another wave hit us; the ocean swirled whitely around us. I went under again; she went with me. In the glimpse I got of her, her face was dark, almost purple. Her features were hideous, unrecognizable in their terror and violence.

"Untie me...and...I'll...untie you!" I screamed in huffing gasps when my head broke the surface. "We can...help...each other."

I was thrashing the water around us into a frenzy, trying to make her listen, trying to keep my head above water. Kim had her arms wrapped around my neck. Her mouth was open, but no words came out. Her eyes were demented, insane with fear; blood vessel-streaked whites gleamed at me.

We went under again. Sunlight sluiced through the black water, the rays slanted down, following us as I let the air out of my lungs slowly. Let myself sink, pulling Kim down with me. She'd gone rigid with terror. Her body seemed turned to stone it was so heavy.

We kept going down. Five feet…ten…fifteen. She stayed stiff, clutching me, tighter, tighter.

Bubbles swirled around us, as I let out the last of my air. Twenty feet. Twenty-five. Kim had fastened her hands around my neck in a grip so tight I felt like she might decapitate me. The weight of her water-sogged clothing and my escaping breath were sinking us both.

She suddenly released me, shoved away, waving her arms frantically. Her blond hair streamed in the water. She opened her mouth, as if to scream, but I heard nothing. A gush of air came from her, and she stopped thrashing. I watched her fall through the water, plummeting downward. She looked small and stiff, like a doll. Her body was rigid, her face glazed, moronic, eyes seeing nothing.

I swam back for the light with thick, choppy strokes. When I reached the surface, the *Mystic* sat fifty yards away, the waves rocking it. I put my face down in a dead-man's float and let the air in my lungs hold me up just beneath the surface of the water. When I came up for another breath, I heard Rick, yelling on the radio.

"*Mayday. Mayday.* Here is the yacht *Mystic.* We are foundering. We have no life rafts. We have people overboard…"

I didn't hear all of it, but I heard enough. Rick was telling the tanker the situation was disastrous; there were women in the

Death Game

cold north Pacific water. He was injured; he could not control the sailboat. There was no time for a Coast Guard rescue; they must stop their tanker. Use one of their lifeboats, use their rescue craft, use whatever they had.

His voice was cracked and imploring, but he sounded reasonable. He explained carefully why the tanker must help. He couldn't throw us life preservers—his back was broken. It would be inexcusable not to stop, there would be deaths; the tanker's officer would be blamed.

I heard the radio stutter, and a voice came from it, clipped and flat. I couldn't make out the words, and I glanced toward the *Luista*. Two seaman stood at the top of the gleaming black hull. One had binoculars. He scanned the waves, found me.

A minute went by. The tanker was passing; I saw her gigantic prow, huge anchors dangling near the waterline. I saw her insignia flag—a green diamond-shaped white field with a gold bird flying above it. Below that, in gold, the letters ST.

The *Luista*'s marine engines powered down, the propeller wash slowed; the tanker was stopping. Waves buffeted me; my thoughts were scrambled, but…the letters ST, a gold bird. Why did that seem familiar?

My head snapped up. I lifted an arm, waved it desperately.

"Keep going!" I screamed, helplessly, foolishly, at the tanker. There was no chance—not one in a million—that anyone aboard could hear me. My voice wasn't anything like powerful enough to cut across the open ocean.

I kept screaming anyway.

"Keep going! Keep going! Damn you, keep going! Don't stop!"

Seawater broke across my mouth and nose. Saltwater spray was in my eyes. Churning hard with my hands, I forced my body higher. Panic was at work in me now, a worse panic than I had ever known.

I kept screaming. *"Keep going,* Luista! *Don't stop!"*

My voice weakened.

"Keep going! You must keep going!" I croaked feebly.

There was the stink of diesel and a grinding sound as the prop reversed. It was too late; she was going to stop.

Chapter Twenty-Four

THE FOUR-HUNDRED-FOOT-LONG TANKER WAS A QUARTER-MILE AWAY before she was able to completely halt her forward progress. A covered lifeboat was lowered over her steep black side. When the *Luista* was fully stopped, they launched it.

The lifeboat, not much bigger than a one-man fishing boat, headed directly for the *Mystic*. I figured they'd lost sight of me, but I hadn't given up. I kept throwing one arm over my head, waving it. The effort would send me yards underwater. Coming up, blowing water out of my nose, I hoped to see the lifeboat angle my direction.

Each time I went under, I'd count to thirty. Force myself up over the surface of the water again so I could thrash my arm back and forth. There wasn't much chance the men on the lifeboat would spot my occasional appearance, but any chance was worth taking.

The lifeboat kept its heading toward the *Mystic*, never swerved. They were too low, they couldn't triangulate on me. Even in the best of conditions, it's damned hard to spot the head of a person from a small boat, with waves heaving around. You need to be either nearby or high enough off the surface to have perspective. It's the main reason people so often drown when they fall off sailboats.

When it reached the *Mystic*, the lifeboat nudged up alongside. No one was in the cockpit—the men had gone below and were lying in wait. I made another effort, despair gripping me. Propelled myself as far as I could above the surface, thrashed around so I could get an occasional glimpse of what was happening.

A man in gray seaman's dungarees made the lifeboat fast, lacing a line into one of the sailboat's bow cleats. He cupped his hands over his mouth, hailing someone aboard. Another man stood next to him. They waited a moment, tried again to raise someone.

When there was no response, they boarded.

A wave tumbled me over. When I came up, I was looking another direction. Disoriented, I started flailing. The waves were powerful, and the water was freezing. My heart was pumping too fast, exhausting itself trying to keep warm blood flowing to my extremities. Energy and warmth were fast flowing out of me and into the cold of the ocean.

I'd been breathing too hard, struggling in the water, fighting it. I tried to relax, let the waves roll over me. Grab air once in a while with as little effort put into kicking and moving my arms as possible.

I thought of my pa's words again: *Out-endure them, Cooper. Just out-endure them.*

I kept trying to see what was happening on the *Mystic*, but hypothermia was setting in; I was losing my control of my arms. Neuroelectric jitters spasmed my leg muscles. The humping thrash I'd been using to get my head above water became less effective. My body felt as if someone had poured buckshot into it. Saltwater got into my mouth in great stinging gallons.

I kept at it, working hard at pretending there was still some hope. *I can do it, Pa. I can out-endure—*

Death Game

There was a spasmodic shuddering from my lungs. I tried to move my arms and couldn't. A vice seemed to grip me, slowly screwing up tight. So tight. I felt as if my sternum and spinal column will break. *Out-endure them, daughter.*

Sorry, Pa, I can't. Just can't...

Time slowed. Sights and sounds became muted, distant. I knew I was underwater, but I started to feel like I should go ahead and open my mouth, breathe in anyway. I fought the instinct, but my mind was betraying me, making it seem logical. Holding your breath is killing you, so why not go ahead and breathe? Chemical sensors in the brain, triggered by a lack of oxygen, started to force an involuntary breath.

This is it, then, I thought groggily. It had all wound up, somehow, with this idiotic compulsion to breath underwater, with only one or two minutes left to live.

I felt calm. The vice had released; the chest agony had disappeared. The sensation of water in my mouth and throat didn't choke me; it was somehow pleasant. My brain was functioning clearly again. Thoughts flowed by honey-slow. Warmth enveloped me.

God almighty, I'm dying, I thought drowsily. Thoughts scattered, broke apart. Flew away.

Out-endure them, daughter.

Nope. Leave me alone, Pa.

One more try, okay? Just one more try.

Okay, but then it's over, old man. Leave me in peace.

I thrashed feebly, dark water all around me. Felt something hard bang against my face. A moment later, the ropes around my legs were snagged. A strong tug upended me, yanked me backwards through the water. Another tug. I hit an object with my face again. Something hard. Smooth.

The side of a boat.

I tried to cling, but my hands were rigid and my fingers

wouldn't move. I fell away, was yanked forward again. Hands grabbed me and lifted, but it took several tries to get me out of the water. When I was finally tipped into the cockpit, I landed with my stomach on the deck.

Water came out. Spit and saliva. Vomit. I used jelly muscles to flounder forward, turn my head. The man-overboard pole lay next to me—Rick had used it to snag the rope around my legs. Pull me to the *Mystic*'s hull.

I was battered and winded, the taste of vomit and seawater in my mouth. My heart beat hard and slow, laboring, trying to recover. Rick had a blanket, and he started rubbing me, the way you'd rub a shivering dog. He untied the rope around my legs, kept rubbing.

"I figured they wouldn't be able to drown you," he said. "They tried fire, and they tried water, and you're still around. You're just like your old man, Cooper. Have more lives than a cat."

He wrapped me in the blanket, told me to go below, get out of what was left of my clothes. I peeled soaking jeans and underwear off with fingers I couldn't feel. Found a warm sweater, jacket and pants in one of the lockers. I was frozen, I felt ill, but at least I didn't feel like morgue material.

When I came back up on deck, Rick sat disconsolately behind the wheel.

"Bastards destroyed the VHF radio," he said. To prove it, he punched it gently with his fist. The radio emitted sparks and a crackling noise. "And they cut the fuel line, so we can't motor."

I barely understood him; I felt disoriented. I pulled the jacket tight around me, tried to stop shivering.

"How did you find me in the water?"

"I hit the man-overboard button on the GPS as soon as I could after you went over. All I had to do then was follow the little flashing marker on the screen. It took me right back to you." He smiled grimly. "Nothing to it when you got a GPS."

Death Game

"Modern technology," I said, shaking my head. "Amazing stuff."

His face had been bleak, but he brightened slightly.

"And I've got steering again. Those fuckers didn't know I had a spare steering cable stowed below. It always pays to have a spare."

I noticed then that the sails were back up, not flapping around on the deck. They were neatly trimmed, and we were moving cleanly through the water. Rick had turned the sailboat around; we were going upwind. The tanker was in front of us, and he was following it.

"You're going after them?" I asked, startled.

"Why the hell not?"

We dipped over a roller, and he wiped salt spray from his eyes.

"Way I see it, if we don't stop these guys I'll be lucky to get a job afterwards selling used cat litter. If we do stop them, maybe I'll even be a hero."

"I thought you were in league with them." I wasn't just surprised; I was suspicious.

He cleared his throat. Made a nervous motion with his hands.

"Sometimes you have to shave the dice to survive, Cooper. You were in the water. They would have killed me."

"But you came aboard willingly. Until the very end, you acted like you were helping them."

He turned his eyes to me. They were intent and clear.

"I didn't understand what was going on. I thought it had something to do with Walter's business. Kim told me Walter had hatched a scheme to disable one of his tankers. Frighten everyone that it would be scuttled, turn into a huge oil spill disaster. That would drive the stock off a cliff, Walter would scoop it up at the bottom, make a huge profit when the disaster was averted. It was a dirty business deal, I admit it, but I wasn't

264

sweating that overmuch."

"It's a goddamn tanker, Rick. And those people are terrorists."

"Yeah. When I saw you, it was pretty clear what was going on wasn't quite what I'd been told." He looked out over the water. "At first I thought it was a godsend, Kim coming along. A silent partner, a gorgeous woman, what a sweet deal." He screwed up his eyes, as if in pain. "Hell, I can't believe how fucking stupid I was. I told myself I'd buy her out again in a couple years, once my law practice took off. Told myself in ten years I'd be living in the tropics, maybe even own my own island."

"Things are never that easy," I said.

He looked at my face, looked away.

"I'm not making excuses. I let myself be enticed into a spider's web, and I got what I deserved. Ended up an empty husk, the blood sucked out of me."

"What'd Kim expect in return for her partnership interest?"

His face colored. "Only my soul. She kept bringing me these people she wanted me to hire. Jala seemed harmless, and he was willing to work for almost nothing, so I let that slide. But Waleed…one look at that guy and I knew he wasn't a Boy Scout." He gritted his teeth. "But she kept hammering on me. She never actually told me why she wanted these jerks hired, and I never asked. To tell you the truth, I didn't want to know."

"And Viktor? What did she tell you about Viktor?"

"Not much. She told me she knew this Russian guy who was a computer genius. All I had to do was rent an AVID machine for him, and he'd do reenactments for me. But then he shows up and he's not about to do anything I want him to do, that's pretty clear. It meant I could hire you, though, so I told myself it wasn't such a bad deal. Viktor didn't tell me what the hell he was working on, but Kim's money was paying the bills, so I just let it go."

Death Game

I frowned. "But you did know what Viktor was doing. You had his office wired, a hidden camera in it. You could have seen what was going on."

He looked ashamed. "If I'd checked...sure. But one thing you learn as an attorney—don't look unless you want to know. Not doing so just might save your ass, if you get hauled in front of a judge someday.

"When you accused me of having Viktor create porn, I was plenty relieved. It explained everything and got me off the hook. I figured Kim, Viktor and the rest of them were part of a porn ring, and were using my facilities and equipment to manufacture sleaze. I told myself I'd put up with it until I started generating some real money. Then I'd pay her back and throw the whole lot of them out."

Rick gazed over the ocean, at the *Luista*. The boat was so huge she dragged a hump of water behind her. He ran his tongue over his lips.

"The poor suckers on that tanker's bridge are probably already dead."

"Maybe not," I said hopefully. "There were only six of them, after all. How could they take control of a tanker?"

He shook his head. "You don't get it, babe. Tankers are run by skeleton crews; just about everything's automated anymore. A boat like that, there'd be six, seven men at most, assigned to the bridge, half of them off-duty. In their cabins, sleeping, eating, watching videos—none of them suspecting a thing. Probably went down easy as pie." He paused, sounded puzzled. "I wish I knew what they were really planning. You think they're going to scuttle the thing?"

My mouth had gone dry. I gripped the railing and felt my body go stiff.

"They're planning to destroy the Golden Gate Bridge. And as much of the San Francisco waterfront as they can take out with

Cheryl Swanson

it."

He stared at me. "What?"

"Viktor's DVD, the one I wouldn't give back to you? On it was an image of a room with six radar stations."

"You think it was the control room of that monster?" he pointed at the *Luista.*

I forced my fingers from the railing. "Is it possible, Rick? Could a tanker bring down the Golden Gate Bridge? They didn't take any explosives with them, so they must be planning to use an impact to create an explosion."

"Not if they just bump it," he said grimly. "But if they strike with force, amidships, that would smash the tanker's bulwarks and shatter the tanks. The ocean would rush in, raise the pressure. The tanker would go up in a fireball. That would bring down the tower and set the waterfront ablaze. The devastation would be incredible."

"Kim was their link with Sea Transport," I said. "She probably snuck them what Viktor needed to create a pilot training program. As well as shipping schedules, so the timing would work out. I saw schedules like that when I searched his office, as well as blueprints of a bridge. This has all been carefully and painstakingly planned. Probably for years." I licked my lips. "It wasn't until I remembered where I'd seen the flag the tanker was flying—a flag of Sea Transport—that it all added up. When I realized it was one of Walter's boats, I finally got it."

"Damn," Rick said. He sounded admiring. "Blood runs true, doesn't it?"

"What do you mean?"

"Your old man. He was in counterespionage, wasn't he? Worked for the State Department? You must have inherited his spook genes to figure something like that out."

I stared at him. "How did you know about my pa? That's a family secret."

267

"I'm family." The admiration was gone; he seemed miffed.

"But how would you know? *I* didn't even know until four years ago."

"I've known for ten years—your mother told me right after I married you. She said she knew she could trust me with a family secret."

"She tells you the minute you become her son-in-law and dies without breathing a word of this to her own daughter? That's just like a mother, isn't it?" I snapped. "Damn her, anyway. She always had a soft spot for you."

He knew better than to respond.

A moment later, he let out his breath in a long sigh.

"Cooper...I swear—I *swear*—I had nothing to do with what happened between your brother and Stephen."

"Why should I believe—"

"Listen! Will you listen to me?" He sucked in a breath. "Here's what happened. Here's exactly what happened. Kim called me a few hours after Stephen was killed. She was hysterical. She said she'd found Stephen's body on the *Sea Dream*. She freaked when she found him. Didn't try to get help, just ran off the boat."

"You believed her?"

"Just a minute, let me finish! Once she was off the boat, she realized she'd been filmed. Caught by a surveillance camera standing over her brother's dead body. She was terrified, scared out of her mind. She thought that would make her father think she had killed Stephen. To prevent that, she wanted me to have Jala go to the *Sea Dream*. Get all the tapes and cut off the ending of the one that showed her standing over Stephen's body. Preserve the rest of the tape so the cops could see what really—"

"She sounds like she did a lot of clear thinking for a hysterical woman." My tone was sarcastic.

"She wasn't thinking clearly at all. It was a stupid idea. The cops would have seen the ending of the tape was cut off. That would have been like a red flag to a bull. The truth would have come out eventually."

"So, you helped her. You engineered a cover-up," I said, angry. "You made a duplicate of the tape because you knew I'd notice the ending was missing. Then you switched the tapes after I left. Blamed me for the damage to the tape. You set me up, Rick. It's been your fault all along that Harmon treated me like I was in league with the devil."

He stared out over the water. The tanker was speeding up, starting to steam away.

"We can talk later," he said. "Right now, maybe we've still got a chance to pull the plug on this. Make your old man proud. What do you say? Want to try?"

"They've got control," I said. "Everything is proceeding according to plan. There's a tanker depot in Oakland. Tankers go under the Golden Gate Bridge all the time."

"The Coast Guard won't authorize a loaded tanker into the bay without checking it out. They'll order them to stop, send one of their cutters to board and see their papers."

"They'll refuse to be boarded. Or they won't even answer. Keep going. The Coast Guard has no way to stop them."

He shuddered. "There's over a hundred thousand tons of crude oil in that thing. A gaseous vapor will hover over the spill and the fumes will detonate. Not just the bridge. Fort Point, Crissy Field, the municipal pier, the waterfront—they're all at risk."

"If they turn that thing into a floating bomb thousands of people will die."

The tanker sailed serenely on.

"We're going to have to catch up with those motherfuckers," Rick said.

"Piece of cake," I agreed, showing a confidence I didn't feel. "Uh...and then what?"

Death Game

"I'm depending on you for a brilliant suggestion." He gave me the helm. "In the meantime, just do your best to steer a straight course for once in your life, will ya?"

Chapter Twenty-Five

WE BOTH DID OUR BEST. MAYBE MORE THAN OUR BEST.
Rick picked out our heading, and I spun the *Mystic* into it and let her go. As an ever-increasing rush of air came over her bow, she seemed driven by some invisible propulsion system. She lifted her wings and took off. We flew up the coast, and the distance between us and the *Luista* slowly lessened.

As the winds increased, sailing became difficult. Getting the most out of a sailboat requires an undying eagerness to tweak dozens of lines that change the shape of the sails. An unquenchable keenness for making constant slight changes to the heading. A keen fervor for watching every cat's-paw ruffle on the surface of the water and taking advantage of it.

And that's when conditions are reasonably calm. When the wind is high and you're being fishtailed about by crosscurrents and big ocean rollers, sailing is like being a playing card caught in the blades of a clattering windmill. Everything you think you know goes right out the window.

We were headed upwind. As our speed increased, the waves started banging us. The *Mystic* cavitated—slamming, roaring, bashing my teeth together, collapsing my spine. It was punishment for my sins, mashing my bones, sticking knives in

271

Death Game

every bruise. The wind bit into our faces, ballooned and buffeted the sails.

Rick spelled me at the helm as the conditions rapidly passed beyond my skills; once I put the bow corner under a wave, and we almost flipped.

As we got closer to the *Luista*, Rick bore away, which looked like a mistake until I realized that, otherwise, we would have been caught in the tanker's fouled water. The progress we lost we rapidly regained.

I was a rank amateur at sailing compared to Rick. He paid attention to every wave and gust, desperately trying to win the race. Even though it was cold, perspiration glistened at his hairline, dampened his hair. Veins stuck out in his forehead and neck. He yelled at me constantly to make slight corrections on the sails. I scrambled around, yanking at the lines and plying the winch until I thought my arms would fall off.

He kept yelling. Screaming out our speed. Screaming out instructions. My hands turned raw, started bleeding. Our eyes turned red from fatigue. We peered through the sun and haze, staring at the monster ship, fighting monotony, weariness, the pitiless glare of the sun, the mighty breath of the wind. We screamed at each other, started to hate each other, screamed some more.

An hour before sunset, I found Rick asleep at the helm, his eyes shut, his head slumped over. Except he wasn't sleeping, he was praying. I'd never seen him pray before.

"I thought you didn't believe in God," I said.

He looked at me with red-etched eyes

"I don't. But I believe in you and you believe in God, so I thought I'd give it a try." He took a deep breath. "We've caught them, Cooper. We're ahead."

I looked at the *Luista*. We weren't on the same heading, so we weren't anywhere near her, but he was right—our relative positions had changed.

"So long as the wind holds, so long as we don't blow a sail or lose the tiller, we'll beat those bastards to San Francisco Bay," he said.

I went into the galley, wondering why he wasn't happier. Made large mugs of instant coffee and poured it in travel mugs. We sat in the cockpit, gulped down the coffee.

Dusk came, deepened into night. The monotony returned. Rick became even more intense; his jaw tightened until a ball of bone stuck out on his left cheek. By then, I knew what was eating him.

There was a Coast Guard station just below the bay. We could pull in and warn them, but what use would that be? The Coast Guard didn't have anything that would stop a tanker. Short of dropping a bomb on it, how does anyone stop a tanker?

A nearly full moon rose bland and chill, bathing the yacht and the sea around us in bluish-white. Lights glimmered coldly on the shore, lights that seemed to mock us.

As we approached the bay, the wind got stronger, the waves steeper; sailing became a complete bitch. Rick had been forced to turn into a heading that put us at right angles to the waves, which pushed the *Mystic* over at a sickening angle, holding her pinned helplessly sideways. I held my breath, hanging on to the railing as she rolled. Farther, farther, farther—each time I was certain she'd leaned over so far she'd just keep going.

Just after nine o'clock, the harsh voice of a monstrous seagull sounded out of the darkness, startling us. It was the mechanical larynx of Point Bonita's foghorn, audible four miles out, serving as a proximity warning for the San Francisco harbor to approaching ships. The piercing sound repeated, getting louder, a constant reminder that time was running out.

There was a fogbank to the north; otherwise, it was a clear night. The tanker was plainly visible against the night sky; her

273

Death Game

prow cut a phosphorescent wake through the dark water. She was behind us now, but she was making a disheartening steady rate of progress.

When I saw the dim outline of the opening to the harbor—Seal Rocks on the right, Point Bonita on the left—I felt my heart sink. Our options were rapidly narrowing. Once the tanker reached the curving turn where the Pacific Ocean poured into the bay the bridge would be less than a half-hour away, and we still hadn't thought of any way to stop the tanker.

A wave roared up, heeled us over. While the *Mystic* wallowed slowly out of the trough, I made the lines fast on the self-tailing winches and crawled hand-over-hand to the bow pulpit. Hanging on at the extreme front of the boat, a thin piece of railing the only thing keeping me from the pitching and rolling water, I strained my eyes, tried to find any indication of another boat. Hard showers of spray buffeted me. Needles of icy-cold ocean stabbed into my ears.

The air smelled faintly of smoke, and there seemed to be some sort of dark blur in the fogbank to the north of us. I blinked to clear my eyes, squinted hard, thought I saw red-and-green running lights coming out of the fog. After another look, I was pretty sure there was nothing there. I blinked again, kept staring.

Turning wisps of fog hung over the spill of dark water in front of me. Maybe it was a projection, a phantasm in my brain...

The sound of a growling motor caught my ears, faded away, became louder, continuous.

"It's a tug! A tug!" I heard a wild voice yell into my ear.

Rick had lashed the helm and come up next to me. He grabbed me in a bear hug, started dancing me around the bow pulpit.

"Do you believe it, Cooper? It's an answer to a prayer. A goddamn oceangoing tug!"

The *Mystic* heaved, knocking us off-balance. He grabbed me

just before I pitched headfirst into the water. Dashed back to the cockpit, the deck at an impossible angle beneath him, while I hung on to the railing, straining my eyes. Not just a tug—a tractor-tug, more than a hundred feet long. It roared south, moving fast.

Rick turned to intercept; in a moment we were cutting a sharp course toward it. The *Mystic* stopped bubbling along and started roaring herself, moving smoothly downwind, surfing the waves.

The tractor-tug stayed on a collision heading until it was about fifty yards away, ignoring us. Being the bigger boat, they expected us to change course, get out of their way. When we didn't, they angled slightly east so we would pass behind them. Rick immediately hove the *Mystic* directly back into their path.

I was on the foredeck, waving the yellow jacket from a set of foulies over my head. I could clearly see the face of the pilot in the glass-enclosed, lighted pilothouse three stories above the water. He shook his head, blasted us with his horn. Three long blasts. Decoded, that meant *Get out of the way!*

The tug pointed lower this time, but Rick immediately edged the *Mystic* to maintain our collision course.

"They're going to keep going," I said with despair, dropping the jacket. The tug had changed course again. "They think we're drunk or crazy. Maybe both. They won't stop. They'll pass right by."

"No, they won't." Something about his voice…

I turned my head.

"Get down, baby love," he said hoarsely. Salt spray dripped off his face. "I'm going to jibe."

I measured the angle and distance. "If you jibe, we'll smash right into them."

"Get down!" Rick screamed.

At the same instant, he threw the helm hard over, sending the *Mystic* into an extreme right turn. The mainsail smashed

Death Game

sideways; the boom hurtled across the deck and into the shrouds. I threw myself flat, grabbing for the toe rails with my fingers; the boom had missed me by inches.

The *Mystic*, obedient to her helm, carved a tight arc onto a new course, heading directly for destruction.

Another head popped up in the tug's pilothouse. Faces stared; fists were shaken. With a slamming clunk, the tug reversed its engines, but it was too late.

The full-speed impact, hull-to-hull, was seismic. The deck gave a wild lurch. The *Mystic* hit the tug broadside, Rick having aimed behind the bumpered bow, where there were nothing to cushion the blow.

The sound that came from the sailboat as she slid away from the tug was almost human—the grinding, groaning scream of a woman in pain. It was as if she was trying to protect herself, but it was too late. She'd been gut-punched.

Supporting posts, beams, bulkheads collapsed. Boards splintered around me, water poured in everywhere; there was no hope for her.

The groaning got louder, and I heard the shatter of glass as windows popped out. I held on to the toe rails with all the muscle power I had in my body as the boat started to fall backwards in the next wave. A wall of water hit me with a crash. The deck twisted under me. A cresting shower of foam poured over me.

I heard Rick shouting something, but I couldn't tell what. When the deck started to shed water, I could move again. Despite the bone-cold chill of the water, I was sweating with relief as I pulled back into the cockpit.

A wave heaved the *Mystic* back into the tug again. When she struck the second time, men on the deck of the tugboat tried furiously to fend her off with poles. She was leaning forward, taking on more water, mortally wounded. Planks had been completely sheared away—any moment she was going to lose the battle. Do a solid nosedive.

"Cooper! Get your ass over the side!" Rick screamed, and I realized he was no longer on board. He was on the tugboat, and he didn't even look wet—he must have jumped just before the first impact.

I waited for the next wave. When it shoved the sailboat against the tug, I took a flying leap. Landed with both arms clinging to one of the tires on the side of the tug. Scrabbled and wormed up the rest of the way until I was safe on deck.

I looked back. The mast had fallen. The rigging was a tangled mass of canvas, metal, lines and wires. Her bow was underwater, and her stern riding free. She slipped farther; her stern pointed upward. A wave rolled over her, and she was gone beneath the dark water.

Rick was on the deck a few feet away, strangely calm.

"She was a hell of a boat, " he said. "I'm going to miss her."

They whisked us up to the pilothouse to face the captain. He was steely-eyed, with triangular features and a jaw like the bow of an icebreaker.

"That's the stupidest maneuver I've seen in forty years on the water. You're lucky you lived through it."

"I had no alternative," Rick said.

He plunged into a description of the emergency, his voice fast but persuasive, the words pouring out. While he talked, the captain's eyes went from his face to mine and back again.

Through the pilothouse windows I could see the tanker making a long, curving turn into the bay.

"Rick," I said, involuntarily gripping his arm, "we have to hurry."

The captain spoke to the mate behind him, who was piloting the tug, calling him Liko.

"I'll take the helm. Radio the Coast Guard and see if there's anything to this."

Death Game

Liko was surfer-boy laconic, enough tattoos to be a Maori tribesman, bleached blond hair sticking up in tufts. He went to the back of the pilothouse and started a radio transmission. As he spoke into the receiver, I caught an occasional word.

"Go ahead...Hey, dude, don't get bent...What?...Man, that is foul...Confirm, uh...Okay, uh, affirmative..."

I kept my gaze riveted on the tanker. She was now bearing inexorably toward the city, had already passed the channel buoy that marked the actual entrance to the harbor. A Coast Guard search-and-rescue plane banked and darted directly in front of her prow, flying low, just twenty feet or so above the waves.

"Never seen a search-and-rescue plane do that to a tanker," the tug captain said. He gave Liko an uneasy glance, but Liko was still on the radio. "We just returned from Portland," he said to Rick. "We're headed for a job with an oil platform down south. Even if what you're telling me is true, I don't know what we can do about it."

"You know the harbor, though?" Rick asked.

"Like the back of my hand. I've worked tugs my whole life. Must have dragged a thousand barges out of the port of Oakland." He gave the tanker a worried look. "Your story sounds nuts, but I can see something is going down. That tanker is going way too fast to enter the narrows."

Liko had finished the radio transmission.

"The Coast Guard dudes said they're trying to stop the tanker. Said they've ordered them to stop, but they aren't listening. Said anything we could do to help would be greatly appreciated. When I asked the weird dudes what they thought the problem was they said they couldn't tell me. It was classified."

"It's okay to get killed trying to do the right thing, but it's not okay to know why," Rick said. "It's a long-standing military tradition."

"You ex-military?" the captain asked Rick.

278

Cheryl Swanson

"Marines," Rick said. "Force Reconnaissance."

The tug captain seemed impressed. "One of those devil dogs, huh? I did a couple years in the Merchant Marine myself. Never saw any action."

The plane was making another pass. This time it shot off warning flares; white smoke streaked in front of the tanker. The *Luista* didn't slow, but all her exterior lights flipped off. In the darkness, she now looked eerily similar to a long, sleek black sword slicing through the water.

Two Coast Guard cutters raced out from under the bridge. Both shot up a series of flares.

"We can catch her, but what good will that do?" the captain muttered.

"Your tug could shield the Golden Gate Bridge," Rick suggested. "If you can get between them and the bridge, you might be able to absorb the shock, keep the tanker from exploding. It's going to take a pretty big impact to make that ship detonate."

I looked at him. Exhausted as he was, he had lost none of his gung-ho aggressiveness.

"A stunt like that could rip this tug to pieces," the captain said. "I could lose my boat. And my crew."

Liko spoke up. "The *Alan G*'s an ace boat, captain. She can take that tanker."

"She's not built to muscle tankers around," the captain said irritably. "She's a barge boat, not a tug escort. Too underweight."

"So, we end up in the boneyard," Liko said, shrugging. "At least we tried."

"It might work," the captain said, chewing his lip. "We can't push a tanker, but we can nudge her. The *Alan G*'s a lot more maneuverable than any tanker. We nudge her just right, maybe we can steer her away from the bridge."

"Ask your crew if they want to try," Rick urged.

279

I saw the captain struggle with the decision. He was the authority on the boat—he didn't need the crew's approval for a decision—and in the end, he was responsible for their safety. He was also striving to preserve his options a bit longer.

The radio crackled. Another crewman had come up on deck, name of Mike. He took the call.

"Coast Guard asking for help, sir," he reported. "Saying the situation is critical. Saying they don't have any means available to stop the tanker. They don't dare drop explosives this close to the city."

"Get the rest of the crew up here. Pronto."

Mike sent out the call through the intercom. The captain waited until the rest of the crew—two more men—showed up in the pilothouse.

"Carlos, you speak first," the captain said, winding up a quick explanation. "You've always got an opinion."

Carlos looked like he had been in a deep sleep thirty seconds before. He was Latino, black bangs to his eyebrows, a desperado mustache. He rubbed his eyes.

"The *Alan G* breaks up, we'll be crushed. A bunch of meat pies."

"Joe?" the captain said.

"She gonna bring the Golden Gate Bridge down? Really?"

"Possibly."

Liko spoke. "Always thought that bridge was the most righteous thing I ever saw. I say we go for it."

The rest of the crew nodded. Carlos shrugged, rubbed his eyes again and yawned.

"Guess we have to do something."

The captain radioed the Coast Guard. Told them we are going to attempt to broadside the tanker. A moment later, he said, "Liko, you're my best helmsman, you take her. I'll give you what advice I can."

He positioned himself next to Liko; Rick and I moved aside, getting out of the way. Water churned behind us as we started to close quickly on the tanker. Two city blocks behind...one city block. Pretty soon we were passing. Directly in front of us was the Golden Gate Bridge.

Mother of God, I thought, looking up.

Lights soared on its two towers, seven hundred incredible feet above the water. More lights dangled on the steel cables, burning with clean intensity, shimmering, glowing, gleaming against the night sky. Cars poured over it, headlights, taillights—a streaming river of light. The bridge was so full of light it tore the darkness away.

Liko swung the *Alan G* in a tight circle and positioned us under the bridge, just in front of the south pier. The pier was the foundation for the south tower, which rose directly above us. This was the pier the tanker had to aim for. The north pier was in much shallower water—she couldn't approach it.

I heard police sirens overhead; the city cops had been alerted to the danger and were trying to close the bridge down. They weren't going to be able to do it quickly enough.

The *Luista* kept chugging forward, but she was starting to make a sweeping right turn.

"They're heading away," Carlos said. "Dirty bastards changed their mind; they're not going for the bridge."

"They're just angling her so her midsection will smash first. The midsection is where the tanks are," the captain told him. "With all that crude oil sloshing around, all they need is a good bang in that area and..."

Words failed him. Dead in front of us was the tanker, so deep and black it looked like a wall between worlds.

The captain's attention was focused alternately on the tanker and the tugboat, gauging angles and distance.

"The *Alan G* won't survive a genuine collision with that

Death Game

monster," he said to Liko. "Here's what you do. Head out, but be ready to go into reverse fast, just before we touch. Let it get in harmony with us, let it push us backwards a bit. When I tell you, slam it in forward and pour on the power. Just be goddamn careful." He smiled grimly. "We push too hard we'll all wake up in oblivion."

"I'll be as careful as a maitre d' sliding a chair under a businessman's big fat ass," said Liko, grinning.

The tanker was still moving sideways, angling toward the pier, the long black slope of its side swinging. The tug growled forward to meet it. As the distance closed, one of the men, positioned on the bow of the tug, started calling out the distance: "Forty feet...thirty...twenty...ten..."

The *Alan G* nestled its bumpered bow against the huge black wall of the tanker's side. There was a moment of apparent stillness.

Then the crew went crazy. Liko got pummeled on the back, punched on the arm joyfully.

But the brief moment of triumph ended. The tug started shuddering and rolling—the huge tanker was pushing us backwards, shoving us effortlessly like a slow-moving freight train pushing an empty ore car.

"Full power, Liko," the captain ordered. "Make those seven thousand fucking horses do their job."

Liko pushed the engine control forward. The engines caught and roared into life, the water behind us started to churn. The tug took on a thirty-degree angle; black water crossed our foredeck. A grinding metallic sound started that sounded ominous.

Bam! A heavy metal object exploded through a window like it had been fired by a gun. A brass fitting tore free, careened off the opposite wall. The tug shuddered violently, slowly being crushed by intense pressure.

"Back off!" the captain screamed. "We're sliding right under

282

the hull! Back off! Back off!"

"Man, dude! Impact zone!" Liko yelled, grinning like a madman. Slamming twin levers down, he pulled us back to safety. Temporary safety. The moment we were free, he moved us forward again, aiming for a different spot, trying to find some seam, some point where he could use leverage and thrust to overcome the tanker's raw power.

But we were running out of time—the high arches of the bridge were almost directly above us.

I looked toward the city. Compared to the blazing reality of the bridge, the city of San Francisco seemed fragile, a city in a dream.

As we approached again, the steady, throbbing chop of the tug's motors was drowned out by the deep sullen roar of the tanker's propellers. If we got sucked into those raging fans, we'd be ripped open like an angler's knife opens the belly of a fish. If we made a hole in the side of the tanker, the oil would gush out, any spark could ignite it and an inferno would zip from the ship to the city.

I couldn't bear to watch anymore, but I had to. Had to.

The tug shuddered, trembled, pitching and heaving. Water smashed, rolled, spilled, scattered and fled in the moonlight. The tanker…the tanker never went absolutely still. There was a moment when it seemed as if was undulating, flexing dangerously. A moment later we were moving it backward. Pushing it away from the bridge.

Liko gave a howl of victory that split our eardrums, but once again, there was no time to rejoice. We heard a mechanical hum. Something grinding, which ended with a clang and then a slow chug. The tanker propellers slowed, stopped, reversed. Her prow turned away from us sluggishly. They were changing tactics; the bridge was no longer their destination. They were backing off but not giving up, aiming for something else.

As the *Luista* moved away from the superstructure of the

Death Game

bridge, two Coast Guard choppers seized the opportunity to nudge up close to her forecastle, where the control center was. Two men dressed in camouflage rappelled out of the choppers, automatic rifles strapped to their backs, sidearms slung on their waists.

"They've got to wrest back control of that monster," Rick said. He turned, started pointing. "Mile Rock Lighthouse…Point Diablo—even the edge of a cliff near Point Bonita. Any of those could still serve their purpose. They hit any of those hard enough that tanker will go up like a Roman candle. The blowback will take out a lot of the waterfront."

A gust of hard wind caught the men in camouflage. One was launched sideways, as if fired from a circus cannon, directly into the side of the tanker. The second man was bounced across the surface of the water, as if he were a skipped stone. The chopper went into a rapid climb, pulled him out of danger.

"They need help," Rick said. "This damn corridor is always a wind tunnel. They'll never board that ship from the air. We have to help them."

"We've done all that we can," the captain told him.

"Those motherfuckers will still win if we don't do something," Rick insisted. "I…" His voice turned strained. "I…feel responsible."

"I don't see what we can—"

"I've got it." Rick snapped his fingers. "You have grappling hooks? Guns?"

"Down below. But—"

"We're boarding her. We'll snag some of the superstructure near the forecastle with the hooks, pull ourselves up. Once aboard, we'll make a move on the bridge. Take control."

He explained the rest of the details, getting more excited as he went, raising his voice, pointing to a low spot on the tanker.

"There! Right there! That deck is only about twenty feet above ours right there. Twenty feet to climb on the rope and then we're

284

over the railing. We move fast enough, we'll catch them by surprise."

Liko was grinning. "I'm with you, dude," he said. "Always fancied myself one of them action heroes." He glanced at Carlos. "You always say you got the biggest cojones north of Mexico City. You ready to prove it?"

"Next to me, you're gonna look like a gutless shit," Carlos retorted. "You're gonna be so embarrassed you'll go home and enroll in ballet lessons."

The rest of the young crew laughed. They were nodding their heads, looking excited.

"Trying to board a tanker that's heaving and sliding around in the waves?" The captain shook his head. "Unless you got a death wish, you'd better forget it."

"I'm not going to bullshit you," Rick said to the men. "Your captain is right. We got about as much chance as five stray dogs crossing a freeway during rush hour. Most likely, they'll be ready for us. Long before we get to them."

The men weren't listening. Liko nudged Carlos in the ribs with his elbow.

"Hey, bro. A Franklin says you won't even be able to drag that fat ass of yours up the rope."

"I'll pay for your ballet lessons if you don't point a gun the wrong way, surfer boy. Shoot one of us in the nuts."

The captain gave them an exasperated glare.

"For God's sake," he exploded. "Don't get snared in the ropes. You get snagged between the tug and the tanker you'll be ripped to pieces. Here," he said, grabbing the helm. "I may be too old to climb a rope, but I can still pilot a goddamn tug. I'll nestle this baby right up against her."

The men clattered down the steps, following Rick. A high-intensity flare, sent out by a Coast Guard helicopter, lit up the night sky. The chopper was hauling up the man who had hit the

Death Game

side of the tanker. He hung limply at the end of the rope.

I grabbed Rick's arm at the foot of the steps. "Rick, try to stay...alive."

He took my icy hands in his, kissed them. I was breathing hard, tears rolling down my cheeks. I was trying to be calm and it wasn't working.

"You forgive me, Cooper?" he asked. He searched my face with his eyes, as if he was looking for something.

"Not if I have to attend your funeral," I said thickly. "I'll never forgive you for that."

He grinned. "There's no way I'm going to die. I haven't done enough bad things in my life yet."

He grinned again. His eyes swam with excitement. There was no denying it—he wanted to do this.

Sure, he felt responsible. But mostly, he didn't want to miss out on the thrill. The thrill he had felt in Force Reconnaissance. The thrill he had felt chasing deadbeats with a surveillance camera. The thrill he felt battling it out in the courtroom. The thrill—hell, even the thrill he felt chasing cheap women. This was how he was. The regrets, the morality, even the logic were never as strong as the raw, primal impulse.

He squeezed my hands.

"Just one thing. I'm just totally fucking in love with you— always have been, okay? It's about the only thing I've been certain of in my life."

"Hey, bro, you can plow that field later!" Liko yelled. He had come running up, ropes slung over his shoulder, a grappling hook in his hands. Carlos, behind him, held four semiautomatic pistols.

Rick took a pistol, checked to see if it was loaded.

"Nine-millimeter Browning," he muttered. "Well, hell I remember these, used one when I was a meathead, chasing bad guys. You ever shoot anything?" he asked Carlos.

286

Cheryl Swanson

Carlos shrugged. "Drilled a shark in the backside once, least I thought I did. Can never tell with those big mothers—they take a bullet like it's a mosquito bite. Flick their tails, swim away."

Rick was tying knots in the ropes. He tossed them back to Liko.

"We live through this, we're going to be brothers for the rest of our lives," Rick said. "We're gonna talk about this night a thousand times. We're gonna name our sons after each other."

Carlos grinned widely, flicked black bangs out of his eyes.

"I ain't naming no son of mine Liko. That's the stupidest name I've ever heard."

I saw a muzzle-flash. Heard a *tzzee-uk, tzeee-uk.* Ammunition spattered the side of the tanker—one of the choppers was firing on it. Bullets ricocheted off the steep steel sides. A bullet sang past my shoulder, cut a hole in the siding of the pilothouse.

"Get off the deck, Cooper" Rick said, turning to me. "Go inside."

"Rick. What you said. About still being in love with me. I…"

He grabbed me, put pressure on my elbows, shoved me backwards.

"Rick, I—"

"Get back!" he screamed.

The motion of the deck had become violent; the *Alan G* was up against side of the tanker. Overriding the diesel stink of the tanker's engines was a sharper stink—the smell of crude oil, sloshing around inside the holds.

The deck bounced and buffeted me. Gusts of turbulence slapped my face, plastered my clothes to my body. Another bullet whined past my ear, and I ducked behind a huge steel winch.

When I looked up, Liko had thrown a grappling hook in a high clanking arc. Beginner's luck—the hook caught. A moment later, he leapt free of the deck, a pistol shoved in his belt like he was a pirate. Scrambling, churning, his arms and legs moving like a

287

windmill, he climbed the rope, using the knots for handholds, disappeared over the railing.

Carlos was just behind him; he crab-walked up the side, grabbed with both hands at the top, yanked himself over. Two more tug crewmen shimmied up next.

Rick was the last; he knew the technique, but he was out of shape, older than the rest by more than a decade. At the top, he braced for a moment against the railing. Then he slipped over the dark edge onto the tanker's deck.

Engrossed in watching, I didn't notice the coil of rope behind me. Caught in the tail of my eye an upward strike, like a snake uncoiling. Realized—too late—I was between the winch and ground tackle that was sliding off the deck.

The line unwound with a hissing whine, caught my foot. The jolt threw me forward, and I skidded toward the edge of the deck. I tried to grab something. There was nothing there.

Chapter Twenty-Six

HARMON CAME TO SEE ME IN THE HOSPITAL; I WOKE UP TO FIND HIM sitting next to my bed, drinking coffee out of a big Styrofoam cup. His tie was slightly loose, but his slacks were creased, his dark-gray blazer unwrinkled, his shirt crisp with starch.

I sat up in the bed and rubbed my eyes.

"Did you bring me a coffee?"

"Would have, but I didn't want you to spill it," he said. "Burn yourself or something."

I shifted in the bed a little. I felt very tired. I had a couple of broken ribs, and the doctor had taken several stitches in my lip. They felt like tiny plastic railroad tracks when I moved my tongue across them. And the long swim had left water in my lungs. It had given me a type of pneumonia.

I had been sleeping almost round-the-clock for two days, ever since the Coast Guard pulled me out of the bay. When I was asleep, I had strange dreams. I dreamt the surface of the sea was over my head, and I was too weak to make another effort. Seconds ticked by, and everything started to close down, like a camera lens shutting in my brain. I saw strange things—waves bursting in spouts of foam on some distant tropical beach, boulders ripping loose from the ocean floor and shooting upward like rockets, a flurry of silver fish rising from the mouth of some

Death Game

underwater cave.

"I did bring you this," Harmon said.

He pulled a ring out of his shirt pocket and dropped it in my hand. It was a man's ring, cast out of heavy Mexican silver.

"I bought it for Rick on our honeymoon in Baja," I said. "We couldn't afford regular wedding bands. He never took it off. Not even after we split up. Just kept wearing it like nothing had happened. Stupid, huh?"

He didn't respond.

One of the nurses had told me Rick was dead. She'd also told me that Walter Ludlow had died—natural causes, in Walter's case. She'd seen his death reported on the evening news.

"I never knew the two of you were married. All this time, and I just found that out." Harmon sounded annoyed.

"Different last names," I pointed out. "Plus neither of us wanted you to know."

He grunted, took another sip of his coffee. "Would have found out if I'd wanted to. I just never put my mind to it."

"I saw something about the tanker on the news," I said, "but they made it sound like an accident. Terrorism was never mentioned."

I thought back to what the newscaster had said.

"An accident in the engine room of a tanker has led to the unfortunate deaths of a half-dozen seamen…"

Harmon grunted again. "The true story never got out. The powers-that-be must have decided to squash it. What really happened is gonna be buried forever by some top-secret military committee." He picked up a stirrer, swirled it in his coffee. "There have been rumors, of course."

There didn't seem to be anything to say. The government was deceiving the people, and California's Fourth Estate was too busy reporting on the latest movie star fondling preteens to notice. What else was new?

Cheryl Swanson

As I thought further about a cover-up, though, my heart bumped. My fingers tightened round the ring.

"Rick's body. There *is* a body? I'll be able to bury him?"

Harmon nodded, and my hope slipped away.

Rick was gone. There was a sudden emptiness in my chest, as if the strings that held my heart had been sliced through. Even holding his ring, I hadn't been able to believe he was gone, not really. Now I knew.

My eyes were burning. I put up my hand and checked—no tears.

"I'm glad you came to see me. I won't get all drippy on you, I promise."

"We caught up with your brother," Harmon said. "Right in the city. Few miles from your house."

"He's been in the city all this time?"

"Nope. Been living in an abandoned car park down in Los Angeles with some homeless kids. Came back a couple days ago. Told us he wanted to talk to you and that he was planning to turn himself in."

"He confessed to killing Stephen?"

Harmon took another sip of his coffee. "More or less. A few things don't match up, but he admitted he killed Stephen Ludlow. With his confession, the DA's office will have no trouble making the case."

I looked out the window next to the bed.

"Jimmie didn't do it. He didn't kill Stephen. He thinks he did, but he didn't."

"You care to explain that?"

"Jimmie fired only one shot, and that bullet missed Stephen. Someone else picked up the gun, fired a second shot. That second bullet was the one that killed Stephen."

He put his coffee down for a moment. "You know about the second shot? We found a slug in the hull of the *Sea Dream*. Came

291

Death Game

from the same semiautomatic pistol that killed Stephen Ludlow."

"You didn't tell me about this second slug before," I said. "As much as we talked, you never told me."

He looked at me calmly. "You keep getting that part of it confused. I'm the one who's supposed to ask the questions, not the one who does the telling."

"Just wondering why you didn't tell me," I said.

He turned his hand and inspected his fingernails. They were clean. Neatly trimmed.

"Next time I need help on a case, maybe I'll call you in, Ms. O'Brien. Just so I won't have to go it alone." A moment later he seemed to regret his sarcasm. He shook his head slightly, picked up his coffee and took another sip. "That extra slug probably means your brother just missed the first time."

"On the surveillance tape, Jimmie fired only one shot. Not two."

"The tape, right after he fired that shot and ran off, was damaged. The end was torn off. Maybe the part that was missing would have showed him coming back and firing a second shot."

"You never told me about the surveillance tape being torn off, either."

"I told Mr. Capra. He told us you must have done it. Said you tried to destroy the tape."

"If I had been trying to destroy that tape I would have destroyed it," I said.

"Yeah. Took me a while, but I figured that out for myself."

"Jimmie fired a shot, but he didn't aim the gun. He couldn't really bring himself, face-to-face with another boy, to kill. So, he turned the gun slightly aside at the last moment. Stephen was ducking to save himself, and he fell. Jimmie thought he'd actually killed Stephen, so he ran away. Ditched the gun.

"Someone was watching to make sure it all came off. They picked up the gun Jimmie dropped. Fired the shot that killed

Stephen. Then they planted the gun at my house."

"You got any proof of this?"

"Jimmie told you he only fired one shot, right? He's confessing to the murder, so he's got no reason to lie to you, but you ask him repeatedly and he keeps insisting 'only one shot?'"

Harmon nodded.

"Jimmie doesn't even know about that second shot. And you've realized that already. That's what you meant when you said a few things didn't add up."

"Assuming you're right, and we're just assuming here, who was it that retrieved the pistol and killed the boy?"

Kim, I thought. It had to be her. She'd claimed to Rick she'd wanted the ending of the tape destroyed because she'd been caught innocently standing over Stephen, but that wasn't the reason. She wanted it destroyed because the ending showed her finishing the job. Killing her brother.

But I had no proof, and Kim was dead and could never be questioned.

Finding the extra slug wouldn't help Jimmie. Unless...there was a way to prove that the shot Jimmie fired on the surveillance tape ended up in the hull. Not in Stephen's forehead.

"The blood spatter, fragments of the skull—the trace evidence," I said, "wouldn't they show where Stephen was standing when he was killed?"

Harmon didn't even hesitate. "We compared the tape and the blood splatter and you're right. Jimmie's first shot went into the hull. But the DA thinks your brother simply fired a second round."

"The DA thinks that, but not you?"

He shrugged. "I can't clear your brother."

A nurse came in then and took my temperature. It was one of those electronic thermometers connected to a small pack on her belt. She noted it on the chart, smiled and left.

Death Game

Harmon had finished his coffee. He got up and tossed the crumpled cup into a wastebasket. I thought he was going to leave, but he came back and stood at the side of the bed. Looked not at me but at the wall on the far side of the room. He was as quiet and impassive, as if he'd turned to stone.

I'd thought of something. "Bernard Tuck was DSS, wasn't he? I got that right, at least. How'd he get in the middle of things so fast?"

Harmon shrugged. He wasn't going to deny it.

"Mr. Ludlow was being pressured by suspected terrorists, there'd been a threat against his son's life. Tuck was on his way before the boy was even killed."

"The wording of the threat. Did it go something like this? *The way Stephen Ludlow will be killed, it's the first time anyone will ever be killed that way. The world has just found a new atrocity, a brand new way of killing.*"

"Close enough. But none of this means anything in terms of an actual trial. It won't help your brother."

I looked him in the eye. "If you trust me now, that means something."

"Not a question of trust." He pursed his lips as if he were weighing alternatives. Grunted and reached into his jacket pocket. Pulled out two folded sheets of paper stapled together. "There's this, though."

"It's in Russian," I said, looking at it.

"We had it translated," he said. "Look at the next page."

I flipped to the next page and started reading.

"'When I was a zek, I learned that the death giver is beyond limitations, beyond blame—he enters another realm of experience. I know this because I am part of the Brotherhood, and we know secrets that other men dare not seize...'"

"I don't understand. What is this?" I asked.

Harmon took out his half-glasses, put them on and pointed at

294

the address block.

"It was written by Viktor Kirnov and sent to some individual in London. We think he was a middleman. One of those shadow people who deal in drugs and illegal weapons."

Kim's man in London, I thought. I went back to reading, my interest quickening.

"'You ask who can be trained as an assassin, and I tell you any young boy the age of a trainee in the army. In the Russian Army, we could force these boys to watch and participate in the secret training camps. We would put the trainees heads in a vice. Force them to see violence and bloodshed until they lost their revulsion to it.

"'In America, we will not be able to use the vice, so we must find a boy who will watch horrors being done willingly. In our testing, we found that there are boys like this. Boys who do not need the vice. Such a boy has a hole in his soul. An orphan, one whose parents have been taken and imprisoned, whose family is lost, that boy will learn to kill easily and quickly. Such a boy is full of rage.'"

I stopped reading.

"A boy who has a hole in his soul," I repeated. I felt like someone had socked me in the stomach. "A boy who's an orphan, a boy who is full of rage...Jimmie. That's why they thought it would work with Jimmie."

Harmon didn't say anything. He'd put his glasses back in his vest pocket. I went back to reading.

"'As we agreed, I will find this boy and use the training program to turn him into an assassin. We will need an English name for this training program so we will call it Enigma. Winston Churchill, that fat old Englishman, he once called Russia a riddle wrapped in a mystery inside an enigma. He did not know what he was talking about, but I do. Enigma, the great truth hidden in mysterious form. The truth that Lenin and Stalin discovered.

Dead men, they have no significance. Only the killing has meaning. The timid, the weak, in their stupidity they may feel horror, but the strong find joy in the killing. The primitive brain knows this. And it is that brain that will triumph in the end.'"

When I was done, I fell silent. Roused myself only with an effort.

"How did you get this letter?"

"A woman gave an envelope to someone to mail to the San Francisco police after she left the country. The letter was in the envelope."

"A woman? You mean Natalya Kirnov? She's okay?"

"We believe so."

"Natalya's gone? She went back to Russia?"

"She's gone. We're not sure where she went. We're trying to track her, but I don't have a lot of hope about that."

I handed back the letter. He folded it up carefully. Put it in the inside pocket of his jacket.

"She knows they killed her husband. That's why she sent it."

Harmon didn't speak.

"Can this letter be brought into Jimmie's trial?"

"I don't know. That's a question a judge will decide."

"With evidence that it was the second shot that killed Stephen, the ending missing from the tape and this letter, is there any chance a judge will reduce or drop the murder charge?"

"Maybe. Nothing is one hundred percent certain, Cooper."

"Something is one hundred percent certain," I said. "They were using Jimmie as an experiment to see if they could turn young boys into sleeper assassins. It was one hundred percent successful."

Which means they'll try again, I thought, and with a bigger target. Maybe they'll try to snuff out a political candidate next time. Or target a religious figure, like the pope. If we get lucky, maybe it will even be some overpaid bureaucrat in the

Department of Defense.

He was leaving.

"You called me by my first name," I said as he reached the door. "Was that an accident?"

He turned. There were faint parenthetical smile lines at his mouth. They deepened slightly.

"An accident," he said. "It won't happen again."

"Take care that it doesn't, Detective Harmon."

The smile came into his eyes this time. He glanced down the hallway and gave me a thumb's-up.

"Nice day outside. Rain finally stopped. Maybe you should think about getting up and taking a walk."

"Yeah?" I said. "Maybe tomorrow I will."

An orderly brought me a dinner of neoprene chicken, watery mashed potatoes and Day-Glo yellow pudding that smelled of ammonia. I shoved it aside and watched the wheelchairs go by, watched the nurses carrying flowers, watched the old people and young people coming to see family.

Eventually, I shut my eyes. I didn't want to see people; I didn't want to think or do anything. So, naturally, I started to think about Rick.

Rick had destroyed the only piece of evidence that clearly demonstrated Jimmie's innocence—the ending of the tape. With a small shock, I realized he had tried—too late—to make amends. Those close-up pictures of the *Sea Dream*'s hull—he'd been trying to find evidence to clear Jimmie.

"You forgive me, Cooper?" he had asked, his eyes searching my face. And then he'd cut his losses. Gone to die a hero's death.

His death was enough—hell, for me anything would have been enough—to do what he asked. Only I wasn't the one to forgive Rick. It was Jimmie he'd sold down the river.

I opened my eyes, blinked, shook myself. I was exhausted, but I didn't want to fall asleep.

Death Game

Do you forgive me, Cooper? Do you forgive me?

A nurse entered on soundless feet, came to the head of the bed and looked at me.

"Is something wrong? Your face is white."

"Was someone here?" I asked, licking my injured lip. "I heard...I thought I heard someone talking."

A wrinkle formed between her brows. "Visiting hours are over," she said. "You were dreaming. Go back to sleep."

When she left I turned my head to the window. The sun was setting, and the city of San Francisco came up out of the sea like a glorious firebird. Russet and scarlet rays of light danced on her bridges and towers. I kept watching until the sun dipped behind the hills, and the view dissolved into black trees and wavering shadows.

But I could still see the city in my mind's eye. See the white egrets nesting in the sand along the beaches. See the old brown pelicans a-wing above the silver-bright skyscrapers. See the seals with their cunning faces wrestling each other for a favored perch on the rotting planks under the wharves.

I saw it all, saw it until the whole city turned into spinning fragments, a spiraling diffusion of dreams.

END

ABOUT THE AUTHOR

CHERYL SWANSON PENNED HER DEBUT NOVEL, *Death Game*, when her life took a turbulent turn with a diagnosis of breast cancer. The author of three non-fiction books and an expert in esoteric technologies, including remote surgical and image manipulation systems, Swanson had just turned fifty when she found the lump in her breast. At that time, another great challenge was staring her in the face—adopting a daughter from a third-world country. Already, Swanson had been questioning whether she could really make a difference in a child's life when a demanding speaking schedule kept her away from home more than sixty days a year.

Instead of backing away from the twin challenges, she changed careers and started writing a novel, while continuing to pursue her objective of adopting a child from Guatemala. A year of cancer treatment later, her debut novel was almost complete and her prognosis had improved to the point where it was feasible to travel to Guatemala.

Swanson believes her cancer simply meant that she had an opportunity to do something special.

"It's a new phase of my life. It's not always easy, but it's impossible to wallow in self-pity, when you have a four-year-old running around the house. Journeys are never in straight lines; your pathway has many curves and stops. The important thing is not to give up, but to turn and find another path."

Hard at work on the sequel to *Death Game*, and always close enough to give her daughter a hug, she is taking her own advice.

ABOUT THE ARTIST

MARTINE JARDIN HAS BEEN AN ARTIST SINCE SHE was very small. Her mother guarantees she was born holding a pencil, which for a while, as a toddler, she nicknamed "Zessie"

She won several art competitions with her drawings as a child, ventured into charcoal, watercolors and oils later in life and about 12 years ago started creating digital art.

Since then, she's created hundreds of book covers for Zumaya Publications and eXtasy Books, among others. She welcomes visitors to her website: www.martinejardin.com.

Made in the USA